WHEN THE HOUSE BURNS

A TWIN CITIES MYSTERY

PRISCILLA PATON

Priscilla Paton

coffeetownpress
Kenmore, WA

A Coffeetown Press book published by Epicenter Press

Epicenter Press
6524 NE 181st St.
Suite 2
Kenmore, WA 98028

For more information go to:
www.Camelpress.com
www.Coffeetownpress.com
www.Epicenterpress.com
www.priscillapaton.com

Cover design by Scott Book
Author photo by Brett Dorrian

When the House Burns
Copyright © 2023 by Priscilla Paton

ISBN: 978-1-68492-081-5 (Trade Paper)
ISBN: 978-1-68492-082-2 (eBook)

Library of Congress Control Number: 2022941478

Produced in the United States of America

For David

ACKNOWLEDGEMENTS

When the House Burns is a work of fiction buttressed by research. For sharing their time and expertise, I wish to thank Paul and Kathy Anderson of Amaximmo Realty, Doug Beussman of St. Olaf College, Greg Casura of Stock & Barrel Gun Club, Paul Gardner for context on the Twin Cities Army Ammunition Plant, Mary Ella and Rick Jones of Jones Associates, Daren Maas of Boldt Construction, and Suzanne Terry of Edina Realty. I am indebted to the Twin Cities Chapter of Sisters in Crime which, conveniently for this book, hosted speakers on fire investigation, firearms, law enforcement's collaboration with social workers, and homelessness. For being sympathetic readers, I thank Jill Ewald, Michelle Kubitz, Krishna Lewis, and Timya Owen. As always, I am deeply grateful to Jennifer McCord, Coffeetown Press, and Phil Garrett, Epicenter Press, for supporting Erik and Deb in their adventures.

Places in the book are a mix of fact and fiction. The Father of Waters statue is real, and the Survivors Memorial in Boom Island Park is the first in the nation to honor survivors of sexual violence.

My family sustained me through the challenges of the pandemic time, and I dedicate this book with love to my husband David.

"Home is the place where, when you have to go there,
They have to take you in."
"I should have called it
Something you somehow haven't to deserve."

—*Robert Frost, "The Death of the Hired Man"*

"Who is good if he knows not who he is?"

—*Epictetus*

CHAPTER 1

THE ONLY FOREVER HOME IS DEATH. Yet the manner of its purchase—natural, accidental, suicidal, homicidal—can be put to trial. Not that once gained, one loses ownership of death, but among survivors there will be winners and losers. Those who profit would cancel out any lien against death's aftermath and demand a deed free and clear, while the losers cannot even measure the loss. Impossible to fix are the boundaries of absence and grief.

Detective Deb Metzger shivered off a haunted feeling as she stood where a body outline had been. That's what made this condo unit cheap and available, the sudden death discount. Deb spread her arms, her blazer sleeves receding from her wrists, and attempted a spin in the open-plan room. Her athletic six-footer self couldn't swing a dead cat in here, if she had a dead cat to swing. She went to the window hoping to see a swath of October foliage flaring across Minnesota's Twin Cities. The view this Wednesday consisted of an early morning drizzle on the gray lanes of Highway 100, which ran north-south through the inner ring suburb of St. Louis Park. "Inner Ring" sounded magical, though the magic Deb experienced was a sinister chill seeping from the walls—likely a ghost from the past, given that the décor remained stuck in the 1980s of sponge-dabbed paint and tile countertops, in this case a counter harlequined pink and green. The chill sucked the life from the room, and Deb shivered again. Spaces should *breathe*.

It was her partner in crime-solving, Detective Erik Jansson, who insisted that spaces breathe. She should receive hazard pay for working with inscrutable Erik at Greater Metro Investigations. Greater Metro, G-Met, was *not* the transit police, *not* a delivery service, *not* a booster organization. It was a fully-fledged public unit pushed out of the nest by other regional law enforcement agencies. Deb and Erik *could* see eye-to-eye since he was 6'2" in shoes and she was 6'2" in stacked boots. It didn't work out that way. Erik handled crises with a sleight of hand, mind, and body that twisted him out of trouble, whereas Trouble with a capital T shined a spotlight on Deb, tossed her in a thicket, and left her to whack her way out with a machete. During a close call when Erik almost didn't twist free and Deb's whack was off target, she had an unnerving exposure to her partner's phobia about tight spaces. She mocked him, non-blond taciturn Scandinavian that he was, for conceding that. In this death-discount condo, she understood what he meant about room for air. This stagnant box was not what she wanted at all.

She wanted *acres*. Space to shake off the day's resentments, to let go the traumas of her domestic violence and homicide cases, to push away dismay over the world as it is. Six hundred square feet wouldn't cut it.

Deb shut her eyes only to experience vertigo. She opened them and yanked at her bleached hair spikes. She should take a gander at the bedroom, where it didn't take much space to engage in fantastic sex. It would take the woman of Deb's dreams whoever, wherever, she was.

The real estate agent had disappeared, either sucked into the vortex of the mysterious chill or scared off by her admission that she pursued murderers. Ah, Deb remembered, the young man had stepped out into the hall. He'd been willing to show her the place at 6:30 a.m., before she was due at work, but deserted her to make phone calls or fall asleep standing up. He was not making a sale here. Desperate as Deb was for a place to live, she couldn't get over her spook about this one.

Death by misadventure—that was how the previous owner died. Indirectly, it was death by spider. The elderly woman had complained to management that the place had been invaded by green-eyed wolf spiders. Nonsense, wolf spiders live outdoors, management replied, and did nothing. The investigators who came when the elderly woman was found dead recorded evidence of spiders, species undetermined, above the kitchen cupboards. The supposition was that the resident, 5'1" in nyloned feet, had stood on the tiled counter with an arm wrapped around the frame of an open cupboard. She aimed Raid, pushed the misaligned nozzle, and sprayed her face. She fell, and that was that.

The very idea of spiders drove Deb from the kitchen area to the bedroom. The closet provided room for two people's wardrobes, providing they wore tank tops no matter the season. Deb had been dreaming of a place big enough for two. Instead, an ocean separated her from a potential beloved, a relationship strained to morbidity by distance. Deb's heart sunk with homesickness for a home she didn't have and lovesickness for an attachment never formed. What astounded her was how hot the real estate market remained during the Time of Terrible Living—the time when that pandemic stopped life-as-we-know-it, a pandemic that stalled when it should have exited—the time when the Twin Cities witnessed police killings of people of color, looting, arson, and distrust. Minnesota Nice went kaput. But was there mass migration outward leaving residences emptied and devalued? Heck no. Soon after the Twin Cities had the worst housing shortage in the nation. That left Deb in her thirties, an Amazon warrior with some form of biological clock ticking, solitary and homeless.

Not that homelessness was rare in St. Paul and Minneapolis. Tent cities posed a humanitarian problem that resulted from economic problems, disparity problems, post-pandemic problems, crime problems, mental health problems, almost any problem you could name and several you had never known. Deb could move into an encampment, an officer of the law living with the people in greatest need. But that was too much like Northwoods camping with a tent situation that combined spidery critters with unwashed reality.

She took one step into the unit's bathroom. On a field of action, Deb moved with swift efficiency; in this box she was a race horse in a pony stall. She couldn't wet both elbows in that shower. She stepped back and banged one of those elbows against the door frame. Here she was, all by herself, not even a chair, in a place too small to swing a dead cat and too cramped for her dreams.

Enough already with the pity stew, the dead cat meme, and a crime of spiders. Deb rubbed her funny bone and blew a raspberry just as the realtor reentered.

"I can't take this place," she told him. "It's criminal."

The realtor, whose maroon sweater set off his white skin, dropped the salesman smile. "Because it was seized from native dwellers?"

"Excuse me?"

"Public buildings acknowledge that it's Dakota land. It should never have been ours to sell. It's like the draft in here—"

"You feel it too?"

"—is the spirit of my ancestors."

"Wait, you're Dakota?" Deb knew that native descendants were disproportionately homeless or in substandard housing.

"Twelve percent, but I was raised totally white and shouldn't be double-dipping into that whole privilege thing with tribal rights too. See, my dad took a deep dive into genealogy and discovered that his father's birth mother was Dakota, from Prairie Island, I think. But she, my great grandmother, died young, leaving behind my three-year-old grandfather—he wasn't my grandfather when he was three—and my great-whatever married a white woman and they forgot about the Native side. I guess it was better to act all white so the kid wouldn't be sent away to Indian boarding schools whose point was to take the Indian out of the Indian. Tribal people, lots of them, need better housing resources. That countertop can be replaced, you know, and this is the only unit where you could negotiate a lower price."

Deb wanted to blurt, *are you in the right profession?* Instead, she said she was sorry about his grandmother, or great-grandmother, and asked if he had more properties in her range.

The answer was a *bringg* from his phone. After asking what's up, the realtor listened in horror, eyes bugging out at the spider lair above the cupboard.

"A spider update?" Deb asked.

His legs trembled in his corduroy trousers. "There's a single-family home. Close. Now."

"I have to get to work."

"It would be work, your work." He seemed unsure if the call had ended and extended his phone to arm's length. "The place comes with a dead body."

The second he said "body" Deb's G-Met number dinged. She was summoned.

CHAPTER 2

THE RAIN BECAME HEAVY AND SHEETED ACROSS THE St. LOUIS PARK neighborhood of small bungalows maximized by trendy remodels. Lawn-proud residents had cultivated their postage stamp into a collector's item, but the flowers had gone to seed and frost blackened the leaves. Detective Erik Jansson could hail from the North Sea with his chiseled bones set against the elements, although his Viking forbears lacked his impermeable yellow raingear and Xtratuf boots. He squished across the yard to a plain house decorated by a "For Sale" sign. The crime scene team had already constructed a tent around the victim in the driveway which sloped down to the road, and he tramped up the slope. When Erik had called Deb Metzger, she knew of the body because the patrol office had called the agent listed on the sign, and Deb chanced to be with that agent. Deb chanced to be in many unexpected places. If theirs was a yin-yang relationship, both yinned when one of them should have yanged. He should get combat pay for working with act-first-think-later Deb.

Erik, steps away from the tent, lurched back when it burst with light and the tree above caught fire. He'd been tricked by an illusion—a tech had switched on portable lights inside the translucent tent which gave the maple leaves above a lurid gleam. Blue absorbent snakes hugged the tent's rim, but the crime scene within had already been well rinsed. By the time a dogwalker had spotted the body this morning, the rain had diluted the blood into rivulets, and the CSI team couldn't risk losing more evidence. Erik could see down the street to a median and beyond that state Highway 7, which dissected St. Louis Park as it ran west to Minnetonka. Beyond the lanes stood a Kohl's. With a noisy highway and mall nearby, neighbors might not be aroused by a sudden pop or car squeal occurring on a dreary Tuesday night. By the time their brains processed the unfamiliar sound, the returned quiet quelled any suspicions.

A St. Louis Patrol officer in a black slicker and patrol cap rocked from one foot to the other by the tent flap. He was short and when he tilted his head back to greet Erik, water ran around his ears. He spoke up to be heard over the precipitation hitting the tent. "You're Detective Jansson, right? I heard you're a marathoner. I can see that. I'm Officer Dave Bremer." Bremer was young enough to be a recent academy graduate and green enough to turn whey-faced from the double shock of cold rain and a corpse.

"Yes, good to meet you. I'm waiting on my partner, Detective Metzger. She's experienced with domestic scenarios, if that's what this is."

"Sure. Med techs are minutes away. The photographer's in there with the, uh, woman. We called you G-Met guys because we're overloaded at the moment and don't handle much homicide here. SLP's murder rate is zero percent."

Erik smiled. "Was zero."

"Still zero if you round down." Bremer spoke to his phone: "Divide one by 49,000. See." He held the wet screen to Erik.

"Hmm, two-thousandth of a percent of your population. She still counts as a full person in need of justice. Do you know her name? Is she the owner of the house?"

"The owner was a man in his eighties who died a few months ago and family put it up for sale. The realty office is checking yesterday's showing appointments. The woman, the decedent, could be an agent or prospective buyer. She, the decedent, is in a down jacket, not waterproof, so the killing likely happened last night before the rain. Nothing like a purse around. My first impression is that she was shot from about six feet away, possibly by a nine-millimeter bullet from a small pistol."

"You've a good eye, Bremer."

"Well, I'm glad G-Met could send you. I don't hear much about you guys. I called the Bureau of Criminal Apprehension first. Their special agents are in so much demand nobody could come. The BCA receptionist said you guys were the adequate alternative."

Erik controlled another smile. Greater Metro Chief Ibeling would prefer a label like "performance-driven professionals" to "adequate alternative."

A car door slammed across the street.

Deb Metzger loomed up from her Prius, donned like Bremer in black raingear, and splashed forward, talking nonstop. "What's with the yellow, Partner? You a school crossing guard?"

"Not since I was ten."

"Hey there, St. Louis Park dude, I'm Detective Deb Metzger. Don't let my partner fool you with his blank face—he's remembering everything including your hat size. I'm not as tall as I look, not as scary either."

That rendered Officer Bremer speechless. "This is Officer Bremer," Erik filled in.

Deb extended her hand, and Bremer recovered by running on, "Yeah, Dave Bremer here, SLP, obviously, you're funny, ha, nice to meet you, Metzger, Deb. From what I saw, I'd say our vic here was shot at a six-foot distance, no shell casing found. I'm thinking the shooter used a lightweight handgun like a Springfield XD-M or XD-S. Easy to conceal, great little pistol. I just bought one for my girlfriend—I'm about to propose. I thought I'd pop the question and offer the Springfield. I don't have the ring yet. The Springfield XD's a great model for competition, reliable. Think she'll like it?"

This rendered the detectives speechless. The falling rain accentuated their silence until Erik uttered, "You must love each other very much."

Deb shot Erik one of her looks. "It sounds, uh, great, Dave. I'm no expert at proposals, believe me, but I think the ring should come first? You can propose at a special place like a gun range, but you have to bring the romance, not that a gun range can't be romantic."

Erik broke in, "Med techs are here." A relief since it was unreal how Bremer linked guns and love in proximity to a woman killed with a bullet. When the hooded techs ducked past, one shoved sets of plastic coveralls at the G-Met detectives. The photographer left the tent as Erik stepped under the plastic awning to pull on the coverall.

"Oh, it's you, Jansson," the photographer said. "I'll send the download link as soon as I'm in my dry van. Not your favorite kind of corpse, but not bad." He patted Erik's arm, which earned Erik a second look from Deb. A med tech signaled them into the tent, and Bremer went to his car to check radio updates.

If the scene inside the tent occurred in a Marx Brothers movie, it would be hilarious. People in absurd gear struggling in each other's way, everyone bent low under bright light, each obsessed with a seemingly trite activity. Instead, a head rested on the coagulated blood that hadn't washed away. The woman lay on her back, her face twisted to the right and up. Her eyes were nearly closed, and her red hair was soaked strings. A bullet had entered her left check, a tech explained, and exited above the right ear. After exiting, the bullet lodged in the maple tree, and ballistics would later recover it and plot out the shooter's position.

As far as murder scenes go, it was tame: common for a woman to be killed, likely by boyfriend or husband, banal in its commonness, horrific because of that banality, and yet unthinkable. Erik knew what it was to be in a blind rage at a woman—he was divorced—but that woman was the mother of their son and had been loved. Was it a peculiar joke on himself that Erik was a homicide detective for whom homicide was unimaginable? He stepped back into the downpour, Deb calling after, "What's the rush?"

Erik stepped back into the tent, affect flat. "You should take—" he started, "I should take," Deb said over him, and they chorused on "the lead."

Erik waited for Deb to speak, he knew she would, and she did after sucking in air. "I should take the lead on this one, Partner, having seen plenty of dead women in my time. Yeah, well, not much to see at the moment. Maybe in her late forties? Puffer jacket, scarf, jeans. Middleclass woman in standard fall look, except for the bullet hole." She bent to peer at the hands before they were bagged. "No sign of defensive wounds. The rings don't look like wedding bands, oh, maybe that one, covered by the red bauble. Single shot, could be an execution. Except she doesn't look the type, and this isn't really the place for that kind of crime."

"She could have been looking away from her killer and not seen the gun," Erik said.

"Or she saw the gun and instinctively turned away. Could be a robbery because there's no handbag. Wonder if she has a car parked up the street? Maybe the key fob is underneath her. Or the killer took the vehicle? There's a spate of car jackings, mostly south of here with teen perps. You'd think then she'd be closer to the street than the garage, and I don't think a teen would do this, unless totally panicked or high." The techs were rolling the body to check the back for damage, and one shook her head no at Deb's key idea. There was no sign of injury other than that one head wound.

Erik left the tent while Deb stayed for a few words with the techs. Neighbors had forced pets out in the downpour, willing to live with wet-dog odor to check out the scene, and Bremer left his car to question several. A couple in a Kia Sedona obliviously zipped around the official vehicles to pull up close. A pregnant woman heaved herself out of the passenger side as the man rushed around to hold an umbrella over her.

They had taken two steps up the drive when the woman realized something was terribly wrong. She grabbed the man's free arm and stared at Erik. "You're not Karma!"

Then she saw the blood rinsed by rain from Erik's plastic-covered feet and collapsed.

CHAPTER 3

Karma's ivory fingers clenched the heated steering wheel of her Acura TLX. Fear had driven the blood from them, and the steering wheel's artificial heat burned without warmth. The fear worsened when an ambulance sirened past too fast and too close to her idling car. It soon sirened itself back within the speed limit, suggesting that what was happening couldn't be too bad. St. Louis Park wasn't high drama, except for soap opera type dramas like the one she'd experienced this morning.

Karma Karas Byrnes had left her house in a fury, her hair a hazel frizz, her gloves forgotten, and now she waited for the police officer to signal her forward. She saw through the thumping of her windshield wipers that other cars were rerouted. Lucky her, she'd received a call from the officer asking her to wait because there'd been an incident at the house she was scheduled to show to an expectant couple who were "being checked out." The woman might be giving birth in the ambulance. If that was the case, why did the police need her?

She revived her fury. Just as Karma had turned on the shower this morning, her mother called to say she would visit this weekend from Rochester to have an amazing time with seven-year-old Sylvy. Karma could go off and amuse herself to allow for grandmotherly bonding—not that Karma's mother let herself be called "grandma"—she was emphatically Nina. When Karma nixed the plan, her mother repeated her mantra that Karma needed Zen in her life to calm her childish temper. "Later, Mother," Karma fumed. She was no child. She was a successful, attractive, *desirable* woman who had only recently passed the thirty-year mark. Whenever her beautiful peaced-out mother—not *that* peaced out—started lecturing, Karma decided it was the CBD talking.

She stopped clenching the steering wheel to twist her hair, her mother's habit. Karma replaced her hands on the wheel. There had to be more to life than not becoming your mother.

There was being pissed at the man-who-could-have-been-the-one dumping you for his high-school sweetheart. Grow up already she screamed at him when he pleaded through crocodile tears that his first and deepest love was back in the picture. She could've spit at the sap that what you feel at sixteen isn't love, it's a hormone tempest. Karma flexed her fingers on the heated wheel. Let him get married and find he's in a bed of depetaled roses, let him get that I-told-you-so divorce, and see if she would take back his sorry self.

And thanks, no thanks, to Jean, her co-worker "friend" who had introduced them. Since the man was Jean's cousin, she had to know he was tripe. When Karma made that point about the cousin in a less tripey way, Jean with her know-it-all smile wagged a finger. The finger wagged that Karma had hit bumps in the road, lost her way, but life's a journey with breakdowns, and, finally, Karma's woes were on Karma. It would please Jean to see Karma stuck in the rain and waiting for news that couldn't be good.

She was jolted from her mood when a drenched officer rapped on her window. She rolled it down a few inches to avoid being drenched herself.

"I'm Officer Bremer, Ms. Byrnes, the one who called you. If you could drive past the CSI vehicles to park on the left. You could be a help."

"Do you want me to identify a body?" she quipped.

"Thank you. Thank you, ma'am, for volunteering." He said into his radio, "I'm sending her ahead to meet with the detectives. Ma'am, go ahead, please."

Karma's blood stalled in her veins and a knock came again.

"Ms. Byrnes, you're revving the car. You need to shift into Drive to go forward."

Karma didn't want to go forward. She wanted to go back three years in time. If only she had that choice.

SHE MUST HAVE PARKED AND LEFT THE CAR. A woman patrol officer held an umbrella over Karma whose trench coat was designed for a photogenic mist, not a raging downpour. They splashed up the driveway toward a tall woman and tall man in coveralls who made five-foot-seven Karma feel short. The tall woman, phone to her ear, rushed back to the line of vehicles. The patrol officer left Karma with a stern man who introduced himself as Detective Erik Jansson. She nodded as he confirmed that her name was Karma Karas Byrnes and that she worked for Lake & Isles Realty. He made remarks that didn't register. He leaned closer, touched her sleeve, and she caught on. His partner, Deb somebody, was checking with realty agencies about showings for this house scheduled for yesterday—Tuesday—and for today. There was a tent—of course, there by the garage—and in it a woman's corpse. It was a tremendous thing that Officer Bremer had asked of her, but could Ms. Byrnes see if she recognized the person who was perhaps another realtor?

She must have consented because she was led into the tent. Rain splatted obscenely on the roof and harsh lights exposed the body. A squeak, more squeaks, *she* was squeaking that the body was Jean's, Jean Nerstrand from her office.

Then she was in an SUV, the detective's, his coverall replaced by a slicker. When he leaned to turn up the heater, his profile was cold and exact. The blowing air inside and the rain attacking outside made it difficult to hear, but Karma preferred that to eerie silence with a stranger. The windows fogged up—to outsiders, it must look like a make-out session. He switched the control to defrost, even noisier.

"Ms. Karas Byrnes," he said, "I'd like to go over the information again. You identified the woman as Jean Nerstrand, another agent at Lake & Isles Realty here in St. Louis Park."

"Jean . . . she's separated . . . her husband." Karma couldn't go on, remembering another body on the ground, her own husband, a body angled wrong with a face that was no more a face because the person behind it was gone. She choked on tears.

The detective turned down the fan, reached for her, she flinched. No, he reached between them to the back seats and pulled out two thermoses. He lifted the gray one—"water?"—then the blue—"hot coffee?" She reached for the latter, in a thermos imprinted with a photo of a boy in a kayak. With hands shaking, she poured the coffee into the mug cover and sipped—startling strong and black. The detective's coffee, and she'd leave a lipstick smear, dark russet, on the mug. Because her mother's call left her to rush, Karma hadn't done eye make-up so at least mascara wasn't streaking down her cheeks. Here she was, worrying about mascara, and Jean, Jean who guided her—

The detective brought her back to the moment: "Did Jean share anything about her schedule? Is there a manager at your office to contact?"

"Paisley, office assistant. The number—" she should be able to rattle it off. "My phone, my bag. Where's my bag?"

"Here." He—what was his name? Detective Jansson—reached toward the back seat again to pull forward her tote, which he must have carried for her. Then he rummaged in a cardboard box and pulled out a towel. He was seeing things about her that she couldn't process, her face wet and her hair a dripping mop. He set the towel on the shift barrier and took from her the empty mug and thermos, which he pitched into the box which once stored mouthwash.

She tried to make light of the situation—"You're prepared, a true boy scout"—to be surprised that speaking hurt her throat.

"You can never prepare for everything. Would you like me to take you to your office or your home?"

Home, where there's heartache.

"Would you like a medic to check you over, Ms. Byrnes? It's quite the shock." His voice had melted into a soothing baritone, a nice voice. Her husband had had a nice voice.

"I'll call first. The office, I mean." She had not, however, warmed from the coffee and her icy fingers couldn't activate her phone's touchpad. "Could you put it through, uh, please?" She gave him the code to unlock the phone. The screen saver came alive, displaying Karma and daughter in swimsuits on Lake Minnetonka. The photo, taken by her seldom-seen brother, was a wonderful pic of Sylvy. Karma had not noticed when she uploaded the shot that by leaning over Sylvy she'd exposed most of her breasts. Detective Jansson's eyes lingered before he asked, "Lake & Isles in contacts?"

Before she could answer, her gut lurched, she shoved open the SUV door and tumbled out. Her hands and knees on the rough pavement, she gagged up coffee which mixed with runoff to whirl down a storm drain. The red stenciled words by the drain grate blazed, *Minnehaha Creek Watershed*. It meant nothing yet felt like doom.

CHAPTER 4

LEAVING THE CRIME SCENE TO THE COMPETENT TECHS and the distressed Karma Byrnes to her partner Erik, Deb Metzger zipped through a yellow light on her way to the Nerstrand home. As a rule, justice for women motivated Deb to throw her all into a case. Deb would have to throw a barrel of her all at this case because she wasn't sure if Erik could handle it. With an inch of seniority over her, he generally took the lead but had turned to stone at the sight of a woman's body. Deb was about to lay into him about giving the scene his "full and undivided attention" when she saw the photographer touch him with concern. What gives? They'd never looked at a dead body *together* before. Was he a homicide detective who couldn't handle a corpse? In grabbing the lead, she'd given Erik the benefit of the doubt though she hated giving the benefit of the doubt. It was a stupid phrase, like how much doubt and what kind of benefit? A lawyer's phrase, except it lacked the syllabication that went into legalese. Deb impressed herself in thinking of "syllabication" and "legalese." Her word-a-day email subscription was paying off. But couldn't Erik just spit out what he felt? Act like a soap opera star and drop a bombshell before the commercial break so they could move on to the next act?

On first arriving at the scene, Deb had called the listing agent, the culture-guilt guy from the condo showing, to learn that a realtor from Lake & Isles was scheduled to arrive. Deb told Erik that she'd take the lead and begin by checking in with missing persons and later contact the deceased's closest relations, once she was identified, and directed him to deal with the arriving agent. That was before Deb realized the agent was a hot woman. Let Erik use his cornfed Iowa gallantry to learn what he could. (They both grew up in Iowa, meaning Deb was entitled to say what she wanted about the great Vowel state.) Then Erik could pass the realtor along to Deb because, first, the woman might prefer confiding to another woman, and second, might know of a perfect property for Deb. Giving orders proved she could be lead, a role she'd never had at G-Met. Deb was used to being the bird of a different feather, the risk-taker on the edge, the irritant to usual order of things. She was used to speaking with pointed force and could hold down the fort when she was the fort's sole occupant. But she didn't always know which point to force and had never commanded a fort full up with independent egos.

Her GPS announced a change to the "fastest route" and added ten minutes to the ETA. The hot woman, Karma, said that Jean's husband worked from their home in the Minneapolis neighborhood of Tangletown, an address the couple shared even though separated. Morning traffic slogged, and Deb should use the time to rehearse her approach.

Except the routine questions slipped from her thoughts as they circled back to last night. Since joining G-Met a few years back, she'd never had a proper home. She had sublet a St. Paul apartment from a young couple who left to assist Doctors Without Borders, but they came back during a cease-fire in some nation's civil war. She bounced to another sublet, which turned out to be short-term. With the complication of a pandemic, she never found an apartment to her liking. Last night Deb had been sleeping on the couch of her long-term stay unit when a text alert caused her to roll off. The text from Jude declared, "we need to talk." Deb thrilled—maybe the never-quite-a-relationship wasn't dead, only comatose. Except nothing said, "let's break up what we never really started," like "we need to talk." Deb had met stocky suave Jude on a previous case but had not heard from her in months.

The dilemma: Jude was in Paris with her elderly employer, Nancy. Nancy LeClerc had gone to France for a stay at one her hotel company's resorts. Jude, her right-hand woman, left newly-met Deb because Nancy Maintenance was Jude's job, and who wouldn't go abroad with all expenses are covered? Then came the pandemic. Nancy became deathly ill in the luxurious fourth arrondissement. The hotel matriarch had survived her father murdering her mother, her husband dying, breast cancer, and a trafficking scandal at her hotels. For a long time, it appeared that Nancy would not survive the virus, and Jude stayed through the touch-and-go months of her employer's convalescence. Deb's brother in Iowa suggested that she arrange virtual candlelit dinners with Jude. They would sit down at their computer screens to enjoy a tête-à-tête. The first attempt was as disastrous as a blind-date arranged by dungeons-and-dragons geeks. With the time difference, Deb was lighting candles at four in the afternoon while Jude was yawning at eleven p.m.; Jude enjoyed escargot with fine crystal and donned a silk blouse. Deb, in a setting created by Target, ate Hy-Vee take-out and wore a tee that onscreen appeared stretched to limpness. She was the bad example in a laundry soap commercial.

Finally, came Tangletown.

If Deb had a life partner (incredible sex!) and a passel of kids (where'd that idea come from?), living in Tangletown would do. The winding streets, unusual for the grid that was the Midwest, had homes built during the Tudor Revival of the 1920s. A pop-up on her GPS informed her that the nearby water tower had supplied the Washburn Memorial Orphan Asylum. The orphanage was long gone—there goes the passel of kids—but the knights of yore remained built into the tower, and the local pub was dubbed St. George and the Dragon.

She made the sharp turn onto Rustic Lodge Road. The neighborhood patrol car Deb had contacted waited several houses down from the Nerstrands' and followed Deb to the multilevel bungalow. The yard lay open to the neighbors on the left. On the right, the lawn banked down to a dying hedge by the driveway and a two-story garage, and behind the garage stood a shed. The upper garage story had curtained windows indicating an apartment. The rain had ceased, leaving curdled clouds overhead. Deb left her car and greeted the patrol officer, "Officer Pete," who noted that his kids knew the Nerstrand kids, though the adults weren't close. He led to the door, made and released fists, pushed the buzzer.

Officer Pete was about to ring again when they heard barking, a shouted "*Bounce*," noises best described as lumbering, then Bruce Nerstrand answered to door. He slumped, his face puffed like dough, his beige sweater stretched over his belly, his shoes missing, and his hair sticking out like shredded cardboard. "Officer Pete, what the hey?"

Officer Pete nodded glumly as Deb showed her credentials. "Mr. Bruce Nerstrand? I'm Detective Deb Metzger with Greater Metro. May we come in?"

Bruce slumped further and let them in. The interior, with walnut wainscotting, saffron walls, and leaded glass windows, would have been a craftsman showplace had a whirlwind come through and sucked up digital devices, chew toys, and abandoned sneakers. Deb's raingear dripped, and Bruce Nerstrand said, "You can use the coatrack, if you can find a spot." The wrought iron rack was heaped up with school-pride jackets, so Deb dropped her raincoat on the entry mat and looked up the stairway on the left. The stairway broke from mission style with a blue wall stenciled with the tail-end of a dragon. The rest of the dragon writhed up to the halfway landing and out of sight. Deb wondered if St. George waited at the top to slay the beast.

For the matter at hand, she had to play the avenging knight. "Mr. Nerstrand." Her voice quaked and she halted.

The man rubbed his fingers against his thumb. "Has something happened to Travis? Tessa?"

Damn, there were kids. "I'm here about your wife, Jean, Mr. Nerstrand."

"We're separated, and first I took the garage apartment, only then she wanted it. If her car's in the drive past the hedge, she's home, I mean in the garage. Or she's at Lake & Isles. Wait, why?" His eyes bugged. "Was there an accident?"

Delivering this news was ripping a band-aid off a wound that required a thousand stitches. "Mr. Nerstrand," Deb said slowly, "Jean was found dead this morning. I'm so sorry."

"An accident? Her Volvo's safe, it can't be." Bruce hulked, unconvinced.

"Mr. Nerstrand, she was shot. She would have died immediately without suffering."

"You saying someone shot her in the heart? It's not Jean. You've got the wrong person. No one would shoot Jean—I've wanted to strangle her sometimes, not for real. There are lots of Jeans. You have the wrong Jean."

Officer Pete blurted, "She's dead. Bruce."

Bruce staggered and Deb grabbed his arm to direct him through an archway to the dining room, where the table held computers and a printer occupied the hutch to spoil the craftsman appeal. She sat him where he could steady himself against the table. Officer Pete leaned against the archway between the rooms. Deb began with the driver ID photo on her phone. "This is your Jean, Jean Nerstrand?"

"Driver IDs are terrible pics."

"The woman found dead at the scene was identified by a realtor from her office. Karma—"

"I know who Karma is. Good Karma, Bad Karma, Jean called her. She thinks she's a House Whisperer. Don't know if that woman can be trusted."

"Mr. Nerstrand, Bruce, I'm going to show you a photo from the scene. We didn't call you at once because we couldn't access Jean's phone. Her phone and her Volvo haven't been found yet. I know this is hard, but please, could you take a look?" The cropped photo on her digital tablet showed the eye, nose, and mouth area with a tiny edge of the wound.

"*Jeezus!*" Bruce jumped up, his legs gave way, he fell back onto the chair which screeched, covered his face with his hands, and cried. This part of the job was the pits for Deb—being sympathetic while remaining aware that the intimate partner was the first suspect. Love, commitment, separation, violence. As for fitting a killer profile, Bruce wore socks that didn't match.

Deb needed to move him through the misery. "Um, Officer Pete, could you get Mr. Nerstrand water?"

The officer pushed on the swing door to the kitchen and with a "whoa" tried to swing the door close—too late. A Golden retriever scrabbled toward Deb, and his front legs were on her thigh, her shoulder, then he was licking her ear, cleaning it like it had never been cleaned before.

"Bounce, down," Bruce ordered without feeling.

Bounce lapped Deb on the mouth.

"*Bounce!*" Bruce leaned out of his chair to grab the dog collar and pull Bounce to a sit. Dog and man crumpled to the floor, Bruce hung onto the collar and sobbed. Bounce, in confused and delayed obedience, slid into full down.

Officer Pete helped Bruce to the sitting area couch where he shoved aside a sweatshirt for Bruce to sit, then dismissed himself to finally get that water. Bounce trotted to Bruce and slid into another down at his feet. Deb moved a game device to sit in a chair and, aching for something better to say but drawing a blank, offered the standard wishy-washy condolences.

Officer Pete returned with waters, and Bruce downed several gulps.

Deb used her soft voice, soft in the way a softball is—you still don't want it to hit you in the head. "Mr. Nerstrand, did Jean own a handgun?"

He sniffled something about hunting rifles in the basement safe.

"So your wife did not carry a handgun?"

Bruce exploded, "She had to be seeing some fucker! That's why she wanted the garage away from the kids, that's why she wanted to keep that crappy hedge. He did it, that fucker."

"What's his name?" Deb asked as if it wasn't a big deal.

Bruce shrugged. "There has to be a fucker. Wait, you said her Volvo's gone? Is she dead because of the Volvo? What kind of criminal steals a car with 210,000 miles on it?"

He sobbed with full-body shakes, and Bounce, with round doggy eyes, pleaded with Deb to do something. When she didn't react, Bounce put down his head and gave a "go-away" snort. Before she could go away, she had to know where Bruce was the previous evening. She asked, and he babbled about the kids and a school event. She also asked if he had a key to Jean's garage apartment.

He snuffled, "Tessa has it. Her room's upstairs, first on the left."

Deb stood, and in an aside to Officer Pete, directed him to reach out to someone for Bruce. Maybe there was an aunt or uncle who could help break the news to the poor kids. Deb followed the stenciled dragon up the stairs and through the turn. At the top, the dragon's maw opened wide not to confront St. George but to swallow a life-size Wonder Woman. Or Wonder Woman in her blue top and striped panties was propping those deathly jaws apart, which was exactly how Deb felt.

Leaving Wonder Woman to fend for herself, Deb hoped to hit the jackpot and find the keys in the daughter's room. She pushed open the door to an orgy of clutter. Clothes covered bed and floor; school binders overloaded the desk; fingernail polish, photos, and snarled jewelry littered the dresser.

It had to be faster to contact a locksmith than to find a needle in the haystack of adolescence.

CHAPTER 5

AFTER THE UNREALITY OF THE CRIME SCENE, KARMA LONGED for the ordinary, and what better place for the ordinary than her office. But as she dripped her way in, Lake & Isles Realty had the unreal brightness of a TV studio. Karma paused to let her eyes adjust and saw that the u-shaped reception desk sat abandoned. She assumed the receptionist Paisley had gone to the storage room and would soon appear. Detective Jansson, who followed her here while she drove like a drunk, had shifted his attention from the glare of a housing display to a photo box of agent headshots. He focused on the top shot of Realtor and Office Manager, Fallon Lordes. The woman, perpetually in her late thirties, had hair that sun-kissed shade common to sorority sisters and in her navy blazer could've stepped off a yacht. Karma watched the detective shift to Jean's photo, ten years out of date.

"I see you have diversity in your group." He noted the photos of Marvela Salas and ebony-skinned Jackson Williams. "I understand that remains an issue in real estate, an issue everywhere really."

"That's an understatement." Karma didn't care to explain that those agents spent most of their time working out of another Lake & Isles office in a less pricey, more mixed neighborhood. Not that St. Louis Park wasn't open to all. The suburb's diversity was most evident in its Jewish population. Jews had lived in Minnesota since the 1800s, and in 1946, a historian claimed Minneapolis as "the capital of anti-Semitism in the United States"—not that there wasn't keen competition from every major American city. St. Louis Park, however, had been without discriminatory covenants, and its Jewish population grew, ranging from ultra-orthodox to those who displayed Menorahs next to Christmas trees. She knew this from her Jewish stepfather, ex-stepfather, the one who didn't realize the luck of his escape from Karma's mother.

Paisley giraffed her way in from the back. Though she was only in her forties, the beginnings of arthritis gave her neck a forward tilt and her long legs an odd gait; her hair, curlier than Karma's, was gathered in two knobs on top of her head. She dressed in camouflage couture. "Oh, Karma, back so soon? Are you with Karma, or can I help?" She cheerfully acknowledged Detective Jansson, who was about to speak when Karma blurted, "Jean's dead."

"Of course." Paisley fluttered her lashes until the news hit her. "Wait, *what* are you saying?" Her knees buckled and Karma, weak-kneed herself, moved to catch Paisley and they tumbled against the desk, a corner jabbing Karma's thigh. Paisley laughed hysterically as Detective Jansson steadied them and the laughing turned to gulping.

He assisted Paisley to her chair. "Please, take your time. I'm Detective Jansson, Greater Metro. I met Ms. Karas Byrnes—"

"Did you say Greater Metro? G-Met? Ibeling's your chief, right? Almost Allwise Ibeling? Who pays you anyway, city, state, feds? Gah, Jean's dead, and I'm *babbling!*" Paisley wept and Detective Jansson reached for a Kleenex box on the desk, saw the box was empty, and offered Paisley a handkerchief. He'd offered it earlier to Karma, but she had buried her face in a tissue wad. It bothered her now that she hadn't accepted it.

"I would like to talk with you"—Detective Jansson glanced at Paisley's desk placard—"Ms. Schulman, after I've spoken with Ms. Karas Byrnes."

"Just Byrnes," Karma snipped. She dropped the double name most of the time because the Karas belonging to a father who'd never wanted her. And what was all this polite nonsense with the *I would like to*? He was police. He'd do exactly what he liked.

She wordlessly went to her private office and he followed. The room had more photos of her, no swimsuit shots anyway. If the detective had a discerning eye, he could see that she used to weigh ten pounds more, a fact her chunky orange sweater was meant to disguise.

Detective Jansson seated himself across from her, eyes on one photo. "Is that your daughter? What lovely hair."

A strawberry-blonde nimbus floated around Sylvy's sweet face. Karma couldn't bring herself to explain the child's red hair and didn't have to because Paisley entered with two steaming mugs of coffee.

"Here you go, Erik." Paisley had assumed a first name basis. Having defrosted into a human, he thanked her for the hot brew. Karma decided Detective Jansson was one of those people who run hot or cold, which could be mistaking his temperament for hers.

Paisley said that she would inform the agents coming in and divert clients for the next hour. She left with a mystifying thumbs-up. Through a pinched throat, Karma asked if Detective Jansson minded that Paisley called him "Erik."

He smiled. "That's fine, but most people this close to a case find it reassuring to say 'Detective.' I'm a detective in this situation before I'm a friend or anything else."

Karma's shoulders dropped; she hadn't realized she'd been bow-tight. It *was* reassuring to know that there was a detective. She allowed herself to observe that he was good looking with disconcerting blue eyes. His gaze caught hers, she bent her head to have tears plop in her mug, then sipped to stop feeling whatever she was feeling. The coffee was heavy with sugar and cream. Paisley had determined that Karma should fat up. Karma was *not* anorexic. Not by choice had she come close to the bone—it was the anxiety diet.

He asked again, "She is your daughter, isn't she? You have the same face shape."

"Yes, Sylvy, almost eight. Her hair's like her dad's who—" she burst into tears. *When would this stop?* "Excuse me, I'm a widow. He died three years back. I don't know why I'm bringing it up." She grabbed tissues from her ample supply.

"You've been through a shock, and one shock can bring back another. I'm so sorry."

She rattled on to a man familiar with death. "My husband Chris, he fell out of a tree trying to rescue a stray kitten. Sylvy, so little then, was all worked up over 'sad kitty' and begged Daddy to get a ladder. He climbed up to the branch. The cat went higher. He sent Sylvy inside for a bowl of milk to tempt the cat down. I was pouring the milk when the tree cracked in half like it'd been struck by lightning. Horrid sound. His neck . . . It was dumb rescuing a kitten that wasn't even ours, a silly way to die. We bought the house for its 'mature landscaping' not knowing it meant trees that killed." Karma blinked at her coffee. "It's . . . silly."

"Fate has an odd sense of humor. My ninety-eight-year-old grandfather died when he fell off his roof."

She looked up. "What was he doing on the roof?"

"He liked the view. He'd been warned against such foolery, but he was a stubborn old Swede—the grandpas are Swedes, the grandmas Norwegian in my family. If he felt like being on the roof, he'd get himself there."

They could talk nonsense like this until Detective Jansson's time ran out and he'd leave her alone and Jean wouldn't matter. "What was his name?"

"Elmer Jansson. I console myself that he died doing what he loved best."

She tilted her head in question.

"Going against everyone's advice."

Out came a laugh followed by a hiccup. Karma wiped her eyes and felt an urge. "Excuse me, I'm going to the restroom. I can also get fresh coffees."

Hers without the sweetener. "If you'd like me to take your cup, Erik." She had her hand on his cup before she realized that now she'd called him Erik. Soon they'd be having the 'is she Good Karma or Bad Karma' discussion.

Her desk phone buzzed an incoming call. Holding two cups, she couldn't hit the silence button and the call jumped to voicemail. An upbeat man announced, "Karma, Dominic here. Where's Jean? Can you have her get back to me, or leave a message with Edward? Rafe, I mean."

The coffee cups sloshed, and it went dark.

KARMA WOULDN'T LET DETECTIVE JANSSON HAVE HIS WAY. She'd refused medical attention after she gagged up coffee at the crime scene and refused it again after her two-second faint in her office. She admitted that she'd skipped breakfast "because of my mother," and he was about to run out for energy bars when Paisley proved to be the better prepared scout in fetching a snack pack and water from the supply closet. Karma sipped and ate a cracker. She felt vague, submerged. Paisley, in contrast, was pronounced as she explained to Detective Jansson that for the agency to release Jean Nerstrand's information, the supervising realtor would likely require a court order. Paisley let it slip that Jean had no scheduled showings for last night. Then in his presence, she ordered Karma to go home, and Karma agreed.

Preparing to leave, Detective Jansson asked, "By the way, who's Dominic and the men named in the call?"

He'd lit a fuse. Karma reddened and Paisley rushed to answer for her, "Dominic Novak, a big man in several ways. He looks like he played football before going a bit soft. Handsome, wouldn't you say, Karma? He's big in development. His company Landvak Properties specializes in making problem sites profitable." Her enthusiasm dimmed—"His wife Renee used to work here"—and revived. "I'll be happy to get you Dominic's numbers. Best to call his cell because he's on the move scoping out properties. Call his office and you'll have to talk to that British twit, 'Edward.'"

"*Rafe*," Karma insisted. "Rafe LUTjenz. Here's the spelling." She scribbled *Rafe Edward Lutyens* on a post-it and handed it over for Detective Jansson like it was a note sending him to the principal's office. "Rafe is a young hire at Landvak."

"Jean used to argue with him all the time. He gets the facts wrong," Paisley said.

"Ask him again," Karma rebutted, "and he gets them right. Dominic calls him Edward because—"

"Edward is a name you can trust," Paisley finished. "Who'd trust a 'Rafe'?" Karma pouted. "Rafe's his name."

"But," Paisley started.

"Thank you both," Detective Jansson interrupted. "I'll take the contact information for both Novak and Lutyens."

Karma softened—"Paisley will"—the softening weakened her, and she shot a wild glance at the door. The other two caught it, and they left her alone. Good. She took a deep breath to soothe herself, exhaled, and felt worse.

CHAPTER 6

Deb Metzger, relieved to distance herself from Bruce Nerstrand's grief, zipped into the lake-of-a-puddle that was the G-Met parking lot and saw Erik heading into the building. She needed to know what he knew. Not *all* of what he knew which could be obscure, just what he'd learned of Jean Nerstrand at the real estate office. She splashed across the lot and at the door caught his boot heel with her toe. "Social Distance, 'Partner,'" he warned. Whoa, she called *him* 'Partner,' not vice-versa. She stepped on the heel of his other boot. Erik, now inside, sneezed a reprimand. The G-Met building, a mistake from the 1970s, had a funk that grew funkier by the day, and Deb sneezed back at him.

Impatient, Erik signaled her ahead and kept a distance so they'd avoid being at each other's heels like debt collectors. When they reached their office, he wiggled the key in lock of the warped door, but before he could open it, their phones beeped. Deb checked hers. "We're summoned, The Chief, Almost Allwise Ibeling, the one and mighty."

Erik shoved the door with his shoulder and lurched inward, Deb tripping after. The phones beeped again, and he checked. "Unsummoned, a delay."

Before Deb and Erik reached their desks, arranged in a V to avoid constant stare-downs, a Black man strode in, fellow investigator James Bond Smalls. He was handsome, despite undereye circles, in a suit that his colleagues labeled "Damn Fine."

"So, Jimmy, you're wearing Damn Fine." Deb sat down to a squeak. "Are you waiting for the call from MI6?"

"They appear to have misplaced my number. Damn Fine will have to wait another day for that glory moment. I should keep it here for court dates to avoid the adornment of my little darling's spit-up." Jimmy's wife had recently given birth to their post-pandemic delight, a baby girl to join two brothers in the Smalls family. Jimmy loosened his tie, which retained a dab of drool. "Why's there no good air here?"

"The new HVAC system died, too pure for this existence," Erik said.

Jimmy leaned against the doorframe. "Too pure, like our forensic accountant extraodinaire, Naomi. Where'd she go?"

Deb panicked. She had a crush on Naomi. That Naomi was married to a man didn't matter. "Is she in labor? She's pregnant. She's been pregnant since I came."

"This is baby two, or three." Jimmy counted on his fingers. "Maybe she fled home with extreme queasiness."

Erik squared his jaw. "Don't mention queasiness in this fetid den."

Detective Metzger," Jimmy Bond Smalls deepened his voice, "Your partner Wonder Boy can stand about anything out there in the field. Want to push him over the brink? Vocab's the clue. Repeat the following, queasy, gaseous, nauseous, bilious, barfy."

Erik put up his hands. "*Enough* with the synonyms."

"It doesn't smell like cinnamon," Deb said. "I wish it did, hot rolls—don't wave me off, a gal can dream." She coughed. "Are we living with mold? Somebody should ask the chief. Good job for you, Partner."

Jimmy added to the demands. "While you're at it, ask Allmost Allwise about raises for us. Only lately, he's been Curmudgeon-in-Chief. It's on you, Wonder Boy Erik, after that 'cultural sensitivity' workshop you put us through, the synonymy one about 'triggers' and 'subtext.' Made me want to subtext somebody right in the gut."

Deb ganged up with Jimmy. "There weren't even lemon bars."

Only to have Jimmy turn on her with a tug on his lapels. "Say, Deb, aren't you on the Committee for the Greater Good, the committee to bring the racist, sexist, numbskull children of humanity together and fix everything?"

"Duct tape fixes everything," Deb said. "You're on it too, Detective Bond Smalls."

"What I'd do to deserve that? Wait, I know, it's my beautiful mahogany tones. Second thought, you, Detective Metzger of the Duct Tape, should ask Allwise Ibeling about raises because he likes you."

"He *does*? How can you tell?"

"You're not fired," Erik said.

"Need better evidence than that, Partner."

"Ibeling's a bulldog, tenacious, loyal, on your side, but there'll be snorting."

"Snorting," Deb said.

"Snorting," Erik repeated. "And somewhere along the time-space continuum he said that his wife Greta didn't mind talking to you."

"See?" Jimmy confirmed. "If former black-ops maven, current caterer, chief spousal unit Greta likes you, you're in. Be yourself, Metzger of the Duct Tape, lighten the mood, throw Ibeling for a loop. You're good at yanking people out of mood ruts. You should have seen Erik's moods before you came."

"I thought they were better," Erik said.

"That's his funny face," Jimmy reassured Deb before turning somber. "Okay, I'm done with playing hip cop. Got court." He saluted farewell, and Deb and Erik's phones stereo-ed with the re-summons from the chief.

CELESTE IN THE OUTER OFFICE DIRECTED ERIK AND DEB TO WAIT in the hallway because "Detective Drees is with the chief now." She had not said, "Drees, that neebly blond Adonis who acts as if he's better than everybody," but that's what she meant.

Erik paced, his motion interrupted by Deb asking, "Where have all the knickknacks gone?"

Her nose pressed against an empty display case. The case had held The Softball of Joy (when G-Met won) or the Glove of Doom (when G-Met lost), the passive/aggressive plaque when it wasn't on the desk of a deserving recipient, a bronze doughnut, and a Bambi figurine with the sign, "the buck stops here."

The display mood changed during the Time of Terrible Living with a pandemic virus and endemic violence. Then the case featured a hand-carved dove, a black fist emblem, a blind justice figure broken, a weeping angel, a plaque listing G-Met investigators killed in the line of duty, and last, the case was filled with battery-run candles. *All gone.* Erik shrugged as the smooth form of Drees exited the office. Drees opened that mouth of aligned ivory but was at a loss for words after an encounter with the chief and for once simply left. *A bad sign.*

Ibeling braced himself behind his desk. He wasn't tall, didn't have to be, and suit jacket off, he rolled up his sleeves and crossed his arms per usual. Not per usual, he shouted as the detectives entered, "*What the hell's going on! A real estate agent dead. People being shot down on calm streets. People who decorate with Ikea. People who decorate with Ikea don't get executed.*"

"I'd decorate with Ikea," Deb said. "But I think Jean Nerstrand preferred Mission-style oak. It's durable."

"*Durable?* Do you know what G-Met has to endure? We've been outed." Ibeling snorted to the side, "should've retired" and stared slit-eyed at his phone.

Deb as lead nudged Erik, and he asked, "You mean the news and social media have become aware of us, sir?"

During the Time of Terrible Living, G-Met's burden increased as the police forces of Minneapolis and St. Paul suffered traumas, too many self-inflicted.

The press discovered and lauded G-Met for having a better behavioral record. Erik explained to Deb that G-Met's clean sheet was not necessarily owing to their superb moral fiber, but to the organization's relative youth and random factors. He couldn't answer Deb's follow-up question, did that make them randomly moral?

Ibeling gripped the cracked leather of his chair. "Yes, Jansson, the media are *aware*. They're questioning our funding, asking if our charter has a sunset provision. Want to know if we, by that I mean the two of you, are a good use of the taxpayer's money."

Erik and Deb evinced zombie status rather than tax worthiness.

Ibeling frowned. "Aargh. Ignore my bark but remember my bite's worse. Your case, likely a straightforward domestic. I understand you're the lead, Metzger. Act like it. The metro area is under attack for not protecting ordinary people in ordinary circumstances. Yes, there's a bias that the *non*-ordinary marginalized can't expect the same standard of safety. That the middleclass who follows the rules, which they made, should never have a problem. It bothers people when a 'decent' person is murdered. They forget how they keep others from decency. Christ, what a world." Ibeling slapped the top of his chair. "And this takes the cake—the media calling us a 'boutique' agency. Boutique! Like we have useless stuff."

If Deb had a gift for lightening the mood, why not try? "We did have knick-knacks, sir, but they're gone. You know, the Bambi? The buck stops here?"

The chief's steel-wool eyebrows twitched. "Metzger, if it makes you feel better, take that with you." He indicated the singing bass plaque on his wall. Rumor was that it'd stopped singing. "Jansson, no wallowing in inner space. Hell knows, we're all wallowing in this sty. And smile, dammit. Not now. Metzger, don't look like a lost unicorn. Not that bite-your-head-off look either. Both of you, find the next of kin for this Ikea victim."

Before she could correct Ibeling that the husband had been contacted, her partner gave a warning step on her boot. They were about to back out when Ibeling saw phone updates that should've popped up earlier. "Good, next of kin contacted. Jansson, pick up anything at the real estate office?"

"The victim, Jean Nerstrand, had been working with a developer, Dominic Novak."

"The tennis star? No." Ibeling mulled. "Novak, as in Landvak Properties? I know of the wife's family in White Bear Lake. There's an ongoing arson investigation dating back to spring about the burning of a Landvak apartment complex. Corpse of a homeless man was found in the wreckage. The presumed arsonist is a subcontractor. Theory is that he was furious when Novak threatened to sue him over failure to deliver so he set the complex on fire. The theory never turned up evidence. Arson cases have a notoriously low closure rate. It's still an angle to pursue, that the Novaks have an arsonist after them and their associates."

With that, Ibeling went to the wall, took down the fish plaque, and held it out to Erik and Deb. Neither reached for it. "Just as well," he grumbled. "Can't have you fighting over it. Go."

At the door, the detectives heard behind them, "should've retired."

CHAPTER 7

TIME OF DEATH FOR JEAN NERSTRAND WAS ESTIMATED TO BE between nine and midnight on Tuesday night. It was now Thursday morning before eight. The advantage of showing up at a house unannounced is that the resident doesn't have time to prepare a face, let alone wash it. Erik was curious what face Dominic Novak would present. Paisley from Lake & Isles had provided a schedule that showed frequent contact with Jean over the past weeks. Calls made last evening to Dominic Novak's phone numbers went to voice mail, and the answering message said that Novak would be in the office Thursday. Erik and Deb acted on the assumption that he returned home last evening.

Erik reviewed files on his tablet while Deb drove the G-Met SUV from the G-Met building, which straddled Minneapolis and St. Paul, toward St. Louis Park. Because Deb was still reaching out to members of Jean Nerstrand's huge Midwestern clan, Jean's name had not yet been released to the public. Deb went over what she had learned from the sisters in Wisconsin. Jean had been optimistic and outgoing except for a low spell that preceded her separation from husband Bruce. The sisters couldn't believe that anyone had reason to kill her, although they admitted that Jean dropped juicy hints about dates with unnamed men. Erik, squirming in a suit, confirmed for Deb that warrants were being processed for Jean's phone and email records. As for the arson angle that Ibeling dropped into the case, Deb decided that since Erik had an eye for fraud and a taste for herrings, red or pickled, that doubtful angle would be his.

Entering the enclave at the north end of St. Louis Park, Deb tapped the steering wheel. "So I want you to take the lead with Dominic Novak, that man-to-man bond. Nice neighborhood he's got. Private."

Erik scanned the area: The American dream, a family home in Pleasantville. Divorce had displaced him from that dream, a regret he submerged. "Dense tree growth, hidden drives. You could think backwoods hermits live here until you see a Frank Lloyd Wright façade. There, on the rise at the end of the cul-de-sac."

"Ooh, fancy talk, Partner, 'façade' and 'cul-de-sac.' Now here's words you don't see together often." Deb pulled up to the curb by the "All are Welcome" and "We Support Police" signs at the end of the driveway. Clouds scudded overhead, casting the lot in shadow then in light. The prairie-style home hunkered down on a stone base, sage siding blended with the landscape, and the muted horizontals were lifted by tall windows outlined in white. Deb stopped the vehicle. "Think either of us could afford this joint?"

"If you move the decimal point from a Mil to a K."

"So that's a no. The fence on the garage side, hiding a pool?"

"Or keeping the attack dogs corralled."

Not dogs but blue jays yakked news of their arrival when Erik rang the doorbell. The paneled door cracked open, and a woman in her mid-forties with a highlighted bob showed her face and smiled. Erik recognized that smile as a requirement of respectable Midwest women. The upcurve of the lips was so deeply conditioned that there was no question of whether it was fake or real. It simply was; the result of culture intersecting with a certain genetic structure. The genetics, curiously, traced back to Northern European immigrants who in tintypes were doomsday sour.

As agreed, Erik took the lead. "Good morning. I'm Detective Erik Jansson with Greater Metro Investigations. This is my partner, Detective Deb Metzger. We'd like to speak with Dominic Novak, please."

"He's had a delay returning from a conference in Albert Lea. You can reach him later at the central Landvak office. If it's urgent, I can pass on a message. I'm Renee, his wife." The smile stretched wider, the door did not.

Erik tossed Deb a surprise, the lead. "Detective Metzger has questions for you as well, Mrs. Novak. It's important. May we come in?"

"Yes, may we come in?" Deb echoed with gritted teeth.

"I'm hardly prepared for company." A crinkle in Renee's brow offset the lip smile. When she let them in, an aroma wafted forth—apple pie in the oven.

"Do you mind taking your shoes off, detectives?" She pointed to a teak boot tray.

"Sure. Not that there's hidden knives in them," Deb joked.

"Excuse me?" Renee tightened.

Deb blushed a *never mind*. As she bent to remove her boots, Erik squatted by her to untie his shoes and hissed, "have *fun*, be yourself." What Deb hissed in return shouldn't be repeated.

The Novak home appeared not only company-ready but photoshoot-ready. Renee wore pointed house flats that added polish to her trim jeans and Irish-knit sweater. She was small and shapely, and her tapered hands waved the detectives to the living room area. "Please, take a seat."

Erik and Deb took tufted side chairs leaving Renee the pristine eggshell sofa. Deb began, "Mrs. Novak, we understand that you used to work at the Lake & Isles office off Highway 100 and that your husband has ongoing business dealings with the realtors in that group."

"Yes."

Deb plunged in. "We have somber news. Jean Nerstrand in that office was found dead yesterday morning."

"*Ohh!*" Renee clasped her hand over her mouth and gasped through her fingers. "No! That can't be."

Deb restarted in a strained voice, "Jean Nerstrand—"

"She was healthy, wasn't she? You should talk to her husband, Bruce."

"I have. He and the children, her sisters—" Deb broke off, tears welling.

Erik hadn't prepared for Deb's time with grieving family taking its toll. "Mrs. Novak," he said, "Jean Nerstrand was shot. Her body was discovered at an empty for-sale house south of here."

Renee's narrow shoulders heaved. A buzzer made them all convulse, and she jumped up, croaked "timer," and rushed to the kitchen. If an intruder hurtled in from that direction, Erik and Deb would have to defend themselves in their stockinged feet. The cinnamon-apple smell intensified, and then there was a slam.

Renee returned holding a dish towel which emitted oven warmth. She draped it over the sofa arm and sat. She checked her manicure to hide her filling eyes.

Deb took a deep breath and restarted, "Mrs. Novak."

"Renee." Renee's gaze dropped to Deb's socks which had a Muppet pattern. "Renee, you used to work at the same office as Jean Nerstrand."

"Yes, but I left eight months ago."

"I see. Were you close to Jean?"

Renee delayed for a moment. "Used to be. I'd say she's, she became much closer to Karma Byrnes. She discovered Karma."

Deb perked up. "The House Whisperer?"

Renee, with prim smile and forehead frown, considered this. "Karma used to be a personal shopper at Nordstrom's. That's how Jean met her. Jean was often in a rush, and she'd gained weight and needed things for an event. She never looked so good as in the outfits Karma assembled. Jean said Karma had a gift for seeing what would please people, which is important in home purchasing, and offered to help her become an agent. It was a while before Karma showed up. She'd married; then her husband died in a freak accident, such a tragedy. That's when Karma joined us, but the loss of her husband set her back emotionally. The last conversation I had with Jean, she was speculating that Bruce was having an affair. I shouldn't think him capable of an affair."

"He seems like a loyal puppy dog," Deb agreed. Renee did not react, and Erik became preoccupied with the state of his socks. "I mean, is Bruce Nerstrand too clueless to carry off an affair?"

"How odd you are, Detective Metzger."

The dig didn't slow Deb. "So, when's your hubby returning again? Is the pie for him? It smells fantastic. We need to trace Jean Nerstrand's movements on what she was doing for your husband. When he checks in, have him give us a call, anytime. Well, up to midnight, and we'll try to reach out again. By the way, was he at his conference Tuesday night, Renee?"

"Of course, and I was at bridge club."

Deb brightened. "I played bridge for a time in college. Did better with the action sports. How'd it go for you that night?"

"I was going to say," Renee snipped, "if you're going to call, do so early. We're in bed by ten-thirty. Really, Detectives, if you don't mind—"

Erik interrupted. "Mrs. Novak, why did you leave Lake & Isles?"

Renee smiled the smile of a saint. "The place was not conducive to good work. Dominic would drop in when I was there, and it became too homey, what with the two of us discussing dinner plans. Also, I couldn't be selling properties on the seller's behalf to my husband's company. There are laws about that, and I don't cut corners. Also, I couldn't spend the day meditating myself into a state of calm."

"Why's that?" Deb persisted.

The smile compressed. "You must know, Detective Metzger, that certain people fuss over the littlest thing. I was exhausted by being the only grownup in the room. Jean—" she put her fingers to her eyes. "Jean and Karma would get into these catfights, one certain the other was poaching clients. They were best friends and then not exchanging a word."

"Like middle school all over again," Deb said. "Queen Bees and frenemies."

Renee's smile turned downward.

Erik took the opening. "What about the others in the practice?"

"Those two took all the attention, along with the office assistant, Pressley."

"You mean Paisley?" Erik asked.

"Whatever she names herself," Renee said with a hint of disgust.

"Like Paisley took that joke seriously," Deb said. Give yourself a stripper name by naming yourself after a pet, your gerbil 'Paisley,' and I forget the rest."

Renee ignored her to address Erik. "I worried Karma, Jean too, would use being coy to take advantage of people. Karma has more of a chance with those looks of hers. Oh, I shouldn't be saying this." She snatched up the dishtowel and buried her face in it, muffling her words. "Jean, don't get me wrong, she could be a friend, but she had a rapacious side."

"Do you know if that rapacious side affected her family, her husband?" Deb asked.

Renee choked behind the cloth. "How could something like this happen?"

Deb sent Erik a let's-go look, and they stood.

Renee dropped the dishtowel into her lap. Her face was blotchy, and she didn't move.

"We're sorry about your friend," Deb said. "It's an enormous thing to take in."

"We'll see ourselves out. There is another matter, however," Erik added. "The arson investigation involving the Landvak Penn Avenue apartment complex. Any updates on that?"

Renee raised herself, bunching the towel in her fists. "That was a terrifying time. Dominic tried to shield me from the awfulness and that evil man! We had to have a round-the-clock security detail here at the house. We thought he might come after us next."

"By 'man,' you mean Jack Cardenas, the subcontractor initially suspected of starting the fire?" Erik asked.

"The state fire marshal tracked him to Canada. The marshal said Cardenas cooperated, which I find hard to believe. That investigation wasn't worth a dime because they let Cardenas go. They said they didn't have any 'concrete evidence on the contractor,' like the 'concrete' was a construction joke."

"What about the dead man found at the arson scene?" Erik asked.

Renee's blotchy face paled. "You don't think Cardenas is back, do you?"

"No, no sign of that." Erik shouldn't have taken this path. "I didn't mean to worry you, Mrs. Novak. I'm sorry. If you ever have concerns about your safety, please reach out and we'll do our best to help."

"Yes, my partner is sorry," Deb said like it should be a perpetual state for Erik. Then her voice cracked. "Jean Nerstrand—if you think of anything, you know." She sniffed. "Thank you for speaking with us. Is there anyone we can call for you right now?"

Renee mutely shook her head no and mutely showed them out the door.

ERIK'S INNOCENT EXPRESSION DID IT. Deb slammed on the brakes the second they were out of sight of the Novak house. "*Way to throw me under the bus, partner. Way to follow my plan.*"

"Buses don't run on this street, and I may have erred," Erik admitted.

"*Rrred*? Is that how you say it, like a cat's stuck in your throat. I could cram a feline down your throat, only then I'd be rrrr-ing. I assign you the lead on *one* interview and you throw it back." Deb stomped her foot. As happens, it was on the accelerator and the vehicle leapt ahead three feet. She thrust the gears into Park.

Erik rubbed his brow.

"That's it, rub your brow. Pretend you're thinking."

Erik stopped rubbing. "Renee struck me as extremely proper, and it can be hard to break through that propriety. If I started asking questions, the only answer I'd get would be, 'Jean was nice.' You, on the other hand—"

"Could plow right through that *propriety*? You set me up to be the loose cannon, Partner, *ugh*." Deb banged her head against her hands on the steering wheel and let it rest there.

"I apologize. It bothers me that your reaction to Jean Nerstrand's death was stronger than Renee's."

"It's been a long twenty-four hours for me, us, and she hasn't absorbed it yet. Then there's that 'propriety.'" Deb looked sideways at Erik. "Renee had no trouble mean-mouthing her 'friends' Jean and Karma after I successfully annoyed her by 'being myself.' I *hate* it when you get me."

Erik laughed. "Likewise. Then I kicked off her terror by mentioning the arson. Can't imagine any link yet between that case and ours. Does it still seem like a domestic to you?"

"Yeah, kinda. You wouldn't believe the number of men on Jean's Lake & Isles contact list. Most are business contacts, but she was also looking for a good time. Death by midlife crisis?" Deb stared at the windshield, head still on hands. "You go at Dominic Novak when he returns and find out what he knows. Heck, find the murderer while you're at it. You know what, it's totally empowering to order you around." She snuck a glance—Erik had slipped into a trance. "You *with* me, Partner?"

He drifted back. "Find the murderer . . . My farm grandmother made pie before breakfast. It'd be nice to come home to a wife who made pie. You'll say that's sexist."

Deb rolled her head on her hands. "Actually, you had me at pie."

Their pie dreams poofed away with the phone ringing over the SUV speakers. Renee, sounding tentative, "You might check out Edward Lutyens at Landvak, sometimes goes by another name. Edward would've worked with Jean on cost projections." The tentative tone ended. "I wouldn't trust him to swat a fly."

CHAPTER 8

Late Thursday afternoon, Rafe Edward Lutyens would destroy the Landvak office—if it came to that. Sear away hard drives, suck Cloud files into a black hole, denude the wires behind the outlet to set the wallboard smoldering. Rafe had been smoldering too long. Screw Dominic Novak, his sheep-faced accountants, and his female Harpies, all living it up at a seminar with a tax-deductible Happy Hour. When Dominic walked into a room, women were ready to bear his children and men to build his fortune. When Rafe walked into a room, people hid their valuables. They were disconcerted by his ravenous intelligence, which should be cause for respect. Case in point, Rafe was left behind because he had the "competence" to handle any situation. *Right*. Rafe would *not* be the one they shut out. No, he would be the one they didn't see coming.

In the back room assigned to him, Rafe twisted his slim frame in a high-design, low-comfort office chair. The chair's fabric, an infected pink, clashed with his tan skin, brown eyes, and dark brown hair. How could they even invent a shade that clashed with brown? This wasn't the career that he had imagined as a "Lead for Development and Acquisition." With his plummy British accent and responsibility as strategic planner, he should be a vice-president, not a boy Friday. However, Landvak was a small subdivision in the mega-city of residential development. Only twenty employees, with several being parttime, worked out of this central office. Landvak couldn't support a roundtable of presidents and their vices. Rafe had left giant profitable Prospectus, a leader in the affordable housing industry, for a position of greater creativity and influence at Landvak. Yet here he was in a cul-de-sac of dreams—not yet thirty and thwarted in his future. This was about wealth creation, and not Dominic's wealth—his.

Upon hiring Rafe, Dominic bragged on him as the best thing since sliced bread. Then he tried to sway Rafe to invest his recent windfall into the company. That would have been appealing if Dominic had put full partnership on the table. Rafe had made the money through a black swan event, a trading scandal that was an up-yours to hedge fund managers. Dominic teased that Rafe owed it to the stability of the economic system to back away from barely legal maneuvers to invest in Landvak. Rafe dodged the opportunity.

He kicked the clogged paper shredder—nothing. This room, "Edward's study" according to Dominic, was *terra incognita* for clients. They were escorted to Dominic's showy office with its designer chairs, not to Rafe's windowless cube of mechanical monsters. Don't let the villagers see who works in the pit. Don't let them see the coal-dusted canary—Rafe coughed at the paper dust when he opened the shredder. With shredders, computers, printers radiating heat and no emergency sprinkler where one should be, his "study" was a firetrap.

He kicked the shredder again, and whining, it gnashed the Landvak documents stuck in its craw. The shrieks of dying data set Rafe's teeth on edge, and he shoved his pink chair into the wall to have it ricochet back. In frustration, he rubbed the bridge of his crooked nose, that *bend sinister*.

Rafe should never have told Dominic about that British phrase, how *bend sinister* signified a slant to the left on a coat of arms, but also evil, the mark of a bastard. That his nose slanted left meant nothing. He was not the unwanted brother in a tale. His gorgeous American mother was not monstrous, merely the princess eternally plagued by a pea. When Rafe first joined Landvak, he'd neglected to return his mother's calls when she and Da, his London-born Anglo-Indian father, were in California. In a huff, she called Landvak's main number and insisted on speaking to "R. Edward," the name she called Rafe when she wanted to manipulate him. Dominic henceforth declared that Rafe be "Edward" in the office, a low blow because no woman cries out *Edward* in the throes of ecstasy.

Rafe Edward Lutyens squeezed his eyes shut. He opened them to glare at the sole desecration of the room's utilitarian purpose, a reproduction of John Constable's oil painting, *The Hay Wain.* What a thrill to make that burst into flame. The nineteenth-century landscape depicted farm workers in a wagon crossing a stream, image placed here by Dominic to remind Rafe Edward of the sceptered isle. But Rafe, who as an adolescent pled to be released from the British boarding school system, preferred prairie horizons to perpetually overcast skies.

The real reason Dominic hung the landscape was so he could swagger in and say, "Hey Wayne!" like Rafe had yet another middle name. People died for less.

The office phone dingle-dingled. Why Dominic couldn't keep a full-time receptionist Rafe didn't know. Instead, his boss had Sela and Carina, parttime

record keepers, fulltime Harpies. Sela if riled, and the sight of Rafe riled her,
squawked. Carina, who clad her fire-hydrant form in men's suits and honed
her gray hair into a Mohawk fade, tracked his moves like a predator. Why not
employ a sexy young thing who didn't want a man who marched to the beat of a
different drummer, but the man who *was* that drummer? Someone *had* to look
past the Bend Sinister on Rafe's face to see his exceptionalism. Several women
had come close—he'd even been engaged to elope with one of them. Until she
decided she couldn't do that to her family as an only child (Rafe wished he'd
been an only child), and their romance died in the Abyss of wedding planning.

The phone demanded Rafe's attention. He plopped in the chair and rolled
over. The number seemed familiar but lacked an ID. He employed his posh-
est tone. "Landvak Development and Estates, Vice-Principal Ra—Edward
Lutyens speaking."

Dominic's voice cracked, "Jean's dead."

"What?" Rafe was rarely a man of one word.

Dominic stifled sobs. "I'm with Renee, she needs me." That's why the
number was familiar, it belonged to Dominic's wife, stylish Renee of the tart
tongue. Dominic struggled on, "Jean Nerstrand, you know Jean. Been finding
properties for us to flip?"

Air left Rafe. Yes, he knew who she was, Jean of the big mouth.

"Edward, you there?"

He sucked an inhale. "Yes." This upset did not go with Rafe's scheme for
everyone to stay calm while he deviously carried on. "Was she in a car accident? She smashed it when she drove. I mean, she drove fast. You're positive
it's Jean?"

Dominic made guttural sounds. "Murdered. Detectives will call the office
for information. Take care of everything, will you, Edward? I got to be with
Renee." The call ended.

"Take care of what?" Rafe queried the boy in the Constable painting. The
boy in the wagon had been pointing the finger at Rafe the whole time. The
answer was a buzz from the outer door.

AFTER THE INTERVIEW WITH RENEE NOVAK, Deb spent the day running
down Jean Nerstrand's recent Lake & Isles clients and assigned Erik to check
"other stuff." He'd spent the Thursday figuring out that Jean's Volvo had been
in the shop Tuesday and she'd taken a loaner, subsequently found a half block
from the murder site; both her Volvo and the loaner were being inspected by
forensics. Then Dominic Novak, returned from his conference, called him
and sounded gut-punched over Jean's death. Novak said that anyone working
late at the Landvak office could provide a list of properties that Jean had been
scoping out for them.

Now in a Landvak meeting room, Erik surveyed the architect's desk and poster paper easels, a place where kindergarten skills meet high design. The afternoon's last light blanched the remaining employee, Rafe Edward Lutyens. Lutyens seemed to have crawled out of a coffin and was surprised to be among the living. Erik suggested the young man make himself coffee or tea at the beverage station, which created a moment for observation.

As detective, Erik had to make judgments about people in a snap and, if countered by further evidence, delete them in a snap. Part two of that equation was harder. Also mind-wracking was determining which details signified. At the realty office yesterday, something about Paisley niggled at him, followed by Renee Novak's dismissal of her. He realized on the drive to Landvak that it was Paisley's broad hands. Paisley's gender at birth may have been male, and she could be a transgendered individual. If that was true, it had no bearing on the case, though a trans bias might explain Renee's dislike of Paisley.

Rafe, shaking off his coffin stupor, was stunned that the detective said his name correctly and launched into an explanation. His first name, Rafe, was often spelled as Ralph in the U.K., but pronounced with a long *a* to rhyme with *lake*. Lutyens was pronounced *LUTjenz*. Rafe stayed with that pronunciation, despite American discomfort, because he was distantly related to Sir Edwin Landseer Lutyens. That knighted *LUTjenz* was a famous architect who designed monumental buildings in Britain and India. Erik could check that on Wikipedia under "Lutyens' Delhi."

Erik concluded that Rafe had issues and that the British failed phonetics.

Also, Rafe Lutyens with his nose set on compass west looked like the guy who'd lost the fight, picked himself up, dusted himself off, yet didn't know how to start all over again. He paused at the beverage cart. "Machines are no good for Darjeeling. Donut Partner it'll be." He popped a pod into a machine and set it burring. It stopped when the "no water" indicator flashed.

"I'll take a walkabout," Rafe said, and Erik, a fellow pacer, acquiesced. Rafe walked back and forth and spoke into the hand that he'd put over his mouth. "The other women in Jean's office, are they in danger?"

"Do you have reason to think they are in danger?"

Rafe dropped his hand. "You don't *know*? Marvela, Paisley, Karma Byrnes, are they safe?"

"Mr. Lutyens, perhaps we could sit and focus on Jean Nerstrand."

Rafe didn't sit. "Just 'Rafe.' Dominic would know more. Women take to him. What's the connection? Oh, yes, Renee, Dominic's wife used to be in that office, Lake & Bile, I mean Lake & Isles. We're real estate developers as you obviously realize, but let me provide a context." He slowed and made eye contact. "Landvak develops and operates apartment complexes that have between fifty and four-hundred units. Most are in the Twin Cities, with a few in metro areas of Wisconsin and Iowa. Locally, Landvak has become inter-ested in smaller buildings to rehab. Existing apartments of ten units or fewer and old houses that could be converted to condos, long-term rentals, and short-term for the for-rent-by-owner model. For the last, the regulations are *insanely* prohibitive. I know from my own experiences with a unit that I rent out when family isn't using it." He put hand to mouth again.

"Do you have a record of properties that Jean Nerstrand was scheduled to show Dominic recently? Lake & Isles didn't have a complete list."

Rafe swiveled and headed down a t-shaped hallway. He opened a door and was peeved that Erik followed. "I would have brought the information to you, Detective."

Erik was cryptic. "Saving time."

All available space was taken up by work devices, printed spreadsheets, and an oversize painting. What the room lacked in oxygen it made up for in the humming heat of the machines. Rafe clicked rapidly to close the displays on monitors. Erik interrupted the activity with a remark. "I visited the UK once. I was told that Constable got the clouds exactly right in his paintings, and I saw how true that was. Out in the real landscapes, I wondered when the clouds would break for a clear blue sky."

"Didn't happen, did it? Little use for your SPF on the tour." Rafe was anx-iously amused.

Erik indicated that Rafe should take the one chair, covered in a sick pink. Rafe in turn gestured Erik to the chair. Both men eschewed the chair to lean against worktables.

"Rafe, can you think of anyone who'd want to harm Jean Nerstrand? Anything that might make her . . . vulnerable?" He almost said, *a target*, an inept phrase for a woman with a bullet in her brain.

But Rafe was already on that track. "You mean what might make her a target? Buyers and sellers can worry that a realtor is ripping them off and get their knickers in a twist. Owners who have property heading to foreclosure can be livid if a realtor takes it off their hands for cheap then turns it for a big profit. An area might be zoned for rentals, but residents get into realtors' faces about selling houses for that purpose. Cities want to choke out vacation rental by owner. But that's a way for a regular Joe, as you Yanks say, to get a footing in real estate and start generating income. But neighborhood associations, which are death to choice, can be vicious and argue that short-term renters are troublemakers. Maybe Jean made a neighborhood association mad."

"Murder by Nimbys?"

"Upon consideration, the 'not-in-my-backyard' sort don't go in for mur-der. Death-in-the-doorway would hurt curb appeal." Rafe's glibness was countered by his contorted body language.

"That list of properties Jean was viewing for you?"

Rafe took the pink chair, tapped away, and mumbled "bloody hell" when the download stalled.

"How did you get along with Jean?"

Rafe looked to Constable's clouds. "She was bossy, on me to get things done at *her* command. I know we're not to call forthright women bossy, but compare Karma in that office. No one pushes her around and she's not bossy. Jean made me feel like a naughty schoolboy. Wagging a finger at me, smirking 'I see what you're up to.' If her information was incorrect, she'd act like *I* was in the wrong. When I was in a torture chamber of a school, I'd pretend-shoot teachers like that behind their backs. But murder a woman because her mannerisms are those of an odious teacher? I think not."

Erik let the moment sit. Jean had annoying mannerisms; his partner Deb had annoying mannerisms; he had annoying mannerisms like dropping into silences and pacing. It'd been annoying to watch Rafe rub the knob on his nose. Bright and British when it suited him, American and casual when it fit, a chameleon with two names who had drive. A drive to go where? A stomach gurgled, Rafe's or his, and Erik had a strong drive to go home for dinner, and a drive to work in one more twist. A printer buzzed to life and churned out a document. Rafe handed it to Erik.

"Thank you. What do you know about the arson at Landvak's Penn Avenue complex?"

Rafe's scowl screamed, you *bloody American twit*.

CHAPTER 9

THE ORANGE PORCH LIGHTS CAST AN EERIE GLOW across the table wrapped for surgery on a Thursday evening. Karma, a butcher knife in hand, wished it brighter. A canvas jacket and kitchen prep gloves offered scant protection for what she was about to do.

"Aren't you gonna stab him, Mommy?" Sylvy in a green fleece jumped about in a stiff-kneed goblin dance. "Stab Jerry on the lines. See where I drew them?" Jerry was the larger of two pumpkins. The other Sylvy named Jilly, but she hadn't outlined the face yet. Karma would have preferred tracing a stencil, but her mother had inspired Sylvy to do her own craftwork. Karma's airy-fairy mother, never around when the real mess had to be made. The second grader's outlines squiggled off center.

"Shine the flashlight here, Sylvy. We have to remove the top and scoop out the seeds." Karma plunged the knife in near the stem. It didn't pierce the thick shell. She waggled it out for a second attempt.

"Stabbing Jerry, stabbing Jerry," Sylvy sing-songed. "Mommy cut an eye-eye, Mommy cut an eye-eye."

"Still working on the top." The pumpkin rind resisted again. She pulled the knife out, readied for a third plunge, and a knock on the porch door startled Sylvy into a shriek and Karma into stabbing the side. Beyond the screen door, Dominic Novak lightened the entry with his blond hair and neon wind-breaker. Sylvy skipped up to let him in. "You scared us, Uncle Dom!" Dom, an honorary uncle with no children of his own, doted on Sylvy.

"Hey, Pumpkin!" Dominic knelt to poke Sylvy and she giggled. He lifted a swollen face to Karma, said "I heard," and burst into sobs.

"IT COULD'VE BEEN RENEE," DOMINIC MOANED after Karma settled him on a stool at the kitchen counter. When she sold the house where her husband had died, because he'd died, Jean helped her find this place and Renee helped redecorate. Karma liked that the white-and-steel kitchen faced a comfy family room with a fireplace. With no fire tonight, it seemed cold and empty, as did Dominic whose ruddy complexion had turned to pancake batter. Karma shooed Sylvy to her room—so much of her survival as a single parent depended on her daughter's self-operated video device. She turned to Dominic, couldn't meet his eyes, and busied herself wiping the clean counter.

"I have an infinite supply of herbal teas, thanks to my guru mother." She sounded strangled. "Though I guess brandy's the kind of thing people drink in moments like this, only I don't have any." She crossed to the refrigerator and checked inside. "Umm, left-over chardonnay."

"Plain water's fine, Karma. Please don't fuss." Too large for the stool, Dominic resettled himself in a compromise between sitting and standing. Karma liked solid men. Her husband had been one, rounding off her edges and centering her. Dominic, big as he was, seemed ready to collapse under a straw's weight. Karma pushed against the fridge's dispenser and water spished into a glass. She put the glass in front of him, and he drank it down.

"Where's Renee, Dominic?" Why are you here, is what she wanted to ask.

"She called me about it, Jean. Next thing I know the police are contacting me as I'm driving back from Albert Lea and then a pair of detectives catch up with me at a construction site." He pushed the glass forward in an unconscious gesture and Karma refilled it at the fridge to another loud spish. "You know Renee's on that board, the foodbank one? I told her to take it easy and stay in, but tonight's a big vote on something. It helps her to get out of the house, but she wanted me to drive. God, is she spooked. I saw that she was inside the community building, and decided to relax by driving around, have a look-see at the Halloween decorations, and I found myself here. Guess I wanted to check with my own eyes that you're all right. Not that you wouldn't be." His eyes roamed the kitchen before settling, wide and wet, on Karma.

She had never seen Dominic so undone, not even after his Penn Avenue apartment complex was destroyed by the vicious sub-contractor from hell. He was staring at her hands, and Karma checked her pantry for a distracting crunch like potato chips. None to be found—candy corn it had to be. She dumped the candy in a bowl and set it out. Without comment, Dominic scooped up a bunch. Karma filled a waterglass for herself, sat beside him at the counter, and grabbed candy kernels. Somewhere along the way from her childhood to this moment of grief, candy corn had traded the flavor of bright colors for that of Styrofoam.

Dominic shuddered as he stuffed candy in his mouth. "I apologize for barging in like this. Here I thought I'd be a comfort. Carjacking is my best guess. Don't see how it could be her husband."

"They separated," Karma said. "But I'm with you. I can't believe that Bruce could do anything like . . . that."

"Bruce. Don't know him well, but he's got to be devastated." Dominic shuddered again. She should've fixed him a hot spiced drink. He closed his eyes, his lashes tipped with tears, and clenched his mouth. For a second, he resembled a camel baring its teeth. "Carjacking, that has to be it," he repeated. "We'll miss Jean, won't we, Karma. You and Jean were sure close, weren't you?"

The faucet of her tears came on full force.

"Oh, Karma, I shouldn't have come." He leaned in for a one-armed hug. Other times he smelled of fresh laundry; tonight he smelled of burnt coffee.

He came to a full stand. "I'd take this a lot better if it weren't for Renee. She's vulnerable and hides it by being busy. Watch out for her, will you? She'd appreciate a word. You guys are close too."

That stemmed the tears. Karma and Renee were close the way maple syrup and tabasco are close on a shelf. Not that it'd always been like that. Dominic, whose default setting was generosity, brought out the sweet kitten in Renee and was blind to the cat with claws. Karma murmured something consoling and walked back out to the porch. Passing the stabbed pumpkin, Karma had a flash that if Rafe had been here, he would have made a show of carving it for Sylvy. Dominic, hair the color of a Creamsicle under orange lights, paused at the screen door.

"I had a dream when I was driving around, a nightmare really, that it was that contractor, the arsonist, Jack Cardenas. No reason for him to hurt Jean. No reason. It disgusts me that the law couldn't get it together and build a case against him. We used to fish up in Canada, Cardenas and me." Dominic's voice cracked. "Oh, sorry, Karma, that's idiocy. Take care of yourself and if you ever need, you know." He squeezed her arm, which turned into a hug, and then he was out in the dark.

Alone on the chilly porch, Karma twitched with an electric charge. Jean's sudden death had shocked Dominic, shocked them all, but it was more than that. His voice hadn't cracked in grief, it cracked in terror.

CHAPTER 10

CERTAIN ROUTINES SHOULD NEVER HAVE BECOME ROUTINES. Deb's shoulder war with Erik on Friday morning, for example. They charged at doors from opposite directions, preoccupied with phones or in Erik's case with that secret universe in his head. Erik had broad beams atop a runner's build. For Deb, Iowa State Cyclone shotput champion, being a propulsive mass came naturally. The end result—they collided, as they did at the entrance to the Cyber unit, home to mild-mannered Cyber Paul. Somebody had to be mild mannered or it would all explode, and it couldn't explode until Deb had her hands on yet another killer of women.

First, a chest pang said she should escape the G-Met building funk. Cyber Paul made a noble attempt by adding a HEPA air filter and a robotic vacuum to his warren of techie equipment. The vacuum, at Paul's feet under the work-table, stopped humming when Deb and Erik jammed the door.

"Hey, Paul," Deb said. "Most people have a cat to warm their toes."

Cyber Paul's golden skin pinked. Unassuming Paul could pass through places unnoticed except for the glow he attributed to Danish-Dutch-Polynesian ancestry. "Facilities complain they can't clean around all the computers, and while they don't seem like spies, you never know. I clean everything myself." Paul moved the air purifier into the hall. Then he moved out the vacuum, activated it, and like a curling stone with a mind of its own, it slid away.

Paul's assistants had taken the chairs to the warren's inner recesses.

"We don't need to sit, Paul," Erik said. "We can stand on either side."

Paul pulled back.

"It's okay, Paul," Deb reassured him. "We won't hulk over you. How about I send Partner here to follow the vacuum?"

"Or as Team Spirit Leader, Deb," Erik said, "you stand by Paul while I lurk in the doorway and block Janitorial spies."

"Deb, you're the lead?"

"Yes, Paul. I'm the lead, no need to tremble in your shoes. So far, thanks to your digging in the Jean Nerstrand case, we know that two months ago the owner of the house where she was found died of a stroke at eighty-three—the owner's age, not the house address. His adult son in Los Angeles listed the house with Lake & Isles and hasn't an idea what might have happened. The neighbors report that realtors come and go—"

"Talking of Michelangelo," Erik finished.

Deb eyed Erik.

"He's quoting a T.S. Eliot poem to lighten the mood," Paul said. "Not that a poem on male impotence is an obvious mood lightener."

Deb pulled her hair. "Remind me, poet-spouter, why did you become a detective? And don't tell me it's because the dead adore you."

"I bring out the best in my partners."

A stunned pause, then Paul doubled over laughing. "Pah-hah! Th-that's why you're a G-Met Lead so fast, Deb, his partners—"

"It's not funny, Paul." Deb sucked in her lip.

"They love my lack of humor," Erik continued straight-faced.

"No laughing, Paul. You're encouraging him. What I need to know, *Partner*, do you have my back?"

"24/7. I'm a real convenience store that way."

"Okay, okay," Deb fought laughing. "I think I like your silences better. So are we serious now?"

Both men gave her a thumbs up.

"Okay, scene of the crime, neighbors claim to have important lives that prevent them from being busybodies about what happens in other people's yards. No security cameras, no traffic cams. So. Here we are, clueless. Throw us a bone, Paul."

"Here's what I have. According to forensics, it does not appear that the house at the scene was entered that evening. Prints on the door handles are traced to realtors who showed the house days earlier and who have alibis for Tuesday night. Now, for the cars and the weapon. As you know, forensics retrieved Jean Nerstrand's Volvo SUV from the repair shop and found her loaner down the street from the scene. They're still processing both. Ballistics took measurements of the scene and retrieved the exiting bullet in the trunk of the maple tree. The bullet's too damaged to match to a weapon but it's a nine-millimeter."

"SLP Officer Bremer called it, the type of firearm," Erik said.

"Could Jean Nerstrand have been carrying the gun?" Deb speculated. "Is she a registered handgun owner? It's possible she could've been killed with her own weapon."

"Grabbed from her, you think?" Erik asked. "Usually that's how the grabber gets shot in the gut, not the head."

"*Or* a mugger seized her bag," Deb followed through, "and found the weapon when she was about to scream."

"Maybe she didn't have a gun," Paul said. "She's not in the concealed carry registry."

"Sure, Paul, burst my bubble," Deb said. "What about Jean's phone records?"

"Lake & Isles just forwarded a list of those made on the office landline. I suppose you have to chase down every client?"

"Already started with help from patrol," Deb said. "That smart intern of yours, Paul, Ms. Mahdi, she could do background checks on names from the past three weeks. See if anyone has a prior or is a chronic complainer to authorities or has made a public ass of himself, herself, or theirself."

Paul squinted one eye. "We're to look for public asses?"

"Not too broadly, Paul," Erik amended. "It'd be a long list. But, yes, Deb's right."

"'Cause I'm the lead. As lead, I can state the obvious. A woman is dead, the physical evidence washed down a storm drain, the list of people to question is the length of Partner's arm added to mine, and no one stands out as a sore thumb of a suspect."

Erik braced his arms against the doorway. "Now that's a mood killer."

Paul raised his hand. "I have a question. Deb, you're on that committee to, what is it?"

"Oh, that." Deb tugged her hair again. "The committee to change everything. Stop racism, sexism, ageism, LGBTQ plus baiting, anti-ethnic hatred, religious hatred, and, um—"

"Whining," Erik said from his doorway.

"Whining," Deb repeated.

Paul hesitated. "I just wanted to know if it's true that we're going to play card games and board games."

"*What?*" Deb asked.

"Advertisements show up online for these game decks, the anti-bias stack, the de-programming stack. See." Paul pulled up an example on his monitor.

"Social Justice Monopoly?" Deb guffawed. "I don't think so."

"Isn't 'social justice monopoly' an oxymoron?" Erik asked.

"Moronic for sure," Deb agreed. "So who loses at social justice?"

"Everybody wins and no one goes to jail?" Paul offered.

"The problem's coming up with rules people will play by." Erik picked up a foot to make way for the returning vacuum. Red light flashing, it jerked back to Paul's feet.

He gasped, "It's clogged! She's new. That was her maiden voyage down the hallway."

"There's no 'maiden' in Social Justice Monopoly, Paul," Erik said. "Because your beloved has value even if no longer a maiden."

Deb dead-eyed Erik again. "This is bringing out the best in me? How am I so lucky to be with Partner Deadpan? Try cleaning the filter, Paul."

Paul cradled the machine like a broken Christmas toy, and Deb patted him on the back. She wished she knew what was making G-Met a cesspit and what psychic damage it was causing. The lack of case details fogged her brain. She had to assign Erik a task and ready herself for the most dreaded of encounters, a conversation with the children of a murdered mother.

A SCHOOL LOCKER ROOM WASN'T MUCH OF AN UPGRADE on Greater Metro's drab confines, but the Nerstrand children, thirteen-year-old Tessa and ten-year-old Travis, wanted to meet Deb there before lunch period, away from their stricken dad, and the authorities permitted it. For adult ballast, they had Tessa's cross-country coach, a man whose eye crinkles and swept-back hair suggested a life spent running into the wind. The coach, who lived down the street from the Nerstrands, had told Deb that he was up to speed on the legal ramifications of the children's situation because his wife was a family practice lawyer. Deb almost blurted, "family practice is her qualification, not yours."

But Deb owed school coaches. When she was a middle-schooler, a woman coach had seen potential where her peers saw clumsiness. In gym classes, Coach Sue had made agonized faces at calf-like students undergoing every awkward phase of pubescence as they fumbled rope climbing, dodgeball, human Pac-man, and gymnastics (don't ask about the balance beam). Deb scored high on bruises acquired, and classmates hurled "goof" at her. She heard worse when playing by the rules she blocked a guy hard. Coach Sue blew her whistle, told the pug-faced male that he'd survive, and hauled Deb aside. After squinting into Deb's soul, she made a single nod. "Metzger, you got potential to plow down the opposition. We'll work on that. Meanwhile, leave your classmates standing." Deb did grow into herself and klutz became speed. There was the added benefit that working with gruff Coach Sue was as close to preparation as Deb would ever receive for working under Almost Allwise Ibeling.

In this locker room, Deb breathed through her mouth to avoid smelling gym stink. The matter at hand was grieving children, lives forever altered, and what they knew of their mother. Deb and the coach sat in folding chairs while the kids sat on a changing bench. Tessa, in a school hoodie with running tights on under shorts, jiggled her legs up and down. She had pulled-back hair that a Shetland pony would envy. Travis wore baggy joggers and Chuck Taylors that squeaked across the floor. Everything about him slumped downward except for his standup hair which resembled the sprouted volleyball in the movie *Castaway*. The coach, in a coach habit, handed out water bottles.

Deb generally spoke with the directness of a line drive. Not a good call here, so she threw a curve ball. "Tessa and Travis, I know you're suffering. It's terrible what happened to your mother, and it's my job to do something about that. You've both seen enough TV shows to understand that I need to ask the standard questions and go through a process of elimination. No pressure."

Travis formed his hand into a gun and pretend-shot the cracked tile at his feet. "Tessa prob'ly knows more. She and Mom were girl-buds."

Tessa stared at the spot shot by the imaginary gun. "Not like so much lately. I got school you know, and Mom, she has her own life." She didn't correct her tense. "She likes going out for 'adult' fun."

Travis jerked himself straight. "They were getting back together. Dad said so."

"No, they weren't! Mom said no way. She said 'maybe' like one time after wine that they might reconcile—I bet she and Dad got drunk the night before and did it. But, you know, Dad can't stand when it's terrible, and he didn't want us to feel like crap and—"

The coach steered the girl away from the grief-pit she was digging. "Tessa, was your mom seeing different people, men I mean?"

"That's stupid people talk. But yeah, maybe." She slugged back water then ranted, "I saw cars in the driveway but not at night I think not at night and she was all secretive this summer for a while she was into swimming and then not and Mom doesn't didn't like doing things all by herself she has to have a buddy."

The coach leaned toward Deb. "My wife noticed a Lexus SUV and a British Mini." (An attentive wife who discarded her lawyerly discretion for neighborhood surveillance.)

Tessa squeezed her water bottle until it buckled. "Yeah, I met the Mini car guy. He said he couldn't find Mom and it was business."

"You shouldn't be talking to a stranger," the coach admonished.

Tessa, gripping the bottle, wiped her eyes with the edge of her fist. "He was cool strange. Rafe, whose nose points west. That's what he said, 'my nose points west.'"

"It can't always be pointing west. He's gotta be moving around," Travis corrected from his slump.

His sister didn't acknowledge his existence. "He had a Harry Potter accent and was like younger than Mom. He was one of those people who do the boring stuff about selling a house. Titles, whatever."

"Did you get the impression that he was special to your mom?" Deb asked.

Another rush from Tessa. "Nah, when she showed she was nice to him in that way where you smile but are dying for the person to leave, I shouldn't of said dying, I talked to him because of his accent and he was funny, told me right off that his degree was not from Hogwarts, that Harry Potter thing again, but he went to a one-name school kinda like Hogwarts that tortured you into being educated."

The coach was lost. "What's a one-name school?"

"First name school? Like Yale, William, Mary, whatev—like he's the kid who's a doofus until he lands at a fancy college where he goes all brain."

"Are you talking about me?" Travis's smirk clashed with his red eyes.

"You're not in college, smarty pants."

"Time out." Deb made the signal. "That man is on our radar. Okay, another tough question—was your mother in any particular mood lately?"

Travis hauled himself up. "Kinda happy, I guess. But into herself. You know how parents usually want to hear all about your day, drag it out of you? She kinda stopped doing that." The boy squeezed his eyes tight—he'd wanted his mom to drag the story out of him. "We've been eating dinner with Dad more than her."

Tessa added, "She said she was *busy* with work."

Travis picked at a thread on his joggers, and Tessa looked like a teen ripped away from her phone. Deb rebooted. "This will be hard for some time. It's about justice for your mom and helping you. Anything you can say."

The answer was feet shuffling, bottle scrunching, and nose sniffling. The coach pushed his hands through his hair creating side wings. Finally, Tessa spoke up: "It was like she had a crush on someone. Like giggly. When she moved to the garage, she'd like bake on the makeup and whip up the hair."

"I wish she'd looked nicer for Dad," Travis grumbled.

Deb heard outer doors opening and closing. Sweaty kids would be streaming past. She was about to stand when Travis roused himself and leaned against a locker. "Why the fuck did this happen!"

"Why the fuck are you saying 'fuck'!" Tessa leapt to her feet and punched him in the arm.

"It wasn't Dad's fault. He likes that woman from his work, the laughy one, but it's *nothing*. But Mom, what was she *f-freaking doing*? She should've just been Mom." He pushed Tessa, and they wrestled until the coach separated them, tucked a kid under each arm, let them cry, and cried with them.

Deb waited for the next move from the coach. After releasing the kids, he said he would take them home—turns out they'd only come in for this interview. From what they said, Deb would have to take a closer look at Bruce. Travis mentioned a woman his dad liked yet stayed convinced his parents were reconciling. To reconcile or not was a disagreement that could prove fatal.

They were heading to the outdoor exit when the coach stopped. "How could I have forgotten this. Back in September Jean asked my wife about restraining orders. Did your Mom take out a restraining order?"

Travis's mouth went slack. Tessa's look said *call-on-me*. "I got it! A homeless dude was stalking her. But like, he didn't have an address or a name? Like what could Mom do? Nobody could stop him if he was nobody who lived nowhere."

"A homeless guy wouldn't kill her, would he? Would he, Detective Metzger?" Travis looked to Deb as if her saying *no, of course not* would bring back his mom.

She couldn't give that answer, and her smile faltered. When you falter, all the more reason to forge ahead with every ounce of mental and physical muscle, and she promised the children that she would do her best.

CHAPTER 11

URDER INTERVIEWS DRAW BLOOD, AND NOT JUST FROM the questioned. Erik paced in the G-Met office Friday after Deb had left to interview the Nerstrand children. He anguished that another interview with Karma Byrnes would terrorize her, undone as she was by memories of her husband's death and the killing of her friend. He also had to remain on guard. Karma's tiff with Paisley had brought a gleam to her tiger eyes, a warning that he should not underestimate her passions or her appeal. It was on him to dig into Lake & Isles internal affairs because office politics could brutalize anyone.

Erik called Paisley who set up appointments with the real estate agents, beginning with a one o'clock meeting with Karma. This left him time to stop at his Linden Hills apartment along the way. That morning he'd cut short his morning run to rush to his ex's house, formerly his too, because she had a lawyer crisis and Ben was dragging. Erik directed his son to hurry up with the peanut butter toast because no, they were not stopping for Pop-Tarts on the way to school. Ben's crusts had been his sustenance. Back at his place, Erik scarfed up leftover porkchops, chomped on an apple, and set up his computer to strategize about Lake & Isles.

Strategizing morphed into gazing out the window at the beautiful October day. Erik dragged his attention back indoors. The teal walls seemed dull and the couch cheap. It *was* cheap because first he'd been certain that he and Kristine would reconcile, later that he would upscale, or recently that there might be another Someone. The very idea of realtors triggered memories suppressed beneath a blanket of denial. He and Kristine had dealt with them in buying the Linden Hills house when the future was a golden sunrise of sex romps and baby buntings. A starter home and, in terms of their coupling, an ender. They hadn't counted the psychic cost of never-done dishes, newborn illness, sleepless nights, a criminal case of his colliding with a legal case of hers, *and infidelity*. After the divorce and a stretch in a resident hotel, he relied on a sympathetic agent to find a "temporary" apartment. Erik's older sister, the banker, forced her way into his decision-making and counseled, beware The Temporary which becomes The Permanent. She twisted his arm, as she did in their childhood, to invest in a condo.

Then arrived the worst day of his life, worse than being stabbed in the arm or betrayed by an old police partner. The day Erik moved out for good.

On that day, he couldn't pack his own damn underwear. Let the *ex*-wife dump his ragged tees. The king bed's duvet was stained by a coffee spill, though he'd never cared much for what was on top of the sheets, just what happened *between* them. And *that* man, bastard-mentor-lawyer smarming his way into Kristine's marital distress, had slipped between them. Erik jerked out a dresser drawer dumping his sweaters on the floor. He tossed them into a laundry basket for transport and jammed the drawer back in. In a change of heart, he tossed the underwear into a trash bag, including the valentine's day silk boxers which he'd worn at Kristine's insistence—she was most warmly his wife then and he'd been quickly relieved of them.

He couldn't make the rest of the packing go fast enough. Jimmy Bond Smalls had unconvincingly volunteered help, but Erik insisted on being alone. He wanted no witness to the sorting of his socks. His wedding suit; God almighty, what does a man do with old wedding clothes?

He made it to the curb and loaded the pickup borrowed from a friend. He drove to his new place, this place, less than a mile away. The apartment-condo with a bedroom for Ben was fine. A decent compromise, if you were satisfied with life as a series of decent compromises. He carried up the first box and dropped it to the floor. He grasped a folding chair, wavering between opening it to sit or throwing it through the window. That's when a knock came at the door. Carl, his running buddy, had circumvented the building's security to show up with sandwiches and beer. Carl was labor law, not divorce, but wise to the fact that Erik should not be alone.

Avoiding the computer screen, Erik assessed the current state of the apartment. It had taken on damage during the Time of Terrible Living, thanks to Ben's pandemic puppy, Stripe. The mutt had a blaze streaking down his nose like a Bernese Mountain dog, but the owner insisted to Ben's mom that the dominant breed was Sheltie. She compounded gullibility— *how could an unfaithful-lawyer-ex be so gullible*—with a failure to check the big puppy feet. Stripe soon outgrew the size of a Sheltie and the size allowed at Erik's place. Erik's marine training—he hadn't accepted a commission to then become a marine—proved useful as he became adept at smuggling in a large squirming object.

The memory of an embroidered sampler that hung in his childhood home came to mind, *In this house, Love is the Host, Love is the Child, Love is the Guest.*

This "house" had never been what Erik desired. He wanted the noise of children, the aroma of food, a shared bed as a haven for rest and platform for passion. A naked woman in the bed… all right, she could wear a flannel nightgown with rickrack trim, as long as it could be whisked away.

He left for Lake & Isles unprepared.

THERE ARE ABRUPT TURNAROUNDS. DETECTIVE JANSSON, in a suit with tie, entered the Lake & Isles office bearing a large floral arrangement. Karma happened to be by reception. wearing a dress with a cunning design, and her lips parted in curiosity. She flinched as he approached though, and neither spoke until she broke the silence, "Detective, you brought me flowers?"

"To see that smile—I mean, I met the courier outside, and to be helpful—" He bumbled to a stop when the yachting realtor entered with clients. The group passed slowly, as if waiting for a kissing-cam moment. He shielded himself with the flowers until his nose began to itch.

"Erik, Detective I mean, it's wonderful to see you." Paisley swanned in from the back in a blouse that happened to match the flowers. "What lovely asters and roses. I'll dig out a vase." She snatched the notecard from a plastic holder, handed it to Karma, and returned to the back. He cradled the flowers while Karma brightened, opening the note.

She read it and dimmed. "The flowers are for the whole office, condolences on the loss of Jean. They're from Dominic."

Detective Jansson, acting as if one of the office clique, asked with a tease, "Remind me, Dominic?"

"What am I thinking" Paisley stepped in front of Karma to put a vase on the reception desk. "We talked about him last time, Detective. Dominic Novak, the developer at the Landvak company. The property list I sent you, Jean was compiling it for Dominic. He has a crush on my ladies." Paisley took the flowers and shot him a meaningful look. The meaning escaped him. "His wife Renee doesn't work here anymore. Botanical scents make her gag."

"Paise, you make us sound like a harem." Karma jerked back when Paisley, fussing over the flowers, bumped her.

He stepped in. "Yes, we've reached out to Mr. Novak. I'm here, Ms. Byrnes, for a fuller picture of Jean Nerstrand."

He followed Karma to her office and saw that her dress hung loose. Perhaps he wasn't the only one who lost weight during the Time of Terrible Living, when hope became roadkill. Protein shakes had been his cure, along with Ben and the destructo puppy Stripe.

Karma sat behind her desk; he seated himself and locked eyes on hers. "I'll get to the point, though I'm sorry I have to ask this. What do you know about Jean Nerstrand's private life? It was common knowledge that she was separated from her husband, and my partner has heard that Jean had new interests. Do you know who she was seeing?"

Karma shifted back, and he fought the urge to close the gap between them. "These investigations are difficult. Would you like me to get coffee or water?"

"I can buzz Paisley." She hit intercom on her office phone. "Paisley, could I have my usual, not too sweet, and—"

"Black."

Instead of replying by intercom, Paisley popped in. "Right, coffee, a white and a black. Anything else? No?" She made a point of shutting the door behind her.

Karma drooped. "I feel I should be more grateful to Paise than I am."

"It's a challenge to be grateful to a person, however helpful, who monitors every breath you take."

"That's an unusual thing to say."

"What's unusual?" Paisley must have premade the coffee to make such a quick return. She brushed Erik in setting down the mugs, and he answered flatly.

"Unexpected deaths."

Paisley departed pronto. Karma, touchingly pathetic, wrapped her hands around the mug for warmth.

"Ms. Byrnes—"

"Stick to Karma." Her tartness dispelled the pathos.

"Karma. By the way, we recovered the vehicle Jean was driving, and carjacking is no longer in the picture. My partner Detective Metzger specializes in domestic violence, if that's the situation here. That means we take a hard look at those closest to the victim—husband, lovers, anyone she might have rejected."

"Until the past few months, Jean used to be incredibly open. She'd say anything. The first time I met her, I was a personal shopper, and she was desperate to find an outfit for a cousin's wedding. It was a Saturday—I preferred midweek for personal appointments and was in a blue funk. I tried to cover it by asking how her Saturday was going, and this is so Jean, like she wanted to cheer me up. She joked that she woke up to 'The Great American Moment.'"

"The Great American Moment?"

"Yes. Saturday morning, and the husband wanted sex, the dog walkies, the kids pancakes and cartoons, when all she wanted was to escape to the mall."

Detective Jansson burst out laughing. "*Pah*, many Americans, myself included, have been in that moment."

Karma smiled as tears pooled in her eyes. "I guess I have too. I met my husband when he was helping his pregnant sister shop . . . that's another story. Anyway, I hit it off with Jean, and she said I had a talent for seeing what worked for people. That's how I got here." With both hands she carried the coffee mug to her lips. Her arched brows tightened as she sipped. "Gosh, what can I say? When Jean first separated from Bruce in the spring, she was excited. She was an upbeat person, always teasing everyone into a better mood, though when that backfired, she became bossy. She did have a low spell, but for the past month she'd been upbeat again. I asked if she'd found someone, and she winked like she had a juicy secret. I wish I had more for you besides 'she winked.'"

He wished she had more, too. Throughout their talks, Karma's moods had camouflaged what she might know. All he'd picked up were more suspicions about Jean's behavior. Time to move on.

Before he could, his phone dinged with an alert, and he begged leave of Karma to step out into the hall to learn of an about-face in the case.

INTERVIEW OVER, KARMA COULD RELAX AT HER DESK before her next appointment and not cramp from eating lunch in a rush. She had picked up a chicken-salad croissant after dropping Sylvy at school, her favorite kind of sandwich. She removed the insulated container from her tote and opened it. Something was off.

Loud knocks at the door and back in the chair without asking was Detective Jansson. The sharp-eyed detective, not the warm-voiced man. He was direct: "Ms. Byrnes, Karma, we've learned that a homeless man may have been stalking Jean Nerstrand. We know that she volunteered at a homeless encampment with others from this office. You went with her to the Deerhorn Camp, correct?"

The tuna odor in the air sickened her. "Yes, the end of September. Do we need to discuss this now?"

"It's essential." Detective Jansson's nose twitched. "Oh, tuna fish. You're eating lunch."

"It was supposed to be chicken," Karma complained. "Not cat food."

"I'm sorry about that, but I need to ask what happened at encampment. When did you and Jean go there?"

"At the end of September to distribute food and winter clothes. I wasn't paying close attention."

He waited, how irritating.

"I mean, Detective"—Karma swept the tuna croissant into the trash—"I didn't want to dwell on how awful it was. One woman, I don't know if she'd seen a dentist in her life, or maybe that's what Meth does to teeth. It was upsetting. Everyone should have a home. A home is—I don't know how to say it, a place of safe people, a place where people are safe. I distracted myself from the worst by talking to a young woman. She wore sweats yet she caked her face with makeup out of a fantasy movie, purple and green around her eyes, spidery lashes. She told me she'd been homeless since she was fifteen and was hooked on heroin." Karma pressed her fingers against her tear ducts. "I blocked out a lot, tried to smile and be done with it."

"A smile can make a person's day." Detective Jansson had gentled his voice. "Do you remember a specific man taking an interest in Jean?"

"Women in the camp pair up with a man to stay safe from other men. Did you know *that*? We might as well live in the stone age." She spread her fingers across her face. *Go away go away go away.*

"Is a particular memory distressing you?"

Karma dropped her hands to shoot him a withering look. He didn't wither. She lifted the mug of coffee—cold. She had to give him something the way women always do. "There was a man who was right in our faces. He looked like you'd expect a hobo to look, frayed green jacket, knit cap, worn-out boots."

"His race? His face?"

"White, but with that skin that looks permanently dirty. He could've been forty-five or sixty-five. I couldn't process, Jean—" Karma caught his eye then dropped hers.

"Everything helps. Do you have any impression of his voice?"

"Wheezy, on the high side. His name was like out of a myth, a wanderer."

"Cain from the Bible?"

"No, Greek. My father's name is Greek, Karas, he walked out when I was young, but I don't know much about Greek culture, though I guess we read myths in school."

"Odysseus, Ulysses?"

"That's it. Homeless Ulysses maybe?"

"And this Homeless Ulysses was looking for his Penelope?"

Karma bristled. "You seem overeducated for your job. Penelope?"

"The long-suffering wife Ulysses left behind to fight the Trojan War, the war with the wooden horse. My mother was a teacher, is a superintendent. For a brief moment in time, I understood the comma."

She shouldn't have smiled over the comma comment, shouldn't let a detective get to her. "I think he just wanted attention."

His eyes stayed on hers. She glanced away, acting as if she couldn't go on. It wasn't an act, she realized, and attempted telepathy—*go away go away go away.*

He didn't go away. "Can you remember anything else about Homeless Ulysses?"

Act relaxed, don't cramp. "He wanted to know how to reach us, to thank us he said. Jean said he could contact the charity. He touched her red hair. She ducked and laughed it off."

"Did he try to touch anyone else?"

"I have an appointment, and it's too late to change it. You have to leave." *Go away go away go away.*

He thanked her, and she walked around to escort him the few steps to her door. An inch from him, she jolted when he, rather a card he held, grazed her hand.

"This is my partner's card, Deb Metzger. As I said, she's experienced with domestic violence and stalking. If you have any sense that someone is watching this office, don't hesitate to call. If you *ever* feel unsafe, call."

She reluctantly took the card. They were at the door, their hands bumped reaching for the handle, he apologized, yet didn't go away and had more to say. "I'll contact Dominic Novak again about Jean Nerstrand. I understand he's caught up in an arson investigation."

"If you need to know about that, talk to Rafe. He said you'd met." She withdrew her hand from proximity with his. "He's smart like a snake—you two should get along." Karma nearly pushed him out her door, and closing it, realized she was trembling.

She wanted to be left alone, but *being* alone left her in a terror.

CHAPTER 12

NOT MUCH LATER, EYES, GLOSSY AND DEAD, STARED AT KARMA. Deer eyes. Whatever the thing was called—a rack, a mount, a beheading—it had been left in the basement laundry room by a shelf sticky from detergent spills. A string of party lights festooned the poor creature's antlers, and sunshine streaking in through the high filmy window glittered on the bulbs. Karma seethed. At the other end of the basement, the egress window had been boarded up. Disrepair and grime everywhere—she should have changed out of her princess-seamed dress with its paired jacket. She hugged her tote bag to her side. She had slipped off her office flats for Hunter boots, which meant she clumped around the empty house like an ogre. This Friday was a disaster. There was that horrid interview with the detective—a handsome veneer wasted on a snake who faked concern. Then there was appointment cancelled when the pregnant client decided that her pangs were genuine labor. Next that veggie pita that Paisley placed on her desk without asking. Finally, this place with white vinyl siding hiding the shambles within, a disaster that should be a teardown.

With one exception, Karma had inherited Jean's listings, including this four-bedroom horror. The exception was the site of Jean's murder. According to Paisley, the office manager had followed Paisley's advice in taking it off the market for the time being. Paisley may have intended to be the fairy godmother but came across as a nag in fine clothing when she grilled Karma about what happened in her private time. Karma's privacy was further invaded when last night Dominic tried to draw her into consoling Renee. While Karma had zilch desire to be a go-between in the Novak marriage, she recognized that Renee could teeter between tough and fragile, as if her shellacked fingernails bled underneath. She used to a powerhouse at Lake & Isles until, like that, she had a sixth sense and was out the door.

Renee's sixth sense could have been about Jean Nerstrand attracting trouble, or attracting men who *were* trouble. Karma scolded herself for overthinking Renee's moods and the liabilities of this house. Jean had made a note on a listing printout, "Dom flip or donate?" Last year, Dominic's company had donated a rental building of six units to a nonprofit, which converted it to housing for veterans. That was before the arson at his big investment, and currently Landvak might not be in a charitable position.

The deer continued its dead stare, and Karma reached down to remove the tangled light string. *Ow*—blood bubbled across her palm. She sissed through her teeth as she wrapped the hand with a tissue, a mere scratch, but a sharp pain clenched her sternum. That pain used to ambush her before marriage, marriage to Chris banished it, it returned as chronic in early widowhood, it subsided during her recent fling, the fling with Jean's cousin that ended with the man's proposal to another woman. Real heartburn she could treat. This constriction's source was undefinable instinct.

She needed to flee this space haunted by a beheaded quadruped. Dominic would arrive soon, along with Rafe. She couldn't figure out what made that partnership work, the young geek itchy wool and the mature man plush fleece. Dom could be right that Rafe should stick with the name "Edward" to enter the realm of respectable business. Karma could butter up Rafe to agree, except she chafed at people "advising" that she adopt Karen or Carmen to avoid confusion—erasing her for the ease of a familiar label.

Karma, and always 'Karma,' tramped up the narrow stairs and out the door into a brilliant October afternoon.

SHE STOPPED UNDER A RED MAPLE WHEN SHE HEARD A CAR SLAM—Dominic walking up from his Yukon. "Karma! You look so much better than the other night," he grinned. His grin usually came with merry crinkles around his eyes, but today the eyes were worried. He must have seen her face drop because he gave her a quick hug.

Before both leaked tears, she rallied. "It's coming out into this dazzling sunshine. It's summer returned, even in this shade."

"Let's check out the landscaping. The backyard edges a woodland."

Karma rounded the corner to the west side and halted, mouth agape.

A thousand wasps pinged off the radiant heat of the white siding, their frantic bodies hitting and hitting again, next bouncing off her arm, and she backed into Dominic. "Wasps! It's a horror show!"

Dominic pulled her back to the shade. "It's all right. They aren't following us. We'll call a pest guy."

"You don't need to." Rafe startled them, slithering up like that. He walked past them into the insect-filled sunshine and thumbed away on his phone. "Paper wasps are beneficial. This season's queen has already succumbed, and they're swarming because they're lost without her and are about to die." He tilted his head for another perspective. "You know, if it weren't for the wasps, this could be an Edward Hopper painting. Sunlight on the side of a house, the American scene at its best. Not that a Hopper comparison will sell this place, though an entomologist might bite."

Karma giggled, Dom did not. Rafe could be that obnoxious know-it-all you wanted to smack, and with his crooked nose it looked like smacking was a frequent occurrence. However, his curiosity had its benefits. The first time he'd trailed Dom to Lake & Isles, Karma asked Dom if he and Renee wanted to join her and Sylvy in seeing an exhibition at the Art Institute. She wanted to know more about art without involving her boho mom. Dom begged off, while Rafe in his posh accent volunteered that like Earl Grey he'd been steeped in the classics.

"Rafe." Dominic called him 'Rafe' if no buyers were around. "Check out this property while I talk to Karma in my Yukon." Three vehicles lined the driveway, her Acura, Dom's Yukon, and a British make that was a big little car. Because a developer's vehicle is a travelling office, Dominic had to shift folders and spec sheets to the backseat for Karma to sit. The sun-heated interior enhanced the citrusy notes of Dom's aftershave. Instead of opening the windows, he switched on the AC "to keep the wasps out."

"Karma." Dom shook his head with regret. "This property's a no-go. If you want, I can have Rafe run cost models and get a reno estimate from Bob Ott." Ott was Landvak's preferred general contractor. "But it'll be a waste of time and money."

"Oh." Karma wanted a sale, not that she was broke, but she had Sylvy to support and a future to manage. Her resolve couldn't make it past a lump in her throat.

"Jean"—Dominic's voice broke—"when she last . . . called me, thought I might be able to turn into this into two or three units. I checked the floor plan online. I don't see it."

"It's hard to talk about her." Karma clutched her tote on her lap. "Jean thought you'd be interested in this as a nonprofit home for veterans."

Dominic pulled back and looked at Karma as if seeing her for the first time. "You're a good woman." He reached over and patted her tote though his big hand inadvertently touched her thigh. "Ott might come up with a way to make it work." Then he seemed to collapse, overcome, which left Karma struggling with his distress as well as her own.

"Dom, how's Renee doing?" He remained still. Jean and Renee may have been tighter than Karma realized. When the three of them were Lake & Isles colleagues, everything tumbled along in the up-and-downs of a busy workplace. Then the office assistant retired to be replaced by Paisley. Renee became tetchy around Paisley—nothing to do with Paisley being transgendered, Renee insisted after Jean and Karm pushed her on the matter. Then Renee turned tetchy with Karma. "You're a dear, but unprofessional." Paisley, tetchy in return, summed up Renee, within her hearing, as a witch with a designer broomstick. Karma couldn't dwell on which witch was which when she had to boost up Dom.

Rafe jogged by to retrieve an SLR camera from his car, which stirred up Dominic. "What's he up to? Oh, Renee, give her a call? She's burrowing into a dark place, wants me close but not too close."

"That's grief," Karma said. "After my husband, that freak accident, I wanted to hide."

Dom watched Rafe, SLR camera in hand, run back toward the wasps. "I never told you."

"Never told me what?"

Dom turned the AC off and half whispered, "We had threats, before and after that arson."

"I did hear something like that."

"What you didn't hear, and it's private, was how the threats targeted Renee to get at me. Security had to follow her around."

Karma gasped. "You can't be thinking that someone, like that arsonist, went after Jean thinking she was Renee?"

"What, hell no. Where'd you get that idea?" Dom's eyes were as round and glossy as those of the house's dead deer.

"I, I made that up." But hadn't Dom suggested it the other night? Disorganized thinking—she saw in him the disintegration she'd experienced when newly widowed. "I've been watching too many scary Halloween movies, Nightmare on—what's this street? It was a drive by, they're thinking." That was a lie. She couldn't read Detective Snake.

Dom's phone vibrated on his dash, and he checked it with a hint of amusement. "Uh, how about that. My calendar's not going to let me mope around, another appointment. Sorry to run out on you, Karma."

As she opened the Yukon door, he leaned over for a lightening kiss of her cheek, and when she out, he sped through a K turn. Karma felt jolted as she walked to her Acura, but her chest was free. It was phantom pain earlier, like Renee had phantom fears about Jean's death. She was settling her things when there was a rap on her window—Rafe with his off-center smile beneath his crooked nose. How had she forgotten him? She brought down the window halfway.

"Hey, Karma, a big Cheerio to Sylvy, and take care of yourself."

"What a sweet and straightforward thing for you to say, Rafe Edward Lutyens."

"I astonish myself with gallantry." He scrunched up his nose in concentration.

"Is there something about the house?" Karma wasn't sure she should trust Rafe without Dominic around, not that he posed a physical threat. In fact, she and Rafe connected the way two kids do at summer camp when they both discover that strawberries give them hives. They both had loving mothers inept at motherly care. His with her "born to be a princess" attitude, and her boho-sprite mamá urging flight from convention while rebounding from one conventional husband to the next. The best had been Mark, Syly's honorary grandfather. Why couldn't Karma meet a man like Mark, only young, with hair and sexy? No snakes or braggarts. Rafe had bragged once that he aimed to be vulpine in business. She had to ask what that meant, which flustered him, and he answered, cunning like a fox. Dominic should watch his back.

"Genius idea," Rafe was saying. "Sell this place as a wasp haven. Remember when things were closed down, we telepartied with a Netflix series?"

"Yeah, Sylvy loved it." Rafe's snark had made it all funny and he arranged for Sylvy's favorite pizza to be delivered.

"There's that Regency one now? Women oppressed into corsets, men pop-eyed in starched collars, and speed sex on stairways?"

"*Rafe*! Why don't you watch it with your British mum?"

He spoke Cockney: "It's me Da that's Brit. Me Mum's a Dallas Cowboy Cheerleader." The accent shifted. "Mum was born in Hopkins, Minnesota, and couldn't decide between being a midriff-baring cheerleader or the cosseted lady of the manor. Mum would get into the speed sex and gross me out."

"Same for my mom." It'd be a gas to watch the series with Rafe, and the idea made her giddy. No, the giddiness came from escaping Dom's anxiety. "Rafe, you can't be serious."

"Yes, I can." He made a serious face.

She suppressed a smile. "I'm worried about Dom, Dominic, because of"—she almost blatted *the bullet to the head*—"Jean's death." Rafe, studying wasp closeups on his camera, waited for her to say more. "I can't do a series now. The funeral's soon. Anyway, I had no idea Dom was so fond of Jean."

Rafe soured. "Too fond if you ask me. 'For to be wise and love exceeds men's might.'"

"Huh?"

"Love is unwise."

That did it. She slammed him—"What a terrible thing to say, even it is famous author blah-blah. You can't be saying Dom loved Jean."

"He was rearranging appointments to be with her."

"*Rafe*, grow up, have a heart." Karma sent up her window, jabbed Start, and revved the engine. Rafe's nose took a grotesque twist. Without a nod, he stuffed his camera-free hand in a pocket and wheeled away.

Rafe could be such an asshole.

CHAPTER 13

IN THE TOMBSTONE HOUR OF FRIDAY AFTERNOON, TIME STALLED. Deb wandered the G-Met halls like an ostrich who's lost the egg, the egg being the homeless stalker who had emerged in the Nerstrand case. She'd just outsourced to Cyber Paul's team the digital search for a restraining order. She drifted back to the office to find Erik suspiciously quiet at his desk. As lead, she decided they needed a verbal tussle to wake up their wits and dawdled where she could see his screen.

"Whoa, are you watching a James Bond flick? We have a murderer on the loose, and you're off in a fantasy of superhero men and the women who go gaga over them."

"It's the Norwegian team in a biathlon." Erik hadn't raised his head. "It's serious stuff."

"Serious, huh. This is me being *dubious*. I know what dubious means because I get a vocab word a day in my email. So"—she pointed at her face—"this is *dubious*. On top of that, I have a mental catalog of your eyeball vocabulary—that, that look right there, that's *your* dubious look. Now it's *super* dubious."

"Guess this one."

"That look, I'm not saying it out loud. Oh, this next one I don't get."

"Forbearance. For all the bears I meet."

"I wanted to say the 'bear' part. Okay, not the death stare, but clue me in." She pointed to his screen. "Ouch, he fell right over. You want to do *that*, which is what?"

"I'm training for a winter biathlon. Cross-country skiing and shooting."

"You can shoot already, but aren't we focused on de-escalation, not going off all gun crazy? Oh, I see 'forbearance' again."

"It's about managing your heart."

"You want to keep your heart from going wonka-wonka at the sight of a woman you wish you could have but don't? Wait, I'm talking about me." What Deb wanted was to whine about Jude and their disconnect. She'd settle for permission to procrastinate, and Erik caught on.

"Here, watch this."

She loomed over his shoulder. "So a guy skis, shoots, skis and shoots again. Isn't there a joke, eats shoots and leaves, so he's like a panda who skis? Anyhoo, he stands for one shot, wooshes off, then throws himself down on the snow, which just seems dumb."

"It's the challenge. Target's at fifty meters. For a standing shooter, the target's four and a half inches wide. For a prone shooter, the target's less than two inches wide. Skiing cross-country hikes up the heart rate and causes adrenalin surges, which makes fine motor control iffy. See, this one's the fastest skier, but he rushed his shot there and missed the target. You've been through Field Shooting 101—hard breathing and pumping heart aren't good for hand-eye coordination. You need to regain control over your reactions."

"You're thinking this is a way for an Erik-type dude to stay in shape and be smart with a firearm."

"Women compete too."

"Ah, you're intending to meet Annie-Skiing-Oakley out there. What's this? The guy has to ski uphill at the end because everything else wasn't hard enough? It's a Bond fantasy all right."

A whap against their open door. "*Hey*, you two fantasizing about the wonder that is me?" Jimmy Bond Smalls. "FYI, you're wanted now. Doesn't the intercom work in these parts? Our beloved Chief Ibeling, in his almost allwise way, wants to see every person in this building. Required school assembly, no spitballs allowed, haul your butts to the big bad conference room."

They hustled because a sudden muster meant a crisis. Several occurred when G-Met had to step in as outside investigators in hot-button cases, and one occurred when a G-Met investigator died mysteriously at a scene under circumstances that remained mysterious.

Deb, flanked by Erik and Jimmy Bond Smalls, joined other investigators and staff on the auditorium seats. The lighting popped and flickered. When the chief entered from a side door, Jimmy nudged Deb. "Damn, Ibeling's in a *suit*, must be bad." He shushed himself as Ibeling stomped to an unstable podium. The chief hacked to clear his throat; the hacking devolved into coughing. From a trouser pocket, he hauled out a flag-sized handkerchief, grumble-coughed into it, then nodded to a petite woman in the front row. Utter speechlessness had forced Almost Allwise to cede authority.

It was ceded to pretty Naomi, forensic accountant extraordinaire. Deb's breasts rose and fell. Pregnant Naomi stepped up and removed a facemask.

Naomi was the unacknowledged darling of G-Met, because acknowledge it to her face and you'd be slapped.

"Thank you for coming, though soon we'll all be going. Not from our jobs but from this building." Whistling and woohoos began, and subsided when Naomi continued, "Because I discovered the problem, Chief Ibeling asked me to explain. I imagine some of you have become aware of the problem as well."

Deb hissed at Jimmy, "the funding shortfall, the old computers, tattletale Drees?"

He whispered, "I don't care what she has to say as long as she says it pretty."

Erik side-eyed them both as Naomi spoke *sotto voce* to Ibeling before addressing the assembly.

"In my condition, my sense of smell is my superpower. Lately it's smelled like we were living in a sewer, no symbolism intended. The HVAC system initially absorbed the, um, *noxious circumstance*." She put a steadying hand to her bosom. "In short, I reported to the chief, he ordered an inspection, and we *are* living on top of an open sewer. The old drainage pipes have corroded away."

There were mutterings of "damned" and "doomed."

"Condemned." Naomi fought retching, grabbed her baby belly, and faded to pea-green. Lola Scheers, anti-trafficking taskforce head and former fake hooker, escorted Naomi outside. As wave of nausea swept the room, people wobbled in their creaky seats.

Ibeling gnarred, "Everyone *out*. Instructions will be emailed when they're known. Until further notice, you're evicted."

"What, no plan?" Jimmy froze in a half-stand. "How can we solve anything without a base? We can't solve mysteries just in our heads—our heads ain't that stretchy. We need *externals*. A murder board, monitors, a breakroom with doughnuts."

"Where do we go?" Deb moaned.

"Where do we go," Erik frowned, "when life's a noxious circumstance?"

THE G-MET DENIZENS RECEIVED A REPRIEVE. They could finish the workday if they could do so without using the plumbing or overrunning the facilities at the nearest Starbucks. Deb and Erik headed to Cyber Paul's lair. Like Naomi, Paul had adorned himself in a facemask and offered spares to the detectives. Death by Mold was an ignominious way to go.

Paul sucked in his mask and blew out. "Here's the thing. After Deb inquired about a restraining order requested by Jean Nerstrand, I called in a favor at that precinct, and they sent me a document recovered from hard drive trash. The form had been filled out, but never filed for lack of information about the alleged stalker, aka Homeless Ulysses."

Paul clicked open documents on his screen. "Jean Nerstrand reported that she met him in the Deerhorn encampment early September. She described him by his army surplus coat, wrinkled face, and gray matted hair. She also said he didn't move one of his arms much, like it hurt, but was unsure which arm. Pretty much typecasting for generic homeless guy. He wore a Gophers maroon knit hat, you know, the University of Minnesota's mascot. She remembered that because she asked if he went to the Uni—she meant as a student—and he said they didn't like his sort on campus. Finally, and Jean Nerstrand thought this odd, he had a dreamcatcher, that willow hoop with feathers, hanging from a 'grody' backpack."

"I suppose when you're homeless, you don't have a window to hang it in," Deb said. "What else, Paul?"

"She first spotted him a day after the encampment visit across the street from her house and told him to move on. At the end of the week, he's hanging around the Lake & Isles parking lot. That's when she gets worried. He knows where she lives, he knows where she works. He came at her from behind when she was unlocking her car. He grabbed her and said, 'You need.' She didn't hear the rest because she hopped in her car and 'skedaddled out of there.' That's when she came in to make a report. The authorities couldn't fill out sufficient details to submit the order, and she called back two weeks later saying drop it, she didn't see him around anymore."

Deb tugged at her hair spikes. "Sometimes the obsession just ends, or he found another person to stalk. What could have happened this week is that he renewed attention to Jean. Killed her when she rejected him."

Erik stretched with restlessness. "I'm wondering how he got around, if he has a vehicle or scored a bus pass."

"As low-income, he might have received a bus pass to travel for medical care and necessities," Paul said.

Deb had both hands tugging at hair chunks. "Neighborhood where Jean was killed, people notice strangers. He wouldn't fit in."

Paul cocked his head at the computer. "How would he come by a handgun? Doesn't seem like he'd have a valid address for a permit. Oh, right, lots of illegal weapons on the streets."

"Unfortunately, yes," Erik stretched his arms to a giant's height. "A homeless person might find a gun that someone ditched after a crime. Great for the original user since if the weapon's found with homeless guy, homeless guy is likely to be charged for a crime he didn't commit."

"It might be Jean's own weapon that was taken from her," Deb said. "Jean pulls a gun on her stalker but can't go through with it. He seizes the gun and it's *that* scenario."

Paul clicked and skimmed the screen. "Hot off the wire, the ballistics report. The uneven ground and possible movements on the part of the victim and shooter make plotting the trajectory difficult. The shot was likely fired from six feet, and a guesstimate for the shooter's height is from five-foot-two to six-foot-two."

"So not a midget or NBA player," Deb yawned.

"But why be at that St. Louis Park empty house at night?" Erik yawned back. "That sounds like an opportunity for a tryst."

"A tryst?" Deb eyed him.

"A good vocab word," Erik eyed her back.

Paul stifled a yawn. "A homeless stalker might not be the killer. But could the stalker have witnessed something?"

Erik came to abrupt attention. "In which case, this Homeless Ulysses might be in serious danger."

"Oh gosh, this case gets worser and worser," Deb moaned. "What's more, I have to pee. What about you guys?"

And that's how Case Leader Deb gave urgency to their Friday night evacuation of G-Met.

CHAPTER 14

DETECTIVE DEB METZGER WAS BACK ON THE JOB SOON ENOUGH, and it felt like being dunked in ice water. After yesterday's summery temps and the clear sunrise this Saturday morning, she figured her favorite yellow sweater would keep her toasty. She failed to register last night's frost warning. After walking a hundred feet from her car, she ran back to choose between the emergency rain poncho or a blood-stained G-Met fleece. She grabbed the fleece figuring the stain could pass as ketchup.

She was early at the agreed-upon corner of Deerhorn encampment and under her frosty breath swore at Erik for not showing up already. He had some frigging *legitimate* excuse like chauffeuring his son somewhere. Darn, if only she could play the parent card, a joke on herself that suddenly felt serious. She rubbed her arms in the fleece to keep her blood from congealing. Her sleek boots with their stacked heel could kick ass but lacked fuzzy warmth. Worse, she had to acknowledge that she had it absolutely bougie compared to the people in tents. Though at the rate she was going in her personal shelter search, she might end up joining them.

"Are you waiting for Godot?" she heard at her back from smart-aleck Erik.

"What does that even mean?"

"It's a play where nothing happens. Whose blood on your fleece?"

"It's 'ketchup.' I wanna wrap up the case pronto for the sake of the Nerstrand kids. Not to mention, I need time to find a place to live. Can you believe it, I've put in three offers *above* asking price and I was outbid every single time."

Erik screwed up his face. "Nothing fair in love or real estate."

"For sure. Where's our guide to the encampment? I need to find a suspect to drill, and you, Partner, are lost without a game to play and a chain to yank or you'll start yanking mine. Doctors have a bedside manner. Do you have a tent-side manner? Wish I had hot cider." Deb tossed her head and stamped her feet.

"Would you like my fleece, instead of stomping about like a fjord horse?"

"If your inflated look means you're layered with a Norwegian sweater, why not?"

Erik removed his fleece to reveal heavy blue wool with a snowflake pattern. She covered her blood-stained fleece with his. "Gloves?" he asked.

"Thanks." Deb thought he meant extras stuffed in a pocket, not the ones on his hands which he gave her. They were warm inside. "Look, monster claws." She waved the long fingertips at him.

Erik was distracted by a woman in a wheelchair leaving the Deerhorn encampment. "There's a classic movie where a spoiled debutante goes looking for a forgotten man. That's what this feels like."

"Are you often mistaken for a debutante? Where's your tiara?" Deb dug through his fleece pockets. No tiara, not even a KitKat bar, just a body cam on a lanyard.

"The forgotten man becomes the butler for the debutant's ditzy family. The girl regrets her treasure hunt and says something like, 'if a person's a person, you should treat him like a person.'"

"Then, duh, they fall in love. Hard to be loving here," Deb said. "Gosh, whole forgotten families."

Erik shoved his gloveless hands up the sleeves of his sweater. "I had an argument with my poet sister. Meaning I listened while she railed on that I was a tool of the oppressors. She said laws make you a 'criminal' if you have no place to stay. You're warned out of shops, libraries, parks. It's under the bridge for you like a troll."

"Trolls charge fees, so they have an income source." Deb in Erik's fleece squeezed herself to warm up faster. "Is this our guide?"

Coming toward them was a young woman in a blanket coat with skin and hair the color of sand. "Nell Gundersen with Shelter Alliance. I take it you're Detectives Metzger and Jansson." She grinned at Erik's Norwegian sweater. "I see that you're in your home uniform, Jansson. My dad has a matching one. He traces his roots back to Sognefjord. My mom traces her roots back to here, a member of the White Earth Tribe. I'm also a tribal member, and that's what pulled me into housing issues. 'Native' land with so many unhoused natives on it." Nell started walking them into the camp. "It's a mix of people, here brown, black, white. I believe in cooperation all the way around, with residents and authorities, and expect that it takes uncomfortable work to keep that cooperation fair."

Nell looked from one detective to the other, sizing them up. "I suppose the two of you know about uncomfortable work. You say a murder victim volunteered here? What a terrible thing to happen to a person of compassion. This man you're seeking, Ulysses—his regular case worker is on medical leave—can he really be a suspect?"

Deb answered, "I admit it's not *probable* that a man in Ulysses' situation could have committed the crime. Today is about retracing the victim's movements. Also, Ulysses may have witnessed something that could help our investigation. Could you take us around? This population doesn't always, um, welcome law enforcement."

"Depends if the police are bringing supplies or booting everyone out. I can get you started, but on my way here I was updated that per city order this encampment must be emptied in two days. Our organization has been working for months to move everyone to better shelter by the first of November." Nell's cheer downshifted to exasperation. "These residents have to be talked through any kind of change, and with this new demand they might just take off and hide and then it's, it's . . ."

Frustration had tied Nell's tongue, and Deb jumped in, "So why the sudden action? Finding shelter's a bitch—I mean, wow, tough."

"The group that owns the apartment complex across the street has filed a lawsuit against the city. The lawsuit claims the city is derelict in its duties, and residents of the complex have complained of having cars broken into and being confronted for money. The suit also claims there's a negative 'aesthetic impact.' To quote, 'people rent at this address to be adjacent to a park, not a Hooverville.'" Nell threw up her hands. "Sorry, we do worry about crime here, we want to keep drugs out, and people need addiction treatment. We've ignored the safety of the unhoused for long enough. There, I've done it, worked myself up."

"Any chance of negotiation with the owner?" Erik asked.

"Endless and pointless, according to my supervisor, but my motto is stay positive." Nell's look, however, was defeated. "What's that, Deb? A body cam? You're entering someone's home, their safe space. Out of respect, can you keep it off? Second thought, be prepared to flick it if an incident happens. I guess that's a mixed message. I'll start you at tent number three. She makes good coffee. Maybe I can bum a mug for a restart."

Nell bucked herself up to wave at a resident leaving the camp and wish him a good day at work. "Lots of people here lived through better times and are doing all they can to get back to them. By no means do all homeless suffer from addiction or mental illness. However," she lowered her voice, "be careful around Agnes who considers herself the Wrath of God."

"Yup," Deb said. "Ready, Partner?"

No, he was not. Erik stared into the distance, and at Deb's nudge he asked, "What's the management company over there, the lawsuit one?"

Nell looked like she'd swigged vinegar. "It's run by Dominic Novak."

Deb's arms dangled, and a glove slipped off a hand. "What a coincidence."

Nell was taken aback. "You know Novak? Do you by chance have clout with him? Oh, my phone's buzzing. Our pro bono counsel about the eviction. Gotta take this." She hurried off and shot back a warning. "Erik, you've gone wolf-eyed. Let Deb lead."

Here Deb thought she was already leading, and Erik had narrowed in on Dominic's building. She whapped him with the gloves she was about to return.

Eyes distant, he stated a truism, "In detective world, we don't like coincidences."

If he'd gone wolf-eyed, Deb looked like she'd swallowed cough medicine cut with fish sauce. As they moved into the encampment, Erik was about to ask if she was all right when she flipped on her zippy switch. "*Hey*, how are you?" Deb greeted the first people they encountered. "We're looking for a missing person." More than one Deerhorn resident scrambled to hide in a tent, and others overshared their stories. From those, Erik gathered that some couldn't make the right choice to save their lives, some couldn't process the difference between the right choice and the wrong, and many never had a choice at all. Needed were hope, hot water, and dental work. Dental records likely didn't exist for these victims of neglect.

Even neglect had its gradations. The two made a hairpin turn down a tent row that was the low-rent district of the encampment. In the center, a tall man perked coffee and cooked midmorning hotdogs on a picnic grill. At six and a half feet, he branched in every direction. He glanced up, his face brown except for white around the mouth like clown lips and white around the eyes like a peeled sunburn. Erik winced and wished he hadn't. The man had vitiligo, a condition that leeched melanin from the skin. You had to get used to seeing him not to feel that you were gawking and not to feel that you were dismissing him as strange.

Besides the towering cook, a white man with a face like a ferret sniffed the hotdogs. "Hey, Tree, you're turning 'em to charcoal. Yo, what in crud's name are the pair of you?"

Erik stepped back to let Deb enjoy the lead. "Hi, I'm G-Met Detective Deb Metzger, and I'm looking for a missing person."

"Oh, you're the cops we heard about," Ferret sniffed. "Not interested in your chitchat."

"Yeah, but—"

"Yeah but you ain't got warrants, Missy." Tree hissed through his nose and leveled his barbecue fork at Erik. "Sure you're not a killer cop? White male serving the public with hate and cruelty." Erik tightened—hard to evoke rapport when a three-inch tine is leveled at your heart. Tree pulled his elbow back quick as if to stab.

"Whoa." Deb lunged between them and pushed back the fork. "Whoa whoa whoa, back away, Tree, and turn those dogs or they will be charcoal."

Tree stabbed hot dogs, scowling at Erik like he was dead meat in need of a skewer. "What you got to say for yourself?"

"Killer cops don't wear sweaters." Erik pulled the wool away from his chest, which made the thumping of his heart less evident. "Killer cops wear orange jail suits, knitwear not being standard issue, and . . . this a present from my grandma."

A Black man with deep eyebags joined the group to a "what's up, Joe?" He put a finger to Erik's chest. "Did it snow? Is that why you got snowflakes on your pecs? Did I miss the snow?"

"He eats, shoots, and skis," Deb said with a quiver. If she meant to be helpful, it backfired because Tree, Ferret, and Joe gave Erik the stink eye. He would've backed out of the room except they weren't in a room.

He made a snap judgment. "The three dogs on the end are done."

"The hell, yeah." Joe snatched a hot dog barehand and blew on it. Tree and Ferret honed the stink eyes on Erik.

"You'll have to excuse my partner's face," Deb interjected. "It can look guilty and innocent at the same time. That face goes back to a misuse of glue in his Sunday School days."

Ferret stood on tiptoes to stick his nose in Erik's problem face. "You got good symmetry with your cheekbones, but this ain't Sunday school. Why you here?"

"We're here about a volunteer, Jean Nerstrand, who was killed," he said.

"No one murdered here," Tree growled.

"Righto," Deb went upbeat and showed photos of Jean. "Jean was *seen* here, maybe with a resident called Ulysses. Did you pick up anything about them?"

A growing ragtag audience glanced at the photos, though their true purpose was to be on hand for the divvying up of the hotdogs

Time to shake things up. Deb said he liked games, so Erik would play one. "Another thing, Detective Deb here needs housing. She has to move and can't get into a place with the market the way it is."

Tree goggled at Deb. "You want to live *here*?"

"So those apartments across the street," Deb picked up the tune and nodded toward the complex owned by Dominic Novak. "What gives over there?"

Ferret held a hotdog in his mouth stogie-style and snatched a second for a pink-haired woman who appeared out of the nonexistent woodwork. He lisped mid swallow, "Thuckth."

"True that," the woman said. She brought her low self close enough that juice from her hotdog dribbled on Deb's, that is Erik's, fleece. She tilted her head back to take in Deb. "You got big eyes up there. How come you didn't stop growing?"

Deb took it pleasantly. "No one told me to."

"You should marry Tree," the woman garbled with full mouth, "and raise a forest together. Little Trees everywhere, ha-ha-gack!"

Ferret, slapping his girlfriend on the back while holding his hotdog in his mouth, lisped information. "That plathe ith run by Dominic Rathole and hith atthithtant."

The choking woman nodded. "*Ack,* the assistant's on Masterpiece Theater only he's got someone else's nose on his face."

"Dominic's popped in and caught on that he's not welcome. The assistant came back asking what it would take for us to leave." Tree pointed his hot-dogged fork at Deb. "Take this, Detective Deb, because you don't know where your next meal is coming from."

Ferret, dog bites swallowed, commiserated. "Man, you're homeless? Is that why you're wearing that fleece that looks like one your grandpa was going to toss? Mr. Sunday School here has a nice sweater from his grandma, and you're in a hand-me-down? Hey, Mr. Sunday School, loan her your gloves."

Erik loaned them to Deb for a second time, and since she was obligated to chew the hotdog, he asked, "Did you see Novak or his assistant with Jean Nerstrand?" He held out his phone, giving everyone a second look at Jean.

The pink-headed woman hmmed. "She talked to that Ulysses guy from the other side of the camp. He's done gone AWOL. He liked the pretty woman who came with the dead one. She's *The Young and the Restless* type. She's hot enough to set somebody on fire."

Deb swallowed hard. "Did you catch the other woman's name?"

The woman scrunched up her face. "Soap opery name?"

Tree poured coffee thick as molasses with a smell as strong. "Her name wasn't a soap opera name. Real opera, *Carmen.* She died."

"Jean's friend died?" Deb gasped, and Erik went on high alert.

"No, the woman in that opera. Saw the performance in the park last sum-mer. Carmen attracted too many men and her lover killed her." Tree falsettoed and dum-de-dummed his way through the opera's famous seduction aria, the "Habanera."

Swaying with the melody, Pink-haired woman stroked Erik's sweater sleeve, and out of the corner of his eye, he saw Deb messing with his glove. He rushed to the point. "Does anyone know if Ulysses is all right? Where and when did you last see him?"

The direct questions ended the party. Pink-haired woman muttered, "I got business," and with the crowd receded to nowhere.

Ferret, Joe, and Tree lingered, uncertain. Tree gangled his arms around, sludging coffee over his mug. "Well, it's hard to say about Ulysses, thanks for asking. He's chronic homeless. Most of us had a place at that Penn Avenue complex until Dominic Suckface went and upscaled it. Serves him right it got burned down. Ulysses comes and goes depending on his meds. He got some kind of PTSD."

"Is he a veteran?" Deb asked. "Knowing that would be a help."

"Can't say for sure. He talk about strange things." Tree sipped his coffee like it was alive and resisted being drunk.

Ferret warmed his hands over the grill embers, which loosened a tremor. "Ulysses was spooked because he saw a man killed before that arson, that's what he says. Dominic wants to pull in millennials, why he's kicking us out of here. Those millennials, they'll pay five bucks for a coffee. For five bucks, Tree can make coffee for a month."

"Tastes like it too." Tree poured his sludge on the ground.

"Did Ulysses report the killing?" Deb asked.

Tree pulled a packaged wipe from his pocket to clean his hands. "Ulysses gets mixed up, says he and this buddy Tom from the Native side of the camp were around before the place went up in flames. When somebody hit his buddy with a wrench, Ulysses ran. A body was found, done real crisp after the fire. Ulysses frets the same will happen to him."

"You're saying that last March, he was a witness to the murder and the arson at the Park Avenue apartments?" Erik asked.

"Don' know that anybody knows that Ulysses was a witness. Don't go ruinin' it for him. He's got no safety net." Tree pulled dental picks from another pocket and went to work on his teeth. "Maybe Dominic's not the bottom of the barrel, 'cause I can see people taking advantage of him, him being Mr. Sunshine with his poufy hair. That English-accent dude, can't make up my mind about him. He gave me a phone 'cause I'd used up my minutes on the old one. They're spooked about their buildings." He waved toward the nearby apartments. "You police never rounded up the arsonist. That's on you."

"I got it! I know what happened," Ferret chimed in. "This arsonist followed Ulysses and the woman—whack! Two dead bodies."

Deb grimaced. "I see, um, thank you for the input. So far it's just one dead body."

Tree delivered a rumbling omen. "There's always more dead bodies. You, Detective Deb, don't go to dark places. Young man in Grandma's sweater, Sunday School can't protect everybody. Hell's bells, I went to Sunday School and pray every day. Look at where I am."

The detectives stood in quiet acknowledgement. Then Erik offered a card to Tree. "Keep in touch about your move here. Our unit can't stop it, but we can track down boxes for you and help out." Boxes being stockpiled at G-Met for their own move.

Tree caught them both off guard with a lunge at Deb, which became a bear hug. "This is your home, Debbie, whenever you need it. I'll make tacos next time."

Deb looked more sick than thankful and rushed a goodbye. She tossed Erik's gloves at him and speed-walked to the street. He caught up, extracted gnawed hotdog out of his glove, and dangled it in her face.

Deb walked faster. "You can finish it. They were spooking *me*."

"Debbie!" Ferret shook like a scarecrow as he ran after them. "I remembered something. Ulysses went to a spa, 'cause he had a gift card. A spa in E-dina."

Then a greyhound of a woman rushed out of nowhere and knocked Ferret to the ground. Deb swiveled to help. Ferret screeched, "Agnes, no!"

Too late—Agnes sunk her teeth into the flesh of Deb's hand and wouldn't release when Erik grabbed the woman from behind. A look flashed between the detectives, Erik raised Agnes into the air, her jaw clamped on Deb's hand, Deb tapped her foot on a spot, Erik brought Agnes down hard, Deb stomped on Agnes's sneaker, Agnes yowled, and they ran to Erik's Highlander. As he drove to Urgent Care, Deb wrapped the sleeve of his fleece around her bloodied hand and said through clenched teeth, "I thought the hotdog from hell was the low point of my life, until I met the Wrath of God."

CHAPTER 15

Saturday, and Rafe couldn't be bothered by calls from Detective Jansson. The detective left a message that he needed to talk with him "at the earliest possible convenience." It would never be convenient, not when Rafe had so many irons in the fire. The current iron that he fought to keep hot was the Promise Creek Commons Development.

Despite Dominic's claim to love a vision, it had cost Rafe to help him see this one. The vision of the Commons, a mixed-use development, was far from realized as the two of them plodded to a fenced construction site bordered by power lines. Brown fields surrounded them because of the late season; brownfields lay beneath their feet because of the former pollutants.

In Rafe's first days with Landvak, he'd begged for Dominic to consider the Promise Creek project north of the Twin Cities. Instead, his boss assigned him a multitude of other properties to investigate. Rafe worked overtime to cover Promise Creek as well, but when he wanted to attend hearings on the project viability, Dominic scheduled conflicting meetings. Rafe secretly zoomed in via phone. He included a cost/benefit analysis of the project as an addendum to other prospectuses. He talked up the "positive optics" with Dominic, with construction manager Ott when he dropped by, even with Renee, and realized that it's difficult to be persuasive when you're a snarky twit. He dignified the concept with quotations about phoenixes rising out of ashes. Heads turned away. Rafe talked tough, like in American movies—if you're not in, you're out.

In the eleventh hour, Rafe dreamed up a mission statement because every company wants a mission statement, whether or not they live by it. In defending the project's cost, he had discovered its value. The Promise Creek project, he declaimed to anyone in earshot, was *the* opportunity for Landvak to prove itself a team player in civic betterment, a leader in affordable housing, and a forward-thinking participant in environmental restoration. How often does the chance come along to transform a World War II munitions plant and Superfund Cleanup site into a green and pleasant land of sustainable living?

Dominic listened, took charge, and with Ott Construction bought into Promise Creek. A short-lived victory for Rafe because then the civic stakeholders sued each other over how many residents to allow and what percentage of the units should be affordable housing. Those living farthest from the Commons wanted high residency with a minimum of twenty percent of units as "affordable." Those nearest the Commons wanted low residency and a maximum of ten percent affordable—a standoff and delays. Dominic came down on Rafe to the point of viciousness. Ott saved the Landvak investment, grudgingly saving Rafe in the process, by reminding Dominic that the commons would happen because the housing market was ravenous. The civic stakeholders eventually played nice and compromised, after a judge decreed they must.

Which brought Rafe and Dominic to the site this cold morning, where they peered through a chain-link fence at the footprint of the apartment complex. The muddy location did not inspire the feel of a vibrant village. In the commercial section, a ramp descending to a broad pit indicated one of the most expensive elements, underground parking at over $20K per space. The Landvak apartment area was an expanse of ditches, concrete footings, and modular work trailers. Center stage, a giant crane rose over one-hundred-fifty feet to guard the site.

Dominic set aside his grief over Jean's death, a grief that surprised Rafe in its depth, and smiled with the expansiveness of a man well-pleased with himself. The pleasure faded when he looked skyward at thin clouds. "Is the first blizzard's coming? I'd thought Ott would have been more advanced by now." Dominic unsnapped the down vest he'd layered over a birds-eye sweater. Rafe cooked in a puffer coat, flannel-lined chinos, and work boots that he'd made a point of buying at a factory downriver in Red Wing.

Rafe threw his shoulders back to regain confidence. "Frozen ground's not an impediment with modern equipment."

"It's the working conditions. Men can't work in a sleet storm." Dominic had chastised him before for not thinking of the intense stress of construction labor and the high rates of mental illness, suicide, and substance abuse. Chalk up another point up to Rafe's insensitivity.

"Edward"—the name choice marked Dominic's annoyance. "Are you sure that your 'stakeholders' know what they're doing? Reassure me, what did Heartland Construction accomplish?"

Promise Creek Commons grew out of public/private partnerships with the master developer, Heartland Construction and Renovation; subcontracted companies including Landvak; Ramsey County; the City of Arden Hills; the U.S. Army; and additional investors motivated by just cause or projected profit. Rafe checked his phone so Dominic wouldn't accuse him of inventing facts. "It was like the labors of Hercules. Heartland removed one-hundred-fifty-thousand feet of piping and fifty miles of materials that look like a different kind of piping, dug up building slabs, tore up railroad tracks, and in all removed four-hundred-thousand tons of material, over ninety percent of which was recycled. Also, the Army will continue cleaning up the groundwater."

"That last part bothers me." Dominic tapped his boot on the ice that skinned a puddle. "Unless you Brits want a cup of this polluted tea." He laughed and undid the padlock at one of the gates into the Landvak section. He slapped Rafe on the back. "Good work. I had to make you prove yourself. To think," he swept his arm back toward the commercial area, "that this will be a place of organic salads, yoga classes, and craft brews. Amazing. What used to be an ammunition plant that helped win wars will be chichi living."

"Before that the Dakotas—"

Dominic waved off Rafe. "The government entities will put our tax dollars into expedient signage. Ah, I get it. You want a big woody sign because you're part Indian."

"The other kind of Indian. My paternal grandmother was Bengali."

"Gotcha! Can't you tell when I'm pulling your leg? I smell the cumin in your microwaved lunches. To me cumin smells like body odor. Just about every immigrant who landed on these shores was oppressed. Ask the Irish, like Renee's ancestors on her mom's side. They escaped from famine caused by Brits like you." Dominic was ignorant of the Bengal famine of 1943, also blamed on Brits, which Rafe's grandmother's family had fled. "I'm bringing Renee by later."

They zig-zagged around ditches to the modular unit. Inside, multicolor schedule grids and punch lists lined the doublewide interior. Dominic waved Rafe to a chair and took a seat behind the desk. He retrieved water bottles from a minifridge and banged one on the desk near Rafe. Rafe, once the runt at a British prep school, knew how to assess a bully. Dominic of the soft exterior wasn't exactly a bully, but when push came to shove, he solidified, an immoveable mass cemented in place by his favorite contractor, Bob Ott—favorite since Cardenas "allegedly" burned down the Park Avenue apartments. Ott emitted a "don't even think of bothering me" vibe and flexed muscles hardened by construction labor. If it came down to Rafe fighting Ott, Rafe's best hope was that after decades of punishing work Ott would throw out his back.

Dominic pulled papers from the desk drawer to review. Rafe went back to measuring himself against others.

There was that shrewd alpha-male, Detective *Call-me-at-your-convenience* Jansson. Women might *ooh* over his physique. Poppycock. Women preferred imperfect men—what other kind was there when you think about it? Rafe, in time, reached 5'10," as tall as a James Bond actor. His eyes could be deemed poetic; his nose, if not the usual shape, did occupy the usual space. *No Quasimodo he.* But that detective moved like a Dobermann disguised in oxford cloth and coiled to spring. If only every battle took the cerebral form of Double Jeopardy. From bruised experience, Rafe accepted the wisdom that discretion is indeed the better part of valor.

Dominic gulped water and belched. "Just scanned your report on that Deerhorn Encampment. The city's evicting them in two days. Prepare a statement to feed the media if they harp at us."

"You outsource that to professional PR people."

"You went to the camp, upfront and personal. You reported that a drug dealer approached you, and we can't risk dealers approaching our tenants or our tenants' children."

"Landvak could help with the transition. Did you see that a number of the homeless lived at the Penn Avenue complex before we, Landvak, bought it? There's lingering resentment." In the unheated trailer, Rafe was sweating.

"All the more reason for a word nerd like you to take over. Text me a draft first thing Monday. Focus on Landvak's support for affordable housing, and help out at the evacuation."

"Right, we support affordable housing."

"Sarcasm is not the path to promotion." Dominic laced his fingers behind his head and plonked his boots on the desk. "Affordable housing is not, I repeat, is not a last refuge for those in the gutter. Affordable housing is a two-way street, affordable for low-wage earners and fixed-income retirees *and* affordable for us to run. Which you should know, with your per-foot cost models based on using laminate flooring versus a Brazilian wood with an unpronounceable name."

"Ipe. The unhoused—"

"The homeless can't be homed unless there's fucking development. I can't be Mr. Nice Guy for idealists supported by mommies and daddies. Nonprofits exist only when there's profit to support them. Protesters yack that development is the spawn of Satan." Dominic swung his feet to the floor. "The opposite of 'development' isn't 'Eden,' and human beings were 'evicted' from Eden. The opposite of 'development' is toxic waste unless the big bucks come in to fix it. And you, *Edward*, trotted off to Tent City where you were supposed to 'focus' on the impact on our tenants. Instead, you ask tent folk what bothers them. *Jesus*."

Dominic's cursing was nothing compared to the obscenities flung at Rafe at the encampment. "In preparing this statement—"

"No questions. Do it."

"I do question the security at this site. No cameras, no guards."

"For fuck's sake, Lutyens. I've been over this with you. THIS IS NOT A HIGH-RISK SITE. Middle of nowhere. Nothing can be carried off without specialized hoists. There's a fence, locks, a regular patrol. I'm not draining my pockets for your whims." Dominic scratched under the arm of his sweater where the vest was snug.

You wanker Rafe wanted to spit. "The investigation of Jean's death has thrown everything off balance. You two were close, visiting properties—"

"*What* are you implying?" Dominic burned beet red. "God, you're a nasty prick." He lifted his bulk to come down on Rafe only to sag. "Jean was spending as much time with Bob Ott."

"With Ott?" Rafe wormed low in his chair.

"He's going through a divorce and needed his own place, needed, *needs*, our emotional support."

"Wouldn't Ott's idea of emotional support be blowing somebody's head off? *Shit*, I take that back. I meant, Ott would probably go to a shooting range to blow off steam."

"What do you know about shooting ranges?" Dominic asked coolly.

"It's where Americans express themselves." Rafe had gone for a laugh. Instead, Dominic was ready to plug him. He waved him away, and Rafe struggled to walk calmly to the door. Keep calm and carry a grudge.

One last blast from Dominic: "You're in over your head. No poisoning our projects."

Rafe kept his upper lip stiff. "Of course not." An ambiguous statement because of course he would not go against his own mind, and Dominic could burn in hell. Hell, unlike Eden, welcomes all.

LATE SATURDAY AFTERNOON, THE LAKE & ISLES OFFICE was deserted under a sky that had turned from sapphire to iron ore. Usually, a few realtors lingered doing follow-ups after an open house, but Karma had been alone. The baseboard heating clicking on and off made sounds like rattling chains. She was anxious to pick up Sylvy from her play date and spend the evening addressing the pumpkin problem of Jerry and Jilly and convincing her daughter that they should draw faces rather than carving them. They'd have spaghetti and meatballs, Sylvy's favorite dinner, and watch her favorite movie. Sylvy identified with a bookworm-of-a-girl who attained a Cinderella moment where she twirled in a gold-leaf ballgown; a polyester-leaf ballgown was Sylvy's Halloween costume this year.

Karma dug through her bag for keys. The key chain, a gift from Renee when Renee feared for the safety of female realtors, was a metallic kitty-cat head with pointed ears that could gouge an attacker. Renee had given Jean one as well, which proved useless. Karma shrugged on a cocoon coat, locked her office door, unlocked the exterior door, relocked the exterior door, and hurried to her car.

She ran right into him, he grabbed her arm, and she pulled away hard. A dark coat and knit hat, that's all she let herself see—it could be anybody. She pushed 'alarm' on her fob and was in the shrilling car hitting auto lock. Her nostrils burned with the tang of body odor. She shifted—wrong gear—shifted again, gunned the car over a parking barrier, and squealed onto the street. A block from Sylvy's playdate, she pulled over until she could stop her heart from beating to escape her body.

THAT EVENING, FIDGETING IN HER PORCH CHAIR, Karma watched Sylvy watch Rafe. Her daughter's Anime eyes followed Rafe's hands as without guidelines he carved personalities into the pumpkins. Last thing she needed was Rafe encouraging Sylvy to have freeform fun with sharp instruments, though he was happy with his hands busy. He'd arrived as "Mr. McGrump Face" in Sylvy's words. He lightened at seeing Sylvy and set her to work readying the porch table for pumpkin carving while the grownups went to the kitchen to devise a plan. Instead, Rafe carped that Dominic had taken the credit for his ideas and berated him for a problem that Rafe did not create. Sylvy, who'd slipped into the kitchen, had to ask, "What's wrong with Uncle Dom?" Karma rolled her eyes at Rafe and told Sylvy that bosses were hard on workers to get the best out of them. It wasn't easy being part of a team. "Unless it's Team Pumpkin," Rafe said and danced Sylvy back to the porch. He was a wizard with Sylvy.

Finished, Rafe positioned a battery candle and swiveled the jack-o-lantern to grin at Karma and mimicked the grin. Good after all that she'd asked him over on short notice.

"How'd you know to do that?" Sylvy traced a scrollwork ear.

Rafe puffed himself up in mock pride. "I had an expensive education."

"Oh, you're the Beast! I *love* that movie so much I could *marry* it." Sylvy bounced in her seat. "Mom, can we watch it next?"

Karma had never seen Rafe so bewildered and laughed, "*Beauty and the Beast,* the Disney movie with real actors. Next, she'll ask you to sing, 'Be our Guest.'"

"Mo-om, Lumiere sings that, the candlestick, not the Beast. The Beast sings about being in his lonely tower."

"But mine is a concrete silo-tower," Rafe joked, "that held grain for cows."

"You don't have cows! You have tea biscuits. Can we come back?"

Karma didn't remember how she had Sylvy had ended up at Rafe's place once, all one thousand feet of it, three rooms on three levels. The apartment complex was a winner for location, location, location, situated between Lake Bde Maka Ska and Lake of the Isles. It was a winner in innovation with its stylish exterior. Rafe softened the concrete interior with wall hangings designed after medieval tapestries and mandala patterns. The building's history couldn't have been more Midwest since the structures had been grain elevators rising out of a field in the 1970s.

Rafe was encouraging Sylvy to trick-or-treat there, but Karma protested that most complexes discouraged strange kids, strange anybody, coming in.

"You seem worried, Karma. Is everything all right?"

"A man spooked Mom. That's what she told Leslie's mom." Sylvy wasn't supposed to have heard that.

Rafe's big dark eyes went bigger and darker. "Did you call the police?"

Karma brushed off his concern. "People take their dogs into the trees behind our building, where they think they can get away with not scooping the poop."

"Sylvy, could you set up the movie choices to show me?" Rafe's request sent the girl scurrying into the house proper.

Karma raged, "You CANNOT tell my daughter what to do."

"You CANNOT have a stalker around without calling the police." Rafe raged back.

She was shaken—he'd never been mad at her. "Listen, Rafe, I can take care of myself." She wouldn't admit that a certain man might be following her. She'd been devious in avoiding a man before and was ashamed of her tactics then.

Rafe wouldn't let it go. "Jean Nerstrand's murderer is out there. You called me about a crisis, turned out to be a jack-o-lantern crisis, and I had to change a date with a civil engineer. I arrive, and you're white as the proverbial sheet. I'm happy to stay but you must tell the police. Call that detective, Mr. Handsome Noir."

She bristled. "I'm not even sure I saw somebody"—she'd run into a body—"It was gloomy and I was in a mood. It's no business of yours."

"Call the police. The worse that can happen is that they'll mock you and scorn you and tie you to a stake and burn you as a witch."

"Not funny, Rafe."

"I read that because women underestimate stalkers, law enforcement urges them to take it seriously. The police used to ignore it, but not after studies of how stalking escalates."

"Don't throw your expensive education at me. Life's not a quiz for you to ace."

"Bloody hell, Karma. Here I am trying to be *sensitive*. Don't put me in the man role of being a clueless dolt unable to grasp that your precious experiences are beyond me."

"Out, you *twit*."

"I am not leaving until . . . Hey, don't fall through the floor. You're shaking. Do you want water? I'll leave, but your mother would want you to call, the spirit of your husband—"

"YOU CAN'T MENTION HIM."

"What happened to U.S.A. freedom of speech? See, my coat, on. My knives, packed. Use battery-powered candles in the jack-o-lanterns. Think if Sylvy had been with you. I'm *out*." The porch door slammed.

Karma was quaking in the wicker chair when Sylvy came out. "Where's Rafe? I'm hungry. Mom, did you fight? You shouldn't fight. Can we have spaghetti now?"

"As soon as I make a phone call." She told herself she needed better advice, opened contacts on her cell, and was about to hit "Dominic" when a call came through from her mother. Karma would hear enough advice on the topic of her mom's choosing that she could hold off on mystery men and Dominic.

CHAPTER 16

The THREESOME WERE IN VARIOUS STAGES OF DRESS and distress during the seven a.m. Sunday video chat.

Erik Jansson, against the backdrop of his kitchen, wore a hoodie over a white dress shirt and paced with coffee. Cyber Paul, against the virtual backdrop of a European canal, had an air of concern as he pulled an apron over his waffle-knit Henley. Deb Metzger, the frazzled originator of the call, used her bandaged hand to wrap a smoke-gray robe up to her chin. "So," she exhaled, "I crawled from bed to make this video-call because I want to see your honest reactions."

"Honesty, honestly?" Erik arched a brow. "Shouldn't honesty come after a shower?"

"Is that your way of honestly saying my hair's a rat's nest? Paul, you look, what's the word?"

"Quizzical," Erik supplied.

"Quizzical," Deb confirmed. "Did you have a question?"

"Are you in a hotel room? I recognize the painting behind you. Also, I thought we were taking the day off, and what happened to your hand?"

"I'm getting that honesty's overrated. I'm in a long-term stay unit though I'm about to be ejected. Yeah, it should be a day off, and I'm supposed to look at condos later and help a friend. So, Cyber Paul, knower of all things, why are human bites"—she waved her bandaged hand—"worse than an animal one? I'm on infection watch."

"A human bite could carry HBV, HCV, and HIV."

"Only letters I recognize were the last." Deb made a face. "If I die, it would solve my housing problem."

"Burial sites are at a premium," Paul added.

Erik settled at his table with a steaming mug. "Deb, do you want time to make coffee?"

"Okay. I wanted to make sure I caught you before you started having fun without me. I'm leaving the screen. Talk quietly amongst yourselves."

When she left, Erik explained to Paul, "Yesterday, we learned that 'Homeless Ulysses,' Jean Nerstrand's stalker, had a gift card to a spa in Edina."

"Isn't the whole place like a spa?" Paul asked.

"You're thinking of Wayzata. Can you generate a spa list for Edina?"

"Shift in priorities, Partner." Deb returned with a hotel cup proclaiming, *Shine!* "The reason for this sunrise session is that Tessa, Jean Nerstrand's daughter, called me at 2:30, 3:30, and 4:00 a.m. She wasn't sleeping so why should a responsible adult get shuteye?"

"Poor kid. How's she doing?" Paul cracked an egg into an unseen bowl.

Deb rubbed an eye with her bandage. "It was mostly crying. She's barely holding together."

They were stilled by the girl's misery.

A dog popped up by Erik, a white blaze between eager eyes. Front paws scrabbled on the table and he licked the screen. Erik hugged the dog away, "Hey, Stripe, down." Stripe was up again, paws on Erik's lap. Erik snapped his fingers, and Stripe sat. "Go get Ben." The dog bounded off.

"He understands?" Deb asked.

Erik transitioned to earbuds. "He understands that if I don't feed him, he can jump on Ben until Ben gets his food. You were saying, Tessa called you."

"Teen angst over a phone number. She was scrolling through her texts and contacts because friends had changed numbers because of hackers or trolls. One mystery number threw her, and she called me to do her thinking out loud, three times."

"She wanted someone to talk to." Paul whisked an unseen mixture.

"I get that," Deb said. "She couldn't figure out why she had that number, then she remembered her mother had texted her from it a month ago. When Tessa asked why the new number, her mom said that she'd picked up a friend's phone by accident. But it happened again, Tessa responding, her mother texting back, 'forget this number.' So Tessa asked her mom *in person* about the mix-up, and quote, 'Mom got all high and mighty and told me to mind my own beeswax.' To get down to it, what was Jean doing with a mystery number, and is it worth it following through on the theory of a grieving kid?"

"No one tracks phone use better than her demographic," Paul said.

"Go for it," from Erik.

"Then the question is, did Jean Nerstrand have a secret phone for calls to a 'special' friend? Or did the phone belong to that special friend, aka Unknown Lover? And another thing, Tessa went on about her mom using perfume,

Opium or Guilty, the past few months, and then not. Maybe she switched men and the second didn't like perfume. But what was I saying about the phone number?"

"A real possibility," Erik said and turned around as his sleepy son behind him fed Stripe. "Breakfast in ten, Ben." Ben pulled his ear to signify he'd heard and trudged back to his room.

Paul moved away from his screen and sizzling was heard. "My team's asap task is to trace this number to an owner."

"Because that owner could be Jean's killer." Deb clapped her hands together, and a section of bandage flapped. "Ah, this won't stay wrapped. Duct tape time."

"We have a direction, we're happy," Erik said as Stripe reappeared with a leash in his mouth.

"Happy," Paul echoed from off screen, a female voice was heard, and his connection went dead.

"Paul has company? Huh." Deb shook off a yawn.

Erik, trailed by Stripe, pulled pancake mix from a cupboard. "And it's time for you, fearless leader, to sleep until noon. Peace."

"Peace," Deb signed off.

FURY PROPELLED RAFE ON SUNDAY MORNING. Fury at Bad Karma, Spoiled Princess Karma, Center-of-Attention Karma. On top of that, Detective Jansson had become a voice-mail nuisance. Had Karma had taken Rafe's advice and called him? Rafe floored the accelerator, transversing the Twin Cities Metro. (His Austin Cooper Countryman never reached warp speed). He'd stormed out of Karma's yesterday into a real storm, and thunder made him toss and turn through the night. The rain had stopped, but not the thunder in his head.

Rafe pulled over by affordable housing units in Minneapolis's Longfellow neighborhood, which butted against the Mississippi River. Observing how the units blended in a mixed-income area was the purpose of the drive, and there was money to be made at all cost levels. During his four years of residence in the Twin Cities, he was drawn to touring the many neighborhoods from city centers to the sprawl overtaking cornfields. Close to the truth, he did so because of his development position with Landvak. Closer to the truth, he might chance across self-advancing opportunities. Closest to the truth, impulse drove him. He had the curiosity of an explorer, when not distracted by impossible women.

Of his four Minnesota years, Rafe had known Karma for two, and she entranced him as a many-faceted gem until recently when she seemed brittle. He understood that her husband's death destroyed the life she'd chosen.

She rallied to be fun-loving, even as other women dissed her vitality. Renee had said, barely out of Karma's hearing, that Karma was going about being a widow all wrong. (Had Karma worn a red dress to her husband's funeral?) Jean had adored Karma but condescended to her. A cousin of Jean's (never met him, would hate him if he did) swept up Karma and dumped her. Being dumped did not correlate to enhanced wisdom, as Rafe knew with his dresser drawer of female avatars stuck with pins for the women who'd dropped him.

Fury dissipated as Rafe drove his Countryman the five-mile route along Lake Street. The drive, level in altitude, was steep in rising social status. He passed a police precinct that had been burned by rioters, businesses catering to immigrants, Ingebretsen's Nordic Marketplace, and legal aid offices. When Rafe drove under Interstate 35, East became West. The intersection of Lyndale with West Lake divided the have-less from the have-lots, with an upscale sex toy shop near an orthodontist practice. He veered onto Lagoon Avenue. The open house in Uptown showcased a luxury condo building by Lake Bde Maka Ska. In 1817, surveyors had named the lake after pro-slavery John C. Calhoun. When honoring the Calhoun name no longer seemed the thing to do, the lake returned to its native name, Bde Maka Ska, or in Rafe's Anglo tongue, White Earth Lake.

Luck blessed Rafe with a parking spot across the street from "The Highwater." The open house for realtors, investors, and prospective buyers started in fifteen minutes at one o'clock. He would wait for a familiar face, like the agents he knew at Sotheby's Realty or someone from Lake & Isles. *Good* Karma could sell units here in a heartbeat. People would credit her looks, but she intuited better than the buyers what would work for them. Buyers swayed by her would snap up a luxury condo in the price range of $500K to over a million.

Rafe *was* one in a million. One in a million with his grasp of spreadsheets and, more tellingly, what the spreadsheets skewed. He was one in ten thousand with his sensitivity to anesthesia and antibiotics. He rubbed the hump on his nose. Depending on the audience, he would claim damage done by cricket bat, hockey stick, or sculling paddle. The buried truth put the blame on his older brother, but Rafe would never give that brother, his mother's darling, credit for anything, including the lump. Dominic claimed to know who could fix that nasal "twist" to make Rafe better than ever. If there was a twist to Rafe, let it be a twist to success, let *him* be on top.

Dominic nonetheless provided a model of success. Rafe had been scouring Landvak records to determine how Dominic kept costs in line, how he decided upon suppliers, and how he maintained a profit. The margin in property deals could be a squeaker or could skyrocket into the Cadillac and caviar territory. Rafe preferred Land Rover and oysters.

People were entering the building of brick, glass, and steel. Rafe could no longer stall.

The public lounge gleamed with floor to ceiling windows and an inviting bar with stemware glinting mid-air. Away from the bar's crimson carpet, the off-white floor consisted of a marble composite cut in near-seamless sheets. It could be polished with a Zamboni. By the elevator bank, the company's underlings hawked name brochures, and he received a badge, "Rafe Edward Lutyens, Landvak Properties." Waitstaff drifted around offering champagne and mushroom spread on toast points. His stomach rumbling, he took a toast point and chitchatted with an older woman realtor who wore a purple bauble instead of a wedding ring. She gushed about investment possibilities that might interest "Dom." Enough with her crush on "Dom." Rafe extricated himself to check out a mid-priced unit, mid-price for this address, anyway.

Two floors up, a $500K unit offered a view of parking lots, boring. Rafe took an elevator to the top floor to inspect a two-thousand square foot apartment staged with furnishings. He waltzed in to see a panorama of tree canopies and waterways. The view's serenity was shattered by the shrieks of two backlit women in blazers and slim trousers. With a shock he recognized a shriek as Karma's.

He went bold. "Good afternoon, ladies. Why, Karma, how wonderful to see you! And your colleague is—oh, Renee, I didn't recognize you." *Be nice to the boss's wife.*

Renee's smile was abrasive. "Hello, Edward, Rafe. You should pick one name or the other."

"I ha—"

She cut him off, "This unit is certainly nice and open." Her manner wasn't nice and open but two sizes too tight like her pointy shoes. The shoes were silver with an opening slit high over the instep like a gutted fish, and her expensive tote was reminiscent of a creel for the dead catch. "You're staring at my feet, Edward."

"Your shoes sparkle like trout. Quite fashionable, I imagine."

Renee glared. Karma choked on a giggle, her eyes glinting yellow in the light. She was talking now, her lips a moving ribbon. Whether or not he was forgiven, Rafe was grinning.

Renee huffed, "It's important with property showings, don't you think Edward, to adhere to clear schedules. I do realize the need for flexibility because residents and clients have changeable lives. All the more reason to establish as much order as possible."

Karma pinched her shoulders back so that her breasts targeted shorter Renee. "Renee thinks if we, our office, had made Jean take more care with

updating her appointments on the office schedule, she wouldn't be dead."
Tears welled, and Rafe wanted to sweep up Karma, the unit's bedroom door
would swing open—

Renee shattered the fantasy. "You're mangling my words, Karma." She
stood rigid as tears ran along the edge of her chin. "Jean was my dear friend—
she shouldn't be dead. Dom's torn apart, he, we, won't be able to bear the
funeral. This never would have happened if Lake & Isles had *controlled* Jean."

Karma pressed tissues from her bag into Renee's hands, and sniffed
through her own tears, "We're *all* grieving. Lake & Isles can't be blamed."

Renee protested, "Jean was careless, being alone at night, that's just how it
is. And you at Lake & Isles can't keep anything straight."

Rafe intervened before Karma fell into a well of trouble. "Everyone's upset,
Renee, but the only one to blame is the killer. My theory"—why not spout it
to give Karma to recover—"is that a houseowner, self-appointed as neighborhood watch, 'stood his ground' and shot in the dark an unrecognized intruder,
who happened to be Jean. The shooter is too cowardly or fixated on his 'rights'
to come forward. How American, shoot first, question later."

Renee swiveled her pointy fish feet at him. "*You*. I know when you're finished." Those feet stalked to the kitchen area where water bottles were set out.
Rafe was murmuring to Karma about leaving when they heard a high-pitched
"Paa-*ping*." Another ping at the open door. A little girl in a tutu and tiara
waved her pink wand at them. Like the normally dressed parents behind her,
she had Asian features. She chanted again, "Paa-*ping*."

The parents froze, baffled by the room's tension, Karma and Renee froze as
if they'd forgotten a cue in their drama, and Rafe froze in undeserved embarrassment. A woman's voice boomed from behind the family. "Go on in. Open
means open. Do you mind if I follow?"

Instead, the parents and the enchantress daughter vanished, and a
woman of impressive stature stepped in. She had a freshly showered glow
about her, with large eyes in a welcoming face. She also had a hand wrapped
in duct tape.

"Detective Metzger?" Karma's hand fluttered to her lips. "Is Erik, I mean,
Detective Jansson, with you?" Flirting with a man not even present—Rafe
might as well be on Pluto.

Renee gripped her creel-bag. "*Detective*. You don't need to be here. This is
out of your price range."

Detective Metzger was unfazed. "Fair Housing check." She knew about
Rafe since she introduced herself, "Mr. Lutyens, Detective Deb Metzger." She
scanned the place. "Expensive but roomy, and boy do I need room. I have a
lottery ticket in my pocket, so it could totally happen. Is there a cat around?
To swing? Does the furniture come with?"

Rafe hadn't adjusted to the Midwest sentence ender, *come with*, as in, *going for pizza, come with*? He hovered by Karma. Detective Metzger strode toward the picture window to be blocked by Renee, a Goliath and David combination if Goliath had spiky hair and David pointy fish shoes.

"You can't count on the lottery." Renee expressed sympathy, which didn't last. "What you can count on is that you can't do your job right. You should rake Lake & Isles over the coals. Jean"—her voice cracked—"would be alive if they'd controlled her." Head high, Renee click-clacked her shiny shoes past them and out the door.

Would she run to Dominic and squeal that Rafe loafed around gob-smacked while a detective abused her? Job over for Rafe? He shouldn't care; he should be soothing Karma.

Detective Metzger had beat him to it, and Karma was biting back a smile at something she said. The detective winked at Rafe, and with a roll on the r's, snarled, "*Mrrrow.*"

CHAPTER 17

Visiting the CORN MAZE WITH SYLVY HAD SEEMED LIKE the right idea for Sunday afternoon, especially after that horrid open-house where Renee's manicured nails were poised to slash Karma's face. No help from Rafe, who fumbled to protect his boss's wife—what was *wrong* with him? And that woman detective—strong, and funny in a I-could-smack-you way. Karma had rushed home to change into skinny jeans, which she'd never worn better, a cute jacket, and tie-boots with a shearling ruff. That steadied her enough to pick up Sylvy at a neighbor's, and her turbulence subsided when they reached their destination of the St. Croix River Orchard. With pick-your-own-apples, a petting zoo, a food truck, and a corn maze, it promised "fun for all ages," and Sylvy's excitement bubbled up to Karma.

By the time they had made kissy faces at llamas, picked a peck of apples and stored them in the car, the wind had keyed up to a whine. Sylvy jumped in a circle, chanting, "now-we-get-lost, now-we-get-lost, in-the corn maze, in the corn maze." They went past tangled briars, a shack covered in lichen, and a broken ladder leaning against a gnarled oak. At the mouth of the maze, Karma glanced at the hand-drawn map which sketched out dead ends, but it made no sense. She let several groups pass before grasping Sylvy's hand and entering the maze. She had assumed that with her adult height she'd be able to see over the corn. Wrong—the hybrid stalks grew to twelve feet tall.

Karma and Sylvy wandered through the corn forest. Outside it had been golden; inside, the stalks faded to the color of wash rags. A machine-like clanking echoed down the rows, and Sylvy stepped on a mound of pellets. "Deer doo-doo," Karma guessed. The skeleton fronds of corn grabbed at them, and clouds smothered the sun. A boy and girl, fifteen or so, laughed as they ran by and soon ran by again, giddy with being lost. Karma had lost all sense of direction and paused where rows crossed. Cold sweat trickled down her ribs. Sylvy chanted in a whisper, "lost-in-the-maze, lost-in-the-maze. *Look*!" She dropped her mother's hand and pointed to a pink blush caught in a root. "Is it a facemask, so you don't get sick? Wait, I know," she said with a child's authority, "it's litter. We should throw it away." Karma stepped close—pink bikini panties. She drew Sylvy back and lied with an adult's authority, "They clean the maze after everyone's left."

"When they're checking for people who can't get out, Mommy?"

Karma steered Sylvy away from the panties only to collide with screaming boys. Not grown enough for teen crushes, not small enough for kiddie play, they struck a reckless compromise of racing blind through the maze wrecking rows and slamming people. One spotted the panties and dared another to put them on his head. They dashed around the corn cul-de-sac and woo-hooed away. Karma grabbed Sylvy's hand again and trailed their racket to the exit.

The wind blew raw and damp. It was a low time of month for her, the miserable preamble to the main act of cramps. Since her husband died, her PMS had worsened to make her feel soggy and hollow at the same time. Her physician called it a condition to be monitored; "monitoring" was no help in the present. Karma faked delight in winding through the maze with Sylvy. Toy monkeys hung from the stalks at forks in the trails, and a monkey bobbing in the wind hit the back of Karma's head. At the exit, a reverse delta of crisscrossing paths, the gang of boys came tearing through and the tallest, a stolen monkey wrapped around his neck, knocked Sylvy down. She landed on her knee with an ow-ow-ow. The gang squealed on to freedom and pumpkin smashing, while a boy about Sylvy's age in a neon puffer ran up from behind and helped Sylvy up. Karma rushed to check the girl's knee.

A baritone voice followed the boy. "It's Karma, isn't it? Detective Jansson, Erik. Is everything all right?"

She jerked her head up which dizzied her. The detective stood over the boy who, despite lighter curlier hair, was clearly his son. Sylvy stuck her lip out in a show of bravery. "It's okay."

He herded them away from raucous exit and touched Karma's arm. "Are you sure you're fine?"

Sylvy thinly echoed, "Are you fine Mommy?"

"Yes, sweetie, a little chilled. I was spooked by a clanking noise."

"Pheasants, plenty of mast for them here," Erik said.

Karma didn't know what "mast" was but accepted it. She was icy white next to Erik whose rosy cheeks matched his son's. Ben, she heard the name. Erik wore a heavy buffalo-check coat. She had the style of the outdoors in her too-thin plaid; he was dressed for real wilderness. Sylvy was announcing to Ben, "My birthday's soon," and the boy claimed status with "My dad catches murderers," Sylvy saying back, "It was scary in there, but I wasn't scared," and Ben with a "me neither" stomped on acorns.

Erik had touched her arm a second time. "Let's warm up by the food truck." The children dashed ahead to claim hay bales for seats, and after Karma settled on one, he offered to get drinks.

He returned with a tray of two hot ciders, two cocoas, and pumpkin doughnuts. Sylvy, with her strawberry hair flying, popped up and down on the bales. She transitioned from pretend to real and back again in accepting the drink with a thank you and saying to Ben, "You're the ogre, and I'll feed you a doughnut so you won't eat me." Karma's teeth chattered, and Erik moved close to block the wind. He volunteered that he had a blanket in his car.

"Brrr, the drink will help. No, don't go."

"A mylar wrap in my pocket." He pulled from a utility pocket a ridiculously shiny material and draped it over her shoulders. "This will help."

"You're a gallant father and son."

"The king died, Mom's the queen, and I'm the princess!" Sylvy put a damp leaf on Karma's head.

"Is your dad dead?" Ben asked while dropping a doughnut chunk into his cocoa. "Whoops. That's sad. My mom has the nice house. Dad has the bachelor pad."

"Where on earth did you learn that term?" Erik asked, but Ben and Sylvy were competing over who could slurp the loudest.

Karma pulled the mylar close, and her feet tingled with returning warmth. "Sometimes I wonder if it's good for Sylvy, being an only child."

"I wonder the same for Ben. I'd imagined his childhood would be like mine—I'm sandwiched between sisters. With siblings, you learn young how to manage hostilities."

"What does your, what does Ben's mother do?"

"She's a lawyer."

Karma burst out laughing. "A detective and a lawyer? Talk about managing hostilities, no wonder. I'm sorry, I shouldn't. But a honeymoon of cross examination?" A new burst of laughter at his sheepish smile. "Well, 'Detective,' in all your interrogations, what's the smartest thing you ever heard about relationships?"

His blue eyes crinkled. "You can insist on being right, or you can be in a relationship."

She leaned into him with more laughing.

He stiffened.

"What is it?" Karma straightened.

"They must sell pie inside. The orchard produces Haralson apples. Where there are Haralsons, there should be pie."

The children, pinching their noses, pointed at the porta-potties to declare their need. Needs must be answered, parents must move on, and haybales left for another group. After a successful pie quest, they reached Erik's Highlander first. The worsening weather made their goodbyes quick, and Karma saw him answering his phone before he'd even shut his door.

She trotted Sylvy to her Acura a row over. She settled Sylvy and a pumpkin pie into the back seat, hit the ignition, and startled at a rap on her window.

Detective Jansson as his tight jaw made clear, and his Highlander idled behind them. She opened her window.

"Karma, there's serious business involving a phone number under your name and the Nerstrand case. We need to talk as soon as possible. In an hour or so, where you're comfortable."

Caught off guard, she shared her ex-stepfather's address in St. Paul. She and Sylvy were headed there for dinner, and while Mark was not a lawyer, he was a wary accountant acquainted with plenty of legal eagles. She blabbered, in a ploy for sympathy, that Mark Bloomberg, divorced from her mother, was the closest thing Sylvy had to a grandfather.

Detective Jansson faced his vehicle. "The heart knows who's family." He jogged away.

But does the heart know who's foe?

THE EX-STEPSISTER ZAHRA OPENED THE DOOR TO THE LARGE BUNGALOW, and Sylvy ran past her to give Marko, as she called him, a hug. Zahra, witchy with her black coat and corkscrew hair, hugged Karma. "Welcome, Changeling, who hath stolen my inheritance." In reply, Karma let go with uncontrolled sobs. "What's this, Karm, is it your friend's death?" Behind them Sylvy chattered to Mark that they'd been lost in the corn maze and a man and his son helped them and were nice, until they were in the car, when the man came back and upset Mommy. Sylvy went for a big ending. "It's about *murderers*."

Karma, between sobs and nose blowing, explained that detectives were coming to question her about an old phone number, which made no sense to her. Zahra, taking a break from her feckless husband until he recovered his "fecks," whisked Sylvy away to shop for groceries, and Mark sent Karma upstairs to rest. She lingered in the bathroom pressing a steamy washcloth against her face as if her pores could release anxiety. She decided to catnap on the guest bed always ready for Sylvy. When she closed her eyes, the overhead light burned red through her lids, but she too exhausted to flip the switch. It reminded her of a noir film she'd seen, *Laura*. A square-jawed detective grilled Laura under hot lights about the murder of her look-alike. Then the grilling melted into tenderness, the hard jaw into a soft smile. Karma went limp and descended into the black cave of sleep.

CHAPTER 18

Erik Jansson had intended to have a Sunday afternoon free of being a detective, but it was not to be. Having a great time with Ben at the orchard, he ran into Karma and the Nerstrand murder came back at him. Cyber Paul, unable to contact Deb, reached Erik as he was about to leave the orchard; he disclosed that Jean's secret number had been Karma's old number. Erik left half a pie and a whole son at his ex-wife's "nice house," where Stripe, unlike his ex, enthusiastically jumped him. He robot-dialed Deb until she answered. She waffled that she was bushed after raking leaves for a friend, but what-the-hey, why not let her partner commandeer her time? He filled her in about the upcoming meeting with Karma at her ex-father-in-law's house. He ended with "Your lead, of course."

Karma bewildered him. In the cornfield, she was dazed. Not prepared for the weather, not prepared to see him, not prepared to move ahead in life. With a hot drink she revived like a bird in the hand. A bird with a sweet song and sharp beak. She seemed to hold her own in her career and as a mother, but widowhood, shifting economics, and a colleague's murder could throw anyone. Erik's hopes had been inverted more than once. A case in point being that whenever he'd made terms with his divorce, people threw that marriage in his face and dragged him back to heartache.

Six-thirty and dark by the time he parked at the curb in a beautifully restored St. Paul neighborhood. Deb hopped out of her Prius to join him under the streetlamp.

"So, Partner, did you jump out of the Manly Men Outdoors catalog?" She nodded at his buffalo check.

"And you Tough Women Working?" He nodded at her rugged twill jacket.

"Firehard material, the way to go. You know, that company uses real women as models, shows them at work in the clothes. I should apply. Why are you grinning?"

"A catalog shoot at a murder scene?"

"Spoil my fun. So report to me, what's the angle?"

"Paul's unit traced that phone number that Tessa Nerstrand said her mother 'accidentally used.' It's assigned to Karma Karas Byrnes. The bill had been paid by Lake & Isle realty, but for the past six months the bill has been paid by a company, Karas Limited, with a Golden Valley P.O. box. Paul's team will be scoping that out." Erik could still feel Karma huddling against him. "Before we go after her financials, let's hear what she has to say."

Deb poked at her phone. "Yup, seeing that report. You know, I saw Karma noonish at a condo open house. Quite the catfight between her and Renee Whatsername."

"That might explain her mood at the orchard."

"You saw her too?"

"Ben and I happened to be at the orchard at the same time as Karma and her daughter."

"*Ooh.* Fate. Let's keep our focus on the phone number. We'll see later if Karma remembers anything more about Jean and Homeless Ulysses at the homeless encampment." Deb's phone vibrated in her hand. "More from Paul? Shoot, no. It's Tessa again, I gotta take it, can't neglect the child of a victim. A man at the door is staring at us. Start without me."

So much for his partner leading.

AS THE DOOR TO THE ARTS & CRAFTS FOYER SWUNG OPEN, Erik saw Karma descending the stairs, flushed with sleep. She'd changed into sweats and thick socks, but before Erik could greet her, the short man at the door demanded his attention.

"Mark Bloomberg. Call me Mark. I can hang your coat."

"Detective Erik Jansson, Greater Metro. My partner will be—"

"Wait." Mark came up to his face. "I know you! You're Rosen's son-in-law. I was at your wedding—you two were so young, so full of joy. You in a stoic Iowa way, but glowing!"

"Mark!" Karma plopped down on the stairs.

Erik hemmed, "Unfortunately, we're—"

"That's right, Kristine's divorced," Mark tsked. "So sorry. But a lawyer and a detective? You expected that to last? Bah, don't listen to me. I've survived two marriages and am none the wiser. At some point, you got to see the humor in it. Have you met Karma's mother Nina? An incredible beauty, always chasing the dream. I for sure never figured out what dream. I'll have to tell Rosen that I saw you, or if you see him first, give him my best."

Deb Metzger chose that moment to enter. "Hey, Detective Deb Metzger here. Why the red faces?"

Sylvy skipped out of the kitchen in a Halloween cat apron with green glitter for eyes. "I heard! Marko went to Ben's dad's wedding and he was glowing. We're having beef stew, moo moo."

"You're supposed to be helping Aunt Zahra fix dinner." Karma pulled herself up with the banister. Sylvy skipped back to the kitchen just as a *whack* severed something within.

Mark beamed at Karma. "They're G-Met!"

"Yeah, we are." Deb looked to her partner for clarity. He lifted his hands to return the confusion.

Mark ushered them through French doors into the front room, talking all the while. "You two must know Naomi." To Karma, "remember Naomi, my cousin's daughter?"

"Forensic accountant extraordinaire," Detective Metzger gushed. "She's expecting again."

"Yes, she and Peter, their third. What happened to your hand, Detective Metzger, that bandage?"

Erik jumped in for her, "My partner was helping a friend rake leaves."

"Ah, I hope it heals soon, and welcome." Mark gestured them to take seats.

Flames crackled in the fireplace, a Mission-style carpet spread over the wood floor, books lined the walls, and leather furniture offered deep comfort. Karma curled into a corner of the sofa, tucking her legs beneath her. Erik eased into a wide chair then scooted to the edge to prevent falling into a stupor.

His partner whirled in the middle of the room. "Holy cow, it's Clue! The butler did it in the library with the candlestick."

Mark lit up. "I'll 'buttle' and fetch tea. Karma, you're a natural for Miss Scarlet. Erik, Detective Jansson I mean, you're Colonel Mustard, though that's a nice blue sweater you're wearing, matches your eyes. Let's see, Detective Metzger, we'll invent a character for you, with your hair, Ms. Lemon-Spike."

Karma and Erik simultaneously choked back a laugh.

Deb waited a moment for Karma to compose herself then raised the matter at hand. "Karma, new leads in the Jean Nerstrand case involve your phone number, area code 763."

"My old number." Karma's pupils narrowed.

"Still under your name with payments made by the 'Karas' limited liability company."

"I never heard of a Karas company, Detective Metzger. I have two *new* numbers, work and personal, on my current phone. I can explain. I'll get it." She untucked a leg.

Erik raised a palm to hold her in place "Don't get up. We can wait." Deb shot him her don't-screw-it-up look. "Go ahead and explain, Karma."

"When I had that old number, I was getting harassing calls. I'd block the caller, then a call would come from another number. Heavy breathing, 'I know where you live' stuff. The phone company was useless in tracing the caller, and I can't block out unknown numbers on my work phone because it could be clients calling."

Mark entered with a tea tray, trailed by the aroma of braising meat.

"It's okay, Mark." Karma took a cup with a shaky hand. "It's about a number I don't use anymore."

"That's registered to a company under the name of Karas," Deb repeated.

Mark gave her tea and attitude. "Got to be more than one Karas, Karma's father for one. He went to Alaska after abandoning Karma and her mother ages ago. Her older brother eventually followed the father. The boy was a troubled teen, and after I married his mom couldn't hack the idea of a chubby Jewish accountant as a surrogate parent and spit on the idea of adoption. But Karma is *always* welcome here."

"Got it." When Deb saw that Mark and Karma had their heads down sipping, she mouthed to Erik, "Karma alone?" He gave one head shake no. He doubted they could get Mark to leave Karma without spoiling the bit of rapport that had been established. In response, Deb sent him look number seven from their repertoire of looks, the miffed one, and plunged into the case.

"Okay, listen up. It's not like we're a tortured family figuring out who poisoned the patriarch. We're simply tracing a phone number. Karma, you were being harassed. Maybe that's relevant, maybe not. What did you do about that number?"

"Last March Sylvy was with me in the car, and an obscene call came across the speakers through Bluetooth. It terrified her! I drove right to a different carrier's store, bought my own phone with a new number and turned off the old one."

Mark agreed, "She told me that."

"You did NOT trade in the old phone?" Metzger sounded suspicious.

"You don't need to be so suspicious, Detective Metzger. That phone was handled through a Lake & Isles plan. I took it to Paisley to cancel and she did. Hold on, that's not it." Karma shivered. Mark pulled a sheepskin throw from the back of his chair and passed it to Erik to pass to Karma. This was too intimate, and Erik had the urge to shake the story out of her. They should have met at the G-Met station, only they didn't have a station.

Now wrapped in the fleece, Karma closed her eyes. "The touch ID wasn't working right on the old phone, and Paisley and I couldn't disable it. Besides that problem, the assistant before Paisley screwed up my identification numbers when setting up the original contract. Calling the provider helpline was a joke—a recording refers you back to the website. Three of us, me, Paisley, and Jean, couldn't kill that freaking phone number."

"Take a breath, Karma," Mark said. "You don't need to say anymore."

"Karma can speak for herself," Erik differed. And when she did, it better be the truth.

She jutted out her chin. "Dominic and Rafe happened by, and I think Dom, Dominic, tried his luck at Paisley's computer. I was so frustrated that I retreated to my personal office. I had to reach out to my clients by emails and the Lake & Isles general number. I didn't want call forwarding from the old number because of the harassment calls—what a mess. I'm sure I lost sales."

"Is she being set up?" Mark became angry and moved to sit by Karma. "Are you going to investigate *that*?"

Deb held up a hand. "One thing at a time."

Karma stared into the fire. "I remember Dominic knocking at my door and saying it was settled."

"So Dominic Novak fixed the phone problem?" Erik asked, his tone colder than he intended.

She glared at him as if he was the source of trouble. "He told me it was fixed, Detective. I imagine it was Rafe who figured work arounds to missing codes. He could be a hacker, not that he is."

Mark grasped her hand. "Karm, is *Rafe* stalking you? He's obsessed, Rafe is. Well, is he?"

"*No*. Rafe wouldn't, and I *know* his number. He calls a lot about, um, activities for Sylvy."

Erik didn't like Karma's half-hearted defense of Rafe, and Mark's bulldog jaw said he didn't either. Karma, her voice strained, changed the topic and without making eye contact remarked, "If you haven't figured it out, Detectives, Mark knows everybody."

"We'll work on the basis of what you've already told us, Karma." Erik said in an attempt to soothe, only to have Deb glare, *how dare you*. He raised his eyebrows at her to signify *trust*, one of them had to establish trust. He turned back to Karma, who was uncoiling her legs to stand, and Mark was rising when Deb's big alto knocked them back in their seats.

"That fight. The one with Renee at the open house. What bee got into her bonnet?"

Karma balled up her fists. "It's *none*—"

"Renee can be difficult," Mark interrupted. "It was nothing, right, Karma?"

Erik shot Karma a warning look, but she was baring her teeth at Deb who caught the look and shot it right back at Erik. An eyeball war all the way around. Karma raised her voice, "*Rafe* thinks a neighbor defending his ground shot Jean. *Renee* thinks that the case would be solved, or Jean never would've been hurt, if the Lake & Isles office insisted that she submit her schedule and follow guidelines for safe showings."

Deb sighed, "Death by poor scheduling is rare." The room fell into awkward silence.

"Well, there we are." Mark slapped his hands on his thighs and jumped up.

"Thank you, Karma, and Mark," Deb said, but she seemed to wait for another question to form itself.

Erik rose and murmured "take care, Karma," as he let her leave the family room first. She looked back at him in terror.

Coats retrieved and at the door, Erik and Deb said stiff good-byes to Mark with Karma lingering to the side. In telling Karma to take care, Erik had decided that sympathy would take him further than suspicion, yet he was more unsettled than he'd been at the orchard on first hearing of Jean using Karma's phone. At the same time, his appetite was aroused by a whiff of rich beef in red wine, and he wanted to bolt home for dinner, but Mark wouldn't release them. He tapped his chin and squinted at Deb.

"*You*, Detective Metzger, were at a fundraising breakfast, an anti-trafficking thing, instead of Lola Scheers. Lola and I go way back, before she was a fake prostitute. Send luscious Lola my best!"

Karma touched Erik to stop her giggles and a frisson passed between them. She snatched back her hand and blushed at her surrogate father. "You're a living rolodex, Mark."

Deb squared her shoulders. "AS I SAID, we'll continue to trace that number."

Karma's hand flew to her mouth. "Ohh, I just realized. Jean made sales to my clients after that phone mix-up. I was dating her cousin, what a cad *he* turned out to be—never mind. But if Jean had my old number . . . I couldn't think of how she poached my clients last spring, but it had to be with that phone number."

Erik and Deb exchanged the realization look: Karma's admission got her off one hook with the phone number only to hang her on another. Jean poaching clients provided motive for Karma.

She, however, had slipped into the kitchen at Sylvy's call. Mark politely shoved the detectives out the door. Walking to the curb, Deb mumbled to Erik that she was as ornery as an unfed cat and he admitted to being hungry as a wolf. He was ravenous, and distressed by Karma's mood swings. Her explanation of the phone instead of simplifying the case placed her deeper into an intrigue. He had to watch out for her, not watch over her. Karma could lead a man, men—Dominic, Rafe, Homeless Ulysses, and himself—into a very bad spot.

CHAPTER 19

MONDAY MORNING, DEB METZGER STOOD IN THE G-MET PARKING LOT where modular units had mushroomed. She rubbed her bandaged hand, still adorned with duct tape. She was tense from the toe of her boots to the top of her hair spikes.

At tense moments, having a stone-faced dodger of difficulties for a partner was an asset, a partner who could relate a fact that would function as a lie, as when Erik told Mark Bloomberg that Deb had been raking leaves to explain her bandaged hand. It had been neither the time nor place to bring up the Wrath of Agnes. Erik was not providing that asset this morning because without foresight she'd given him an assignment: interview a resident of the street where Jean was found who'd been away at the time of the murder. That left her a lone pilgrim to answer Ibeling's eight a.m. summons, late, because she was flummoxed finding street parking. The modulars occupying the G-Met lot had been assigned to administration and media outreach, aka new employee Frank. Media Frank like Deb was lesbian. Unlike Deb, Frank had a wife and a calming way with words. Deb gritted her teeth on entering Ibeling's modular den. His assistant Celeste "had gone to a better place," i.e., off on a foliage tour. Encounters had been daunting enough in the chief's old office under the watch of the malevolent fish plaque. In the modular unit furnished like a forsaken middle school, Deb fidgeted like an adolescent caught shooting spitballs at the teacher.

Ibeling, arms crossed, stood behind a steel desk covered by three laptops. His frown melded his brows into one steel-wool caterpillar. "Metzger, the notes you texted had gaps. Explain again what you failed to discover at the homeless encampment. Then why you believed visiting a penthouse was a must. And how you ended up at Mark Bloomberg's having tea."

Before Deb could reply, a desk computer beeped. Ibeling snatched a pair of glasses off a pile of folders and balanced them askew on his nose to read the monitor. "Humph. According to Frank, a news article is raking G-Met over the coals for a lack of diversity. One woman and one man of color retired, and like that we're no longer diverse? The article also claims women are paid less than men. Balderdash. More men have seniority with the corresponding pay because of defunct hiring patterns. This journalist exploited the public record. Any idiot who can blunder their way through the civic pay portal can find salaries. One high-paid senior woman retires, and our mean is shot."

"Would this be a good time for me to ask for a raise, to help out with the optics?" Deb, Deb, Deb, she chastised herself, why did you open your mouth?

"It will *never* be a good time unless you stop annoying people like Renee Novak. She has a reputation as gracious and civic-minded. Not that she was gracious on the call after whatever that open house fiasco was. What do they call that kind of yappy woman? A cairn?"

Deb's guts somersaulted. Outraged Renee had gone straight to Ibeling. "A Karen, sir."

"We named our daughter Karen, so not that." Ibeling muttered under his breath, *should've retired.* Louder, he asked, "Where's Jansson?"

"Investigating."

Ibeling's expression could throw a mule. "Metzger, the only thing keeping Renee Novak from making a formal complaint backed by lawyers is that I listened to her theories. She believes that the alleged arsonist, Jack Cardenas, is back to do more harm to her husband Dominic and to her. Days before the Nerstrand killing, Renee had been in that St. Louis Park neighborhood as a design consultant at another property. The killer may have mistaken Jean for her, is her theory. I assured her that we would take her warning seriously. Even if it is crackpot. I, unlike some on this force, had the sense not to say that last part out loud."

Deb rubbed her bandaged hand.

"Metzger, what happened to your hand? Is that *duct tape?*"

"Mad Agnes at the homeless encampment bit me. I'll add it to the report on Saturday's visit."

Ibeling pinched the bridge of his nose. "When Renee was leaving the condo Sunday, she says you said something behind her back. What did you say?"

"*Mrrrow.*"

Ibeling landed hard on his chair. His hands covered his face and his shoulders shook. Was he laughing, crying, having a breakdown? He asked through his hands, "What was your investigative goal in going to the model condo where you ran into this . . . Cairn?"

"My sublet came to an end, and I'm living at a hotel, sir. But Gopher football fans are displacing me this weekend with their advanced registrations. After my, uh, face-to-face with Mad Agnes, I didn't feel the homeless shelter would do and thought, why not dream a little? Boy, where money will land you."

"Are you angling for a raise again?"

"It would take double *your* salary to afford—"

"You know my salary?"

"You said any idiot . . . Anyway, I was hoping something cheaper in the building might work. But 'cheap' didn't describe a thing in that building except my clothes. That realtor Karma Byrnes, her clothes were fantastic without being—"

"*Metzger.*" Ibeling stood.

"I do appreciate your leadership," Deb said. "Sir."

He waited, compelling her to speak.

"Especially since trying to lead Erik, Jansson, sir. He won't be led."

A laugh exploded. Ibeling could laugh?

He wiped his eyes. "Metzger, you're ready for advanced leadership now that you realize it's impossible. I'm leaving for a damned conference in Chicago, then on to another back-to-back. Double damned. Call Greta. You have her personal number? Of course you don't, no one does. She'll call you. There's a"—he circled his hand around to make a word come to him—"a garage overhead-door apartment thing. She'll explain."

Greta, Ibeling's wife, reputedly former black-ops and current deluxe caterer. Was she going to put Deb up at the *Ibelings*'?

"So, like, I'm moving in? For real? Sir?"

"Check it out." He waved her away.

At the scuffed prefab door, she overheard, "should've *moved.*"

AFTER THE MEETING WITH IBELING, DEB HAD NAILED DOWN an appointment with Dominic Novak and met up with Erik in the parking lot. The issue of Karma's old phone number being used by Jean Nerstrand hung in a digital cloud waiting for Cyber Paul's scrutiny; the issue of other men who knew Jean was shelved for the moment. It was time to pressure Dominic Novak because of time spent with Jean and because, as Ibeling underscored, Landvak had been on the receiving end of threats and violence with the arson last spring.

Deb, driving a G-Met SUV, felt a boost to her spirits on reaching Landvak Development, early, and finding a parking space wide enough for the vehicle. Erik, riding shotgun, nursed a mood because he'd lost the coinflip to drive the SUV, had to leave his own vehicle in a G-Met deconstruction zone, and before that he failed to complete his morning assignment. The St. Louis Park neighbor he was supposed to meet had rushed himself to the emergency room after being stung by a wasp. Currently, Erik was contorting his face as Deb eased into the space. Jeez Louise, she wasn't even parallel parking. If he was going to be that way all day, there was room in their partnership for equal pettiness. "I can get out easy," she said to him. "Not my fault there's an RV on your side." He made a big deal squirming over the back seat to exit through the hatch. Deb moved around him to stand behind the RV and in its shadow she reviewed the situation.

Dominic had an alibi for the night of the murder—at a conference in Albert Lea where he stayed the night to attend a breakfast meeting. It was possible that his "intimacy" with Jean had given an UnLuv, aka a jealous unknown lover, a motive. In a stretch, the evil-contractor-arsonist Jack Cardenas killed Jean as payback to Dominic, believing Jean was Renee or believing Jean was Dominic's favorite. Deb had sent out feelers as to Cardenas's current location, and nothing had been "felt" yet.

Erik was all attention until his phone dinged and he became preoccupied with its screen.

"So, Partner, what's bothering your evil eye there?"

"There's no sign of Homeless Ulysses. The city evacuation time for his encampment has been extended, though Landvak is still pursuing a lawsuit against the city about it. The insurance settlement for the destruction of the Penn Avenue Complex is pending and the criminal case remains open. A few years back Dominic Novak was one of Forty under Forty for achievement in business. His company, which worked on housing for vets, received a recognition plaque."

"Whatever happened to G-Met's passive/aggressive plaque? Is that lost in our diaspora? *Diaspora* is my vocab word for the day. Being on that Committee to Fix Everything, I'm finding lots of worthy recipients for passive/aggressive honors."

"One of us will trip over it soon enough. Our focus in this interview is Dominic's connection to Jean, right?"

"Right. I'll sweetly take the lead. You silently annoy him. You already talked to his gopher, Ralph, no, don't tell me, it's—"

"Rafe. Rafe Edward Lutyens. Dual U.S./U.K. citizenship. Smart and smitten with Karma Byrnes."

"I bet she could 'smite' a lot of men. Could Rafe have had a thing for Jean?"

"Doubtful. Also, Dominic calls him Edward because he thinks that name is business appropriate. That's an emasculating change."

"Dashing Rafe versus dull Edward? What are you looking up, Partner?"

"In Old Norse, Rafe means 'wolf-counsel.' Edward—" Erik tapped again at his phone—"can refer to guardian of wealth."

"Does that make 'Rafe Edward' a wolf guardian? I got to wonder what he might do for Overlord Dominic. Anyway, time to pounce."

INSIDE, DEB APPRECIATED THAT DOMINIC WASN'T STUCK on hiring the young and glamorous. A woman in a bowtie with gray hair in a fade checked her out. "Carina" said her name badge, and a tiny woman, "Sela," gave the detectives a beaky smile and buzzed her boss.

A frosted glass door slid open, and Dominic greeted the detectives with a smile. "It's Detectives Metzger and Jansson, correct? Welcome in." The pair had met him at a construction site where he'd been wearing a hardhat and protective eyewear; today he made a softer impression. With a broad handsome face and attired in a rugby shirt and chinos, Dominic exuded the confidence of a one who'd achieved success and wasn't going torture himself with a workaholic drive and missed meals. He seated them in cushioned chairs by a table. Other tables about the large office held architectural models of apartments, reassuring given the housing shortage.

Deb started: "Mr. Novak."

"Dominic."

"Dominic, we asked if you had a record of the times and places where you met Jean Nerstrand."

With the mention of Jean, his head drooped and a hank of hair fell over his eyes. He looked not unlike the Nerstrands' Golden retriever, Bounce. He handed her a sheet of paper from the table. "Here's the printout."

She handed the paper to Erik because when you're lead, you hand things to people. "At any time when you were with Jean, did you sense that you were being followed?" She wasn't going to bring up Homeless Ulysses or a crazed arsonist unless Dominic did.

He didn't. "No. But it's not like we were alone much. When checking out properties, we'd overlap with owners and realtors."

"Did Jean mention that she was seeing anyone, or that someone was bothering her?"

Dominic snuffled, "I'm having a hard time . . . with this. Renee, my wife, is devastated. Jean was *fun*. Can't you solve this already?"

She glanced to Erik, who answered Dominic with a question, "Why were you working together so much?"

"Jean has, had, a good eye for places to flip. I used to check out places with Renee, but Renee's a perfectionist. She'd see the flaws and multiply them. Now my wife is excellent, just excellent, at interior design and staging places. But to find the diamond in the rough, that was Jean's gift." Dominic pinched the bridge of his nose. "I suppose Jean hoped her husband was a diamond in the rough, but the flashy carats never emerged. He's not really a suspect, is he?"

Deb smiled as if in answer to the question but did her own flip. "Were you and Jean having an affair?"

"Wow, hit me with your worst shot, Detective." Dominic gave a pathetic laugh. "Oh, I can see people thinking that because she was a huge flirt. You know why she flirted? To keep men interested in her schemes. She'd tease, bump against an arm, give a kiss on the cheek." He shut his eyes for a few seconds. "You don't get a lot of love in this industry—the competition, the regulation, the media that invents scandals. I liked Jean's attentions, but an affair? Look, Renee's my rock. Jean 'cultivated' several developers, not just me. Gosh, the shock of this ordeal." He stood up to dismiss the topic.

She stuck to her seat, and Erik waited for her move. "I thought real estate agents had the means and opportunities for hookups, all those empty houses."

Dominic's laugh caught in his craw. "Ugh. Urban myth." He stayed on his feet, hands thrust in pockets. "Once I walked in on a couple, not a pretty backside I can tell you that, but it was the exception that proves the rule. People aren't doing 'it' on properties, not with nanny cams everywhere. You might come across a teen and her boyfriend necking in the basement. Hard to turn *that* off."

Erik hit a different note. "Landvak Development is suing Minneapolis over a failure to place homeless people. Your lawyers argue that the encampment not only lowers the value of your adjacent apartment complex but hikes the crime rate."

Dominic scowled. "The city is not doing right by those people."

Impatient, Deb barked, "Are *you* helping? Homelessness sucks."

"*Detective*, my company, Landvak, is doing affordable housing near Arden Hills, Promise Creek Commons where there used to be a World War II munitions plant. There's an area that needs redemption, and we gave that redemption a jumpstart."

The door slid open startling the three, and the rugged man entering did a doubletake. His Carhartt coat had rough use, and paper covers slipped off the lugged soles of his boots. "This is Bob Ott, my main contractor," Dominic said.

"Didn't know you were"—he took in Deb and Erik—"occupied." Ott's voice was hard. His lipless face with high cheekbones was hard. His weathered hands were hard, the hands of a man who'd labored outside his whole life and couldn't give a flying duck about sunscreen.

"I was just telling the detectives about Promise Creek," Dominic said to him, and to them, "Ott's managing that construction."

Deb went to exchange looks with her partner, but he seemed focused on an invisible horizon. She cleared her throat and smiled at Ott. "How's it going?"

"Check the website." Ott's tone said, *eat dirt.*

Dominic caught Ott's hardness. He kept his hands in his pockets instead of offering to shake. "Time's up, Detectives. Ott wouldn't be here if there wasn't a problem. You can see yourselves out."

Erik was at the door before Deb had time to nod goodbye.

Back in the main office, Sela and Carina were pounding whack-a-mole at their keyboards. Deb looked around for wolf-guardian Rafe, no sign of him. Then Erik took her elbow to rush her out.

OUTSIDE, THE CAR THAT HAD BEEN PARKED ON DEB'S SIDE of the SUV had left, but the RV remained on Erik's. She made a concession. "I'll back out and then you can get in. What's with the rush?"

"Sick of the information stonewall. What kind of sideline work do you think Ott does for Dominic?"

"That would be a *great* thing for you to find out." She hopped into the driver's seat and hit start. "You could sit in back, behind me. Boy, that interview was an unsatisfying suck-fest."

Erik crossed his arms and waited outside.

Deb revved back with enough swerve that Erik had to jump. That at least was satisfying. Then, on the drive back to the G-Met ruin, Erik advanced the case by being a mute sounding board to Deb's argument. "Okay, Partner, it's only Monday and we got a whole week ahead of us. Next time you drive and I'll bring your favorite Kit-Kat bars."

He didn't look mollified.

"That's your I-have-demands face."

"The bars and coffee."

"Oh, all right, coffee."

"Fresh."

"You got something against gas-station coffee aged on the burner? That's it, try not to smile. Okay, coffee, fresh. So far we have no evidence that Dominic Novak and Jean were having an affair. Sure some blond hairs were found on her clothing and in her Volvo, along with other strands that could've come from clients, kids, the hubby, the dog. Hair gets around and you need a sticky roller-thingy to get rid of it. Dominic seems to have been genuinely fond of her. What I don't get, people are all upset that a person dies and then won't help the investigation?" Erik gazed out his window. "I see what you're thinking, Partner. You're thinking that Novak's thinking we're wasting our time prying into his business instead of pursuing a phantom killer. Or maybe something's going on with his business?"

Erik leaned back against the head rest.

"You're thinking, Partner, that something's up with his business, but it's out of our lane. Almost Allwise Ibeling keeps bringing up the arson dealy and—"

A call cut in, causing Deb to swerve and Erik pull upright. It was from one of Jean's five sisters.

"Detective Metzger?" The voice trembled. "We talked before? I'm Jean's sister Katie, number four in the pecking order, over in Eau Claire, Wisconsin. I remembered something."

"Hold on a second. I'm in a vehicle and I'm pulling over." Deb turned into a supply store loading zone. "Go ahead."

A man outside rapped on Erik's window. "This is a loading zone."

Erik showed ID. "We're loading information. Out in five." The man swore.

"Katie," Deb said. "Are you still there?"

"My sister's *dead* and she still makes me feel guilty. Jean blamed a lot on me when I was little but she helped me with homework." Katie cried.

"Death makes most of us feel guilty for no good reason," Deb assured her.

"I loaned her one of my handguns."

"*What?*"

"I'd forgotten, it was last summer. We all used to go deer hunting with our dad—though Jean wasn't much of a shot, not like I am. I belong to a sharp-shooter club. I held that over her—if she picked on me, I shoot her to shut her up. That's a joke?" More crying. "Jean came up for a visit last summer without Bruce and the kids. She wanted to borrow a gun to try before buying her own. She said friends had invited her to a shooting range and insisted in the way she does. I wasn't shooting because I'd sprained my wrist when I fell over a Tonka truck. My wrist healed and I went to check this morning, and I remembered."

"What's the make?" Deb asked.

A blood curdling shriek cut off the conversation.

Erik was poised to call 911 and Deb clenched the steering wheel "Katie, are you there, Katie?"

"It's just my toddler but I gotta go." Katie disconnected.

Deb chewed her lip. "So Jeannie got a gun."

Erik made eye contact. "Bad," he said.

"Bad," Deb repeated.

CHAPTER 20

Four o'clock Monday afternoon, Rafe lingered in the Landvak parking lot reviewing property photos. Unlike realtors, he recorded the ugly and the broken. He'd checked out apartment buildings averaging six units each and found several promising if Dominic could negotiate steeply downward. While Dominic could drive a hard bargain, he preferred soothing his way into an advantageous deal. Dominic liked to be liked.

A dealmaker could be likeable when well-guarded, and Dominic had his guards. Lawyers, the lipless Ott, and wife Renee with her menacing chimpanzee teeth—plus the keepers of the books, Sela and Carina. Sela had beakish lips that could spear any office grub. Carina would fluff herself up and parrot, *asap, asap, not your turf, not your turf.* That Rafe ranked higher on the food chain as a quasi-vice-president meant nothing. Rafe boosted his importance in deciding that he was the fox sniffing out the weasly tactics of Landvak's would-be partners.

But Dominic expected too much for too little. He held it over Rafe that the Promise Creek development wasn't promising to be boldly black on a balance sheet. Rafe couldn't compute how Landvak's other projects managed costs effectively, and when he raised that question, Dominic griped, was that business degree of Rafe's legit? That made Rafe hot and ready to be bought off by another job offer. Fixing up his resume, however, was a bed of stinging nettles. The resume could boast a Carlson degree, although there were, to put it delicately, issues of timing.

Neither Dominic's Lexus nor his Yukon occupied the lot. Rafe left his Countryman and girded up his loins to face the Harpies within, Sela and Carina.

Carina peered over her readers at him—those glasses were invented for that look of disdain—and Sela squawked, "Dominic needs your reports, Edward. Better go to your room to finish them. Asap."

"*Asap*," Carina echoed.

Before he could slink there, Rafe felt a heavy clap on the shoulder, and Dominic's voice filled the room. "The great thing about Minnesota is its dual nature, tame and wild. I had a great time up at the cabin fishing. Lousy internet made me take it easy. Ladies, you work too hard, and you'll bankrupt me with overtime. Go home, take it easy. I'll only be here a minute to check in with Edward." The Harpies bobbed their heads, and Dominic gallantly saw them to the door. That "gallantry" was likely why Karma liked him. Rafe shouldn't have thought of Karma. Karma, after all, adored pop music without irony.

His ladies dismissed, Dominic turned against Rafe. "*Give me one good reason why I shouldn't fire you right now.*"

"I know where the bodies are buried." *Oh god*, Rafe cringed, *what am I saying?*

"Do you *hear* yourself? That's the problem right there. You're clever but not smart."

Rafe's face was a blotch.

"I leave Renee behind, and you abuse her."

"No, I . . . I saw her at the condo open house."

"Where you mocked her and took Karma's side."

Rafe didn't remember mocking anyone, unless he always looked like he was mocking someone. "A detective showed up."

"Stay out of their case and stop harassing my wife. You should apologize."

Rafe didn't know what to apologize for and again blabbed the first thing that came to mind, "I thought her silver shoes looked like fish."

"Her shoes." Dominic made an ugly mug. The mug softened. "Oh, *those* shoes."

"Yes."

"You're on a tightrope. Watch yourself. Do you have the reports I requested ready?"

"I just gathered the material."

"Well, don't sit around sulking. I have calls to make. If I'm done first, lock up." Dominic went to his office and slid the door shut. When he used the office line the Harpies Sela and Carina listened in. Rafe would never do that.

Instead, he sat at their station and set up his iPad as if studying it. The screensaver on Sela's computer was a photo of Dominic's lake 'cabin' where unlike Rafe she'd been a guest. The 'cabin' was a four-star lodge complete with guest bunks, boathouse, and dock. It had been a rundown monstrosity that Renee's parents bought to protect their own lake retreat next door.

The Landon family didn't sit on the peak of Midwest high society, if Midwest society had high peaks, but they were successful in the construction business and held tight to their own. The Landons feared the monstrosity might be sold for commercial purposes and be overrun by weekend woodsmen. So they snapped it up and let it sit. The Landons eventually gifted it to Dominic and Renee to relieve themselves of the tax burden. True to his word, Dominic subjected the place to extensive renovation, and the result was a showplace. Rafe knew that Dominic entertained high-end developers and finance gurus in the ancient practice of greasing up the well-to-do and that deals came out of it. Rafe should have been in on those deals.

He clicked away the image and saw a program which Sela failed to shut down. Rafe was on the brink of accessing it when Dominic clomped out. A printout in his hand preoccupied him long enough that Rafe could spin away from the computer and be absorbed in the data on his tablet.

Dominic's anger had dulled to insistence. "Check out these addresses." He dropped the printout in front of Rafe. "The last tenants at the building by Lake Nokomis complained that the gas meter hissed and suspected an outdoor leak. Should've called it in themselves but they were in a nasty hurry to move. Also, see if there's nighttime activity around these other locations. I gotta run. Renee wants me to grill lambchops tonight if it's not too cold. Be done with this list by Friday—Rafe." On his way out, Dominic squeezed Rafe's neck in an aggressive show of forgiveness.

Bollocks, Rafe could spend days running around to the scattershot addresses, including that house with the wasps. Just when he thought he had the measure of Dominic, he was thrown. Dominic had made a sudden cash offer on that house; with cash offers and waived inspections the purchase was imminent. When Rafe was attending college in Massachusetts, a woman professor critiqued a literary analysis he'd written. "People aren't flat," she'd declared in a toneless American accent. "I should know." She was wise to the fact that students reacted to her Rubenesque figure by labeling her the roly-poly prof. He hadn't expected an American to be smarter than a Brit, but the point of college was that you began to achieve the measure of yourself. He perused Dominic's assignment, and like the student he had been, decided to procrastinate. If it got him fired, no big deal.

But being fired *was* a big deal, and the idea made him itch. The itch was probably set off by his Da's texted request that Rafe video-call him tonight at their retirement getaway in San Diego. His mother arranged the calls as a rule, and Rafe worried that something was up with her health or with Da's. Rafe was coming around to doing as Dominic demanded. If it weren't for that creepy neck squeeze.

"IF SHE'D HAD A GUN, JEAN WOULD'VE BEEN SAFE"—that was Dominic's line, the reason he wanted Karma to join him at a shooting range. It'd be his treat, he coaxed. Karma would've preferred a bottle of wine as a treat. It also upset her that Dom called when she was driving Sylvy to her Monday dance class.

Karma was three blocks from the dance studio when that call from Dom came over the speakers in her Acura. After his gun range recommendation, he asked, "How are you holding together, Karma?"

"Fine." Not true since cramps seized her body. "I have Syvly in the car, dressed as a sprite for her dance class."

"Hey, Sylvy!"

"Is Mommy going to shoot a gun? She doesn't like guns. Is Rafe with you, Uncle Dom?" Sylvy favored inventive Rafe.

"No, he's out scouting."

"Like a boy scout?" the girl asked.

"No fire-starting badges for him. Looking for fixer-upper houses."

Karma, exasperated, asked Dom to call back when she was settled at Sylvy's class. She hated men pressuring her. She had barely got her fanny on the chair when Dom rang back to ask if she could recommend grief counselors. He assumed she sought one out after her husband died—true, but she had no intention of sharing that. Before she could manufacture a good-bye, Dom, heavy with sadness, said, "Renee's shutting me out. It would be so kind if you could talk to her."

"She doesn't like me that much."

"Of course she likes you. Why wouldn't she?"

Because I'm younger, taller, sexier, and a mother, Karma thought. When Karma joined Lake & Isles, a story made the rounds about Renee taking in a foster child, the arrangement not working, and Renee becoming brittle with disappointment. Former Prom Queen Renee, a peachy blonde with a tang of sour. Dominic over the call bugged Karma about the counselor again, and she promised to ask around. Dom in turn promised to get back to Karma about gun safety training, and to end the call she agreed.

She'd been so intent on escaping Dom's needs that she wasted an opportunity to ask for advice. Dom had to know about confidentiality laws, like could police secretly check her phone calls and appointments? It gave her the creeps that Jean had seized her old number to poach clients. Did law enforcement take days or hours to secure warrants and subpoenas? Karma checked her phone calendar which highlighted in red double-bookings for tomorrow. Paisley had screwed up. She enlarged that section. Oh, things were rearranged to accommodate Jean's funeral.

The funeral, one week after Karma had identified the corpse.

Karma's lungs contracted and she dashed from her chair, Sylvy in mid-pirouette, to rush outside for air. She slipped behind the building—a fine place for a stalker, she realized. There was a lone tree, and she tilted her head back to see a cracked branch. *Why why why* had her wonderful Chris died on her? She leaned against the tree and keened.

CHAPTER 21

T UESDAY HAD BEEN A DAY OF TEDIUM, BUT WEDNESDAY MORNING, the oxidized colors of fall—rust, ochre, copper—shimmered beneath the blue sky. Erik charged ahead on his run fueled by that brilliance. He desired distance from the killing of a woman—it'd been one week since Jean Nerstrand's body was discovered. When he was a uniformed officer, he hated calls involving domestic disputes, how many were "normal" for the family, how many were violent, how many had children hiding in a corner. As witness to homegrown savagery, you could sink into depression, turn callous, struggle to build empathy the way you build muscle, or react as his partner Deb did with the armor of attitude and forward propulsion.

Erik propelled himself into running around Lake Harriet, letting the movement take over, the heat of his body, the cool against his face, the knot of concerns in his head unspooling behind him to dissipate into the atmosphere. He ran, legs and heart pumping, foot strike and foot lift, until he was motion without ego.

Euphoria cannot last, and back in his apartment after showering, Erik returned a video call from Deb. Her hair sparked up straight in the air while his curled damply against his temples. She bellyached that she'd already had a day of it. She tugged her hair—you'll be bald before the case the case is over, he teased. You'll be bald if I make a bet about who solves it first, I win, and demand you shave your head, Partner. Your only demand, he asked. I can come up with tons more—she slugged back coffee and carried on.

Deb agreed with Erik in dismissing the theory that Jean's killer took a gun from her. Feisty Jean would have fought back, and there were no defensive wounds. Jean could have been carrying her sister's handgun in her bag, but that bag was likely at the bottom of a river. The day's assignment for

Deb was more interviews of Jean Nerstrand's contacts and for Erik chasing a wild goose—a Landvak conspiracy possibility. Both then had to pack the minimum of G-Met paraphernalia to move from the condemned building to vacant cubbies in the Minneapolis City Hall. This sent the video conversation in a new direction. Why can't we G-Met nomads go to the convention center, Deb demanded of Erik. There are conventions there, he retorted. The fairgrounds, she riposted. Do you really want to be in the poultry pavilion, he dead-panned. Deb jumped tracks—the funeral you couldn't attend was jam packed, family clan, business associates, the curling club.

Erik interrupted Deb. "Any jealousies on the curling team?"

Deb chewed her lip. "I understand there were heated discussions at matches, but no beating each other with brooms, and you can't pick up those rocks and toss them at each other. I'd say there's more animosity surrounding her Troll collection."

"How could I forget." When he and Deb had done walk-throughs of Jean's office and garage apartment, trolls abounded. Naked plastic trolls with hot pink hair, trolls indistinguishable from Chia pets, trolls in traditional Norwegian dress, and trolls that were gap-toothed mini-monsters. Jean's boilerplate will made no mention of who would inherit the troll horde.

"I say the kids get them," Deb concluded. "It'd give me the creeps to have those google eyes on me—already got your google eyes on me, Partner. To wind up this call, I'm having trouble putting the handgun angle to bed. Why did she want a gun?"

"It didn't keep her safe," Erik said. "Are you still checking out munition stores to see if she was stocking up?"

Deb took a turn he hadn't expected. "Nah, I'm going for a swim."

To GO UNDERCOVER, DEB HAD TO EXPOSE HERSELF. Tracking down a possible lover of Jean Nerstrand brought Deb to this locker room on Wednesday where she stripped and began to squirm into her swimsuit.

Yesterday, Tuesday, had driven her to so much hair-tugging that she'd end up balder than a doorknob. She'd been checking out area sport-shops that sold ammunition, asking if anyone remembered a cash sale to Jean Nerstrand. Standard answer—"the guy who could tell you is out." That guy is always out and that guy never calls back. That afternoon was Jean's funeral where the tears could flood a prairie. Jean was loved. The reception that followed was a sob-fest and laughing reunion with cousins popping up like corn stalks. Deb saw the sister who forgot she'd loaned Jean a handgun, and the story that hadn't seemed credible over the phone came across as totally credible in context. The sister had three kids, the youngest girl a Holy Terror. The toddler commanded the attention of her older siblings, her mother (Dad hid somewhere), and a packed room with screams that peeled the wallpaper. The Terror was bodily carried off, hair flopping, patent shoes falling to the floor, giggling until she let loose one final shriek as she was released into the wild.

For Deb, it was back to the Unknown Lover angle. Jean, using Karma's old phone number, had called untraceable numbers except for her daughter's and one other. Research on the owner of that number inspired Deb to dig out this swimsuit which at last yielded to her tugging and covered what was meant to be covered. Its design—swirled blocks of blue and black, high neck, racer back—accentuated the breadth of her shoulders and the V-shape of her torso. She snapped on a swim cap and hung reflective goggles around her neck. She stood on unfamiliar tile in the Plymouth recreation center during this Wednesday lunch hour, intending to catch Glen McCrae with his pants down, in a Speedo.

Glen McCrae managed a real estate title company which would have provided cover for interactions with Jean; however, his online schedule put him at a business seminar on the night of the killing. At Jean's funeral, he wore grief like a wrinkled suit and stayed away from Jean's husband Bruce. Glen McCrae was hard not to notice because of his red Brillo-pad hair and because he dropped a ham slider when he rubbed tears from his eyes. Lake & Isles office assistant Paisley informed Deb that McCrae was a registered Masters Swimmer and that his lunch hour was sacred lap time.

High noon, Deb padded out of the locker room into the luminous aquatic area—free lane, far end. Despite the deltoid-flattering suit, she wished she'd grabbed a wrap towel before walking in front of God and everybody. She could weigh three pounds less and had significant breasts which she didn't care to have ogled—except by a very special person who wouldn't leave a Parisian arrondissement.

Bodies flowed agelessly in the water, until age proved inescapable in the next to last lane, where the slow pace and crepey arms revealed the swimmer's maturity. Past that swimmer was an open lane. Deb plunged into the salinated pool and flipped into an easy backstroke. This was more vacation than stake-out. She flipped back to freestyle and after another lap stopped at the edge to thumb saltwater from her nose.

Glen McCrae stood over her, his quads bulging. His freckled pecs and delts were firm, but between that chest and the muscled legs hung a paunch made prominent by Deb's angle of vision and its contrast to the Speedo's paucity. Goggles in hand, McCrae pulled on his white cap though a red fringe remained uncaptured. Deb visualized Bozo the Clown until McCrae spoke with an un-Bozo-like peevishness. "I use this lane, so I can see the wall clock. A lane's opened up two over."

Next to Deb the elderly swimmer, a slight woman, paused at the wall. "Excuse me," Deb said. "The two of us are racing against the clock up there. Is it too much to ask if you could move over one?"

Water dripped from her long ear lobes. "Ten in the bed and the little one said, roll over—oh, I don't mind," she said. "I'm racing against the clock of eternity, but I don't want to arrive too soon."

When the woman slipped under the lane divider, her medical alert bracelet caught, she grabbed the pool edge with her free hand, the hand slipped, and her head bobbed under.

Deb dove under to assist before the woman panicked. The woman rose up, gasping. Mr. Speedo was oblivious because he was setting a sports watch—*he didn't need to see the effing clock*. Deb hauled herself out and pulled up the woman, calm if winded.

She patted Deb's arm in thanks—"That's what I get for being ninety-two"—and walked steadily to the locker room.

McCrae, baffled by his watch, jerked his head in surprise when Deb stepped up to him. He eyed her up and down.

"Holey Moley, you're stacked!"

A flick of tension—with a man. "Hmmph," was her come-on.

"Did you compete?" His eyes came to rest on her chest. "Breaststroke?"

Deb's every nerve fired. "Freestyle. Whatdya say, one hundred meters, four laps, on my count of three?"

McCrae flew off the edge and established a ten-meter lead. Deb stroked hard to close the gap. Water split around her and gurgled past her face. Her body concentrated on clean thrusts at the turn. McCrae had greater muscle mass, but that paunch of his caused drag. Deb's strokes forced oxygen to her muscles, her brain going black, which is why it never crossed her mind to let McCrae win for diplomacy's sake.

She slapped the pool edge and surfaced to see McCrae surge upward. With no official touch pads, the two had to depend on the judgment of strangers, two women who disagreed on the victor. Instead of wrangling over it, McCrae yanked off his cap and shook his red locks like an Irish setter. "We should do that again!"

Deb, heaving and dripping, wheezed, "How about a smoothie first?"

McCRAE, IN A BUTTON-DOWN, CHINOS, AND LOAFERS, slurped a green concoction from the center's snack shop. He slowed to chew on a mystery fiber from his slurpee. "I swear I've seen you somewhere."

"You were at Jean Nerstrand's funeral, weren't you?" Deb asked.

He gagged. "Agh, yes, knew her through work. You?"

"Don't you miss her?"

"Sure, we, um." A flush scalded his cheeks.

"Look, Mr. McCrae, Glen, I'm an investigator."

He relaxed. "You don't say. With insurance or the Department of Commerce?"

"Not real estate fraud. Here, my G-Met ID—no place for it on my lap suit."

"That's for sure."

She shot him a look usually reserved for Erik's *non sequiturs*, but he was studying the ID and asked, "Metro police? You ride the buses?"

"Homicide and domestic violence. I'm investigating Jean's murder."

She expected him to lash out about his rights. He merely appeared confused over the contents his sludge. He swirled the remaining amount around the glass where shreds clung like grass clippings.

"You were close, weren't you?" she prodded.

"Jean was a hoot. Too bad she didn't swim." He leaned back in his chair. "I'm guessing you're wondering if we had an affair."

"You seemed devastated at the funeral."

The awful thing about appearing sympathetic is that people then bare their souls. Glen meandered on about how he and Jean knew each other from business dealings, how he'd been involved in a humiliating divorce case—his wife had not only been unfaithful, but unfaithful in three-ways and four-ways to which Glen was never invited. Jean offered affection and excitement. There'd been "canoodling," but Glen, a stickler for hygiene, was appalled to his core by the idea of hookups in strange bathrooms, unvacuumed cars, elevators, emergency exit stairwells, and hotel rooms unless he'd personally interviewed housekeeping on their practices. He returned to his aquatic obsession. "I hoped to seduce Jean into joining a Masters' swim program—not that she could achieve our speed—wrong body composition." Including Deb and her body composition, how nice. "Jean told me she'd become interested in target shooting. Great for concentration, but hardly aerobic."

"Did she ever say she was being stalked?"

"Not to me. I think another man caught her eye and maybe he was into shooting."

"Who?"

He scanned the snack area for spies. "Are you going to say I said so?"

"I never reveal sources," Deb lied.

"I heard Jean was working with Dominic Novak. Novak has done good things with nonprofit projects, but he's in it to win it. Usually, I can make up my mind about someone like that." He snapped his fingers. "I find Dominic a hard read. People will disagree with me on that because he seems open. But he doesn't have that many repeat associations, except there's one contractor he sticks with, Ott."

Back to Dominic. "What did you think of the arson at his apartment complex?"

"Arson's messy. I buy into the theory that it's that contractor, Jack Somebody, who skipped town. He's mad at the boss, he burns the boss's building, he disappears. Simple. What I heard is that Dominic isn't discriminating enough about his associates. His wife's the tough cookie who insists people be fired for screwups. She hated the arson guy from Day One. Okay, I thought of an exception. If there's a screwup, Dominic blames that 'English lad' in his office, but I worked with the 'lad' on a few closings and didn't see him as mistake-prone. Does look like he lost a bar fight, that nose of his. The kid struck me as hungry, a risk-taker—that can make you or ruin you. Also whip smart—smart people want to outsmart everyone else and stick their noses where they don't belong. You know what else?" Glen leaned in, a co-conspirator. "I'm ordering coffee to go. You want one, Miss Lap Lady?"

Deb jumped up. "Drop the 'lap lady,' *now*. 'Detective' will do. After you get your coffee, I'll walk you out." There could be more to hear about too-smart Rafe.

Glen stood, his hair dried to twisty waves of a Michael Caine in the 1960s, if Michael Caine was a carrot top. "Another thing—"

"Yeah?"

"Think we burned off enough calories to deserve a double-chocolate brownie?"

"No?"

As if Deb's response tossed him in a pit of despair, Glen started to cry. Jean was missed.

CHAPTER 22

WEDNESDAY, MORNING BLISS FORGOTTEN, STUCK IN LUNCH HOUR traffic where the Crosstown met I-35, Erik fought stomach pangs and road rage. Halted in his travels by an accident ahead, halted in the Nerstrand case by a lack of progress, he stewed.

In the week that he and Deb had been on the case, no leads had led anywhere. Patrol officers in the area had been alerted to Homeless Ulysses—no sightings. Deb continued to seek "unknown lovers," but known male contacts of Jean had been cleared. No evidence had popped up of a random shooter. In their morning video confab, Deb and Erik reviewed which steps of the investigation left them most unsatisfied. They landed on last Friday's interview with Dominic Novak. "Novak's the wild goose you should chase," Deb had said between hair yanks. "Employ that twisty mind of yours. Find a conspiracy he's in and—this is the important part—find out if it involved Jean."

A state trooper on foot was waving vehicles to pull up right next to lane dividers and into rough construction areas to make way for a tow truck. A waiting driver leaned out the window to spit out obscenities. The trooper ignored him and signaled the truck to back up to a crumpled sedan. Another driver flipped the bird to the trooper's back.

As law enforcement, Erik was accustomed to receiving messages of hate and revilement. The police system bore the burden of history's sins and too often worsened that burden with crimes against the marginalized. On one of the crimes, Erik had yet to forgive himself. He had no direct involvement, merely suspicions about a white Minneapolis policeman, Meshbesser. Erik had interviewed Meshbesser about his former service partner's bad behavior, and by implication Meshbesser's own questionable acts. Meshbesser stonewalled. Later, during the Time of Terrible Living, Meshbesser had given the go-ahead for a no-knock entry of a house where a Black woman had been shot and killed. The address had been wrong: the murder suspect's house had been numbered 3178, not 3718, and dispatch called through a last-minute correction, but Meshbesser wouldn't listen. He swore he knew there were suspicious activities at this address, charged in, and Meshbesser's partner, on the force for five days, panicked at the sight of the woman—holding what turned out to be her phone—and shot her.

The only grounds Erik had for reporting Meshbesser before the fatal shooting was the officer's bad attitude. If bad attitude were a crime, we'd all be in jail.

But bad attitude can lead to hate crimes. Just when Erik felt he could feel whole again after his divorce, his beloved city went up in flames and came down in ruins. He had never considered himself an urbanite—his true home the outdoors—but it tore him up to see the Twin Cities ravaged. He wasn't utterly surprised when the Third Precinct burned down, a target of outrage and violent opportunism. Later rocks crashed through Fifth Precinct windows with high-charge fireworks thrown at officers. The site of his first placement as a patrol officer. Then again, when you're the one finding the skeletons in the closet and the bodies in the yard, you know no home is perfectly happy.

Yet a happy home was what Erik wanted and faith that he served justice. The trooper signaled him ahead with a wave.

DESPITE THE DELAY, ERIK HAD TO WAIT OUTSIDE the Four Square eatery for Lionel Fowler. He had met Lionel, teenaged, gifted, and Black, in a café shakedown of a drug dealer. Lionel's gifts included an ability to ease and discomfort people simultaneously.

"The grilled cheese is to die for." Lionel came up on Erik's left. "You been in yet, Mr. Detective? See any dudes you put away?" The eatery hired the formerly incarcerated.

"No. I doubt anyone here recognizes me. People I arrest for homicide stay in a long time unless it was negligent manslaughter. Then you're together in the Home Depot tool aisle, backing away from the wrenches."

"I get that, man. They have tables outside here on Minnehaha Avenue. You're cozied up in L.L. Bean and I'm insulated and fly. Want me to go in for you? Classic Four-Cheese sandwich is the way to go."

Erik grinned. "Sure, with coffee. Here's a twenty, no blood on it."

After their initial meetings resolved on good terms with a bloody twenty-dollar bill explained, Lionel, a high schooler then, had asked to chat with Erik about law enforcement careers. When racist police behavior turned catastrophic, Lionel texted that no way could he shoot the breeze with a white officer. Erik understood. When Lionel reached out again, Erik assumed that like most Black people the young man had ample chances to practice forgiveness. Lionel wanted to beef about the housing problems of his relations, which is how they ended up at Four Square waiting for four cheeses. When he returned with coffees and a number stand, Erik asked him about his studies.

"Ya know I didn't end up going to the U. Went south thirty miles, one of those liberal arts places where students come rich with cars, students come poor with scholarships, football's a joke, and the caf serves vegan." Lionel unzipped his puffer to show a logo sweatshirt. "It ain't easy to fall through the cracks with all that situational privilege. People notice you."

"It might be hard not to notice you, Lionel."

"Got that right. I'm up for the day 'cause White Gran's in the hospital, gallbladder stuff. Gran's too crochety to die. Not that she's really my Gran, she's my cousin's, Jaylyn, remember?"

The graceful pianist, so empathetic it put her in danger. "She's fine? I remember she was learning a virtuoso Liszt piece."

"She's Liszt-less now, working on Rachmaninoff for a hot-shit recital. Like, I'm still the youth rep for the equity taskforce on the Northside? I need tips on what to say for the next zoom-zoom meeting, show that I care about you white fuzz, the 'other' side."

That pained Erik. "We're not supposed to be 'other' but—"

"But you gotta stop being Killer Keystone cops. Now I'm het up, which I have every right to be. I duzz think you, Mr. Detective Erik Jansson, are what profs call an 'aberration.' Who'd you want to be when you were a kid?"

"Indiana Jones." As Erik said that, baskets of sandwiches fried in butter were set on the table by forearms tattooed with flaming hearts.

"Huh, Indiana Jones. White dude archaeologist who exploited the natives."

"It was about action with a soundtrack."

"Man, we all need a soundtrack." Lionel beat out a rhythm and sang in falsetto, "*Up where the air*—what, I'm singing Disney. The undercover on that case that about did me in, the Squeegee dude, was he Black?"

"Squeegee was a role, a chameleon whose color and gender changed depending on the need."

Lionel pulled a string of cheese from his sandwich and chewed it. "I sure ain't going to be your cool Black informant. Gotta admit, though, I'd slay it."

"How about being Consultant 'Squeegee'? What're your insights on housing?" Erik asked.

"I've developed this whole theory about why Minneapolis was so good at segregation, that redlining stuff that kept BIPOC people in place. Black, Indigenous, People of Color were restricted to neighborhoods that were then devalued because they lived there. You know what I'm talking about?"

"Watched a documentary on restrictive covenants as one of our sensitivity updates."

"You don't look any more sensitive to me. But take the twentieth century." Lionel framed the picture with his hands. "Jim Crow era. Minneapolis is attracting immigrants, Scandinavian, German, Jewish, you name it, busting with new arrivals. Blacks coming up from the South to the industrialized North. The city's growth spurt came right when white-dude bankers figured out segregation through zoning. They could apply it to new platting, new builds, new federal loan programs. Fresh start on old racism. Lilydales everywhere. That's my theory and I'm sticking to it. Freedom at last, the 1960s, civil rights, and your buddy Walter 'Fritz' Mondale, before he was vice prez, did a deep dive with the Fair Housing Act. Good old Fritz. Did you, like, protest in support of that?"

"In the *sixties*? How old do you think I am?"

Lionel shrugged. "I need an angle on this 'other' stuff. Can't you help me out? Changing culture's like herding rhinos, and folks see this—" he circled his face with his finger—"they hunger for the smart inside."

Erik crossed his knees, wiped his hands on the inside of his trouser hem, and punched at his phone. "Our Committee for All Things Better forwarded a program link. Found it. A woman professor at Yale discusses how to talk past prejudice. Smart, funny, a Muslim woman of color, lesbian."

"That's whack."

Erik doublechecked his phone. "The talk was presented at your college, beginning of the term."

Lionel choked on his coffee. "Oh, yeah, I 'member. Busy that night, like, um, busy. It's not all about the academics. There's other . . . learning. I'm bettin' you did stuff in school that won't polish no teacher's apple."

"No comment."

"Yeah, no comment from Indiana Jones. I'll check the video archive on your say-so."

"I'm stuck on whether a murder case is linked to that housing scandal you talked about."

Lionel tapped his forehead. "It's coming to me. My great auntie got evicted from that Penn Avenue complex that done lit up like a marshmallow. Before that, Auntie was 'duly informed' that the place was sold and under new management, all leases expired. She was 'welcome' to apply for the redone unit. But the cost, hoo baby! The new management sent her a brochure that bragged about the improvement like it was porkchop-on-a-stick. Making myself hungry here." He tackled his sandwich. "Mmm, they couldn't have squeezed a fifth cheese in here if they tried. I can talk with my mouthful, hmm. Can't, too good."

Erik ate his sandwich before the creaminess hardened into glue. It would take a gallon of coffee to wash it down.

"So, Auntie." Lionel swallowed. "She had to cram herself into a shelter and Nana—did you ever meet Nana, my real grandma?—had to give Auntie a chunk of money for a place cause real estate keeps climbing that rollercoaster. Ooh, rollercoaster, shouldn't have thunk of that on a cheese-stuffed stomach. I see by your eye, Mr. Detective, that you want plot only, no nuance, no character development, even though Auntie—okay, spiel onward. Auntie goes back to Penn Avenue because she left stuff in a closet. The rebuild has started at one end. Only she's too late in the day and can't find a hardhat with keys. It's like a maze outside with stacks of flooring and stuff in wrappers. Weren't the 'quality' brands the brochure bragged on. A switcheroo."

"Do you remember the development company?"

"Landrat? That's not it, sounds like it sucks up leaves."

"Landvak?"

"Ta-dah, that your Ark of the Covenant? Wait, there's more. Not more sandwich. Boy, I about OD'ed on dairy. Anyway, Auntie's about to go around a corner but pulls back because she hears two men arguing. One guy sounds like he's spitting tacks and the other's a bullhorn trying to calm him down. Auntie hides between those fake wood stacks, hears the men scuffling and cussing, then a *Wait*. She's too scared to come out but the voices cool down and say, *we can make a deal*. They walk closer, she peeks out. White guys, one with his arm on the other's shoulder. There's talk like *that'll fix the company* and *the money be good*. She thinks it's the mad tack-spitting guy said the last and she can see a bit of him, red hair under a construction hat, before she slips back in the stacks to save her wrinkled hide. Tack-spitter looks like the cat that ate the canary, she says. She's got a cat and a canary. Don't get antsy, it's all facts. Then, after the place goes up in smoke, she sees the photo of the suspect on the news and says he's Tack-spitter."

"Jack Cardenas, the alleged arsonist? Did she talk to an investigator?"

"Naw, because they already had Tack-spitter aka Cardenas and couldn't get a thing on him. You think the other guy was an accomplice, or Tack-spitter turned on him?"

Erik couldn't figure out the take-away of Lionel's story, so he showed interest in character. "Did your aunt recover her items?"

"A psychic helped her remember that she'd given the stuff to Goodwill. Now don't go thinking that cause Auntie sees a psychic she's unreliable. I already edited out her embellishments. Oh, and this was like before Auntie had her cataracts removed. Wait, something wrong? You getting a headache?"

He was. Erik had no idea if any of the story was valid. "I'm fine. So college life agrees?"

"Look, I got to see White Gran before she escapes the hospital and kills me for not showing. College life? It's living large in a sardine can with tests. You, Mr. Detective, keep dodging those bullets and stay out of burning buildings."

"Always my plan."

With Lionel jive-walking to the bus stop, Erik sat for a second. It seemed he'd forgotten something. He went inside Four Square to return the sandwich baskets and order a coffee to go. Behind the counter, a hulking white man, formerly incarcerated, seemed familiar. His squint eye lasered in on Erik. "Do I know you?"

Erik skipped the coffee and beat it.

CHAPTER 23

FOUR O'CLOCK THURSDAY, AND ERIK AND DEB HADN'T HAD TIME to compare case notes for the last twenty-four hours because they'd been moving their paltry G-Met possessions. They should be grateful that the Minneapolis City Hall had found them this shabby room (to be remodeled *after* they left). Instead, they felt taken in like poor relations. Erik could not make himself stable on a folding chair at a rickety table, made ricketier by Deb sitting on the table because *her* chair had a rough edge that caught on her pants. They didn't even have the hospitality of guest internet. Admittedly, they had to bring their own router for security reasons. For the moment, their murder boards were a tablet not much better than an etch-a-sketch and a poster board that belonged at a job expo. The tablet was in Deb's hands being cursed and jabbed. Because the room reeked of disinfectant, Erik opened the door to the corridor. "Dispelling the bleach odor," he said.

"That's me," she grumbled, "and you can't dispel me." She tossed the etch-a-sketch murder board on the table and shut the door he'd opened. "Can't have eavesdroppers wandering by. First, I made a list titled 'How Jean Died.' This should be on the murder board, and I'll shift the order when one theory trumps another." She pulled printed sheets from her bag and flung one at Erik. It read:

DEATH BY:
Spousal Unit
Unknown Lover, aka UnLuv
Random Factor
Stalker, homeless
Conspiracy, arson variety

Deb fanned her face with her death sheet. "I went swimming twice this week and found myself in the deep end of the chlorine. The so-so news, I could have a Type A male swim partner for life. The news that sucks, his chatter about Jean Nerstrand puts UnLuv, unknown lover, in position one on my list. He thinks it's Dominic Novak, but we need that cool stuff called evidence. The news that knocks the ball out of the park, a foul ball, is that Jean was going to a shooting range. That stench isn't me—what died in here?" She kicked the door open. "Investigate *that* before I kill somebody. Argh!"

"I don't know what *that* refers to in your syntax."

"I'll wring your syntax."

"I'll assume you mean that you deeply admire me as your partner and that you haven't come across any information about which shooting range. Anything like that on her credit cards?"

"No. The *point*—she yanked a hair spike—"is that we can't *not* investigate the gun even if it wasn't used against her. Do you want to know what's more?"

"More is better than less, unless the 'more' is aggravation."

"What's *more* is that Tessa ripped a hole in her dad's alibi. That puts spousal unit back at the head of the list. She was telling me after the funeral . . . by the way, your suspect sweetie was there, Karma Byrnes, looking numb and stylish, with Paisley. They didn't come to the reception. Wasn't Karma ready to throttle that cousin of Jean's who dumped her? Why can't sexy women crush on me? Why is one always making goo-goo eyes at you, Partner? Why are you folding that chair up like you're crushing a pop can? Am I getting on your nerves? Sorry, I've gotten on my own nerves, *erg*. Oh romance, wherefore art thou?"

Erik unfolded the chair, slammed it on the floor, refolded it like he was crushing a can, and tossed the chair in a corner with excessive force and clatter. "There, that's better. Has it occurred to you," he said to Deb, also standing now, "that the only women I meet, the only *time* I have to meet women, is on a case? Do you think I *like* that the only interest comes from homicide suspects?"

"Ah, you admit there's interest. I'm in the same effing boat, same smelly office. I tried hooking up with someone after a case was closed, but no-o. A stupid pandemic got in the way. And Paris." Deb pulled a folding chair out of a different corner and banged it down at the table. "How about internet dating apps?"

Erik paced. "Right. Can you see us posting, *Homicide detective wants a live one?*"

Deb giggled. "*After time in the morgue, I need a fresh face.*"

"*When death do us part, I promise to investigate.*"

"*Swipe right and I got your back. Swipe left and it's Miranda rights for you.*"

Deb giggled again. "So, Partner, we're sex-deprived and oxygen-deprived. This case is making me woozy." She plopped on the chair which screeched.

Erik fooled with the chair in the corner, gave up on it, and put his back against the wall. When Deb sucked in air, he counted the seconds until her *So*.

"So, Tessa. At the reception, she was telling me that Jean was bossy but 'the best mom' ever and her dad was the greatest, though always late, like that Tuesday of the killing when he was late picking up her and her brother at a school event. A total contradiction of the account that Bruce stayed for the event. Tessa realized what she'd done, and you can't imagine her agony when she realized she sent her dad down the river. She didn't defend him—just ran off to snatch a lemon bar. The bars were gone before I got there. To me, husband Bruce seems as likely a murderer as Bounce. He'd be late for the event—the victim would've skedaddled."

"Bounce?"

"The dog." Deb had her head on the table.

"You need oxygen, necessary to the combustion of ideas. You, as leader—"

"Who's leading us nowhere. You know, I almost—*almost*—look forward to my committee meeting tomorrow to get my head out of this hash. I got food poisoning from hash once, real bad. Patrol officers and social workers still haven't found that homeless stalker, Ulysses. That arson angle where crazy Cardenas is back to knock off people close to Dominic? Again, Bounce the dog looks better for the deed than a pyro, but hey, we got to check everything. Dream the impossible dream, Partner, go for it. See where the arson report takes you. I'm burned out."

Erik decided to scram to avoid more impossible orders. "I'm going to my alternate office, my Highlander."

"I'm set for my Necessary Alternate Plan."

"N-A-P, you're taking a nap."

"You catch on." Deb stretched her arms across the table and yawned.

Erik stashed his computer into the backpack that was his mobile office. Tempting as it to release frustration by bugging Drees somewhere, he couldn't act like a ten-year-old and had to accept that he must behave like the man of the hour, even if hour was the armpit of the day.

ERIK ATE TRAIL MIX, MATURELY EATING THE M&Ms AS THEY CAME. Working from the backseat of his Highlander with a parking lot view, he read on his laptop the files on the Park Avenue Apartments arson case. Arson investigation happens in stages with multiple agencies. It starts with the observations of the first responder firefighters; police are called in, especially if there was personal injury; the state fire marshal sets up the prolonged investigation; and insurance companies may send in their own teams or provide their own interpretations of evidence provided by law enforcement. Dominic Novak, after getting over the initial shock, speculated that mishandled welding materials were to blame. After the investigation found three ignition points, the consensus was that the Park Avenue fire resulted from space heaters positioned by "streamers" of combustible substances like paper trash. Not accident but arson. The man whose corpse was found fifteen feet from an origin point became the first suspect, until the autopsy indicated that a blow to the skull had felled him. That's when Dominic Novak pointed the finger at his disgruntled construction manager, Jack Cardenas. Cardenas had motive (revenge against displeased Dominic) and couldn't be found for a week after the fire. A traffic cam caught several vehicles in the vicinity of the apartment complex within the approximate time frame of the fire starting; none of the drivers were viable suspects, and none of the vehicles were registered to Cardenas.

Erik needed to go beyond the report. The fire marshal's lead investigator, by reason of death, was unavailable except through a séance. A thirty-year-old woman, as driver of an SUV in the vicinity, was briefly a person-of-interest. She was a scientist who researched the ignition point of industrial components.

The woman, Maria Hartung, told the investigators that she had pulled into the complex parking lot because her toddler son complained of a tummy ache. There were a few other vehicles, but she paid no attention to them. In her transcribed words, "My son had been to a birthday party, and I barely got him out of the car seat in time. He'd ingested party favors that looked like candy. The favors were in the vomit. It's beyond me why parents ignore the warning, 'not suitable for children under three.'" She went on to say that after throwing up, her Micah screamed to have the party favors back. She would not retrieve them from the puddle of vomit. The root cause of his distress ("said with attitude," the interviewer noted) was her recent divorce from his father.

Erik winced at the divorce reference and speculated why so many of his homicide cases involved vomit. Explanation: puke happens.

The summary came back to the scene: Maria reported seeing two men as she walked around her SUV with crying son in hand to calm him. The boy had pointed, "Dere, who's dat?" and "Pawdaws." Maria saw men dressed as if they could be homeless hanging around the fencing protecting the complex renovation; she interpreted the "Pawdaw" as one of the men reminded the boy of her father, the grandfather he called "Pawdaw." She took a second look at the time, didn't see the resemblance, and noted that one man had a stiff arm: end of her observations.

The part about the boy hurling struck a chord. Erik enlarged a selection. One investigator commented that Maria's knowledge of ignition could be significant to the arson, while a second scribbled, "give it a rest."

The University of Minnesota's online profile of Maria Hartung showed a serious woman with a depth to her skin that suggested mixed ethnicity. Erik reminded himself that we're all ethnic from some point of view. The scientist's headshot showed a dimpled chin, black hair in a short ponytail, and a turtleneck. She was unadorned except for earrings that may have been a peacock design. Her research involved adhesives and heat in industrial applications. She didn't respond to two voice messages on her university phone line and didn't reply to his email. She did have late office hours on Thursdays, from four to six.

Erik's left leg never stopped jiggling during his virtual searches. Prolonged computer work gave him a boxed-in feeling, intensified by the enclosure of the Highlander. There was nothing he dreaded more than being in a box. He needed the adrenalin surge of a fresh challenge, and the challenge of finding parking near a university building fit the bill.

Luck rode with him through rush-hour traffic allotting him green lights and a parking space to boot. In the chemistry building, an information desk was womanned by a student wearing earbuds and absorbed in her laptop. After Erik repeated several "EXCUSE ME's," she blinked at him, "Oh, yeah, sign here." He signed a piece of paper no one would ever look at and asked the whereabouts of the Dr. Hartung's office. The student, attention back on her screen, tilted her head in the direction of the elevators. The glass directory was plastered with stickers—*Elvis is dead, Frodo lives,* and *climate warming is hot-as-hell real*—which Erik had to peer under to find an office number.

Erik found Maria Hartung's office where the name plate on her door said "Fellow." Professors claimed to be progressive egalitarians until it came to their own medieval hierarchies, and Erik was unsure of a "fellow's" status. He put his hand up to knock and heard a muffled, "later, please, Matt." Hearing no reply from Matt, he assumed a phone call had ended and knocked. *Nothing.* He knocked louder and announced, "Erik Jansson, police."

Banging came from inside, a "*shit*," and the door opened. Brown eyes hollowed out by an unknown sorrow caught his. Nothing came out of Erik's open mouth.

The first word came slowly from hers, "Yes?" She was on the verge of crying and controlled the impulse by speaking in low, even tones. "Yes? Police? Are you sure you're looking for me?"

"Positive." His answer surprised him. "Yes, I am, Dr. Hartung. For information. I'm Detective Erik Jansson with Greater Metro Investigative Unit, G-Met." She seemed unable to process him. "May, uh, I come in, or make an appointment for later?"

In answer, she waved him in. She stood a little taller and a little fuller than Karma Byrnes—he shouldn't be thinking of Karma. Her small office had the orderly disorder of a professor's nook. One wall was covered with images of switches and components in various stages of melting. A junior ranger badge was pinned to a photograph of the Black Hills. On the desk, a picture of a boy holding a duckling held the one space not occupied by digital devices. She straightened a folding chair that had fallen helter-skelter against wire shelves. He sat in the wobbly chair while she sat on the rolling one at her desk and became lost in her thoughts.

"Dr. Hartung." With the repetition of her name, she focused on him. Her dark eyes shifted from sadness to a dissecting sharpness. Erik cleared his throat. "I'm investigating the murder of Jean Nerstrand in St. Louis Park. One lead is that her murder is connected to the arson last spring back at the Penn Avenue apartment complex. It is a circuitous lead."

"Circuitous lead, meaning circular and straight?" *A nitpicker*. Before he could explain, a man in lab coat and jeans knocked at her open door and acted as if Erik didn't exist.

"Maria, are you all right? I know you're tough but talk to me soon. If there's anything—"

"Thanks, Matt." She stared at Erik's hands on his crossed knee as if they were giant insects.

"Okey dokey, then." Matt thrummed his fingers on the doorframe and, at a lack of response from Maria, moved on. She wasn't big on responding to male cues, Erik concluded.

"Detective, um."

"Jansson." When Erik tilted forward to give her his card, his chair wobbled. Without glancing at the card, she asked, "Do you have several to spare?"

He handed over two more. She folded them into a packet which she handed back. "Put this under the chair leg so it won't rock." As he wiggled the chair into stability, she talked, "I hardly remember that time. You've already checked with the arson investigators?"

"I'm trying to put the reports in a fresh context."

Brringg—the office phone shocked her into a nanosecond of panic. She checked the caller ID and hit decline. "I thought it was . . . Matt." Her delay suggested it wasn't a call from Matt that concerned her. Erik squirmed, his name-card shim popped out from under the chair leg like a tiddlywink, and he had to catch himself.

Dr. Hartung observed him like a scientific specimen placed in a hostile environment. "I could look for another chair."

"It's fine. I only need to double-check—"

"Detective, I'm struggling with focus at the moment." She looked to the picture of the child. Erik should leave, if he dared stand up without having the chair collapse.

"Dr. Hartung, when I read the report, what struck me were your comments about your son's stomachache, which one officer called into question. My wife, ex-wife, has Rules of Life. Number one, if your child says he's sick, believe, act, and prepare to clean up the grocery aisle where you stand."

No laugh. Serious scientist all right. She parted her lips, a pretty shade, and frowned in thought. "I have rules. The first on my list is, never sleep with James Bond in the first half of the movie. You'll die."

Erik burst out with a laugh and his chair collapsed. He grabbed the wire shelf which went off balance and bound files tumbled on top of him.

"I'm not usually clumsy," he said from the floor. Dr. Hartung's mouth quirked as she offered a hand. He ignored it to right himself and bent over the files. "I can sort it out."

"Leave it. It's only my life's work. People step on my life's work all the time. Everything I had to say about that parking lot I've said. I just feel lucky that we were gone before the complex went up in flames."

Erik started to the door, saw it was a mere step away, and paused. "Would you recognize the men you saw? In the report, you said that after your son was sick, he saw two men, presumed homeless, and asked about them. One of them may have been the corpse found after the fire, and the other, 'Ulysses,' is at large. There's a chance that he's in danger or a danger to himself and others. That's the link to my current case. If you saw pictures of the men, could you identify them?"

"No, sorry about that. It's not like I videoed it." She was casual now that her life's work lay scattered at her feet.

"You sure you don't want help here?"

She picked up a folder and clapped it against the palm of her hand. She moved close to him, didn't seem to realize how close. "Detective, how often—" She caught sight of someone over his shoulder. "Oh, Matt, you're back. Detective Jansson is just leaving." She looked at Erik, again with an inscrutable sorrow. As an afterthought she offered her hand. It wasn't a handshake so much as a touch goodbye.

"Thank you, Dr. Hartung. If anything comes to mind, my cards are under the chair." As Erik passed, Matt coughed on him.

If only Maria Hartung had recorded on her phone what happened in the fateful parking lot thought Erik—an absurd wish. Erik was in his Highlander when a less absurd thought hit him.

He texted Lionel: "Did your Auntie video the two men she saw?" A video with a time stamp to identify who was arguing at the arson site the day before it went up in flames.

CHAPTER 24

FRIDAY MIDMORNING, DEB IN THE ROLE OF GREATER METRO Detective and Committee Member had to put the Nerstrand case aside because the betterment of the world fell on her shoulders. Those shoulders slumped when she sat on the base of the Father of Waters sculpture in the Minneapolis City Hall Rotunda, and they couldn't compare to those of the marble Father, a seven-ton Poseidon figure. Granted, the world-betterment burden was shared by a multi-agency committee on inclusion and de-escalation of violence, which had been meeting in an airless conference room. Today's task was planning diversity training. When several on the committee threatened mutiny, a break was declared.

Deb closed her eyes. She opened them as fellow committee-sufferer, G-Met detective Jimmy Bond Smalls, sat his Black self beside her on the stone base.

"I hope we accomplish more than polishing the Father of Waters with our glutes," she grumbled.

"Change happens at its own pace," Jimmy sympathized, "unless you drag people kicking and screaming into a future in which they're not special in the way they want to be. Me, in the future, I don't need to be any more special, except for shaving my head more often to hide the receding hairline and cutting back on ribs and petit fours to maintain my wasp-waist."

Deb's phone dinged. "Huh, another member texting me that the meeting has become a 'garboil.' What's a garboil? Oh, Drees is coming. Act like we're looking at a pdf together." Jimmy put his finger to her tablet.

A handsome form, aka *that tool Drees*, cleared his throat. Drees was insufferably his own idol. "Ahem, how goes it, Deborah? We must get that diversity training underway. It's mandated. I can find a reputable training team if you need—"

"Oh, hey, Drees, didn't see you coming," Deb lied with gusto. "You're welcome to email suggestions."

Drees cogitated like a man who can't decide between two percent or soy in his latte then addressed Jimmy. "Smalls, you appear to have a question on your mind."

"Yeah, why does the Father of the Mississippi River have a pet alligator hiding under his leg?" He jabbed the exposed marble snout. "If there're gators in Minnesota able to crawl up the banks and reach this building, it's a problem."

Drees lifted his brows. "The animal's a symbol that the river runs into the deep south."

"Does that make us the shallow north?" Jimmy surveyed more of the statue. "Where's the Mississippi's mom at?"

Drees peered down his nose. "I suppose you have to amuse yourself to lighten your load."

Deb began, "You're the lo—". Jimmy elbowed her ribs and she slipped to the floor. "*Ow*, my tailbone. These mini tiles are hard."

She regained her perch to see that Drees had been replaced by Erik with a cardboard holder of coffees. Jimmy took one and raised it. "Deliverance!"

"I saw Drees." Erik tossed the cardboard holder into a recycling bin. "What were you up to before he arrived?"

"On a committee break. Committees, where good ideas go to die," Deb explained. "After break we divide into sections. Each group has a task."

"Which is to complain about the other members," Jimmy added. "So far I've learned from the returned questionnaires that self-justification is an artform. Anonymous, but we can guess. Read him the responses, Comrade Deb, rapid fire."

Deb held up her tablet. "Quoting. People just need to be behave. If everybody behaved, it would be fine."

Jimmy—"Old fogey."

Deb—"I don't need a class. I'm woke. I demanded this for you old white men who don't get it."

Jimmy—"Old white guy getting himself off the hook by complaining about other old white guys."

Deb—"A class is useless if it tiptoes around white people."

Jimmy—"Next, it's useless if Black people won't accept responsibility."

Deb—"Finally, real action! The diversity courses *must* be required. However, it's not necessary for me to attend the sexual harassment unit because I'm a woman."

Jimmy—"W-O-M-A-N."

Deb—"Last but not least, it's useless unless you end capitalism."

Erik—"Because feudalism worked so well?"

Jimmy tilted his face to the ceiling. "If this is structural change, we're in for it. Gotta get cool air before committee hot air. See you tonight, Erik, dinner date?"

Erik, eyes shut, was muttering to himself, "Tell me this will be better. Tell me something good can come out of this." He bucked up and rejoined them. "Oh, right, dinner, your treat, Jimmy?"

"Ha, you know that ain't how it works. You're busy, right, Deb? Catch you another time." Jimmy left with a wave over his shoulder.

"Yup, busy." She didn't want to admit that it involved collecting her belongings from a storage unit and heading to Ibeling's garage apartment, which she'd checked last night with Greta. Sufficient for short term with a kitchenette, a sitting area with outdated furniture, a separate bedroom, and a utility closet with a stacked washer and dryer. A painting of a dear little cottage in snow hung on premier wall space. Deb asked Greta if she could remove the painting, hang a whiteboard, and place the table beneath to use as a desk. Greta, complimenting Deb for being "so *feng shui,*" took the painting down. Deb, oddly enough, regretted losing the sentimental image, but she needed the space. This place was a stopgap, not home—a good thing too since her boss lived close enough to shout at her.

Deb rose from her hard seat and rubbed the Father's toe for luck. Delaying her committee return, she quizzed Erik who'd been absorbed in his phone.

"So how'd it go with the scientist yesterday? Was she eager to help?"

He released air. "More like totally unimpressed. She used my contact cards as a shim for the chair I sat in."

"I like her. She's come up with the best use of our cards so far. Walk me to the death chamber. Right, so, Dr. Scientist wasn't helpful. Is she a suspect? A sexy suspect? I'm still avoiding online dating apps. Is she gay, bi? Yeah, I'm being 'incorrect.' Give me a fun distraction. Who's hotter, distracted science gal or stressed realtor Karma?"

"Karma Byrnes, though Dr. Hartung moved with a haunted grace."

"*Moved with a haunted grace*? Like a deer? Don't you shoot deer?"

"Ahem, did you know, 'Detective Metzger,' that deer are more abundant now than in the 1700s? They're habitat destructors with big brown eyes. But I can't shoot anything with big brown eyes, unless it's a charging mama bear."

"You still 'shooting' for that biathlon, ha-ha? Drat, texts." Deb scowled at her phone as they walked down a corridor. "I keep messaging Jean Nerstrand's photo to shooting ranges. No positive response yet." She leaned close to Erik. "Drees is following us with those nosy ears of his. Don't give me a look—ears can be 'nosy.' Why can't Drees stay in his own lane?"

"Because ours is the fast one," Erik whispered and hit a button on his phone activating an alarm. "Fake crisis—run."

They left Drees in their dust.

FRIDAY AT SIX, DEB STOPPED AT A GROCERY ON HER WAY to the Ibelings' bungalow off St. Paul's Grand Avenue. She would pay a nominal rent for the garage apartment to Ibeling's wife Greta. The apartment had been done up for Greta's mother, who died on the day she was to move in—Deb hoped she wouldn't share that fate. She worried that she'd screw up mission of fulfilling Greta's shopping list with high-salaried humanity crowding her at the meat counter and be assigned the doghouse. Except there probably wasn't a doghouse since Almost Allwise's Labradors, retired from cadaver service, snored inside on couches. He'd left for his conference and Greta was preparing a spread for Unknown Diners. Greta, detail-oriented since black-ops and catering were her bailiwicks, had texted Deb a list that required stopping at this place, All The Food You Never Dreamed of Eating and Then Some.

The man in front of Deb retrieved his lobster tails to go, and it was Deb's turn at bat. With those prices, they must put the animals up in the Ritz before whacking them. Greta hadn't said if she'd reimburse her for the food, and Deb should cover the cost as gracious guest. Was this what foster children felt, hope and fear tumbling together in their desperate hearts?

A woman behind Deb cleared her throat as the deli clerk asked and repeated, "Do you know what you want?"

She did and didn't know. Love, home, belonging—the stuff on the list which she handed to the clerk. He handed back wrapped halibut, lamb chops, and frozen squid. Deb's next destination, the Grains aisle. At its entry, she stopped on hearing a familiar voice. "Sure, sure" followed by a belly laugh—a phone conversation. "Oh, sweets, what you put up with! Say, would you like me to buy you those eclairs?" Bruce Nerstrand, and he wouldn't be chatting up his daughter like that.

She came at him, full cart ahead. "Mr. Nerstrand!"

He dropped a bag which split, and grits spread out like ball bearings.

DEB INTERVIEWED BRUCE IN THE STORE'S STAFF BREAKROOM, where he gulped water from a Pacific island and she, water from Norway.

Bruce hulked over the salvaged-wood table. "Back in that lockdown time, all that stay-at-home stuff got to us." His nails scratched at the water bottle, which lacked a label to peel. "Jean had to show places because housing is an essential need but did the paperwork at home. I thought it would be cozy for us to work together at the big table. Didn't think that through, and I was busier than ever. I work on distribution networks, scheduling and mapping on computers. It was crazy, still is crazy, and you can't fix every-thing online, so I was on the phone a lot to Rosaleen at the central office. I get loud when into stuff, and the kids were doing school zooms upstairs, and there wasn't much place to go where Jean wouldn't hear everything. She said headphones couldn't cancel me out. That's when she moved to the garage. When she'd go back and forth, she'd catch our conversations. I, I kinda haven't been so faithful."

Deb spit her pricey water. "You had an *affair*?"

"Nooo." He rubbed away tears with the hand holding the water, which dribbled onto his shirt. "A work wife, Rosaleen—she's married. Like we're bosom buddies, not that it's about her bosom." He glanced to Deb's breasts. "Tessa says I light right up when Rosaleen calls. Probably seemed like I was happier with virtual Rosaleen than with real Jean. But I *loved* Jean. That night she—died, I'd dropped the kids at school and was driving around to work up the nerve to talk to her about seeing a marriage counselor. I tried and tried to call, no answer." He broke down, his face in his hands and his heart on his sleeve.

Deb knew about the unanswered calls and had speculated that they were meant to shore up an alibi. Bruce sure had a hole in his, and now this "work wife." As she waited for Bruce to recover himself, employees slipped in and lingered over prepping a doll-size cup of coffee. Deb employed her gift for clearing a room—"POLICE INVESTIGATION. SCAT." They scatted.

Bruce rubbed his red eyes. "What's the point of tiny coffee?"

"Bruce, what do you know about Jean borrowing a handgun from her sister?"

"I didn't know she did," he faltered. "I kinda knew she was interested in shooting. I think it was July that she and a bunch of real estate people went to a conference up in Wausau, Wisconsin. She said I had to stay with the kids. Anyway, she comes back and talks to me when we were doing yard work—we did that together—that this woman agent from northern Wisconsin does con-cealed carry when she's showing places. The Wisconsin agent said a woman realtor would be crazy not to carry."

"That's Wisconsin for you," Deb said.

"I suppose, those remote cabins. Jean said the Twin Cities agents thought carrying a gun was ridiculous, but several said they had a great time at gun clubs. And like that, she wanted to sign up."

Deb tightened. "Did she say who she would go with?"

Bruce reached for an open package of kettle chips left on the table and crunched. "Maybe Renee what's-her-name, that Novak family. She didn't come to the funeral because of a migraine but she sure sent beautiful flowers. The Novaks are the type to belong to clubs."

Employees knocked on the door, prepared to undertake a siege, and Bruce was done. It didn't sit well on Deb's empty stomach that Bruce claimed not to know about Jean borrowing a sister's firearm. He was also needy—Deb's gut feeling that he couldn't be a killer gurgled to a new awareness. The needy will do about anything to hold on to what they want. In that dangerous logic, the only way to hold something in place was to stop it from moving again, ever.

Deb released Bruce, who went straight to check out without picking up eclairs for Rosaleen. Deb finished shopping for Greta. She acquired Israeli couscous and was on the quest for cardamom and saffron. She discovered the Persian saffron, saw the price, and stunned everyone around by gasping, "*Holy freaking shit.*"

She'd need to remortgage an imaginary house to buy this spice.

CHAPTER 25

I T WAS THEIR CIVIC DUTY, JIMMY BOND SMALLS HAD SAID TO ERIK, to keep small businesses open after the Time of Terrible Living. This was how Erik found himself in a bar light-headed with hunger and surrounded by the aroma of other diners' bistro steaks. After Jimmy messaged that he and his wife and a gym buddy were running late, Erik made his way to the counter to ask for cranberry juice to avoid alcohol on an empty stomach. The juice came tarted up with a lime slice and greenish stick. He turned to the lounge area and saw alone on a curved seat Dr. Hartung.

Her white shirt and russet sweater enhanced the sheen of her skin. Her trousers were standard campus wear, but she traded out the practical shoes for burnished ankle boots. Her earrings sparkled as she sipped red wine. She raised her head and caught his eye. Awkward to slink away, Erik asked if he could join her for a few minutes.

She nodded. "Are you waiting for a delayed party as well?"

"Yes." He sat, not too close. Since they'd met, he realized he had additional questions for her, only this wasn't the place.

"Are you on duty?" she asked. "Your salad drink there?"

"No," he smiled. "Do you know what this is?" He fished the herb twig from his drink.

"A driveway weed." Her slight smile gave way to confusion. "Do I call you Sam Spade, Marlowe?"

"Erik, Erik Jansson, Dr.—"

"Maria." She examined the low level of wine in her glass and appeared displeased with herself. Not so displeased that she didn't take another sip.

Erik forged ahead. "Yesterday, you were about to ask something when Mr. Labcoat—"

"Matt."

"When Matt came by. Do you have a question for me?"

Her lips parted. "Matt came by, trusty Matt, Matt who should show up here any time now."

"Does he have a chance?" Erik asked, for god's sake why.

"A chance?" It took her a second to catch on. "Ha, not one in a cold day in hell."

"I think it's 'not a snowball's chance in hell.'"

She raised her brows "Not a snowball's chance, eh? Matt's married, but he needs to be needed. I do his wife a favor in being an occasional person-in-need. I hope they're here soon—I'm paying a sitter. Matt means well but he's not quite a grownup." She side-eyed Erik. "I suppose in your profession, you hear confessions that have nothing to do with your case."

"Yes." Erik gulped his juice. Wherever he was meant to be in life, it wasn't here with a soul-baring stranger.

"Didn't you say you had a son? Excuse me. My line of work, like yours, involves asking direct questions."

"Yes, in second grade," he answered.

"How much time do you spend with him? You know, forget I asked."

"Some weeks I see him every day. More often it's about four days out of seven. I have breakfast with him and take him to school; he stays over many weekends. What happens to that arrangement if Kristine—if his mother remarries, I don't know. If we'd put half the effort into scheduling our days before the divorce that we put in now to do right by Ben, we probably wouldn't have gotten divorced."

The bar's decibel level ratcheted upward, and Maria's attention drifted. Just as well if she hadn't heard what he said. Her head returned halfway, and Erik bent close to hear. "After the divorce, my ex-husband went to France, and I don't mean France Avenue but the University of Bordeaux. The terms called for joint custody—parenting by zoom—and he expects Micah to visit him four times a year and puts the arrangements on me. That's petty stuff. The day you darkened my door, he'd called and said the arrangements wouldn't work. For him." She swirled her remaining wine. "He 'recommended' dropping the next visit. That's easier on me, but I thought fathers *wanted* their sons, wanted that bond." She took a shaky breath and glanced at him. "Next time I'm hanging out in a bar, I'll try your Erik spritzer there. Nothing like a generous pour of California cabernet to bring out woes about ex's." She finished her wine and relaxed against the back of the seat. Erik's phone dinged with a message that Jimmy was in the parking lot by the restaurant's other entrance. He stood.

"My group's here. The only thing I can say is that I can't imagine my life without Ben."

She made a single nod without looking at him.

"I, uh, do have one more question about the case. Is there a good time to call you at your office?"

"What question? I'm curious." She didn't sound curious.

"Your son said 'Pawdaws' at Park Avenue scene. I wanted to be clear on what he was referring to, if the men reminded him of his grandfather Padaw, if their clothing was similar, a vehicle, whatever."

Maria stood as well, eyes on the bar entry. "They're coming. Give me a call later." When she couldn't find a place to set her wine glass, Erik took it. There was a faint thank you, and she wound her way toward Matt and a woman. The woman clapped her hands on Maria's shoulders and her voice carried, "I hear a Noir Detective stalked into your office and you were short on repartee. Dish the details."

Erik took the long way around the bar. After cheery greetings and the seating of his group, his text alert dinged: Deb Metzger sending him the name of a shooting gallery to check out. Another ding: "FYI, September, gave spa card to homeless man. Spa 50th and France. M.H." Maria was the source of Ulysses' gift card.

Erik pushed it all from his consciousness but didn't feel present in the moment, didn't follow the table talk. He ordered because the others did, and why not share a bottle or two of *Côtes du Rhône*? Though when the juicy steak arrived, topped with chive butter and accompanied by hot salty *frites*, he savored every bite.

CHAPTER 26

Teddy Roosevelt could have rambled in bow-legged and been at home in the gun club lobby. Karma, feeling otherwise this Saturday afternoon, convinced herself she was open to the experience and had nothing better to do while Sylvy had a playdate. It was better than sitting at home fretting about her phone conversation with Renee yesterday, conciliatory on the surface with vipers beneath. Renee invited Karma to join her bridge club, knowing Karma would refuse because she wouldn't take weeknights away from Sylvy. Second stab at mean-girl inclusiveness, Renee told Karma she was foolish in not learning to shoot: "You never know when you need self-defense, especially if you're the type who doesn't know when to be careful." Then Dominic, as he'd promised, invited Karma to join them at the Fox and Boar range. That put Karma in the Wild West of Eagan, ten minutes east of the Mall of America.

Dominic strutted up, strong and woodsy in a chamois shirt, kissed Karma on the cheek, and said Renee and Simon would join them in a half hour. *Simon who?* Oh, screw them to hell and back, this was a blind date. She'd heard of Simon, divorced, older, stable—a toothless horse. Oblivious to her mood, Dominic introduced her to a Fox & Boar employee, a cheerful man named Gary who welcomed Karma. "We're a Guntry club, a country club without the golf," Gary said proudly. "We have the premium indoor range in the region. As you see, we sell logo clothing items, a few firearm models, and certainly ammo because ammo makes the world go round." Karma guessed that meant you had to have ammo to make use of this place where the background of muted gunfire was constant. Gary talked up the rustic grandeur of The Fox and Boar Club with its rough wood walls, plaid chairs trimmed with brass brads, and walk-in fireplace. A brick brew pub angled off to one side. If you went in the pub, your hand would be circled with an ID bracelet to prevent people from drinking before going to the indoor range. Gunshots *before* whisky shots, Gary joked. He pressed into Karma's hand a brochure about "Situational Awareness for Women" and "Proximity Weapons." That last phrase likely referred to items like her pointed kitty-cat key chain. Gary and Dominic chorused that the club emphasis was on safety and sportsmanship for everyone. "Everyone," from what Karma saw, included two Black women turning in rented handguns, a woman working the sales counter who could be Hmong, a mixed-race man with the bulk of "The Rock" actor, and plenty of white men.

Gary left them at the gun lockers where Dominic grunted at his phone. "I wish Renee would get here. One of her bridge buddies is having a crisis. Renee loves this place in winter when the Christmas greenery's up and the fires are crackling, but she doesn't care for the noise and shooting at a humanoid blob."

"The target's human?" Karma was taken aback.

Dominic remained locked on his phone. "Renee can't make it. She has to rush a friend to the ER." He puffed out air. "Simon texted he can't come either."

Karma could faint with relief. She'd prefer being grilled by a detective under a spotlight to a "blind" date blasting weapons around her.

"We won't rent a gun for you. You can borrow Renee's Sig Sauer. I'll load when we're ready." Dominic opened the locker, unlocked a case, and handed her a plain black gun.

"It's light," she said in surprise.

"Small ones, you got to be prepared for the recoil, not like with this beauty." Dominic took a gun out of another case, nearly twice the size of the Sig Sauer with a stylish turquoise grip. "My CZ Shadow special. Great for competing."

Karma was surprised again—the gun *was* beautiful. And from the way big Dominic held it, heavy.

"Remember, this is about your safety, Karma. I worry." Dominic choked back a sob. "If Jean had known how to handle a gun, that husband of hers, any stranger . . ."

She took a gentle hold of his arm. "You were going to show me?"

Minutes later, with eye and ear protection in place, they stood in a lane with wall barriers separating them from other shooters. The targets were standard circles, not human blobs. Dominic fired a few times and impressed her with his accuracy, but the popping from other alleys startled her and she put off taking a turn. Dominic did have her hold the firearm and practice sighting. An instructor dropped by, adjusted her grip, and had her squeeze one off. Her hand jumped with the recoil, and the bullet grazed the bottom of the target. There was nothing transformational about the act—she could live without guns. The instructor left to be replaced by someone pausing behind them. She turned and gasped, "Detective Jansson!" He had a gun holstered on the hip of his jeans.

"It's a good idea to put the gun down, Ms. Byrnes," he said. She clattered it down on the counter and he flinched. "Good afternoon, Mr. Novak. I see I've committed a fashion faux pas." Detective Jansson tugged at his chamois shirt which matched Dominic's. Dominic's torso bulged next to the detective's, which in Karma's dreams had the definition of a Greek statue.

"I prefer a Glock to a Smith & Wesson," Dominic was saying by way of small talk after he didn't take Detective Jansson's extended hand. He was puffing himself—"Now that case with Jean"—when a pang of grief deflated him. "Shouldn't have said her name. Damn. Solve that case, would you, Jenson?"

"We're doing all we can, and it's Jansson."

This was worse than being in an elevator with two ex-boyfriends. Karma's mouth seemed to fill with sand, and it took effort to speak, "Are you here to shoot? You could join us."

"Two per lane," Dominic reminded her. "I bet you have to be a crack shot, Jen—Jansson."

"We have required practice time and safety refresher courses. Being familiar and prepared with a weapon, you're less likely to use it."

"Pfft," Dominic disagreed. "The police record of shootings proves that wrong. Sorry, didn't mean to go there. Tell me, it's about deer season. You a hunter?"

Karma interrupted the male posturing before there was a showdown, "Where's the safety on your revolver, Detective Jansson?"

"None of us is holding a revolver, which has a rotating cylinder for bullets. My nine-millimeter, like yours, has a magazine cartridge and no safety."

"Police want rapid fire," Dominic sneered.

Detective Jansson addressed himself to Karma, "As I told a friend, I don't hunt anything with big brown eyes. Can't do it. Ducks, geese, those little beady eyes, the poop they leave, that's another story."

"Guess you won't be hunting down Karma then, not with her big, beautiful browns." Dominic put his free arm around her. The detective stared into her eyes, hazel according to her driver's license.

She looked down and fidgeted. "I'd have dressed in calico if I'd known you two cowboys would be having a showdown."

"When what you're really interested in is saving the ranch." Detective Jansson's sunny smile from the corn maze came back. Noise broke in from a few alleys down; men had stepped back from their shooting cubbies into the corridor, heeing and hawing. "You sure took out Paper Guy's appendix. Remind me not to hunt with you!"

Dominic glowered, "We don't usually get yahoos here."

"I imagine," Detective Jansson said. "I'm looking for a work colleague. Have you noticed a man in his thirties, medium build, about five-nine, golden skin? Pacific Islander heritage."

"You describe everyone like they're in a lineup." Karma laughed which surprised herself. She was flushing and startling all the time now. She hated it, hated the vulnerability.

"Not a gracious habit, I'm afraid. Mr. Novak, I haven't seen that model of Glock. Do you like the handling?"

"With my big hands, I prefer the heavier gun. I'll show you. Ear buds in place?" Dominic fired multiple shots, well centered.

Detective Jansson compressed his lips before saying, "Not bad. I'll recommend that model to a colleague. Maybe you could tell me, Mr. Novak, did Jean ever talk about investments she was making?"

A shock rippled through Karma—what was *this* about?

But Detective Jansson was backing away. "Strike that question from the record. Have a good weekend, Mr. Novak, Karma." He walked off, his sidearm never unholstered.

The yahoos followed, boots clomping, yucking it up about who'd pay for the first round of beers. Dominic talked through their racket. "He called you 'Karma.'"

"Men take liberties with women's first names."

"Have you been seeing him?"

"Of course not. I did run into him once when he had his son with him."

"And a wife?"

She shrugged a lie.

"He's buttering you up. You think it's about the case, but he wants into your pants."

"Dominic! That's *rude*." She picked up the gun without realizing it.

"*Karma, you're pointing the gun wrong.*" She jerked it higher, and Dominic seized it before she triggered something she shouldn't.

Embarrassed, she asked a dumb question. "Is this about you two wearing the same shirt?"

"*What?* That's silly. He was silly to bring it up, and that nine-millimeter of his is girly."

"Girly? *That's* silly."

Dominic's cheeks were as bright as peppers. "You're defending him, Karma? Have you *slept* with him?"

She went to slap him, missed, and he caught her in a downward spiral.

FLATTERED AND ANGERED, ERIK STRODE PAST FOX AND BOAR reception to the membership desk. When Karma first saw him, her dismay morphed to delight. It would've been more flattering if she hadn't been pointing a gun at his heart then lowered it to his crotch—she knew where to hit a man. Dominic Novak had to go and show off, swelling his barrel chest and hitting bull's eye. Erik was angry at Dominic on general principle and angry at himself for being angry. He'd ticked off the man in interviews and today with a smart remark about matching shirts. Mistakes, he was making mistakes.

Erik wouldn't have to explain his mistakes to Deb because she could figure it out on her own. She had tossed the gun club tip to him because she was delving into the cases of two unidentified men found killed at Deerhorn Park—one might be the Homeless Ulysses. Erik needed to keep his sights on Dominic Novak, who had a habit of being out with a woman who was not his wife. Did Dominic turn vicious if a woman wanted too much or threatened exposure, as Jean may have done? Was this a case of garden-variety adultery that ended with an execution?

The membership attendant was faking it at the computer while his eyes roved over young women entering the bar. Erik rapped the table, and the young man pivoted like he'd been poked. He wore a polo shirt with the logo of a fox on a boar's back, and the sleeves strained over his biceps. He likely called a frat house home. Erik flashed his G-Met ID, so it was barely glimpsed and said offhand, "I'm a detective, and I'd like to know a little more about a couple here, Dominic—"

"I get it." The man pulled close and whispered, "His wife hired you."

Erik glanced to the side as if checking that no one heard their secret.

"If he still has a wife," the attendant said. "Today's woman, I think she would've preferred a movie. Speaking of movies, have you seen—"

"Could you describe the other women?"

"I've been working here ten months, and I first saw him with this tight-looking woman. Your client, the wife, right?"

"Could you be more specific?"

"Blonde, short, would be middle-aged cute if she didn't look like a constipated schoolteacher."

"Next?"

"A redhead, not a fantastic looker, but fun from the way they whooped it up. It's been weeks since I've seen her, guessing she was dumped." He hadn't connected the image in his head with news items on Jean Nerstrand. "The one today rates a younger guy who's in shape." Polo Shirt's biceps jumped. "I'd say Dominic's after a fun time when he brings women in to shoot."

"When he brings in women for shooting practice?"

"What I said, brings women to shoot. It could be he's hunting for true love."

Erik wasn't keen on finding true love at the end of a gun barrel. "What do people here think of Dominic?"

"The owner brags up Dominic as the greatest. Landvak, his company, built this place. There is a regular who blabs that Dominic's a cheat."

"I suppose most of us are seen as devils by some and angels by others."

Polo Shirt disagreed. "Negative. I can read people. You can tell the real solids."

That sounded like waste management. "A great talent. If I need to come back, what are your hours?" Erik intended avoidance.

The attendant scribbled on a card and handed it over. "Dominic must be doing something right, the women, the projects, the money. It's not like he's a government dweeb, a parasite wasting our tax dollars. Look, I have to help these folks."

The "folks," laughing women coming from the bar, hardly appeared in need though Polo shirt rushed to them. Erik left uneasy and not because he feared the character-reader would see through him as a tax-paid parasite. With the Nerstrand murder, he feared that the arson leads were spinning everywhere, business leads spinning nowhere, men and women spinning away from marriages, with bystanders Karma and Rafe caught in the web.

Yes, Erik should have been forthright with the attendant that he served the public and not constipated clients. He should reform his errant character to become as straightforward as he looked. No more feints and dodges, no more tricks on Drees. He realized he hadn't played any decent tricks on Drees lately, and with that he came to his senses.

Tricks had an exuberance, and mistakes could be fortuitous. Erik had pushed enough of Dominic Novak's buttons that something had to pinball in a new direction. Dominic could be tricking them all with an act; time to trick the trickster. It was also time to go home to Ben and that exuberant mistake, overgrown Stripe. Erik's parents were also up from Iowa City, promising to make pasta the "Italian way," and not the "Midwest way" with cream-of-mushroom soup. He could go to bed early on a full stomach, which is about as much as any detective can expect of a day.

CHAPTER 27

IT WAS LIKE WEARING A BRA THAT SQUEEZED and jeans that shrunk. Deb's emotions wanted full naked release. Late Saturday afternoon, she wanted stocky, sexy Jude in or out of her life, not dancing along the edge in cute shoes with tassels. On a previous case, Jude had directed all her flirtatiousness at Deb and post-case they met for coffees and lips brushed. Before their relationship could heat up to passion, Jude's employer like an evil stepmother (in fact a generous philanthropist) whisked her away. Deb had sunk to the depths of dubiousness about tonight's Skype date with Jude signing on as Paris clocks chimed midnight. As for freeing her mind from the case, Deb knew zip about the men murdered in the park, whether one was Homeless Ulysses, because city detectives on the case were stalled over identification. And last night Bruce had blabbed away his alibi—back to his phone account to trace his locations the night of the murder. Famished Deb hungered to build a case that wouldn't blow up in her face.

She warily watched Greta Ibeling clamp down the lid on the pressure cooker. Greta had a professional kitchen in the bungalow. She looked like what she was, a compact grandmother in a denim apron who meant business.

Deb had asked for food advice, and Greta obliged. "This cooker is vintage," she said to Deb. "My mother's second one. Her first one blew up and took out the kitchen ceiling. Today I'm steaming potatoes. With this I don't have to watch them every second and they come out a consistent texture."

"Huh-uh."

"I'll use them to make railway potatoes. It's a curry dish that people packed to eat on Indian trains. You add the cooked potatoes to a tadka, which is mustard seeds and spices thrown in hot oil. The fumes can make your eyes sting, but the flavor's worth it. It's a simple dish, really."

"When I watch the food network, I get hungry by step five of the recipe and order a pizza."

"You want an easy menu for a virtual date, right? Perhaps a pot-de-crème dessert?"

"I was thinking steak frites takeout and my mom's brownie pudding. You know, you dump a brownie mix in a casserole, add boiling water, brown sugar, and cocoa, throw in the oven, and you have chocolate cake with a sauce."

Greta pulled on sterile gloves with a spanking sound and prepared chilis. "You don't seem confident in your menu."

"I think the other party is stringing me along. I'm a fallback for when she returns to the states." She handed Greta a plate holding a raw chicken.

"Some never want to pay the price of making a choice." Greta cleaved the chicken in half. "Relationships are scary. A new one is the great unknown where you're the most vulnerable. What if you make a choice, or somebody forces it on you, and it turns out to be wrong? Disastrous."

"That's dead true in abuse cases. Where do you want these spices?" Deb read the labels, mustard seed, cumin seed, turmeric.

"Right there." Greta indicated a spot. "The first time I met Ebee"—she called Chief Ibeling *Ebee*—"I ignored him." She severed a leg from a thigh. "He hardly talked and when he did, it was three sentences about his military service and two about hunting and fishing. Before Ebee, I'd scared off other men. They acted like plain me was a femme fatale." Deb didn't dare ask if the men knew of her black ops skills, and Greta went on. "Persistence can be sexy, and loyalty in the face of challenges when combined with muscular—"

Deb cut her off. "Renee Novak is incredibly loyal to her husband and her husband's company. I'm not talking about the case"—yes, she was—"but it seems like they have a history, overcoming obstacles like in a Netflix romance."

Greta sliced lemons. "We lived years ago in White Bear Lake, Renee's hometown. Renee's family, the Landons, had their start in the lumber industry. Her father branched off into construction and specialized in building luxury lodges along the North Shore. If I recall the gossip right, I can see Renee believing that women would take advantage of Dominic. He was a beautiful fifteen-year-old when an eighteen-year-old senior seduced him at an unsupervised drinking party. Then the baby came."

Greta told the story while Deb helped set up the *mise-en-place* for finishing the potatoes and marinating the chicken. Dominic's parents paid the girl's medical costs, and the baby was adopted out. At a marriageable age, Dominic met Renee, and both were high on love. Her family agreed to their marriage if Dominic, good looks and promise with no experience, would apprentice with the Landon company. The Landons took life seriously, and it was rough going for a showman like Dominic. Rumor had it that Dominic proved his worth by becoming an expert bird hunter like his father-in-law. When Dominic wanted his own company, the Landons provided startup funds and invested. As for the baby, in his teens he rebelled against his divorcing adoptive parents and appeared on Dominic's doorstep. With no children of her own, Renee was thrilled. She was devastated when the boy chose to return to his adoptive mother.

At this point, Greta heated a massive skillet on the burner. "Now for the tadka. Be prepared for the seeds to pop."

Deb made a mental leap backward to what Tessa Nerstrand had said about her mother's perfumes. "Why would a woman buy an expensive perfume and like that stop wearing it?"

Greta poured oil into the hot pan. "It didn't produce results? The joke is that if women want to attract men, they should smell like pumpkin pie. Or the perfume irritated someone around her." She tossed the spices into the hot oil and slapped on a splatter shield. The popping released pungent odors that made Deb's eyes water. Greta, shaking the pan, mused, "Women have a keener sense of smell than men. A man might not notice a woman's perfume clinging to his shirt, but a wife doing laundry might."

"So Jean stopped wearing the perfume unless her lover be found out. Is it all right if I wet a towel and put it over my eyes?"

"Of course. I forgot the cooking goggles. Skip takeout tonight. French fries don't travel well, and you can sous vide a steak here to rare and later panfry for the Maillard Reaction. That's the caramelized browning."

Before Deb could decide, she doubled over with sneezes. She stayed low for a minute where the odors were less intense. She straightened up to find Ibeling in hunting orange giving Greta a big smooch on the lips. Ah heck, his "conference" was bird hunting.

One arm around Greta, Ibeling pulled from his vest a dead bird. "Not bad for an old grouse." He kissed her again and *then* spotted Deb. Good thing he'd left his hunting rifle in the truck.

"What the?" Ibeling's eyebrows crackled.

"Deb's my sous chef," Greta said placidly.

"And I gotta go." Deb was out of the kitchen before Ibeling could say boo, you're fired.

Back at the garage apartment, she filled the bathroom sink with icy water and dunked her head. Her eyes, throat, nose, and ears burned. She couldn't anchor the Nerstand case. The more she learned, the less direction she had. She prayed that this was the kind of case where one murder was the be-all and end-all. That it was not the kind of case where one murder led to another, like dominoes falling. But homeless men had been killed, and those close to Jean—Dominic, Renee, Bruce, and Karma—seemed stricken. Everyone, except Jack Cardenas, and Rafe.

It was time to assign more tasks to Partner Erik.

CHAPTER 28

FROM SHOOTING GALLERY TO SPA, THE NERSTRAND CASE PINGED Erik around over the weekend without conclusion. Sunday, he waited outside the Hygge Spa off 50th and France in Edina, hoping to learn if Homeless Ulysses had made his way there with the gift card from Maria Hartung. She had forgotten which spa, but G-Met intern Ms. Mahdi had called around on Saturday and found the one. The Hygge, 'hygge' being a Danish word for a nirvana of comfort, admitted to treating "a person in need of hygienic repair." The spa opened at 1:00 on Sundays; it was now 12:45, windy and overcast. He'd rather be at his place with his parents and Ben, though if this spa had a branch in Iowa City, he could take care of his mother's Christmas present.

Lights flipped on inside, and the electronic door lock clicked off. Erik entered a scented domain of soft light and pale crystals to behold a woman moving with ballerina grace. She must bathe in cream to have such opalescent skin. She glided to a rack of robes, and after adjusting them to display their ephemeral patterns, she floated to the counter and lifted her face to Erik.

He was in love.

Her cheese-grater voice knocked him out-of-love. "Hey, I'm Mina. Can I help you?"

"Yes, I'm Detective Erik Jansson, and I'm seeking a man who may look homeless because he is. He has a gift membership here and goes by Ulysses."

Mina's eyes smoked by makeup became black slits. "What's he done?"

"I'm seeking information from him."

A dark-skinned woman drifted in from the private area, her head in a "what's up" quirk.

Mina's nasality increased. "The detective here wants that homeless person."

The second woman was too busy smiling at Erik to comprehend and purred, "What would you like? We'll full service here."

Erik felt certain that the Hygge full service was family rated. He repeated his question, and the woman's purr flattened, "Oh. Ask Anders, our male masseuse. And here he is."

A Nordic god strode through the door, tall, blond, fit. Purr murmured to Mina, "he puts the sex in Sioux Falls."

Erik introduced himself, and Anders told the women that he'd talk to the detective in Massage Room Three. He could have been a twenty-something version of G-Met's Drees, only not plastic. In the room, Anders turned the dim lights up and the background *omm* down. Erik leaned against a counter of lotions, and Anders sat on the massage table. The room reeked of sage which could evoke spiritual rest or the sensation of being stuffed inside a Thanksgiving turkey.

Erik started, "We believe a man known as Homeless Ulysses has information that could help us in a murder investigation. He's left his usual encampment and has not been seen at shelters. He told a street associate that he was a member of a spa."

Anders grinned. "Kinda. He walked in here with the card weeks ago, a quiet Wednesday. Mina was about to call the police 'to assist him.' I looked at his card—man, it was for a thousand bucks—and said I'd help him." Erik decided Maria Hartung must've have been terribly burned by her ex to regift that card. Anders continued, "I was raised to see the 'downtrodden' as envoys of Christ. You know, 'I was a stranger and you welcomed me, I was naked and you gave me clothing.' He signed in as Grant S. Ulysses, and when he wouldn't provide an address I 'borrowed' my uncle's. I told him he should shower first to warm up his muscles, and that as part of his deal, the spa would provide a robe and do his laundry while he was receiving services."

"You made up the laundry part to help him out?" Erik had his suspicions about Anders, which Anders confirmed.

"Yeah, I'm a P.K., preacher's kid—my mom's a preacher back in South Dakota."

"Lutheran? ELCA? My mother's sister is a pastor in Iowa." Though Erik's mother, despite having dragged them all to church, considered herself Druid Reformed. "Forgive my curiosity, but how did you get from a Sioux Falls parsonage to an Edina spa?"

"Long story involving me wanting a job at the pro-club of a golf resort and being sent to the spa because I wasn't 'up to par.' I'd eventually like to work on performance issues with skiers. I've gotten into cross-country and Telemark and grew up pheasant hunting. I've entered a biathlon."

No way Erik would win when Anders had the lightning reflexes of a young Thor. "Back to Ulysses, did he talk about his situation?"

"He said a woman with 'deep eyes' gave the card to him. Whoever it was may have noticed his pain. He must have osteoarthritis, the way he was seized up. He really didn't want me touching him but finally let me knead out the knots in his back. One arm had scars from a training accident in the army. He loved the heated whirlpool."

"Did he talk about anything or anyone in particular?"

"I stayed close to him in case he spooked, and his tongue loosened when he was steeping in the hot water. He said he had to work up his nerve to find a woman who 'needed a father.' She'd brought him food a few times. He said if he were younger, he'd go for her, but joked about being an old rooster who'd lost his crow. He didn't trust the man she was with, said he had to get her away from him."

Ulysses had a stalker mindset, the belief that the woman needs you and only you. "Did he describe the woman and man?"

"No. He obsessed about a business card she'd handed him. The card said Jane or Jean, but when he called that number—he bought cheap phones when he had the cash—'the wrong woman' answered and the one he reached gave him another name, which sounded like candy."

"Do you remember what kind of candy? Strange question, I know."

Anders shook his head no. Erik chanced a word that sounded like Karma, "Caramel?"

"I couldn't say."

"Anders, you're a Good Samaritan and listened with sympathy. How did *you* take what Ulysses was saying?"

"You mean, did I believe him? I did believe that he'd met this 'fatherless' woman and seen her with a man."

"Did he seem delusional?"

"You've got me worried." Anders dropped his voice with a glance at the door. "He came in nervous—who wouldn't be, crossing such a class barrier? This is a comfort zone for the well-heeled, and that guy's boots were garbage." Anders checked his smart watch. "I have a client scheduled. I can claim an emergency."

Erik sneezed from the aromatics. "No need, just another minute. From what you've said Ulysses sounds harmless. His fears could also be justified. He may have witnessed a murder and an arson, perhaps a second murder." He omitted that Ulysses could be culpable. "I trust you won't excite your coworkers here, but if he makes contact, call 911, me, and the Mental Health Crisis Hotline. Paranoia not only imagines dangers but creates them. Have you worked with the delusional?"

"Remember, I've dealt with golfers."

Erik laughed and took his leave. He bid farewell to Mina and her colleague, busy checking in clients, and stepped out into autumnal gray. Mina came after him.

"A gift card," she hee-hawed, "to thank you for your public service. And do we need to do anything?"

Erik took the card, which might cover the manicure of one hand. "Anders will explain. The man in question needs immediate assistance. If you see him, follow your protocol for people in distress. The important thing, stay calm and keep him calm."

At hearing "calm," Mina's opal skin flattened to gauze white. Erik, reluctant to give false assurances, said thank you and goodbye. As for the card, he'd give it to Tree at the Deerhorn encampment.

He hopped into his Highlander, eager to join his family and whatever make-believe game Ben had invented. Erik started the engine, didn't shift to drive. The terrible truth could be that Homeless Ulysses, instead of living in world of make-believe, had known of real and deadly threats to Jean Nerstrand, and to Karma Byrnes.

CHAPTER 29

MONDAY MORNING, WITH SPECULATIONS CENTERING ON Dominic Novak and Homeless Ulysses, the detectives chased down a lead. Erik parked the G-Met vehicle on Bloomington Avenue, south of East Lake Street, in a neighborhood of owned and rented houses. Yellow leaves floating down slowed time, tamed their rush, as he and Deb shuffled through them to the home of Lionel's Auntie.

The red house with dark wood trim staggered up several floors to the pitch-point of the roof, its setbacks and gables like the crooked little home of a fable. An elderly Black woman opened the door. Her face held a history of thought and worry in its lines; her upper and lower jaw, like the stories of the house, didn't align. Her lower jaw shifted left to right before she clipped, "Who sent you?"

"We know your grandnephew, Lionel," Deb answered. "I'm Detective Deb Metzger and this is Detective Erik Jansson. You're expecting us, Ms. Geary, Charlene Geary? We called?"

"'Cause you know Lionel, it's Charlene." She welcomed them into a room that wasn't constructed into existence as much as crocheted. Deb and Erik sunk into the afghan throws on the sofa while she took the rocking chair. She wore beige stretch pants, slippers, and a gold tunic sweater—leftover gold yarn dangled from a craft bag next to her chair. A tuxedo cat on a granny-square pillow shifted attention from a goldfish in a bowl to a canary hanging in a cage. The bird fluttered close to the bars taunting the cat, whose tail switched. In sync with the tail, Charlene's jaw moved back and forth. Deb couldn't tell if her jaw had been injured, if she bought dentures from the internet, or if difficulty after difficulty caused the clench.

"Do you want coffee?" Charlene offered. "I have a fresh jar of Nescafe. No?

I just had some myself, so I'm good. As good as I can be knowing there's killers out there, going after the homeless, and that encampment's practically next door. They should be helpin' the homeless, not hurtin'." She worked her jaw. "Are you armed? Don't tell me. I don't allow guns in my home. Won't allow it. But people do. My friend Doris used to say there's no guns in the Bible. I said there ain't toasters in the Bible either, so what's that prove? I don't like guns, and I don't like killers. I could relax if you'd catch 'em." Her jaw clicked.

"We have colleagues working on that, older detectives." Deb meant the *older* to be reassuring. "Detective Jansson, Erik here, and I are investigating if the recent killing of homeless men has any connection to the killing of a realtor in St. Louis Park."

"According to the news, you sure ain't making progress on that."

"We're here to make progress," Erik said. "It's possible that one or more of these deaths goes back to the arson at the Penn Avenue complex where you used to live. Lionel—"

"He's smart, that boy."

"Yes, he is," Erik confirmed. "He said you overheard an exchange between two men and that you have video."

"Forgot it was on my phone. But you need context. Context for the who and when and why. It's something big. I'm not talking conspiracy with aliens and people called 'Q,' but this screwy housing market, it's got to be a scam."

Deb sat forward on the sofa, dragging a section of the afghan with her. "I'm living it. Can't find a decent place to live and have to crash in my boss's garage."

That was news to Erik, who stared at her. Charlene tutted, "That's no good."

Erik ahemmed, "It's making Deb a better detective, not that she isn't a fine one already. She has insight into the homeless and what drives them."

"Most of 'em don't have much drive, that's why they're homeless," Charlene said. "Listen up, I'm grateful for everything in my life. I'm not poor. I'm not getting a Section Eight subsidy, but I might have to the way the prices gone boom." She mimicked an explosion with her hands. "I have the Social Security I worked my whole life for, and IRAs. That *used* to cover the rent. I had that nice Penn Avenue place where family could visit. Then he kicks us out, this Landvak what's-his-name. He kicked out Black people, white people, Hispanics, retirees. This place here's tiny and my sister, that's Lionel's nana, has to help me, and like I said, I ain't even poor. But one thing go wrong, like my Buick needs a new transmission, I'm hanging by a thread. And I don't like Minneapolis, the crime, the stuck-up city attitude. I like the South."

"Florida?" Deb asked.

"Richfield or Bloomington, as long as you're not right on 494." The cat in a feline spasm sprung on the loose yarn like it was a roiling serpent. "Sylvester, stop that, you ninny."

Deb pulled Charlene's attention away from the cat's violence against gold acrylic. "I understand, Charlene. Unfortunate *and* legitimate. The group that owned the complex sold it, Dominic Novak's company Landvak bought it, and started renovating to meet market demands. Then the arson happened."

"Market demands, my foot. That Dominic wants young pretty people around all the time, thinks pretty means money. My old neighbor there, Doris, was white. You'd trust her I bet. She heard things."

"We trust you," Erik said, "but would you be willing to share her number?"

"She passed. She told me before her heart quit that old management was in trouble because somebody had a gambling problem. I bet that Novak won the place in a card game. Next thing we get the notice to move out. We could come back with a new lease, if we had mega-moola, and they hand out these brochures that brag up the place. But the school district got at 'em because an immediate move woulda meant a hundred schoolkids displaced. That gave us a bit of time. Then they resettle those kids, we're evicted, and I had to stay with my sister. Better than staying with the boss." She shot Deb a look.

"You go back to retrieve items at the complex," Deb prodded. "What happened?"

The jaw slid back and forth. "You can't be on the grounds when they're working on it, so I go late and can't find a single person left to help. I walk right up to these stacks of wood. Don't see no stickers about responsible forestry like in the brochures." She picked up the yarn undone by the cat. "Then I hear cussing and fighting and hide between the stacks. So rattled it takes me a minute to think I could call 911. Then what would I say? I'm an old Black lady and I hear white men at each other? I peek around and there's this man in a hardhat shoving this bigger one and swearing about 'bum deal' and how he'll burn the place down." Charlene stopped with the yarn.

"Could you recognize these men if you saw them again?" Deb asked.

"Honey, the next day I failed my driver's license test on account of my cataracts and decided then and there to go ahead with the surgery. I had nightmares about eyeballs popping out of my head like a ghoul's. Turned out to be over in a jiff and I can see the noses plain on your face, and you got good straight ones. Back at the apartments, I could read the label on the fake wood 'cause it right in front of me." She discovered a knot in the yarn. "If they knew I was talking, would they come after me like they did those homeless people?" She dropped the yarn in her lap where Sylvester stood on his hind legs to bat at it. "Maybe I said enough. You should go."

"Please, one more minute?" Erik asked. "No one except Lionel knows about this conversation. I promised him we'd keep your safety foremost. It would help if you could describe what happened next."

Charlene nudged the cat with her foot. "Sylvester, don't you stare at Tweety like that. These men pushed each other to where they might see me, and I duck, and suddenly it's quiet, like when Sylvester here thinks he's figured out how to get Tweety." The cat clawed the yarn from her lap to the floor with a *grrr*. "I got my phone and think I'll record 'em for protection. That's when they walk past me, like blood brothers."

"Could you show us the video, Charlene?" Deb asked.

"You better promise it won't be all over the internet." Her jaw slid back and forth. "I don't want to get myself killed for being viral."

G-Met could keep Charlene's identity out of it, but if the video indicated who was behind the arson, they'd need to share clips with other investigators. Deb turned to Erik, whose hand to mouth suggested thinking. "Partner, you have an idea."

"Ms. Geary, Charlene," he said. "Could we see the video first? Then we can discuss how to proceed."

She retrieved the phone from a stand near the door and mumbled to herself while hunting for the video. The canary trilled, and Sylvester napped on his tangle of yarn. Charlene trembled handing the phone to Erik. "Lionel better be right about you."

Deb, unable to scooch across crocheting to be near Erik, walked around the sofa to peer over his shoulder. Charlene came over, caught up in their anticipation. Erik hit play. The edge of a lumber stack, no sound, then men's torsos approaching, both in unzipped jackets revealing a solid middle for one and a thicker middle for the other.

"*There*," Charlene pointed. "I didn't get their heads, but there you can see their belts. You can identify them by their belts."

"Possibly." Deb crinkled her nose. The shorter man's chin, reddish from hair or a rash, came into view—he could be Cardenas. The men briefly pressed sides suggesting the tall one had his arm on the other's shoulders. Their conversation was faint.

"Thanks for this, Charlene," Erik said. "If you don't mind, I'll adjust your settings to improve the sound." He tapped on the phone and hit replay.

This time they heard a man grunt, "You'll keep your end of the bargain?" The answer came from the taller: "best for us both, and it'll set the company right up."

"What the! That's—" Deb stopped herself.

"That Landvak fellow?" Charlene gasped and stepped back on Sylvester's tail. The cat yowled, she lost her balance and grabbed the pole of Tweety's cage, it slipped and crashed against the table with the goldfish bowl, knocking over the bowl and releasing Tweety. In the general panic, Deb caught Charlene as she was about to hit the floor, Erik cupped his hands to catch Tweety in midair, and Sylvester caught the goldfish. He spat out the fish.

After containing the critters and assisting Charlene to her chair, the detectives remained standing. Deb, hands on hips, summed up the situation: "We have a short man making a promise he breaks when he burns the place down, allegedly burns it, to spite the nose on his face, though we can't see his nose. Or we have two men in on the arson. We'll work on belt identification."

Charlene started over with winding the yarn. "They say that Cardenas burnt the place down to cover his shoddy work and get back at Landvak for complaining. But the police got *nothing* on him, and they say he's back and up to no good." Her phone dinged and she snatched it from Erik. "News alerts." She froze. "Bless us, they found two dead homeless men this weekend. They're killing people off. I can't let you have this video. They can trace videos to people. I gotta protect myself."

"Charlene," Deb tried to reassure her, "those deaths are already under investigation, but you're right, too many deaths. You've been a big help."

"Helping don't feel safe." Charlene's jaw clicked. "If they figure out who was around that Penn Avenue place, they die, like the man they found burnt to a crisp." She picked up Sylvester and pressed him to her chest, which he maniacally clawed.

"You're right, Charlene. These people are dangerous. Here, let me." Erik took the cat, which liked the advantage of his height for observing Tweety. "We intend to solve this case to protect people like you, and they're not onto our investigation. I reached out to Lionel on a hunch. Arsonists can't figure out the hunches in my head."

"That's for sure," Deb agreed. "I can't figure them out even when Partner here explains them."

That mollified Charlene and Erik set a calmed Sylvester on her lap. "I guess if I remember anything else I'll have Lionel tell you. He knows how to be safe in what-they-call-it, the cyber sphere? Maybe Doris remembers something."

"I thought she'd passed," Deb said.

"There are ways—she left me one." Charlene nodded at a triangular corner table where in pride of place was a Ouija board.

IN THEIR VEHICLE, ERIK SAT AT THE WHEEL and Deb on the passenger side, taking in the fresh pigeon dropping on the windshield. Erik had asked Charlene to let him record her video on his phone. That way the recording would not be a digital transfer but a copy lacking the time/location stamps necessary to qualify as trial evidence. She said she'd think on it. Seeing them out, Charlene said that despite preferring to be south by nine miles, she felt at home in the red house. It did feel like a home. Not that Erik desired a yarn haven with pets on different levels of the food chain, but he could do more with his place for Ben. Like many men, he considered his apartment less as home and more as base camp, the place you left in quest of adventure. Home was where you stashed the underwear, locked up the guns, and packed for the next outing.

Deb broke in on his musings. "How'd you catch that bird without squeezing the life out of it?"

"I have hands like a Labrador."

"Labradors don't have hands. Ha, caught you in a mixed semaphore."

"You mean metaphor. Hands like a retriever's mouth, without the slobber."

"I'd like a pet minus the slobber. Are you thinking what I'm thinking, Partner?"

"That keeping caged birds is problematic?"

Deb groaned. "*Our*, and *our* includes the congealed noodles in your skull, *our* thinking has been that an intimate partner, i.e., Bruce or Dominic, killed Jean. Or the killer is a unicorn, not the kind on girls' pjs, but a one-off event like a drive-by shooting in a suburban neighborhood."

Erik inhaled. "Or someone killed her because she was close to Dominic."

"But," they both started. Deb took it. "I doubt that Charlene as Unknown Informant is in danger, but Jean could've stumbled onto a conspiracy. That's it, Jean may have figured out something she shouldn't have. If she was sleeping with Dominic, she could've come too close to his secrets."

"Charlene's video might have captured a reconciliation between Jack Cardenas and Dominic Novak before a final betrayal," Erik said. "That could mean Dominic's innocent and Cardenas went through with his threat."

"How good are you at identifying belts?"

"Speaking off the cuff, one man wore brown cowhide, thirty-eight-inch waist. The other espresso colored, forty-four-inch waist."

"What, did you work at *Males Are Us, Large and Small*? Without that video, we can't prove much. Can't prove much with it either. Gosh, a conspiracy?"

Erik rubbed his hands on the sides of his nose. "Setting Cardenas aside, it would be hard for Dominic to run a Landvak scam without an insider, like Rafe Lutyens. He's worth putting under the microscope. If anyone can think sideways, it's Rafe."

"Meanwhile, back at the encampment," Deb said, "it's being dismantled today. If we can't find Ulysses there . . ."

She didn't finish. If they didn't find Ulysses, someone else would, and he'd be no better than a lifeless discard at a landfill.

CHAPTER 30

Rafe was not welcomed at the homeless encampment on Monday. His first mistake was to wear a Landvak cap. His second was to look like himself, a youngster of keen ambition who understood in the abstract that people have feelings but was flummoxed when those feelings impinged upon his schemes. As Dominic instructed, Rafe walked into the Deerhorn encampment to volunteer on removal day, thus representing Landvak as sympathetic. At the sight of Rafe's hat, a crumpled woman taking down a tent snarled, "Come to gloat?" When Rafe said he'd come to help, she blew a raspberry at him. Two men in safety vests grumbled, "Do you have instructions?" Rafe said no, and one pointed his thumb to a van emblazoned with the logo of a housing nonprofit. Rafe heard the men mutter behind him, "They should tell him the evictions have already been served." That's when the Landvak hat went into his puffer-vest pocket. If only Karma had come along to make it lovely.

At the command van, Rafe expected the intake woman to acknowledge that Landvak was doing its part. She merely doled out bags, gloves, and reflective vests, and explained protocol if weapons and needles were found. She assigned him trash pickup and didn't look twice at his nose. He felt dissed.

Then sunbeams broke through the clouds to light up a kaleidoscope of shapes and colors, and Rafe's spirits lifted. But it was a kaleidoscope of ratty tents and trash. He was a doomed figure in a medieval painting where naked humans seemed to dwell in a bright paradise, until a closer look revealed the paradise was a clutter of demons.

A woman whose eyes shook, nystagmus, accosted him. "Are you stealing?" Her mouth gaped in a hideous grin.

A female police officer rushed between them. "He's a helper, Agnes. See Jackie over there? She's a saint and will help you with your things." Agnes repeated *Saint* like Jackie was indeed canonized, and the officer said to Rafe. "She's a biter. Follow that group and trash what they don't put in the carts."

What unglamorous charity for sordid humanity. The detritus irritated Rafe's sinuses. He picked up rotted food, blew his nose, picked up unsanitary sanitary products, blew his nose, picked up filthy clothes, blew his nose. He'd sneezed his way to a group of three homeless men, short, medium, and tall, who toasted their hands over a grill that heated a liquid. The liquid, Rafe swore, smelled of eye of newt and toe of frog. He'd landed in *Macbeth*.

"Least Landvak didn't burn us out first," Short said. "Or set fire to their own building across the way."

Tall, who resembled a tree with mottled bark, agreed. "Yup. They never found who killed Ulysses' friend back at Penn Avenue,"

"That arsonist is back. I seen him," Medium said.

"In a crystal ball?" snorted Short.

Medium defended himself. "He's going to kill Dominic and already did in the wife."

"It was his lover that was kilt." Tall hooked a drooping eye on Rafe. "Who you staring at?"

"Trash?" Rafe held out a bag.

"Trash back at you." Medium dumped a frayed sweater in the bag.

"Hey, I'm taking that." Short snatched it back and stuck up his chin up at Rafe. "I seen you across the street. You taking over if they kill Dominic?"

Head down, Rafe hurried off to his destiny.

DETECTIVES JANSSON AND METZGER STOPPED IN THEIR TRACKS before colliding with Rafe, who seemed utterly lost. Erik hadn't expected to see anyone from Landvak and adjusted his National Park cap to gain reaction time. Deb forged ahead like she'd run into an old buddy. "*Hey*, Rafe. Good for you, helping out."

He responded like a peevish child. "It's a mess. Are *you* helping?"

"We're trying to find a homeless man," Erik said and watched for Rafe's response to the name. "Ulysses, he wears a green army jacket. Picked up any information?"

The name seemed to mean nothing to Rafe. "One of the warlocks behind me peered into a crystal ball and saw—*pah*."

"We'll check them out." But Erik stayed on Rafe while Deb trotted to the men.

"There's a woman who bites," Rafe warned after her.

"An old friend of Detective Metzger's." Erik said. "Have you seen the set-up where many of these people are going? Is Landvak involved?"

Rafe shifted again. "The Respite place? *Rich* corporations with tax write-offs are behind that. It's secure units within a warehouse so people can lock up their belongings and sleep without fear. It's about reduction of harm. The homeless come as they are with the addictions they have, and professionals work to get them healthy. You know . . ." Rafe scanned the park. "People talk about what they'll leave behind. A building, a business, a legacy. When what we leave behind is spent bullets and heroin needles." He turned on Erik. "What if there's violence against developers and realtors? Where's the 'reduction of harm' there? Who are *you* keeping safe?" He twirled his trash bag shut and volte-faced to a dumpster.

Deb replaced him, breathless. "Partner, Ulysses was here a few days ago for coat distribution so he has a new look. Rumor is that he served in Afghanistan where he specialized in evasive maneuvers. What'd you do to Rafe?"

A woman screamed that a man grabbed her phone, uniformed officers went in chase, and Bobcat loaders scooped up broken bikes and grills.

Erik crossed his arms and frowned in the direction of the dumpster—no Rafe. "I think the question is, what is he doing to himself?"

LATE MONDAY AFTERNOON, THE ENCAMPMENT BULLDOZED AWAY, Erik felt great relief when Deb happily despaired that their case was going nowhere, might as well go home and put the feet up. Then rumors gave birth to nasty truth: Jack Cardenas, as a person of interest, had been picked up in St. Louis Park in response to the APB. The SLP police were holding him, so could you G-Met people shake a leg and get here already?

The detectives with their digital tablets were shown into a St. Louis Park station interrogation room. Cardenas could be the Landvak arsonist, the killer of the homeless man at the arson site, and/or the killer of Jean Nerstrand. On first sight, Erik thought Cardenas was a contradiction in terms: with Hispanic surname, he had the demeanor of a drunk from Glasgow; rosacea burned across his cheeks but his throat was pasty white; not tall at five-eight, he had a physique enlarged with muscle. When the three sat at a small table, Erik fought gagging at the man's scent redolent of musk ox. Deb across the table choked and slugged water from a bottle. Cardenas centered his scarred hands on the table—he'd win any bare-knuckle boxing match.

"Fucking Mary," he swore. "I've been interviewed by bigger fry than you. Marshals, the FBI, the BCA, that tobacco bureau. What does a tobacco bureau have to do with me?"

"You mean the ATF? Bureau of Alcohol, Tobacco, and Firearms? Arson of a certain scale falls in its purview," Erik said.

"Don't you talk pretty," Cardenas sneered at Erik, then cast his eyes up and down Deb, "You ain't pretty unless they shrink you to fuckable size. Good set of knockers on you, though."

"Cut the crap, Cardenas," Deb snapped and for a second Erik worried that she'd lose it, but her focus sharpened. "Mr. Cardenas, you remain a person of interest in the Penn Avenue Apartment arson, and you're a person of interest in the recent killing of Jean Nerstrand."

"Don't even know who that is, sweet cheeks."

Deb smiled at him—"Funny"—and looked to Erik. "Legal question, how much is the contempt fine?"

Erik played along. "I'm thinking as high as we can go. Compound that with an unregistered vehicle running a red light."

Cardenas slammed down his giant hands. "Zip it, you fucking Marys, or I'll call my lawyer. This is all because Dominic Novak don't like me no more. What a pretty boy he is, but put him on a playground and he'll kick you when you're down. Him and his twisted contracts."

Deb pushed back. "Mr. Cardenas, we're not here to talk about Dominic unless what you have to say connects him to the death of Jean Nerstrand. Then we'll listen like clams."

"Why does she get to do all the talking?" He smirked at Erik.

"Because she's the boss. You don't become boss unless you have guts, but I can throw in my two cents worth. You left suddenly after the Penn Avenue arson," Erik said. "Suddenly you're back."

"Look, I had 'concerns' in Canada that needed tending. When I 'tend' to something, I tend to it fast. I'm a multinational business." Cardenas tilted back, put one leg over the knee of the other. "You're a smart boy. Run along and look up the Fed reports. I have an alibi for that arson time."

Deb glanced at her tablet. "Provided by your girlfriend, Della Stokes. Still together?"

"Women are like cars. You got to upgrade 'em every so often for a new model that works slick."

"So that's a no," Deb said. "Now Tuesday the fifth."

"I was in Bemidji at a poker game. Those guys I shot the shit with aren't keen on sharing with cops, but you can try. Be a scenic drive for the two of you this time of year. Relax out those worry lines you have. Age fast in this job, don't ya? See, I empathize. That sleaze Dominic has you believing all kinds of things. Look, all anybody has against me is Dominic's say-so. Not that I'd take it out on his nearest and dearest. Hell, I'm the forgiving type. I'm forgiving you your dumbass questions right now. Dominic and me might get along again, after I straighten him out."

Deb squinted. "What do you mean, straighten him out? You mean you'd hurt Dominic Novak or someone 'near and dear' to him?"

Cardenas threw up his hands—"you fucking"—and Erik leapt to his feet, inhaling through his mouth to avoid the ox odor. Cardenas waved him to sit down. He did not.

"My partner feels like standing," Deb said. "So do you have plans for Novak?"

"Nah, listen to what I've been saying. I empathize. Maybe me and ol' Dom will 'take a meeting.' Second thought, that's a crap idea because I heard he's got some monkey-eyed twit working his schemes. As far as hurting innocent folk—" Cardenas raised his fists. "If I'd hit anybody with these lately, you'd see fresh cracks. Recess is over. I have work to do." He started to rise.

In two strides Erik was behind Cardenas. Deb, on her feet, ordered, "SIT. Keep up this attitude, and you'll be in detention. But I have empathy too. I'd like to hear more of your story, Jack. SO SIT."

Cardenas, face inflamed, grumbled himself back into the chair. Deb returned to hers.

Erik moved back a few feet and started: "I've read some of your story, Mr. Cardenas. You have a felony assault on record. The husband of a woman you were sleeping with lost an eye after you attacked him. That means you can't carry a firearm."

"Aah, I was a drunk kid then. When there's a disagreement, I use my words now." Cardenas cracked his knuckles. "I don't know squat about arson. I can tell ya Dominic likes to have a harem around. And if I was a fucking Mary like you, I'd go over his records. If some goober figured out how Dominick's profits get fat like him, I wouldn't be surprised to find 'em dead in the street. Now can I be excused to use the little boy's room?"

"Finish your homework," Deb said. "Not only was your vehicle registration out of date, so's your driver's license. Where are you staying?"

"With my girlfriend," Cardenas gloated. "The new model."

"Her name and address?"

"I just drive there, know the look of the place. I don't need a stinking number."

"I'll call her for the address." Deb took out her phone. "Her number?"

Cardenas sniffed. "Maybe I'm not there all the time."

"Oh," Erik feigned sympathy. "Are you couch surfing? Homeless?"

Deb tsked. "That's bad, Mr. Cardenas. It sucks to be homeless. Trust me, I *empathize*. We can find you accommodations in a jail cell unless—"

Cardenas, face more inflamed than ever, screeched his chair back. "I'll give you the number, all right?"

He spat it at Deb.

THE DETECTIVES PAUSED BY THEIR G-MET VEHICLE in the SLP station lot. They didn't have enough to hold Cardenas.

"I could punch somebody." Deb hit the SUV hood with a gloved hand. "Cardenas, what a piece of stinking garbage. Oscar the Grouch would kick him out of the can. He put me in a mood."

"The mood's mutual. Let's get out." Erik jammed his hands in his fleece pockets.

"Before we can blow this popsicle stand, we have to come up with a way to keep tabs on Cardenas. Man, what a prize he is. C'mon, put up your dukes. Let's spar over this." Deb hit her fists together. "Don't give me that 'I'm looking at you askance' face. I never heard of 'askance' until I met you. What, aren't you into boxing?"

"Makes mashed potato of your face and pea gravel of your knuckles."

"I won't make mashed potato of you if you don't make mincemeat of me." Deb threw mock punches and Erik spread his hands as a blocker.

A passing SLP officer called out, "Why don't you two get a room, in a gym." Deb threw a hard right that whistled by Erik's ear.

"*Watch out*, where's this getting us?"

"C'mon, Partner. Turn on that lightbulb in your brain. Dig up a detail that didn't mean squat until you saw it. Cardenas, talking about my 'attributes.' Men! How do you put up with each other?"

Erik avoided her jab. "And women? How do women put up with *him*?"

Deb swung at Erik's chin. "That's it, virtual knock out! It sounds like there's a list of trade-ins, the old models." She bounced and sparred. "Do you suppose there's a social media page, the ex's of Jack Cardenas? There are women who have private groups warning about losers, abusers, drunks, and cads."

"Is that sad or funny?" Erik dodged her swings, his thick hair flopping.

"In support groups like that, the women are usually free from the worst of it." Deb sucked air. "Let's say Cardenas strongarmed a woman to provide an alibi for the arson and the related killing. Next he dumps his alibi provider, and she no longer gives a flying fig about him." She threw a punch.

Erik caught her fist. "Cherchez la femme?"

"Admit it, you've always wanted to say that." Deb slowed her bounces. "Okay, I've had a day of it. Let's go."

Neither moved because their attitudes were too raw.

Deb blew out air. "Is this the part where I say, 'let's get a beer,' even if I'm not feeling it, and you look like you want to head to the territories by your lonesome? What comes next?"

"You say how about another time, and I look like I agree."

"How about another time? You look like you agree. A twelve-hour break's good. Twenty-four if we can get away with solo assignments."

"I'll re-comb the arson reports." Erik ran a hand through his messy hair. "You'll hunt down women scorned?"

"I'd rather be a woman fulfilled."

"Or find a woman to fulfill."

"Easier to solve the case," Deb rolled her head around her neck.

"Easier to solve the case," Erik stretched his arms overhead.

They reached for the driver's doorhandle at the same time.

CHAPTER 31

MONDAY HAD BEEN A TIGHTENING BELT OVER A HEAVY MEAL you never intended to eat. Frustrated that she couldn't detect a lethal pattern in suspects' behaviors, Deb lay face up on the braided rug in the Ibeling's garage apartment and stared at the rafter. It was eight p.m. and black outside. Gorging on leftover pizza had been a mistake. She stretched her limbs, though it was her brain that required stretching, and closed her eyes.

One of the homeless deaths that upset Charlene Geary was a run-of-the-mill overdose—when would opioid deaths stop becoming run-of-the-mill? Then the Minneapolis homicide officers reached out on the other case. The male suspect, an addict, admitted to killing the homeless man but claimed self-defense, an unconvincing claim given that a half hour later the murderer was buying street drugs with fresh cash. Nothing about either case tied to Ulysses or Jean. Those officers had picked up rumors of a homeless man identified as Grant Stewart appearing and disappearing because he thought he was being hunted. Since Grant and Ulysses could be one and the same, a former Army man, Deb had reached out to the Veteran's Administration: nothing yet.

Forensic Accountant extraordinaire Naomi had done a second comb-through of the checking account that Jean set up for herself after separating from Bruce. From the latter, she wrote out three checks of $7,500 to "Karas Futures Investment." If it was true that Karma was ignorant of that company, could it be a hidden venture of Dominic's? There was no justification, how-ever, to subpoena Dominic Novak's personal or business accounts. Then there was Jack Cardenas, Mr. *I-Use-My-Words-Now.*

The icing on the yuck-cake of a day was the call Deb received on walking into the apartment, Mom. Her divorced mom—oh Dad, you flubbed it—had dropped the married choir member she'd been seeing after the wife confronted her with an ultimatum. Mom had to stop seeing the husband or the woman would never again bake pies for church events. Mom confessed to Deb that she'd already given up on the dude but desperately needed someone to talk to. Deb blurted, "Mom, you know everybody and talk all the time." Mom went ahead lamenting that Deb's brother was busy with wife and kids, so couldn't Deb—Deb cut her off with chitchat about a cat living with a canary. Mom jumped on what was not meant to be a suggestion and vowed to come up for parrot shopping.

Deb's thoughts drifted to love lost and regret. There was a saying that the French have no regrets. Or was it cats have no regrets? Did lost love Jude have a French chat? Deb pulled herself to a sit and stared ahead. The bed awaited.

The bedding Greta Ibeling provided was not only of a quality beyond Deb's dreams, it was a quality that could *improve* her dreams. Deb changed into Wonder Woman pjs and crawled in, the comforter embracing her in a queen-size cloud. Totally acceptable to be asleep by eight-thirty. She drifted into soft darkness. *Ank, ank, ank!* Her effing phone—*please* let it be spam. She struggled to free an arm from the clinging comforter, which clearly wanted her to stay, and grabbed the phone from the bedside table. Oh geez, caller ID, Bruce Nerstrand. She jerked upright and pushed "accept."

"He's in my shed! In my boat. That homeless guy, the stalker. He scared the hell out of my daughter. He's lighting a fire!"

"To keep warm or burn the place down?"

"Who *cares*?" Bruce panted, "HE'S IN MY SHED."

"Mr. Nerstrand, do three things. Call 911 to report the man and a possible fire and they'll send patrols and a truck. Call your neighbor, Officer Pete, in case he's handy. Then you and the kids and Bounce stay away from the shed. Do not approach on your own."

Deb dressed in the dirty clothes heaped on a chair and covered all with the trench coat her mom had made her buy. Sometimes it paid to listen to Mom.

TESSA'S EYES WERE THE SIZE OF PLANETS. Her father Bruce and brother Travis stood protectively in the Nerstrand doorway as the girl sobbed to Detective Metzger, "I was taking out a broken andiron and I had a flashlight because I'd lost an earring, and it might be there because that's where I put the rake."

Deb didn't stop for logic. "Go on."

"I pulled up the door, antique not automatic, and like he was right there!" She held her breath as if waiting for a cue.

"Did he say anything? Ask for anybody?"

"No."

"What happened next?"

"I hit him with the flashlight and ran. Oh, I shoved down the garage door?"

"It only shut part way," her father burst in. "I heard her scream and came running out. I looked under the door and saw him scrabbling under the boat cover. That's the kind of thing terrorists do. Where's the SWAT team?"

"We'll go easy first," Deb said. "Backup's right behind me." And they were, two officers, hands on their service weapons.

Officer Pete arrived and stayed with the family while Deb and her backup went to the boatshed that attached to the garage where Jean had lived. Deb acted on the assumption that this was Homeless Ulysses. "It's all right, Ulysses," she shouted under the door. *Silence.* The officers raised the door with a metallic screech and panned a flashlight over a trail of blood leading to the boat. Tessa had done damage, not that Deb blamed the girl. She signaled the officers to ready their weapon and held her flashlight as Tessa had done, to flip like a bully stick if necessary.

She stepped closer to the aluminum fishing boat. "Ulysses? I'm Detective Deb Metzger. I'm worried about you. There's blood out here. Why don't you come out and tell me about Jean and the woman with the candy name?"

There was rustling under the boat cover.

"Ulysses, do you have any weapons in there? You don't want to scare the children, the baby." The baby was an inspired touch.

"What baby?" came a thin voice.

"I mean you frightened the girl. She came out to help, but you startled her." *No response.*

"Ulysses, you like to help people," Deb said. "Throw out anything that might scare the girl."

An arm appeared and pruning shears dropped to the floor.

Deb frog walked close to grab the shears and fell back at a shriek from the boat.

"There's babies!" Ulysses scrambled out and fell to the floor. Forehead bleeding, he cried, "I sat on 'em. I killed 'em."

Ulysses had squished a nest of mice. He was easy to apprehend after that.

EMERGENCIES WHERE SECONDS MATTER TRANSITION TO PROCEDURES where this-will-take-hours. Deb ascertained that the fire was the odor of woodsmoke from a neighbor's chimney, that the garden shears were already in the shed, Ulysses picked them up after Tessa hit him, that he had nothing else that functioned as a weapon, and that he needed medical attention. When EMTs arrived, they said they would take him to a hospital because, besides the headwound, he exhibited confusion and his blood pressure was spiking.

Deb rode in the ambulance figuring out how to keep Ulysses from escaping the hospital—detain him under guard on the suspicion of trespassing with intent to commit harm. The greatest harm he'd done was to himself. A Black woman EMT had administered a beta blocker for the blood pressure, positioned an oxygen mask, disinfected the shallow cut, and insisted he stay calm.

The confusion back at the boat shed uncalmed Deb. Who's dead, Ulysses asked in tears, Jeannie or her friend? Was this Jeannie's house or Caramel's? Jeannie was too young to have an adult daughter—he saw adolescent Tessa as an adult. Where was Jeannie with the light brown hair?

Jean Nerstrand was a dye-job redhead; Karma Byrnes was a sun-kissed brunette.

Ulysses dozed, and the EMT told Deb that the blood pressure had dropped, but if it continued dropping he could slip into fatal shock.

ULYSSES SURVIVED THE NIGHT, AND A BATTERY OF TESTS were lined up for today, Tuesday. Erik joined Deb in the hospital room, where Ulysses had been shifted to a chair by the window. He wore a blue robe over the hospital gown and had an IV feed in the back of his hand. He was drinking a cup of tea, which he lifted in stopped movements like a claymation figure. When asked about the name Grant Ulysses Stewart, he said that *that* man had a family which died and he was no more. However, a social worker informed the detectives that the VA would foot the bill because Stewart served twenty years in the military and was discharged for medical reasons after his wife and daughter died in a car accident.

Erik said softly, "Your spa friend Anders can't join us because he has a class, and you don't have to worry about that IV. It's not mind-control drugs. It's electrolytes to treat dehydration. I've had those more than once. How would you like us to address you, Mr.—"

"Ulysses, just Ulysses. They used to say he was a good general. Now they say he was bad. I found a book in a little library and read about him. He was realistic and depressed. Did people want him to be nice and lose the Civil War?"

"Did you read about the other Ulysses?" Erik asked despite Deb's eyeroll. "He came up with the Trojan horse idea but most of all he wanted to return home to faithful Penelope."

"Is that her name?" He perked up. "I thought it was Jeannie with the light brown hair. She could use help. Big lost eyes." Ulysses sneezed and pulled a handkerchief from his robe so disgusting that Erik handed over his. Ulysses didn't touch it. "Men's handkerchiefs now are done up with polyester swirls. Polyester handkerchief, you might as well blow into saran wrap." He blew hard into his gray stiff one.

"I'll fetch some tissues," Deb volunteered. She canvassed the room and then left to find supplies.

Erik continued, "I'd like to know more about that woman. Is this her picture?" He showed a photo of Jean Nerstrand on a tablet.

"That's her friend, Caramel. Jeannie's prettier."

Deb returned with the tissue box. Erik said to her, in hopes his aside would prompt the man to say more, "Ulysses was describing the woman he knows as Jeannie, who is not the woman in this photo. Ulysses, what was Jeannie's hair like?"

"Light brown and curly. Jeannie's thin. She should eat some of those meals she delivers. It was hard on her, helping us out. She was scared."

"Do you remember what she said to you?" Deb asked.

He slurped tea. "The two of 'em came by a couple of times. The other one talked more, but Jeannie needed a friend. I don't have a way, you know, you probably have that," he nodded at Erik. "A way with women."

"Not always the way they want."

"I was going up to her, and she acts panicked. I said I just wanted to talk, and she fished in her bag—looked like a feed sack to me. She gave me her card. I called a couple of times, no answer, and, uh, found out addresses." He dropped his eyes like a naughty child, and like a naughty child shifted the blame. "Once at the camp that man came over from across the street to talk to Jeannie and her friend. He sucks in his gut when he's by Jeanie. He pretended he wasn't mad about the camp to them."

"A man from the Landvak apartments?" Deb asked.

"I suppose it was Mr. Landvak."

Because there was no Mr. Landvak, Erik presumed it was Dominic Novak and Ulysses' "Jeannie" was Karma Byrnes. With the warmth of the tea, Ulysses' eyes glazed over and his head nodded

"What happened to the woman's card?" Erik asked.

Ulysses jerked awake. "In my coat, somewhere's. They didn't throw my new coat out, did they?"

"It's okay." Deb held up a hand when he struggled to get up. "I'll check the closet." She retrieved a maroon parka. Ulysses poked through the pockets for the card. He held it out but wouldn't release it.

Erik's turn to be confused. "You sure you got this from the brown-haired woman, not the redhaired one?"

"Yup, but when someone finally answered, it was the talky redhead, so I hung up. I was worried like you wouldn't believe and checked Jeannie's house and where she worked, that real estate place."

Thus the stalking began, the stalking of Jean, the wrong woman. Karma, of the light brown hair, had given Homeless Ulysses Jean Nerstrand's business card.

"Ulysses, did you ever approach the talky woman?" Erik asked. He could have approached, Jean pulled the gun, panicked at using it, and he grabbed for the gun which went off. An accidental fire with no intent to kill. "Did you feel you had to defend yourself?"

"At that construction place, where Tom burnt up, yeah. I had an army knife but my hand was shaking and I couldn't work it, why I hid. But that red-face man, he hit Tom with a wrench, and he knows Mr. Landvak, first name something like Dom. That's why I told her to watch out for that man. He hired that red-face guy, the one—"

"Wait," Deb interjected. "You told which woman about the Landvak man, Dominic?"

"The talky one, that day before it rained because I was dry and didn't smell bad. I took a bus to that real estate place and waited outside to see Jeannie, but the redhead came out instead. I told her she had to be careful because that arson guy might be after her and she should watch out for that Dom person."

The two detectives gaped at him, and Deb took it, "So you warned the older woman about that Landvak man?"

"She yelled at me to back off because of the real bad odor and I didn't even smell."

"Could she have said restraining order?" Erik asked.

Ulysses sagged. "I'm feeling real sick."

Erik rang for the nurse, who gave him and Deb the skank eye for exhausting Ulysses. When they reached the elevator, Deb banged her head against the wall. "I can't see Ulysses as a murderer. Can't see him as a reliable witness either, mixing up the two women." Erik agreed as his mind circled back to Karma giving the man the wrong card. The truth in this case was muddied, and it was muddied by Karma.

CHAPTER 32

Tuesday, Rafe Edward Lutyens avoided the office tensions caused by the detectives leaving urgent, and ignored, messages for Dominic. Escaping to in his lair with Constable's *Haywain*, he awaited the role that would make him a man. A man in his own eyes, in his Da's eyes, his serene Da. (In his mom's eyes he'd always be the second son.) A man in the eyes of a woman. Several years back he lauded himself that he'd arrived until a fiancée, whose affection shrunk like a boiled sweater, decided that he was a throwaway. Slippery and shallow, she called him after he explained alliteration to her. He was clever with the degrees to prove it, but cleverness hadn't won her. He was not, he admitted with regret and admiration, on his father's level, his Da, international consultant on suspension bridges. It took more than smarts to escape being undone by others, but what? By others, Rafe meant Dominic's self-enhancing guile.

When Dominic learned that Rafe's grandmother had roots in India, he wanted to claim him has a minority hire. Rafe protested that he'd grown up with every advantage, a child of empire raised in a democracy. Dominic went ahead and listed him as a person of color. But whenever Rafe was about to give up on Dominic, he was handed a plum. If it was a plum and not a pit to do an interior audit. Dominic might suspect Carina of embezzlement but wanted another view before proceeding. Rafe would not only check that $a + b = c$ and that $c - b = a$, he would also dig for the root of a.

Dig deep enough and he might uncover links to Jack Cardenas, presumed turncoat and arsonist. Rafe found it implausible that Cardenas had slunk back to wreak havoc and shifted his suspicions to Bob Ott as bad actor. Rafe settled into his ugly pink chair and with the password provided by Dominic clicked on files.

The spread sheets were pools of swimming figures. The enormity of it dizzied Rafe and he spun away from the screen to settle queasiness. Think of something else. Karma, whose face fascinated him with moments of sunshine, shadow, and outright storm. Rafe now had to cool his blood and did so with a pile of paper invoices. But Karma must be doing better. The news reported that a homeless man had been picked up for questioning in regards to Jean Nerstrand's death, and if that solved everything, Karma could relax.

On one of the paper receipts, Dominic had penned, *wrong routing?* Later he crossed out the question, but Rafe decided to track down the confusion. With an assist from Google and the dark net, he went through a fold in the universe into a parallel budget system with accounts that he had never seen before.

"Rafe Edward!" Dominic blocked his door. "What are you doing?"

"Checking the accounts, like you asked."

"I asked you to do that so you could assure yourself that everything's on the up and up and stop nagging Carina. Now I find you never checked out those vacant Landvak properties like I told you, the ones that might have gas and water leaks."

"What properties? Ohhh, from last week." Rafe had put himself at a disadvantage.

"You brag you don't forget anything."

"That investigation—"

"What investigation? The one involving Jean? That tragedy never bothered you until it's convenient. You're on the short leash, *Edward*." Dominic slammed the door shut.

He'd tear through his assignments today and have plenty of time tomorrow for his lunch date with Karma. He could bring up his birthday then, close to Sylvy's. Karma might turn down a direct date, but a hands-on event making dal with Sylvy for a party—that he could broach.

Tonight would be soon enough for an urgent check of Landvak's leaks.

TUESDAY PROMISED PROFIT AND FUN. Karma had dressed in corduroy jeggings, a tweed jacket, and glossy boots. Very Katherine Hepburn attire for paperwork but she was celebrating that three—three!—house offers had been accepted. She didn't need a horse to enjoy that ride. Also, Dominic wanted to squeeze in a property viewing this afternoon and the timing might just work. She celebrated at noon by picking up a chicken, not tuna, croissant sandwich.

She pulled into the Lake & Isles parking lot in time to see a black-coated figure throw orange paint on Paisley and run.

Over an hour later, Karma seethed in a musky room at the St. Louis Park Police Station. Detective Jansson, he was not nice 'Erik' with that much anger trapped in his face, sat across from her at a table. The table was hardly big enough for his ubiquitous digital tablet and a water pitcher. A camera eye in a corner ogled her.

Detective Jansson, mouth grim, adjusted his position. She'd been a fool to call him when Paisley, paint running down her hair and coat, had already called 911. The SLP police pursued the paint-thrower, suspecting the act to be a vicious prank or a hate crime against a transgendered person. Detective Jansson, who had brought her to the station in his personal SUV, doubted that the attack on Paisley had anything to do with Jean's murder. Despite Karma's insistence, he would not involve himself in that situation. However, he had other questions for Karma. She tried to insist otherwise and saw the end to his patience. He insisted on going through, again, the confusion over the phone number that Jean had snagged from her. She turned the tables and came at him. How could he be sure that the attack on Paisley was *not* part of a series of crimes that included Jean's murder? Karma fumed that Paisley being trans never upset anyone at work except when Renee—"

Detective Jansson cut her off. "I'm sure of nothing until I know more. Explain to me the mean-girl dynamics of your office as they affected Jean Nerstrand."

"They—Jean and Renee—had been close. Renee would encourage Jean, and me, to confide our concerns, whether it be about work or home stuff."

There was a disconnect between Detective Jansson's harsh tone and sensitive content: "Did her advice help, or did simply having her listen help?"

"At first it felt good getting things off my chest. Then I'd feel awful. Like the reason Renee's advice didn't help me was because I was petty. Like she expected more of me and I never delivered. Now that I think about it, that made me feel like I do with my mother. My woodland fairy mother is sensitive to her own feelings, not really anyone else's. Mark pointed that out to me after their divorce, like he'd just figured it out."

"The office dynamics and Jean."

"Jean stayed cheerful around Renee, but she was worked up that Renee wouldn't invite her to play bridge. Not that Jean had time for bridge with her family and her ambition. Paisley saved me. She pulled me aside and said, be careful what you say to Renee, and I caught on. Confiding in Renee was like getting a wonderful buzz from wine and later having a hangover. She wasn't sympathizing—she was making me doubt myself."

"Was Jean having an affair with Dominic?"

"No!"

"Is that what you want to be true, or what *is* true?"

Hot spots bumped up on her arms. "Dominic's a flirt. He's big-hearted like my husband was. He's stressed that Renee in her grief is shutting him out. Jean was always boosting up people around her, except when she was scolding. They worked together, that's all. At the shooting range, not that I need to defend that, we, Dom and I, were supposed to be part of a group. When the others didn't show, Dom talked to me about investing in a new property venture. Maybe Jean was investing in his ventures, I don't know. Dom always needs a sounding board. He's not a loner. Too much a loner, and you don't get other people."

Detective Jansson moved and she flinched. "I was reaching for water," he said, poured two glasses, and pushed one toward her. His eyes had become soft, or tired.

She released an amused sigh. "Maybe Dominic was hoping to seduce me, and I was lonely enough that I was sending out pheromones. I have nothing to hide." He looked at her the way Renee looked at her, her mother, Rafe, even her husband sometimes, and she snapped.

"So what if Jean and Dom had a fling? Don't you, 'Detective,' ever let your feelings carry you away? Or does the idea that people have feelings which you don't like make you angry? Don't you ever want a fling?" He turned scarlet and his gaze shifted to a corner. Karma flashed her eyes in that direction, a spider web, how appropriate. "Flings aren't all bad, the right moment, the right *man*."

If she expected Detective Jansson to cave at her goading, she was wrong. The muscles in his face worked against each other, and he caught her eyes with a directness that made her woozy. "A fling, I suppose, is exciting in the beginning. But the end?"

"A fling's a fling." A frisson made her shiver. "It happens and it's delightfully over."

"Maybe I don't want 'delightfully over.' Maybe I'm not one for flinging. When there's adultery on both sides, Jean Nerstrand separated but not divorced, Dominic Novak married, it's volatile."

Karma, heart racing, edged forward. "*You* can't imagine the excitement of a fling unless it's a fling into danger. What you do is dangerous, prying away at murderers. I wouldn't live with that kind of threat. Fun is better."

"My job is mostly this, difficult conversations, painful. There's also hope for families of the murdered that there'll be justice. Until a murderer is apprehended, fear and distrust stain everything. People panic at perceived threats or panic because of threats in the past."

"I want to go," Karma whimpered.

"You gave a homeless man Jean's business card instead of your own. When that man approached you, why did you hand over Jean's card instead of your own?"

"You wore me down to ask that? You *cad*!" Karma had given the man Jean's card on purpose, couldn't admit it, not if it got Jean killed. She wouldn't say another word but her shoulders shook, her eyes stung, her throat burned, and on murmuring that she was scared, she broke down, again.

HE HAD DRIVEN HER TO THE SLP STATION, and he drove her back to the office in his Highlander with a panoramic rearview mirror. When Karma asked if it was a useful feature, Detective Jansson said it offered the clarity of hindsight. When that was all the conversation she could muster, he started in on a shaggy dog story. It involved him and his father, nearly a decade ago, dropping in on his younger sister's college advisor at Macalester. Younger sister had texted older sister, "the banker," declaring she was "swept away" by her poetry advisor, "a beautiful, mesmerizing man." Word got to Detective Jansson's, Erik's, mother, who passed it to his father, head of campus security at the University of Iowa. His father drove up and retrieved Erik at his precinct where Erik, new on the job, was still in his police uniform. Then father and son popped in on the mesmerizing advisor. The senior Jansson, whose scant conversation generally involved sports, hunting, or "your mother's latest thing," talked of how his "youngest girl" had much to learn. Then he asked how the professor handled impassioned poets like Lord Byron.

"The moral of the story," Karma laughed, "is that the adored advisor never dared lay a hand on your sister."

Eyes on the road, Detective Jansson smiled. "Gauging people's future behavior is not exactly a crapshoot, more of a calculated risk. My partner Deb Metzger understands an abuser's profile. She's interviewing Jean Nerstrand's stalker, 'Homeless Ulysses,' the man who took your card. So far, he's an unlikely suspect."

Karma put her head back, wiped out. "So it's too easy for him to be the murderer. The murderer's still out there."

With the front of Lake & Isles taped off as a crime scene, Detective Jansson pulled into the back entrance.

Karma grabbed the door handle. "I'll let myself out. Jean, I guess she was secretive about what she was up to with Dominic. She'd tease that she was picking up 'tips.' I don't know if that was supposed to be, what's the term?"

"Double entendre?"

"Yes, but Jean did want to make it big on her own. I need to go."

She watched as he drove off without a backward glance. She felt like a Barbie doll with a troll head. Who was she (her mother came to mind) to rant about flings? To talk about delightful endings after she'd fallen apart when dumped by Jean's cousin? She steeled herself to enter the office, and it struck her that nothing had happened to her that was more than talk. Paisley had been attacked, and for her friend's sake it was time to resurrect Good Karma.

CHAPTER 33

D EB REMOVED THE LID FROM HER STEAMING LATTE. "I'm in a funk. How about you, Partner? I can't believe you don't have coffee. Gloomy Tuesday afternoon and you lost your pet cup." She sipped hers then licked the white moustache it left. "Mmm, creamy and strong. Too bad you take it black or I'd share."

Erik pushed back from the crappy table in their temp office and extended his legs, his posture conveying a mood that he was too polite to name.

"So, I had a second chat with Ulysses when Anders showed as moral support. If I were cisgendered up to my eyeballs, I'd tattoo Anders' number on my brain. Anders, the dinner of your dreams plus a dessert so sweet you'd faint. He's entering a biathlon. Same one you're in? Man, you haven't a chance."

"Thanks for your moral support."

"Do I light into you now or in five minutes for your handling of the Karma interview? Letting her take over. You know, I can order black coffee on my app and you can pick it up downstairs in five."

"No thank you. I didn't want to put off Karma more than I already had. Next you'll say that I let women get to me and don't take them seriously as suspects."

"You were talking flings. I could *fling* you out this window. Lucky for you it doesn't open—you think that's funny? Something around here has to be funny, might as well be me."

"You're smarter than Drees."

"That came out of nowhere, Partner, but I'll take it. Yeah, and I get that you were letting Karma say whatever in case it led to wherever. Could be she's having trouble facing Jean's behavior with men. Back to the unhappy lover angle. We should take another look at the for-sale sites where Jean might've met up with her *fling.* Also for fun, let's review everyone's alibi, starting with Karma Byrnes. Home with her daughter. Maybe she's not telling us about a sitter."

"You really want to go that route with a single mother and a seven-year-old?"

"Jean set Karma up with a jerk-of-a-cousin. Jean took Karma's old number and poached clients. It could be the case that Karma was having the affair with Dominic and Jean found out. Karma sets up Jean and shoots her."

Erik let the front legs of his chair crash down. "Don't forget this, Team Spirit Leader, I've seen Karma handle a gun. More likely to shoot her foot than anything else."

"Question mark by her name. Dominic, seen at the finest hotel in Albert Lea, could've done the deed if he had a speedster for a quick turnaround. But he delegates and could have hired a hit-person. I'd say he's more likely to have a body killed if the motive is protecting his business. Could've sent that foreman Ott. If he knew Cardenas was back, he might let bygones be bygones and hired that liar. Or that English dude, where was he?"

"Rafe? That night he was zooming with his 'Da' in California, what a good boy is he. There's an aura of resentment toward Dominic."

"In that aura, he might have shot Dominic's lover out of spite. Should check on the exact timing of that zoom with 'Da.'"

"Renee Novak?" Erik asked. "The first time we met Renee, her apple pie smelled too much of cinnamon, a culinary misjudgment."

Deb took a swill. "Yeah, I'm going to say murder's a bigger misjudgment. Ordinarily, the aggrieved wife is the sub-prime suspect, tipped off by her philandering hubby's tell-tale phone. But Renee's convinced that a scoundrel's after her and has a whole bridge club backing her."

"Would that bridge club have insight into her worries? She could've dropped some details if she suspected Dominic of cheating."

"Point for you." Deb marked a one in the air. "Jean's husband Bruce was driving around during the opportunity window, but he's not in the housing business, so unlikely that he'd set his estranged wife up at a listed house. Last, Ulysses."

"Can he tell one day of the week from another?"

"He's *mostly* cognizant. Anders got him to admit that he had been diagnosed with PTSD. If his anxiety spikes, he experiences blackouts. He's obsessed with that arson at the Landvak Penn Avenue complex. Now get this."

"I'm getting it." Erik pulled one of Deb's moves and lay his head down on the table.

"He worried about 'that arsonist with a face of fire,' which at a stretch could be Cardenas with his rosacea. According to Ulysses, the man paid his homeless buddy Tom to be night security at the site while it was under renovation. The man provided a propane heater and a sheltered nook."

"Nook?" came a muffled response.

"Nook."

Mumbles came from Erik's downed head.

"Right, Partner. It seems that Cardenas was setting up a homeless man to take the fall for the arson. By the way, Ulysses didn't tell his story in any kind of order, but here's how I put it together. The day of the arson, Ulysses lags behind, and Tom sees that Cardenas is up to no good. That's when Cardenas attacks Tom with a wrench. What did you say? Not the wrench but the candlestick? You lose a point. Ulysses, master of evasive maneuvers, gets the heck out of there."

Erik propped his head on his hand. "Not a witness for the stand."

"Half point for you. He's unreliable with the blackouts and PTSD."

"PTSD. I'm pretty sure something happened to Karma Byrnes, not necessarily recent. She acts flirty but there's fear. You should talk to her after this case."

"She could also be anxious because she's holding stuff back. I take your wrinkled brow as evidence of agreement." Deb balanced her coffee lid on one finger. "And remember, you're not the one giving orders."

"A suggestion in the form of a directive."

"Now you've gone all language-y again. Which reminds me, I need activities to get my mind out of its rut. There's a poetry reading coming up, Sonje Jansson. Is that your kid sister? There's a photo—wow, she's a beautiful waif in a Norski knit. Oh, now you're bolt upright paying attention. The Women's Pages announcement says her poems throb with eroticism. Are you going?"

"After that description, it'd feel like incest."

"Why are you two talking incest?" Drees at the door startled them. "Say, Jansson, I hear you're in a biathlon. Up for some practice with a twenty-two? I'm heading to an outdoor range later. I could give you pointers."

Erik suppressed a yawn. "My son has soccer practice and I'm assisting."

"Really," said Drees.

"Really," said Deb. "We have to tie up points in our case before Partner makes like a tree and leaves. See you later, Drees."

Drees lingered. "I hear that your case isn't going well. Also, patrol reports that Jack Cardenas is cruising the Lake Nokomis area. Gotta keep an eye on those updates." He departed with a military pivot.

"Gotta keep an eye on the updates," Deb mimicked.

Erik stretched himself to standing. "I have to rush." Deb stuck her tongue out. "By the way, that scientist Maria Hartung emailed me a list of unexpected accelerants and an article on 'corporate arson.' Arson's figurative in the article for bosses undermining their employees."

"I would never undermine you," Deb said, "just tell your secrets to Drees."

At the mention of Drees, Erik peered out the door for signs of the nemesis. Before he could escape his phone beeped and he lingered to check it.

With Erik absorbed by his phone, Deb put her head on the table—she was having heart palpitations. Too many people were hot and bothered by the investigation, on edge. The case was going to break soon, but how?

Erik was pocketing his phone when it rang, and he answered by rote, "Detective Jansson, Greater Metro. Oh." His voice lifted. "Sure, plenty of time, Maria."

Deb raised up on her elbow and shot him a "me too?" look. He did not put the call on speaker and faced away. He turned back to Deb to mouth the make of a van. She threw up her hands—what was she supposed to do with that?

"I owe you," he was saying with his all-star smile. "I got to fill in my partner, bye." He clicked off. "Maria Hartung. Her toddler Micah had said *pawdaw's* at the Penn Avenue site before the arson started. *Pawdaw* is his word for grandpa. It was assumed that he meant the homeless men looked like his grandfather, which they didn't. Ben at that age was obsessed with trucks and the like, and responding to her email, I asked if Micah might be as well. Maria, Dr. Hartung, tracked down what van her father, Pawdaw, drove at the time. Techs can check to see if a red van of that make shows up on the stored traffic footage of the area. It's a long shot that it'll lead us to the arsonist."

"We don't have any short shots. Good one."

"Time to run." Erik rushed out.

Time for Deb to follow up on that S.O.B. Cardenas except she had an excuse: her mom had come from Mason City, Iowa, to go parrot shopping. Mom played bridge and could give pointers on how to pry gossip loose from Renee's club.

IT WAS RAUCOUS ENOUGH INSIDE THE BIRD STORE AVIAN LOVE without Deb's mom talking over the whistles, squeals, and chatter made by cockatiels, budgies, parrots, and more. While Deb projected a strong alto, her mom Doreen had a voice that dropped into the basement. Doreen unzipped her jacket and fog-horned, "So many beauties. This is going to take a while."

"Mo-om, it's Hitchcock's *The Birds*. I'll start flailing any second." Deb had never seen the movie but got the idea.

Doreen considered this. "You'd be like the star, Tippi Hedren from New Ulm, Minnesota. You could wear high heels and a fur coat, fake obviously, and buy lovebirds to tempt a Ms. Special Person."

"I'd fall off the high heels. Are you sure you want a caged thingy?"

"If they can talk back at you, they'll liberated enough. It'd be like when your dad was sitting in his chair and yakking back, only fun." She made a kissy face at a Mynah. "Can a talking bird give evidence in court?"

"Swearing them in's the trick." Deb said.

"Swearing," the bird echoed. "Get the hell out of here you sons of—"

Deb talked over the Mynah. "Look, Mom, that mother and baby are cooing at the budgies."

"You should have a baby. I know your brother has done his share, but you shouldn't be left out."

"Mom," Deb wheedled. "There'd have to be, you know, a donor."

"You mean sperm?" *Sperm* carried and the clerk stared.

"Life partner first," Deb hissed.

"What happened to that *jeune fille* in France?"

"A fickle fille."

"Labrador retrievers are loyal if that's what you want. Ooh, listen to that one screech! That'd be a great home alarm."

"Mom, I need to question members of a bridge club, but they've closed ranks on me." A parrot squawked, *talk to me*. "I'm thinking if I pretend that procedure requires me to call but what I really want—not what I *really really* want which is to solve the case—but what I want is bridge tips, they'll talk."

Mom rumbled, "What you want is a home. I can't decide on a budgie or parrot. Everyone here is such fun, except for that raven in the corner."

"He's stuffed, Mom."

"The thing about bridge is the rivalries. It's as bad as choir. Crack that and you'll find a talker."

"Talker," a parrot echoed.

Deb brushed a feather from her nose and hustled her mother out of Avian Love. Like in the song, she had worries, whoa-oh, troubles, whoa-oh. Like how to prevent Mom from popping over to the Ibelings to chat it up. Then there was Jack Cardenas. If Cardenas was a vicious arsonist who murdered a man and returned to murder Jean Nerstand because of her involvement with Dominic or Landvak, none of the people the case touched were safe.

"I was liking that small parrot," her mom said when they both slumped down into Deb's Prius, "until he told me to piss off. Did I tell you I invited the Ibelings over for dinner?"

CHAPTER 34

Tuesday evening, streetlights dimly lit the Lake Nokomis neighborhood while jack-o-lanterns cast an orange glow on the stoops. The spookiness didn't bother Erik Jansson; he was, however, unnerved by a message received at five o'clock. Landvak "would no longer accept information requests from Detective Jansson," a statement made by the company's lawyers. He had played the wrong hand with Dominic. He distracted himself from that setback by thinking that this was a place, despite the night's eeriness, where Erik could settle permanently, if he had someone to settle permanently *with*. Shouldn't end a sentence with "with." He emended the thought to someone with whom to settle, which unfortunately downgraded the meaning to settling for less. The neighborhood rated an "A" on real estate websites because it had space for children and quality public schools. Surprising, then, that the two-unit rental house before him stood empty. Paisley from Lake & Isles told him of the property when he'd called from Ben's soccer practice to see how she was faring after the paint incident. She chalked it up to bad juju and relayed that Jean Nerstrand had been viewing this duplex with Dominic Novak because he intended to list it. When he called Landvak to supplement Paisley's information, he was cut off, which likely prompted the legal notification. He had to be discreet in viewing their properties.

Erik scuffed through rotting leaves, slowing himself down. Despite the temptation to rush the case, he had to be discreet viewing Landvak properties. He liked to move fast, in part to create time for a life with Ben, Stripe, and a woman, a life with dog-proof furniture, a stocked kitchen, and a warm bed. As ever, he was driven to solve the case, but he felt outside of it; he hadn't found the thread to pull. Cardenas looked the part of the bad guy and had the bad guy's knack for avoiding the law. He had to stay guarded with Cardenas

on the loose, be wary of trusting anyone touched by the case. He walked up
to the rental with caution, the possible site of trysts, the location where Jean
may have discovered something about Dominic or his properties that he did
not want her to know. For all he knew, Dominic could be there now, with a
woman not his wife.

A single motion-sensor light came on over the entry to reveal a drab
stucco exterior. The more Erik looked, the less he liked. The window ledges
were cracked, the front steps a hazard, the doorbell out of commission. No
doormat, no welcome.

A snap came from the back of the house as if a prowler stepped on a
branch. There were fences around the property, and neighbors had drawn
their shades, meaning no witnesses. Erik carried his long-handled Maglite
over his shoulder and followed a stone path. He paused at the back corner.
The leaves rustled enough that he couldn't hear slight movements or breathing. He took another step.

A straight object flashed down at him. Erik blocked it with his flashlight,
pushed back, another blow came. Erik blocked that and jumped away from
the wall before a blow could connect with his head. A light saber fight. For
seconds, Erik was too busy burning oxygen and parrying with a shadow to
shout *police*. Light again slashed toward him but he grabbed the handle with
his free hand. The assailant grabbed at a trash can lid, but the lid was locked
against raccoons. Erik lunged forward, his flashlight crosswise, to force the
shadow man, not quite his size, against the wall. The man hit his head against
a utility meter and yowled. He came at Erik again, who dropped his light to
grab his opponent's arms and they wrestled in the dark. Erik panted *police*, his
assailant hesitated, and Erik wrested away the man's flashlight. The man lost
his footing on a sunken flagstone and shouted, "Bloody hell!"

"Rafe?" Erik heaved for air. "Rafe Edward Lutyens, what the hell right
back?" Holding both lights, he blinded Rafe, also heaving, who balanced on
one foot while rubbing the ankle of the other.

"*Owowow*, triple bloody hell, Detective. Why'd you come at me?" Rafe
hopped on one foot.

"You came at *me* like the Scarlet Pimpernel."

"More like Cyrano de Bergerac. What are *you* doing here?" Rafe pitched
forward, and Erik caught him.

"As an officer of the law, I don't have to explain myself," he panted in right-
ing Rafe. "Except to my chief, the media, social justice warriors, a grand jury,
and my mother. I'm investigating."

"I'm investigating these meters. The ground's soggy and smells rotten.
There could be a water and a gas leak."

"Isn't that the utilities' job?"

"There've been screwups."

"Do you need a medic?"

Rafe hung his head.

Erik returned Rafe's light. "You're getting one, or I'd be derelict in my duty. Where's your car? I can take you in that." Anything seen in Rafe's vehicle might contribute to the case. "Right ankle? Not sure you can drive yourself until it's wrapped."

Erik draped Rafe's arm over his shoulder and helped him limp half a block to a Mini-Cooper Countryman with racing stripes. The Cooper's malt-brown interior was spotless without a telltale file in sight.

When the men entered the urgent care clinic, furnished in jarring yellow and green, Rafe bared his teeth. The round-faced attendant pulled back from those teeth to greet Erik: "Hey, Detective Jansson. Holding body and soul together?"

"Yep. How about an icepack, and check-in forms for this man?"

They sat out of earshot from the others in the waiting area. Rafe attacked the forms with a pen drained of ink. Erik loaned him one. For thanks, Rafe groused, "They know you well here."

"I'm a frequent flyer."

"Is this like *Fight Club*? We fight and then we're buddies?" Rafe twisted in pain.

"Never saw the movie. I'd rather run than fight, better endorphins and health outcomes. Besides x-raying that ankle, they'll shine a light in your eyes and ask, concussed, or not concussed."

"You've been through this?"

"That frequent flyer status." Erik found Rafe to be an open book in a language too esoteric to grasp. He couldn't fathom the man's loyalties, if he had any, except to sense a crack in Rafe's connection with Dominic. Erik needed to split that crack wide open. He could throw Rafe off balance with a fact that was inconvenient but would not, Erik hoped, blow their fight-club rapport.

"You started at Landvak a month before the Park Avenue arson, and with all that was going on you managed to complete your program with Carlson School of management two months later."

Rafe shifted his icepack from ankle to head. "Aren't you the dweeby fact finder?"

"Is that something Dominic said to you? Did he find out that the degree was listed on your resume before you received it?"

"Dominic wouldn't care. Results are his game." Spoken with false bravado. "The capstone project needed finishing touches, that's all."

Erik didn't pursue whether Rafe left his previous employer because he feared the dodgy resume being disclosed. He went to the reception station to refresh the icepack; on returning, he asked if Rafe believed Jean and Dominic were having an affair. Rafe was terse—Dominic carried separate phones for "business and pleasure," and didn't "remember" to record all his appointments on the company calendar.

"Do you worry that Jack Cardenas, the presumed arsonist, has returned? Because," Erik was honest, "it's worrying me."

"I don't know what to think about that." Rafe held the icepack against his nose bump, which hadn't been injured in their duel.

"Could Jean Nerstrand have uncovered a circumstance that upset Dominic?"

Rafe didn't have a comeback, and he was the sort who lived for comebacks.

"Rafe, have you read an article in the *Harvard Business Review* about corporate arsonists?" It was the article Maria Hartung had forwarded it to Erik. "It's about bosses who invent crises, start 'fires' at work to manipulate employees, and then take credit for dousing them. Was having to check the meters a fire created to keep you busy, and Dominic would take credit for finding a dangerous leak?"

Rafe snorted, "I read the *pertinent* articles."

Erik should give injured Rafe a break. But Rafe was his last chance to get an inside angle on Landvak, and he suspected that Rafe, like himself, survived on dogged persistence. "Rafe, with Jean gone, has Dominic turned to Karma? Did they start an affair?"

That galvanized Rafe. "He couldn't be having an affair with Karma, he couldn't be. Karma's too good. Karma would go more for a guy more like . . . you. She likes dependability with a tight ass. Sorry, she's not crude like that. She's built her dead husband up to an Angel of Testosterone. No living man could compete. Just so you don't think me completely heartless and daft, I would never say that to her face."

"If she feels she can't find such love again, do you think she'd have a fling for fun, say with Dominic?" Who, Erik unpleasantly recalled, reminded Karma of the idealized husband.

"You're talking trash."

"You're right." Speculating about Karma left a bad taste in Erik's mouth. Whatever his confused feelings were, they had to be shelved. Maybe his prying made Rafe feel lesser, which was not Erik's intent. He rubbed his face while Rafe grunted about the wait. He opted for directness. "It's stuck in my head that this case is about sex and real estate."

Rafe smothered a laugh.

"Rafe, are you close enough to Karma to tell if she's in trouble? Paint was thrown on one of her coworkers today, likely a prank, but is there anything about deals made by Jean and Dominic, anything about that past arson and Landvak, that's triggering these events?" Rafe gave him a dazed stare. "Can you tell if there's more going on with Karma than distress about the Jean's death?"

"Having a friend murdered is not an everyday occurrence for most of us," Rafe scoffed. "Since you won't cease and desist, I'll tell you this. I amuse Karma. She likes that I like that imp of hers, Sylvy. Karma's sexy, and don't tell me you don't think that too. To quote a romcom cliché, I don't deserve her."

"Have you tried to deserve her?"

"A divorced detective offering advice to the lovelorn? That's rich."

What the—Rafe knew of his divorce from sneaky research or worse, from Karma. It was thick between them; they were still pushing each other against walls. Walls between people shut out danger, but also possibility. Erik had to be the grownup in the room, a necessary role, and boring, unless you could be a grownup with ingenuity and flair. Erik dropped his guard.

"Then hear this as coming from one who's loved and lost. Love means having to say you're sorry, a lot. When you give your heart, also give your time. Keep the refrigerator stocked with white wine and put down the toilet seat. Clear your head outside. Come up with every caress you can to vanquish the 'too tired for sex' epidemic. Your sweat is not as sexy as you think. Women can be trapped by feelings, too. Verbal fights are better than silence—but fight fair, assuming a fight can be fair. What *you* think is romantic doesn't count, it's what *she* thinks is romantic. And never start a sentence with, 'you should.'"

"I knew all that. Maybe not the sweat one. I could use a shower. *You* could use a shower."

Rafe was called, and Erik settled in for the second part of the wait. He should've driven his Highlander and had Rafe taxi home. If pursuing this case meant pursuing sex and real estate, no telling where it would end. Despite that worry, despite the waiting area's garish lighting, he fought against the greatest seduction of all, sleep.

CHAPTER 35

IF CLOTHES MAKE THE MAN, RAFE ARRIVED on Wednesday at noon. Specifically, he'd arrived at the 50th and France neighborhood in Edina and entered Raga Indian Cuisine. No detectives or bosses in sight. The host, with smoky skin and dusky voice, showed Rafe to a table. If he walked like a gentleman, no one could tell that his sprained ankle was mummy-wrapped. He'd been able to drive himself home last night, popped a Percocet, and crashed like a dead dog. He wakened early and rushed to the office before anyone else arrived, where he was dogged about finding the devil in the details in accounts that were none of his business.

He'd discovered invoices from Callender Plumbing for amounts in the tens of thousands, and from Callendar Plumbing for the same, which led him more valid invoices mirrored by false ones. Embezzlement, payments to shell companies, to a Karas company. That gave him a twinge about Karma, and he switched blame to that Harpy Carina with her tomahawk hair. But did Dominic know? Rafe twitched at a new idea, that Dominic was in on it. When Carina and Sela arrived, Rafe claimed meetings elsewhere, returned home, rewrapped the ankle, took a pain pill, and went to Raga. He aspired to tailored, not formal, for this lunch with Karma. He hung his best tweed jacket on the chairback and adjusted the cuffs on his button-down. His shirt could stand on its own, a slim classic in an engineered fabric that inhibited sweat with no sweatshops involved. If only it were yellow, not blue, so turmeric stains wouldn't show.

Rafe hoped Karma wouldn't mind that he went in to claim a table before the intimate room filled. He faced the restaurant's entrance and bar; the décor was not what his mum called the kitsch of India, but Scandinavian modern with birchwood tables, light walls, and a herringbone floor. Banquette seating in a wavy blue pattern stretched along the back perimeter, and along the top of the seating ran a mirrored border which made the light dance. It reminded him of a lagoon, and when he looked over his shoulder, he saw a mermaid of sorts. Painted on the wall was a woman in profile, face raised, a river of black hair swirling with pink scarves. At hearing steps, Rafe fumbled to a stand as Karma, in a flame-colored blazer, trim skirt, and tall boots came up to him. When he reached for her hand, she was preoccupied with hanging her tote on the chair and his hand dropped. His tech shirt notwithstanding, he perspired. It wasn't like this was a *significant* proposal, only a proposal to help him decorate the common room in his building for his birthday party. He was inviting friends from Carlson and his last job to show that he had them. Karma's eyes scarcely engaged his before slipping past to the woman painted behind him.

Rafe swallowed. "She reminds me of you."

Karma laughed. "Except for the nose ring, sari scarves, and yard-long hair. If that was a compliment, you don't know how to pay one."

"I—"

Karma broke in, flustered. "I'm sorry if I'm late. We have a sister office here and I dropped in. I'd love to work out of this area, but I'd spend *way* too much at the fab shops."

"You don't have to worry, do you?" Rafe's question confused her. "About money?"

"Menus." A young woman stood by them, her vibrant Indian features set off by her Fair Isle sweater. "Would you like drinks before you order?"

"Tea?" Karma asked.

Rafe scrambled to see if the menu listed varieties. "Do you steep Darjeeling?"

"I'll bring over the tea chest, sir." In a derisive acknowledgment of Rafe's British air, she pronounced *sir* as *suh*.

"I'm not knighted," Rafe joked, but the server was out of hearing as servers generally are.

Karma's hazel eyes caught his before they dropped to the menu. "That was rude."

Did she mean him or the server? "I'm paying for the days of the Raj," he joked.

"Your complexion, though it's lighter, and your eyes make sense here," Karma said and immediately looked away at a group of dark-skinned women being seated at table next to her. "It's a Boy" balloons bounced above the chair of honor. "A baby shower, cute!" Her tone sharpened—"No, I don't worry, more than anyone should, about money. I'm closing three house sales this week. But not everybody has a fat inheritance, and you never know what to expect." Rafe was baffled and readjusted his Harris tweed on the chair. He should tell her about the embezzlement. No, he should tell the FBI first; Karma was burdened enough. Her eyes were on him. "Are you warm enough without that jacket?" she asked. "That is a nice shirt."

"And I wear it brilliantly," he mocked himself as server approached with tea. "This'll warm you, the tea, I mean."

The server set down pots and cups and then brought over with the tea chest. Karma picked an Assam and Rafe took a Darjeeling bag. "Is that good enough, *suh*?" she asked.

"Quite fine." He'd fallen into full Brit-twit condescension. The woman took the chest away, returned with crisp pappadum, took their order for paneer in a cinnamon spinach curry, and retreated. Rafe bent forward to catch Karma's sweet-spicy scent. They say home smells like the food of your childhood. He hoped not because his mother was a terrible cook. Karma seemed to be waiting on him. "At least they're not calling me *sahib*. Speaking of sahibs, you've been seeing a good deal of Dominic."

"It's business." She busied herself with her tea.

"I realize. Yet." Rafe stopped before blabbing that he didn't trust his boss with women. He dunked the teabag in his pot releasing aromas of musk and flowers.

"Yet but what?" Karma flared her nostrils.

"But Jean's death has thrown Dominic off track. Thrown all of us. I'm thinking if it wasn't the husband, it had to be a jealous lover."

"Why don't you leave the speculation to the detectives? They're mean enough to wrangle confessions."

"I bet people confess to Detective Jansson's handsome nose."

"Rafe!"

"Listen, Karma." Rafe intended to bring up the Karas shell company, couldn't. "What I'm trying to say is that it may not be the best use of your time to show Dominic properties for nonprofit projects. At heart he's not convinced about a deep dive into affordable housing. He thinks it's a deep dive into debt."

Karma snapped a pappadum and scooped up a peppery sauce. "Dominic's heart is in the right place. He and Renee are into charity."

"Dominic thinks of charity as a onetime gift." Rafe poured his tea—weak.

"You make Dominic's charity sound like alms for the poor. He's sincere."

Rafe gulped too hot tea at *sincere*. "Dominic, arrgh. Yes, charity's lifesaving. In classical art, Charity is a nursing mother with three breasts. Now that I recall, I'm not sure about the third breast. That should be a title, 'The Third Breast.'" As he said *third breast*, the server returned with the food and a hard stare.

Karma briefly smiled as she took her share of the paneer and spinach curry. "Lifesaving, I see that. Short term help, bringing food and clothing, is also needed, what Jean and I did at the homeless encampment." She took a bite that displeased her. Another group of women with hijabs and bubbly Minnesota accents were seated to her left. A white couple who dressed like jocks sat in the banquette behind them. The babble and a muted recording of sitar music sealed Rafe and Karma into a private bubble, though an eruption from one of the jocks broke through, "Talk about a rhinoplasty!" Rafe grimaced and refocused on Karma, who was lecturing him: "If your job's minimum-wage fulltime work, you can't afford decent housing without a subsidy. That's so not right. The market's skewed."

A Vindaloo curry arrived, and the first bite flamed through Rafe's sinuses so he sneezed out, "Ah-*skew*-ed toward profit. That's real estate and that's why you're in it, *choo*."

Karma's eyes yellowed. "Do you do anything besides undermine people? What do you want, Rafe *Edward*?"

Rafe put his elbows on the table, jostling the tea makings, pulled back, pulled close again. "Believe me, Karma. Dominic pursues flings."

"Flings? Who talked to you about flings? Are you talking to Erik, Detective Jansson, behind my back?"

Rafe spit rice at Karma. "*Erik*? Why would he bring up flings? What did the two of *you* discuss?" Her eyes teared up. "Forget I said that. Listen to this, there's a business theory. Dominic distorts what people report to him. He's a flamethrower." His fingers signaled air quotes. "A 'corporate arsonist.' It was an article in the Harvard—you get the picture. Dominic riles people up, talks up unresolved issues into big problems. Fans them into conflagrations and then puts them out by pissing on them."

"That's disgusting." Karma pushed her plate away.

"It's classic. Pissing out a fire's in *Gulliver's Travels*. Dominic's becoming hard, talks to Ott like they have secrets. He's scaring me." The second Rafe said that, he knew it was true.

"You snob. Dominic's not like that." Karma banged her water glass down, and Rafe shook his head no at the server coming from behind to refill it. The server refilled Karma's glass anyway. "Dom's a teddy bear."

"A teddy bear with a jackal heart." The server, back to spirit away dishes too soon, pushed Rafe's last button, and he spouted, "Take Renee, then. Do you know the first thing she told me about you? You're enough of an asset package for Landvak to keep in mind, but essentially a prettified package not worth unwrapping."

"You're lying."

The server set down panna cotta and cookie crisps, though they hadn't ordered dessert. Then again, Karma cooled herself with a slippery spoonful of the panna cotta. She swallowed and then came at him, "What the *hell* do you want, 'Edward'?"

The room buzzed. "I want to know why Landvak was paying for Jean's phone line."

Karma gaped. "My phone?"

"What?"

"Jean reused a number I used to have. It's gotten me in trouble!"

"I told you, she and Dominic were having an affair, a *fling*." Like you and the detective, he almost said, but saying it might make it true.

"He *killed* her?" Karma whispered in shock.

"I don't *know*. I'm focused on the crooked financials."

"Where are you going with this, Rafe? A woman's dead, and you're trying to ruin everybody?"

"No, no, I—" Rafe blubbered. "Someone's going to get hurt. My ankle hurts because I sprained it, but that's nothing to the hurt that will happen if I'm linked to corruption. I don't know why, but Dominic's been asking if the police have caught up with Cardenas. He's been asking about a stalker who's homeless, if he's been found, if he's stalking you. Would he hurt you?"

"He who? You?" Karma stood abruptly, full water glass in hand, her voice shaking. "You're scaring people, Rafe. You're *awful*. You *bastard*." She set the glass down hard, yanked her tote off the chair which dragged the chair screeching across the floor, and was gone.

Everything buzzed and Rafe squeezed his eyes shut—the buzzing worsened. Suddenly icy water splashed against his lids and dribbled down his cheeks. He gasped and saw the Fair Isle sweater girl holding a goblet.

"I thought you were fainting." She'd dropped the *suh*. She picked up Rafe's tweed, which had fallen on the herringbone floor, reset it on the chair, and laid down the bill. The dessert was complimentary. She explained, "If she'd thrown the water in your face, we'd have comped the whole meal." She handed him a napkin to wipe away the water. "You needed closure."

Zero tip for her. Rafe had poked a hornet's nest with no idea what would fly in his face.

KARMA SPED LIKE A DEMON IN HER ACURA. She was not the beautiful maiden poised on the wall of the Indian restaurant. She was the female deity Durga of many arms and hands, a weapon in each. After storming away from Rafe, she'd driven several blocks and pulled over to check her phone for updates. She called Dominic's office—voicemail. Dominic's direct number—voice mail. The number that *used* to be hers but stopped—the police had it. She drove to a St. Louis Park house she was scheduled to show. The prospective buyers stood her up. She checked her online Lake & Isles bulletin board. The sale of the Wasp house popped up. Her listing, how could she not know? She'd go there right now and see for herself if there was a *sold* sign. Dominic must've bypassed her to buy through that Lake & Isles senior realtor who perpetually dressed for sailing. With her many Durga arms, Karma would pitch her mutinous colleague off the yacht.

Rafe—she'd push him into a construction pit. *What did he want?* Her roiled brain screeched, *You, he wants you.* Batshit. Rafe was a clever boy trying to outwit his betters. *Rafe—who got things done, who fulfilled any request she'd ever made, who looked not bad in a tight shirt, who lit up like sunshine with Sylvy.*

Patrol would pull her over for speeding. She couldn't count on Detective Jansson to get her out of a ticket. Bad 'Erik,' ratting on their "fling" fight with Rafe. *Heartless detective, fond father, warm voice in a warm body.*

She accelerated through a turn into the Wasp house cul-de-sac. No signs of life at any of the three houses, except Dominic, in hunting camouflage of all things, heading to a work van in parked in the driveway of the empty Wasp house. A figure slumped in the passenger seat, hat pulled down over his face. Probably Ott dozing. Karma pulled into the driveway and slammed the brakes before hitting Dominic's bumper and rushed from her car. "*Hey!*"

Their bodies collided between her car and his van. "Karma?" Dominic gasped.

"Yes, Karma, the woman you've been hitting on. Karma who'd find properties for you. Karma tricked into thinking that you'd make a deal with *her.* That Karma." Lacking the height to get in his face, she poked his gut. "I thought we had a relationship based on trust, and you're going behind my back."

"Karma, shh." Dominic grabbed her shoulders.

"Hands off me!" She squirmed away, heart skipping beats, *no no no.*

He reached for her. She dodged. "Karma, look, we'll go through you to buy—"

"So you say."

"This is no place to talk. Calm down." Dominic's eyes jittered up and down the empty street behind her. There was a whiff of sewage.

"Are you ninety-percent bullshit, Dominic, or one-hundred?"

"*Karma.*"

Relent and she'd be trapped. "Rafe says you're a flamethrower."

"*What?*"

"You start fires for your benefit. You're a fucking corporate arsonist." Her fists pounded his chest as punctuation.

Dominic caught her arms. She tried to kick, couldn't being off balance on the slanted drive. He weighted each word. "You have to tell me, Karma. What does Rafe know?"

"That detective, the homeless man—"

"They found that homeless freak? The one everyone says is a witness? Did the freak find you? What the hell did he say?" Dominic's tourniquet grip numbed her arms.

"Let *go*." Karma's head seemed to detach from her body until she sucked in air. "Oh my god, you started the fire, the real fire, you burned your own property, for money. Jean found out and you killed her!" She bluffed to save herself. "I told that detective, Jansson, he's got proof of everything. *Let go of me*."

Dominic pressed her against her Acura. A man was coming up from the side—she'd be saved.

A jacket went over her head.

CHAPTER 36

At Ben's school, Erik took hope from the afternoon assembly that children did indeed mature. The Great Pumpkin pageant had gone peacefully without the smashing of each other's papier-mâché costumes, and Ben had flapped black wings and croaked "Nevermore" at the right time. Erik departed pleased and snugged his jacket around him. Not until he turned the street corner did he see that his Highlander had been blocked in. He'd parked behind a Ford Escape, and since then a paneled van had parked behind him, and an appliance delivery truck idled in the driving lane. Paranoia can be your friend, and he paused to text for a patrol to check "suspicious vehicles" at the school. He'd be reprimanded if the vehicles were legit. When he walked around to the front of the delivery truck to assess the situation, a man jumped from the back of the truck, Erik swiveled to check, a shock seized his body, and he collapsed. Tased in daylight with no witnesses.

DEB, DRIVING TO AN APPOINTMENT IN ST. LOUIS PARK, pulled over to receive updates from Ms. Mahdi. The hunt for a red van like Micah Hartung's "Pawdaw's" from the arson site might pay off. She had to admit, Partner Erik was good at long shots. In tracking down the girlfriends past of Jack Cardenas, Ms. Mahdi reached one who had loaned her red van to Cardenas the week of the arson. He returned it reeking of smoke, she nagged him, he wrote a check to cover the cleaning, the check bounced, and he disappeared. She'd found a stained work jacket in the van which she decided to keep as "insurance" and said the authorities could have it "for a price." "We'll deal with it soon," Deb told Ms. Mahdi, put her siren on her vehicle, and sped to her appointment.

When Deb entered the Moose Coffee in St. Louis Park, the woman's tooth-ache face gave her away. She had to be the bridge club member willing to spill the beans on Renee. In her thirties, she wore an Army sweatshirt with jeans and pulled her brown hair into a ponytail away from her face, plain except for its anguish. Deb stopped at the counter for a latte and joined her. "I'm Detective Deb Metzger. Are you Josie Walker? Thanks for seeing me." Josie had insisted on seeing the detective in person, and see her she did with a cold appraisal.

Deb needed a pickaxe to break the ice. "This would be my local coffee shop if I got a condo in that building by Highway 100. You like it here?"

Josie relaxed enough for her mouth to move. "None of the bridge club would lower themselves to come here. It's a chain, and the coffee isn't European enough. Thing is, I was an army brat, later served, and saw more of the real Europe than they did in their spa resorts."

Resentment has its uses. Deb let Josie's steep while she sipped her latte. She opened with, "The coffee's plenty good for me," took another sip, and said. "As I told you on the phone, I'm investigating the killing of Jean Nerstrand. She wasn't a member of your bridge club, but her friend Renee is, and Jean worked with Dominic Novak, Renee's husband. To be—" Deb bobbed her head side-to-side looking for the phrase. "To be circumspect, I'm looking into a link between Jean's death and Dominic's company, Landvak. One supposition, no hard intel, is that someone is going after anyone close to the company and Dominic. That includes Renee. I need context, things Renee might know that she doesn't know she knows. You're the only one in the club who'd give me the time of day."

"They're afraid that talking about trouble would bring out their worry lines. All the members are older than me, savvy at bridge but not champions. I'd been in tournaments, which is why they let me in when I moved to the area. Turns out, the better I play, the less they like me."

"Yeah, I've had experience with pecking orders and being ignored despite merit."

Jodie sized up her again, scuffed boot tips to bleached hair spikes. "I bet you have, Detective." She stirred her coffee with a stick. "Renee worried about a couple of men. 'Jack' is one. She thinks he's the arsonist who torched her husband's building, but no one would go after him. I asked if that was because no one had the balls, and she gave me a look that would curdle your coffee. Next she starts in on the replacement foreman in the company, has a blunt name. Ott, that's it, because I said her husband 'ought not' to have hired him. She didn't like that comment either, but she doesn't trust the guy."

"Did she say why?"

Josie shook her head no.

"Did she mention a Rafe or Edward, British dude?"

"Renee called him a smart ass. If I'd said 'ass,' I'd have been out on mine. He's another one she doesn't trust, but Ott got under her skin, that's all I know."

That sounded final, yet Josie was disinclined to leave. Deb wanted to keep it casual, but her question came out urgent. "What did Renee say about Dominic?"

Josie glanced toward the exit. "She said that women took advantage of 'Dom's gallantry.' Renee bragged about how he doted on her. If my husband doted on me that much, I'd want to know what bitch he was seeing on the side."

"Amen!" a passing woman said.

"Hmm." Deb swallowed coffee dregs.

Josie sipped her brew, cold by now, and avoided looking at Deb. "They blame me when Renee wheezes or has an asthma attack. They say it's my perfume. I don't wear perfume. But I went totally hypoallergenic with shampoo, conditioner, the works, after the first meeting. I kinda wanted to belong. The women help with charities, have business contacts, have each other's back. The one who's my Bridge partner is nice enough, but the rest blamed me."

"Back to Ott. No, wait." Deb's scalp prickled. Everything about Josie said no-nonsense. This wasn't about self-pity; it was about loyalties. You're loyal to a troop for honor and survival, but when does the demand for loyalty become a betrayal? "The time of Jean Nerstrand's killing, when you were all at bridge club—"

"*What?*" Josie sloshed coffee on herself. "It occurred during club time? I didn't know *that*. I just knew from another member that Renee's friend had been murdered so we had to be sensitive. I wrote a note. What is it, Detective Metzger? You look—"

Shocked. Deb didn't catch for several seconds that her phone was sounding an alarm. The G-Met dispatcher checking on the whereabouts of Detective Jansson, last located near a Linden Hills school where he'd reported suspicious vehicles. No contact since. Deb's prickles worsened to a burn. Decision time. Stay with Josie or rush to find Erik? It mattered who had your back—it also mattered when and why.

CHAPTER 37

TERROR DRUGGED KARMA, LEAVING HER WITH NO POWER over her muscles. She must've passed out for a time. She concentrated on her hands and strained against the plastic ties that held them in front of her. No give, and her feet were bound together, ankle bone against ankle bone. The cloth bag over her head, a flannel pajama bag, was loose at her neck. She could smell through it the musty sofa she was lying on. Her head—she focused on that to rub it against the sofa arm cat-like but panicked when the bag tightened. She wriggled on her side and started rubbing again. She hyperventilated into dizziness, and hot nauseous waves coursed through her. She counted her breaths until it felt safe to move. She rolled over and by trial and error worked the bag looser. It caught on one ear and she tossed her head which hurt like hell. Sylvy—she gagged and became aware of tape sealing her mouth. She squirmed into a seated position, the bag slipped over her eyes again, and by arching her neck to the breaking point, she shook it off behind the sofa. She scraped her mouth against the stinky sofa arm where the blue tape, painter's tape, balled up and away from her. She smelled more odors, dizziness threatened her, she'd black out again. She sensed the rotten egg smell of carbon monoxide but also the sweet scent of laundry. She became aware that she was in a crudely finished basement with no bag, no phone, and that she was staring at a man on the floor, bound as she was. Detective Jansson, Erik. He was muzzled with blue tape bloody at the edges and blindfolded with a bandanna. She whispered first, unsure if anyone was around to hear and if being heard meant the end of them. *"Detective Jansson, Erik."* No movement—please don't let him be dead. *"ERIK!"* she tried to scream, but her constricted throat barely squeaked.

Karma slid to the floor, concrete covered by moldy carpet, and wriggled to Erik and bumped his arm with her head. Nothing. She pounded her head on his chest. He moaned. She squeaked his name again. She couldn't paw at him like a dog. Dogs licked people, so she licked the stubble on his cheek. He twitched. She bit at the bloody corner of his mouth tape to pull it off. Not enough to catch between her teeth. She licked the tape corner to loosen it. A muscle in his face spasmed. *Erik, Erik,* she called, *Detective.* She tried again to bite the tape corner and bit him instead. When he jolted to life, she retreated to the sofa and waited.

RAFE DIDN'T CARE IF HE NEVER SAW KARMA AGAIN. He fled to his concrete bunker to lick his wounds after their fight and distract himself with fantasy. His favorite fantasy, besides the X-rated sex one, consisted of FBI agents in tacky windbreakers swarming the Landvak office. Rafe would love to witness that except he would have strategically taken a sick day. However, he had no certainty of that day since he didn't know what would happen with the invoice issues he'd leaked to the authorities. He did know that whistleblowers rarely lived happily ever after in the career of their choice. He tapped random computer keys. He could stream a movie instead of running cost estimates. As he was browsing BritBox, his cell vibrated on the table. He picked it up without checking the number because until the last second he wanted to cling to the hope that it was Karma. "Rafe Lutyens."

Bob Ott blasted him. "What are you up to, you Brit bastard? What the *hell* are you and Novak planning?"

Rafe had never heard more than three words from Ott before. "I'm doublechecking the Promise Creek projections."

"Sure you are. Just so you know, I'm right outside your building and have plenty of maintenance IDs to get past your concierge. Bastard."

"S-stay where you are." Rafe glanced around—no way to barricade the door. He asked feebly, "What plan?"

"Novak says you halted the repair order after vandalism at what you call the Wasp House. Do we own that piece of shit or what? And you told Novak to have me personally gut that Lake Nokomis property, but you didn't call in an order to fix the gas leak, and now that work order is cancelled. You told Novak that those murder detectives are trying to frame him. Next his tight-ass wife wants me to provide a personal security detail. Not my job EVER. This morning Novak wants a 'favor' on something *you* recommended and then turns on a dime and orders me to butt out or I'll hear from Jack Cardenas. What kind of mastermind are you?"

Bloody hell, the man could speak full paragraphs. "I'm no Moriarty, never mind who that is, I mean—"

"Shut up, you smug little fucker, that Penn Avenue arson you planned is going to combust right in your face."

"Aah—" Rafe was done for.

"Are you there, Lutyens?"

"Arson?" He sounded like a chipmunk and couldn't lower his voice without breathing, and he couldn't breathe. "I, I, uh, apologize for the pettiness of my behaviors, past and present, and I'll get right to the point which is, hum, which is if I masterminded anything, it's an honest audit of the books, an honest rewrite of my resume, and an honest, perhaps over-optimistic, appraisal of Promise Creek. I'm lost in deep shit about everything else." He threw himself in deeper. "I know for an absolute fact that Dominic lies. Tell me what he said."

After hearing a clipped account, he hung up on Ott and called Karma, texted Karma, emailed Karma, called Lake & Isles, called Karma again. Nil. Rafe rewrapped his ankle and swallowed four Ibuprofen and a Percocet. Once more into the breach.

RAFE ZIGZAGGED PAST THE HALLOWEEN SKELETONS to enter the office, and startled Carina cawed at him. He barged into a part-timer and grabbed his arm. "Hanlon, urgent, where's Dominic?"

Hanlon paled. "You look like a gargoyle, Edward."

"I'll hex you if you don't tell me. *Where in bloody hell is Dominic?*"

"We got messages to stay away from that building by Lake Nokomis because of safety hazards. He's getting a restraining order against you."

"I'm the very model of restraint." Rafe pushed Hanlon aside and ran out to his Countryman. He zipped a few blocks away, pulled over, and called Paisley.

"Paise, Karm's in trouble."

"Rafe? Hold on."

"Do you know where she is? Can you reach her? Something wicked is happening with Dominic's company."

He was frigging on hold. He pounded his fist against the Countryman's roof. He was about to give up on the connection when Paisley came back.

"Karma didn't pick up Sylvy. The counselor at her school has her. Where's Karma, Rafe?"

"I don't know. Don't trust anyone near Dominic. Call 911."

"What do I say?"

"Dominic's an arsonist." Rafe had zero proof. "Fraud investigators are onto him." Soon enough. He could tell Paisley the address where Dominic might be, but he wanted to confront the ass and gain a court-admissible clue as to what was going on. "Tell police to track Karma's car, her phone, she knows about Dominic." He assumed.

"On it." Paisley disconnected.

The hell, he was getting a call from Sela, who peeped a question, was the security at Promise Creek supposed to be cancelled? No, he insisted, only to hear Carina grab the phone from Sela and hoot, "he's wrong," and slam down the receiver. Carina was helping Dominic scam his own company through the shell company named "Karas," the name stolen from Karma. Karma better be fine.

In twenty minutes, Rafe cruised past the Nokomis property where there appeared to be a renovation permit, probably faked by Ott, the building where he'd fenced with Detective Jansson. He reversed and saw one of the pickups Dominic used behind the building and drawn curtains in an upstairs window. Had Cardenas been hiding here? Rafe parked out of view and slipped across a neighbor's lot and through the boundary fence. Dominic stood between a heap of demolition trash and the utility connections on the back wall. A Red Bull can in a wheelbarrow behind him attracted the last yellowjackets of the season.

Rafe leapt a debris pile, too jacked up to feel pain in his ankle. "Hey, boss, what's up? Have you seen Karma? She didn't pick up her kid."

Dominic's face was hash. "I've been here for hours. Out of my way."

"Your truck engine is hot." He reached back to touch the hood—it *was* hot, and he stood between Dominic and his escape. When Dominic slipped a hand into a back pocket, it occurred to Rafe that he might have a weapon and he lunged to grab his boss's forearms. "*Where's Karma?*" Dom jerked his arms free. Rafe bluffed, "Everyone knows you're a crook, Dominic. Feds have the files. No point in hiding. *Where's Karma?*"

Dominic shoved into Rafe with his full weight. They stumbled and knocked over the wheelbarrow, the Red Bull bounced on a cracked flagstone, and they fell with grunts. A broken board jabbed Rafe in the kidney and a nail scratched his ear. Dominic groaned and Rafe straddled him with a piece of board raised in his hand. He squirmed higher on Dominic's chest until the large man wheezed for air. "Where's Karma, you potbellied toad bastard, or I'll split your toad head and your mushy pea brain will leak out. Where!"

"Wasp house," Dominic gasped. "Too late."

"Address." Rafe bounced on him "*Address!*" He worked his phone out of his trouser pocket with one hand. "Don't you move, Worm Turd." He hit emergency call. "Karma Byrnes is in trouble at"—Rafe bounced harder on Dominic's chest and he choked out an address. "And Dominic Novak needs medical attention at—" he panted out the location.

"Spell your name for me, please?" the dispatcher asked.

"R-A—"

Dominic surged like a whale and Rafe went flying. Dominic grabbed a board from the pile, releasing a squadron of yellowjackets, and staggered to his feet. He raised the board and swung.

The whack hit Rafe like Satan-on-a-stick. Blood gurgled in his fractured nose, filling his mouth with its thickness, running down his throat, and he was out.

CHAPTER 38

A NIGHTMARE HAD LOCKED ERIK WITHIN HIMSELF. He was blind, suffocating, his nerves charred. Ben jumped on him, he couldn't move, Stripe licked him, he couldn't move. Stripe bit his cheek and Erik shuddered the length of his body. His mother, sisters, Kristine, wheedled, Erik Erik Erik Detective. The "detective" jarred him, and he came to on a hard surface, blindfolded, mouth taped, hands and feet bound, so disoriented he couldn't move. A woman urged, get up get up get up. He contorted himself into a fetal crouch and rubbed his temple against the floor until the blindfold rolled off. He saw through a blur a woman on a sofa, Karma Byrnes, and scooted over to rub the mouth tape against the sofa edge. He sucked in dust and collapsed against the bottom of the sofa.

Karma's legs in black tights, no boots, were beside him. His words scraped across his throat "What were you doing? My face is wet."

"I wasn't making out with you!" she cried from above. "I smelled gas and laundry."

"Where are we?" The dingy walls closed in, the ceiling sagged low. Closing his eyes, Erik felt dizzy enough to fall, though at the edge of perception was aware that he couldn't fall from the floor. His earth was flat and tingly. He opened his eyes and the carpet smelled of moldy stew. He was tripping on synesthesia.

Karma looked around. "I don't know . . . yes, I do. This house has wasps, it's a cul-de-sac. We're in the basement den. They took my phone. Can you turn off the gas in case, you know?"

"My hands are tied." His half smile turned to a wince as he brought himself up to sitting, his head resting by Karma's knees. "Someone, Jack Cardenas by the smell of him, crammed sleeping pills in my mouth." He spit out white saliva and more stringed from his mouth. "*Achoo.* What's making me sneeze?"

"Oh, dryer sheets. What a relief, realtors use them as room deodorizers." She contorted to peer behind the sofa. "Huh, a bunch are dumped back here all the way to a space heater in the corner."

Squirming to see he fell over her legs. "I just learned from a scientist that they're an accelerant. They'll go up in an instant if the heater comes on full blast, and it's plugged into a timer. The sheets leave no trace."

"*Shit*. I'll unplug it." Karma moving with wrists and ankles restrained fell over Erik and her chin hit the floor. She rolled on her side gulping and sobbing.

No panicking he'd command if his throat wasn't sandpaper. *Panic kills*. He had to move to fight his own fear though he was nothing but a mass of hurt. He dragged himself by her and on the verge of blacking out, croaked, "Slow inhale one, two, three, four." She sobbed instead of complying. "Karma, swing your legs over mine. Pressure helps. Roll your legs on mine, apply pressure, and hold your breath for four counts." Her trembling legs crossed his—if only that pressure could steady herself, steady them both. "Slow inhale, slower. Exhale spelling M-i-s-s-i-s-s—"

At the fourth *s* her breathing calmed.

"Center yourself, Karma. Now move your legs off, and we'll catch our breath until we know our next move.

She lost it. "Dominic's a *killer*, he's killing us. Get me out, I have Sylvy, *get me out*."

"*KARMA BYRNES STOP*," he rasped as loud as he could.

"It's hopeless."

"There's always hope." For his life's sake, he needed a reason for hope or his heart would pound itself to death. "Hope because they're amateur as criminals. Painters' tape and bandannas, Ben could escape that." Ben. Focus on the job. Courage is doing your job when you don't think you can. "You have a job."

Karma's cried-out eyes went blank.

"You have a job." It was coming to him. "You're a realtor. *You* have to help *me*. Tell me about this property, Ms. Byrnes. Start with this level. Is there a landline?"

She couldn't respond.

"Windows?"

She looked up at a row of clerestory windows. A hamster could escape through them.

"Anything sharp around?"

Another blank.

"What is here, Karma?"

She answered in a rush, "No landline. On this level, there's this den, laundry room, furnace room, bedroom. Upstairs there's a gas cooktop and fireplace. Oh, I cut myself in the laundry room. Over there." She tilted her head right toward an open door.

"What was sharp, Karma? Can we use it with tied hands?"

"A deer head with lights on it. Antlers."

Erik started to squirm that way but stopped when needles stung the length of his leg.

"*Don't die*—let me die first." Karma scooched to lean against him, almost toppling him. "Don't leave me, don't die!"

"The job, our job, is *not* to die." Erik called up energy from every organ and pore in his body. "My leg has to wake up." He shook his tied legs back and forth before scooting to the laundry room. Karma awkwardly followed.

The room was a dumping ground for a bike without tires, a crib section, and broken lawn chairs. A door to the outside was boarded shut. The deer mount leaned against a storage cupboard. Erik appraised it. "That's a ten-point buck."

"What?"

"You'll see." Erik pushed himself up against the cupboard to come to a trembling stand. He tottered around as if to sit on the buck.

"What are you—oh." Karma watched him hook his wrist ties around a point and press down. *Snap.*

Erik landed on his tailbone, hands still fastened; an antler point had broken off.

"Should I try?" Karma quavered.

"I weigh more, greater resistance." He ignored the numbness of his spine to position himself again. Another snap, another fall to the floor, another broken point.

Karma emitted a mousy, "oh, no."

Sweat ran down his face. "Obscenity is more empowering," he panted.

"You didn't swear," whispered the mouse voice.

"I went to Sunday School," he said darkly. He hooked onto another point. The point broke and Karma cried, "*Fuck!*"

Only this time Erik could work his hands free. He hobbled to the cupboard to rummage for an implement other than a broken antler. He fished out a rusty box cutter, and went to work on his ankle restraints. Then, muttering about updating tetanus shots if he nicked her, he cut Karma loose. He gulped water from the utility sink faucet, gulped more—*hydration revives*. He dug around in his pockets, empty except for a smashed energy bar which he held out to Karma. When her mouth twisted in disgust, he opened it and crammed the whole thing in his mouth. She staggered to the outer wall where the utility pipes came in.

"The natural gas shutoff is on the exterior," she said.

Erik swore—so much for Sunday School—and said hoarsely, "Walking out the front door works." He motioned her to stay back and walked noiselessly up the stairs to the main level. A few steps from the top, he listened beneath the closed door and sniffed. It smelled funny. He turned the knob, locked, he shoved the door, no budging. The shadows indicated something massive blocked it. He trundled down to Karma, who was choking on tears and snot.

He pinched her shoulder. "*Job first*, cry later. Other exits?"

They heard the click of the space heating coming on. Karma stumbled to it and ripped the plug from the outlet which sparked. "*Aaah!*" She clasped her shocked hand.

"Egress." Erik pulled her by the good hand into the room that had to have an exit to be a bedroom. Karma sniveled that if he got them out of this, she'd love him forever. No tripping on that, no time for sentiment.

He pushed the bedroom door open and flipped a switch. Plywood was boarded over the window.

Karma gasped, "Bloody fucking *hell!*"

Keep thinking. "Back to—" Erik was interrupted by an alarm upstairs. Four repeated beeps.

"Carbon monoxide detector," Karma whispered, her eyes dilating. Erik lifted his head to the ceiling—low ceilings were a trap. *Don't think that.* Karma chanted, the chant fainter and fainter. "Four beeps gas three beeps fire four beeps gas three fire." Her eyes rolled back.

He grabbed her arms and shoved her against the wall and she fluttered to consciousness. "*Karma, stay*," he crackled. He was seeing black—see color, hazel eyes, hazel hair, pale lips. "Stay. The fork of the bike can be a pry bar."

Just as he released her, there was a tremendous *crack*. A second *crack* from the outside and the plywood splintered, shards flying. Blood spurted from Karma's cheek and she slid to the floor.

Erik squatted and grabbed her again. "*You're alive.*" Think fast—"They can't be coming from outside to, to harm us." Her eyelids fluttered. "It's *help.*" He better be right with the alarms sounding upstairs and him putting all his effort in pulling the plywood back to create a bigger opening. He sensed a commotion, leapt back at a *thwack* and a deep scream of pain, raised his arms to deflect more broken plywood. He looked up through the hole and window well, Ott on his knees on the ground, one hand on his shoulder, the other by a sledgehammer. Their eyes connected, Ott, gray with pain, mouthed, "Out."

Erik raised up Karma, but by the opening, she cried, "no no no," and fell back into Erik. "No no no," she moaned against his chest.

"He's helping, Ott's helping, he's not taking us to Dominic." Erik didn't like the smoke he was smelling, didn't like the crackling he heard, and brought her back to the window. "Ott's hurt, you climb out, *now*."

He boosted her, and she climbed through, clothes ripping against the jagged hole. Erik didn't look back, knew the floor above him was burning. He placed one hand on the window frame and was about to grasp a sharp edge with the other when Karma extended her hand to pull him, and he was out on brown grass, firetruck sirens deafening him, but he swore he heard Ott moan "about time," Karma saying over and over, "Thank you, thank you, thank you."

Erik placed his hand over his thudding heart and was himself profoundly thankful. Then the toxic fumes reached his nose.

CHAPTER 39

Certain routines should never have become routines. That shoulder war of Deb and Erik, the ribbing of Drees (he started it), the mutual button-pushing. The worst were the trips to the emergency room—Deb, Erik, Erik, Deb, Erik again, each time an escalation.

Detective Deb Metzger marched into the St. Louis Park Emergency Unit like she was meant to be there. She *was* meant to be there. She extended her badge and declared she was Detective Jansson's "Significant Partner." The nurses parted to let her enter the stall of beds curtained off from each other. She slipped into the space assigned to Erik where he lay on his back with a forearm flung over his eyes and wearing sweatpants that were too short. He must have begged the clothes from someone when he surrendered his garments to forensics. The hospital gown remained on a hook. She pulled up the one chair and blurted, "Erik."

No movement. She rubbed her eyes and touched the bed. "Partner, I need to know if you're alive for my report."

He stirred, raised his arm to peek at her, exhaled, let the arm fall back.

"Whew. So, you're done in," Deb said. "I'm a little shaky myself, but I can do the talking because you like that so much. You were tased, kidnapped, drugged, tied up in an abandoned house with Karma Byrnes, tried to escape, fire started upstairs, Bob Ott broke in the window, dislocated his shoulder, and you got him, Karma, and yourself out of the way as firetrucks arrived."

Without removing the forearm from his eyes, he made the okay sign with his fingers.

"I'll write that Detective Jansson approved the full details of the report." Deb touched his straight arm. "How are you feeling?"

He yawned. "Not so bad. Thank god Dominic and Cardenas are no better criminals than dabbling ducks."

"I'm not putting in the report that escaping murderers and a burning building 'wasn't so bad,' and I have no idea about ducks and dabbling." Erik had covered his eyes again. "Are you light-sensitive or can't stand the sight of me?"

He smiled faintly. "I was afraid you might be Drees. Do me a favor, use your blunt force for the good and 'persuade' a doctor to prescribe me a hot shower, a meal, and a nap."

"I'll delegate Cyber Paul to the food roundup. I'll ask a nurse for heated blankets. You sure you're okay?"

"Good enough. Add ibuprofen and eyedrops to the list. What about Karma?"

"They took her to the attached women's clinic because it was less crowded than this ER. Banged up and in shock, but she told arriving officers that Dominic and Cardenas were behind it all."

Erik spoke through yawns, "This has been fun, but go solve a crime. You can do it." He rolled over, his back to her, and curled up. A nurse intuiting his needs brought in warm blankets.

"Good to know I got your back and you got mine," Deb said to herself and left because sleeping beauty Erik was right, she had multiple crimes to solve. The conspiracy involving Dominic Novak and Jack Cardenas was one thing, but she couldn't swallow that it had anything to do with the murder of Jean Nerstrand.

HAVING RUSHED BACK TO CITY HALL, Deb felt like it'd been days since she'd gotten out of bed but it was still Wednesday, almost night. She strode through the corridors with refilled water bottles toward her temporary office. Drees flanked her.

"Deborah," he said. "As lead on the Nerstrand case, you're responsible for all involved parties."

"It doesn't feel like a party to me, Drees. There's no cake."

"It's way out of hand. You should check on your partner, Jansson in the—"

"Done, his stoicism's intact."

"The press wants updates," Drees chided.

"I don't deal with the press, unless I like a reporter. My focus is on crime."

"It can take a village to solve a crime," Drees admonished. "A whole village."

Deb checked over her shoulder to see that Jimmy Bond Smalls had slipped behind them. He mouthed, "village idiot" and pointed down at Drees, who didn't notice.

"Drees, if you want to help—Oh, hi, Jimmy."

Having caught up with them, Jimmy spoke into Deb's ear that Charlene Geary had been moved in case Cardenas had any suspicions about her. Then he raced off.

"Thanks for the help," Deb called after him. "Now, Drees, if *you* want to help—"

"I have my own case."

"Then I'll get back to mine." Deb flashed a smile indicating she was ready to eat idiots, and Drees vamoosed.

She entered the office but couldn't sit. Borrowing a page from absent Erik's book, she commenced pacing. The bivouacked office was no less grim, but Ms. Mahdi arrived wearing a vibrant purple hijab that lent the space vibrancy. She sat with a computer ready to compute. Deb gave a water bottle to the intern and gulped from the other. She scowled at lines that didn't connect on the murder board. She'd squeezed in time before seeing Erik to hurry along security camera checks and warrants for all things Renee. Renee Novak had left bridge club the night of Jean Nerstrand's death because of an asthma attack, returned half an hour later, said she still felt unwell, and went home. Had she indeed visited the nearest Urgent Care clinic for a nebulizer treatment? Currently, no one could find Renee.

"Review and update of the locations of persons of interest," she said to Ms. Mahdi. "First, where's your mentor, Cyber Paul?"

"Mr. Visser left to take items to Detective Jansson per your message."

"Well, that answers the question, does Cyber Paul have a last name. You don't need to put that in the notes."

"He's messaging now that he supplied Detective Jansson with a protein-recovery shake and a cheeseburger with fries."

"You don't need to write about the cheeseburger either, but it was probably medium-rare. Add this, Karma Byrnes was treated for a puncture wound and is under observation for shock. She called Dominic Novak a corporate arsonist and he confessed to being a real arsonist. Write that down so I can figure it out later."

"To figure out," Ms. Mahdi repeated and typed.

"Bob Ott." Deb ticked a finger.

"At the St. Louis Police station. He rescued Detective Jansson and Ms. Byrnes by breaking into the basement of the house where they were held. A fire had started upstairs."

"Yup. I joined via Facetime SLP's interview with Ott. Write this down, 'I did not sign up for murder.'"

"You didn't sign up for murder, or Mr. Ott didn't sign up for murder?" Ms. Mahdi asked.

"Guess I signed up for murder with this job, but Ott did not. Huh, that rhymes, Ott-did-not. Rafe Edward Lutyens. A 911 dispatcher sent an ambulance to a Landvak rental where he was found unconscious and choking on his own blood. Still being evaluated at Abbott Northwestern Hospital. Write 'pending.'"

"Pending on what?"

"What the docs say. I hope he makes it, though I'm clueless as to what he's been up to. Wait, when your boss Cyber Paul with a last name returns, pass on that he should track Rafe's computer activities. I bet there's Landvak bookkeeping gobbledygook. Next, villain of the hour, Dominic Novak."

"In the wind?"

"Write 'highest priority.' Make it a threesome, Jack Cardenas and Dominic and Renee Novak."

"Do you think they really are a threesome?" Ms. Mahdi asked shyly. "In bed?"

"No idea and don't want to know unless they killed people to keep it from becoming a foursome. Okay, the veteran 'Homeless Ulysses.'"

"Your notes say, Nordic God Anders knows."

"Good enough. You stay here and forward me updates on above POI's. I've got to shake out, delete that, 'request' information from Landvak employees. On my way."

Deb opened the door to Cyber Paul holding a food tray.

"Paul, you're an angel. So is Ms. Mahdi. I owe you." She grabbed a burger from the tray and was halfway through it and down the hall when Ms. Mahdi called after her.

"Detective, Bob Ott's lawyer is on the G-Met line. Someone's using Ott's credit card and name checked in at Regions Emergency Room. Reaction to wasp stings."

Deb crammed the last of the burger into her mouth. New priority: have local officers close in on Dominic Novak. She hoped anaphylactic shock didn't kill him because a line of people were waiting to wring his neck.

CHAPTER 40

THE SUN HAD SUNK LIKE A STONE HOURS BEFORE, and Deb Metzger coming out of Regions Hospital acted on gut instinct, though why she should trust a gut that knotted itself tight she didn't know. She hopped into her G-Met vehicle, secured a flashing light to the roof, turned on the siren, and gunned the engine out of the parking lot heading north to 35 E and on to the Promise Creek development. If luck was with her, she'd find a murderer or two.

Dominic Novak was beyond questioning that night. After his clash with Rafe, he'd driven a Landvak pickup truck to Regions Emergency in St. Paul and attempted to check in under Bob Ott's name. When Deb ran into the hospital flashing ID to say that the man claiming to be Ott was Dominic Novak, Reception stated, "Whoever he is, his head's puffed up like a mushroom." Dominic collapsed after giving the false name and was rushed into treatment for anaphylaxis. She directed hospital security to treat the man as a violent criminal and flight risk. "Too hooked up to machines to fly anywhere," she was told. Security also informed her that Dominic had left his truck running in the drop-off zone. It'd been moved to temporary parking, and she intercepted the tow truck to claim the vehicle as evidence. She gave the pickup a quick going over before a patrol arrived to secure it. Brochures for Promise Creek littered the seat and beneath them were a set of padlock keys. She grabbed the unmarked keys and ran to her vehicle when she intuited from the hospital's location that Dominic had been fleeing to Promise Creek.

She radioed Cyber Paul to set in process warrants for Dominic's phone and finances. He reported that Erik Jansson had been discharged to return home. Karma Byrne's surrogate father Mark was attending to her and her daughter Sylvy. Rafe Lutyens was in surgery at Abbott Northwestern for a broken nose and possible brain bleed. That hospital had yet to reach his next of kin in San Diego. Jack Cardenas was at large. Before the Dominic excitement, a Landvak employee, Sela, admitted that the security detail for Promise Creek was dismissed at the insistence of another employee, Carina, who subsequently "up and ran off."

Also earlier, Renee's bridge buddies swore that they weren't hiding her and that they were "shocked and appalled" that she could be involved in anything criminal. A sheriff up north was monitoring the Novak lake house, and state patrol had an APB out for Renee's Mercedes. Promise Creek might be a prearranged rendezvous for the Novaks should the shit hit the fan, or more exactly, should Rafe knock the linchpin out of Dominic's scams. Deb had no idea if Renee and Dominic had contacted each other before his collapse or if Jack Cardenas was in the mix.

She exited the interstate in Arden Hills and didn't call for backup because this could be a wild goose chase under a full moon. She left behind suburban streets for empty fields, wooded hillocks, and chain-link fences. Her GPS became confused by the boundaries between U.S. government properties and private construction access. After dead-ending at a gate, "restricted to National Guard personnel," she wound around until a sign fluoresced, "PROMISE CREEK COMMONS." A lower sign listed civic entities and private companies including Landvak Development. Multiple signs announced CAUTION, DANGER, PELIGRO. Security lights shone on the main gate but little else. Deb stuck her head out of the G-Met vehicle window and looked up. Red warning lights blinked on a construction crane one hundred yards beyond the gate. The crane's cross-arm stretched high above like a bridge to nowhere. *No chases up the crane.* A sign dictated that entrants must wear a hard hat, safety glasses, and "High-Vis" item. Only she didn't want to be high visibility in a neon vest, not until she knew what she'd encounter. No sign of human or canine guards.

That gate was padlocked. Deb slipped out of the vehicle to try the keys she'd scored from Dominic's van. None worked. Scaling the fence would be slow going in and deadly slow going out if she needed to escape gunfire. She toned down her lights to parking level and pulled the G-Met vehicle over to an equipment entrance, put on protective Kevlar under a fleece, checked that her nine-millimeter was unlocked in its holster. She put on her body camera which might fail in low light. Maybe an all-seeing eye hung from the crane. Deb faked an internal cheer—*let's do this*—made herself get out, and left the door unlocked. With a Maglite offering pinpoint illumination, she prowled thirty feet to a fence corner. Inside the construction zone, modular buildings stood in clusters, one possibly occupied by Renee Novak. She cast her light over the nearest hulking forms. None of the vehicles registered to

Dominic and Renee were in sight, only parked bulldozers and barrels that read *Flammable*. She slipped around the corner to the wire equivalent of a side door. She didn't have to try the keys because when she jiggled the padlock, it fell open. The lock had carelessly, or deliberately, been left loose. She slipped in.

Modulars dotted the interior perimeter. Stretching between them were dirt mounds, ditches, and squarish pits. Concrete pilings emerged from several pits like stripped tree trunks. Recent rains had turned paths into ruts and water ran in rivulets, a less gruesome variant of World War I foxholes. If you fell into a deep trench, you couldn't get yourself out.

Deb wasn't here to die in no man's land, but she very well could. And she should've turned off the TV every time a preview played for a Halloween horror flick where a solitary woman, busty like herself, became fodder for the monster. She squatted and put a hand down to steady herself against the uneven ground. Why had she effing come? Because she was driven by connection. A wife and mother had been murdered, a homeless man frightened into hiding, another mother kidnapped, and Deb's partner gagged, bound, and left to burn. The image of Erik as a blackened French fry did it. She stood to rush ahead but slipped on her butt. Now her butt, not her gut, was making decisions for her. Staying on her butt, she texted backup to be on the ready, asserting as fact that Dominic had been heading to Promise Creek and that the loose padlock was a telltale breach.

Deb raised herself to a squat and jogged between machines, feet squishing and skidding. The giant crane blocked her view. She jogged to a bulldozer, grabbed hold of its mud-crusted tread, and leaned out to see around the crane. Light spilled from a modular unit. She reminded herself that the National Guard was stationed nearby.

There—a flicker at a modular window, someone was inside. The red lights high on the crane flickered too as the wind came up. A front was moving in, pushing clouds that blocked out the moon. With a shiver down her spine, Deb texted backup that they should come in dark and quiet. She pulled her weapon, reholstered it. Holding both flashlight and gun across treacherous ground was risky. Last thing she wanted was to fall and shoot herself—death by embarrassment. The light could be from onsite security. A guard, or Jack Cardenas, could step out of the unit and wham her right in the kisser. Would she ever pucker up with a sweetie again? *Focus!*

She dashed up to the crane base—*no chases up cranes*. Its ladder ran straight up a steel-bar shaft. Climb that, and she'd be as good a target as a turkey in a bare tree. She scooted behind the crane. Her pounding heart made the body cam thump against her chest, her phone vibrated against her hip, vibrated again, and she checked it. Backup ten minutes out and an awake Erik texting about location. "Promise" was all she relayed because a metal scrunch stopped her, and she peered around the base. The door to the lighted unit stuttered open. A motion detector revealed highlighted hair: Renee, alone.

Because Renee, not Dominic, shot Jean—that idea hit Deb hard, despite being subsurface for a long time. Renee's alibi, the entire evening spent at bridge club, was false. Deb was just ahead of the proof, that's all. Dominic was genuinely upset by Jean's death because he loved her, in his version of love. He had attempted to kill Karma, Erik, and Rafe not to protect Renee, but to protect his fraudulent business. His crimes with Cardenas, as Partner Erik implied with his dabbling duck talk in the ER, were sloppy. Jean's killing had been neat, efficient, ruthless.

"Who's out there?" The question sounded sweet, and Renee's head protruded further from the doorway. The question was repeated minus the sweetness. "Who's out there? Dom, Bob?" The voice squealed upward. "*Detective?* What are you doing?"

Damn. Deb thought she stayed out of sight. Treat this as a volatile domestic, sound like an ally. "Renee? It's Detective Metzger. I'm here to help."

"You couldn't be more wrong," she snarled. "Why are you even here?"

Deb moved as if she had to be close to talk. "I'm coming, Renee. Tell me what's wrong."

A *pah* was the answer.

Without asking Mother-may-I, Deb took three steps. "Renee, where's Dominic? Something's up with the company. When did you last hear from your husband?"

"You're trespassing." Renee moved forward enough that she was backlit, her expression unknown.

Deb had to play every angle until one worked. First, be the confidante to the betrayed wife. "Renee, Dominic hasn't been faithful, has he? He was having an affair with Jean, with your 'dear friend.' Jean had been your friend first and then she began sleeping with Dom. I'm guessing you found his secret phone and its messages. To think, Dominic owes you and your family his success." The wind blew up Deb's back and the chill distracted her from blurting *you killed Jean.* "Then Jean dies, but does Dom run back to you? No, he puts the moves on sexy Karma."

Renee pulled back.

"Renee, Dominic's wandering is just one side of him, isn't it? You could ignore that as long as he stayed faithful to your dreams, your togetherness. Right?"

Renee receded so all Deb could see were her toes and her hair.

"Renee, I can help you find the truth. I imagine Dom intended to be faithful to your family money." Deb had bluffed her way to thirty feet from the door. "But Dom could be careless with money, like he was with women. He lost a bunch of it. He was working on getting it back by any means. Arson insurance."

"Get back!" Renee hooked her foot around the door to open it enough to extend a handgun. "It's nothing to you, Detective. *Get back.*"

Deb froze. "Has he told you that today he tried to burn two people to death and put his partner Rafe in the hospital?"

"Rafe Edward couldn't keep his crooked nose out of what wasn't his business. You're the same."

"You can't save Dom from himself, but you can save you." Deb couldn't outdraw and outshoot a woman with gun in hand, a woman from a family of hunters, a woman known to gun clubs. She stepped to the side to obscure her movements but instead triggered more motion detectors to spotlight herself.

She bit her lip to keep from screaming, *you killed Jean, didn't give her a chance.* The wind moaning through the crane and the blood rushing in her head blocked out other noises, but she could clearly see that Renee had aimed the gun at her. Best tactic so far, lying. "Renee, is Dom with you? Rafe attacked him, and that's when Dom attacked him back. Does Dom need medical care?" No answer. "Is Jack Cardenas threatening you?" Oh hell, could he be with her?

"*You don't know anything!*" Renee screamed.

"Come on out and we'll talk." If Renee wouldn't cooperate, Deb's options were moving forward with a strong likelihood of being shot in the face, or moving away with a strong likelihood of being shot in the back. Her knees jellied and she struggled to keep eye contact across the dim distance. Normal people are less likely to shoot a person if there's eye contact. Maybe Deb made up that rule on the fly. Where was backup, having an effing tea break?

The wind wailed like a siren around the looming pillars. "Hear that, Renee?" Renee's head shifted and Deb put her hand on her weapon. "Renee, put the gun down." Renee sighted along her barrel.

Shit, the bullet went right, pinged off the crane ladder, and seared across Deb's arm as she was about to pull her weapon. "Renee, don't dig a hole for yourself." *For the love of Pete let a sinkhole open right under that insane woman.* "Renee, easy." Deb's voice shook.

Renee's was steady. "Bad things happen at construction sites. People break in to steal. A thief attacked you. That's plausible. That's the way it'll be."

"Like your alibi for the night Jean was shot. Plausible but a lie because you killed her. You set her up. You knew she wouldn't let go of your husband. Renee, drop the weapon *now.*"

That was as good as pulling a trigger—another shot, shots, echoes of shots, a gun crashing down the modular's steps, and a burn through Deb. She fell flat on the ground and sucked mud.

What happened next happened in a blackout state. Deb was told that she surged up and charged Renee like a wildcat to keep Renee from retrieving her weapon. She remembered Erik Jansson standing over her, someone telling him, helluva shot, Erik kneeling by her ear saying time out, off Renee, and let's check that arm.

CHAPTER 41

THE MEDICAL COST OF CRIME RUNS HIGH, and the G-Met tally for the Wednesday of capture set a department record. Two days later, Erik Jansson ticked off the costs as he parked his Highlander by Chief Ibeling's modular office. On the civilian side, Rafe Lutyens topped the list with a hairline skull fracture, broken nose, sprained wrist, and broken finger; he remained monitored for adverse reactions after reconstructive surgery. Dominic Novak, bruised, stung, and on steroids, was released after twenty-four hours into police custody. Renee suffered two cracked ribs from Deb landing on her, and one hand was a bloody pulp from his shot that blew the Sig Sauer from them. Bob Ott was prescribed painkillers and bedrest because he dislocated his shoulder when he took a sledgehammer to the plywood at the Wasp House. The least visible injuries were Karma's psychic wounds; she had after all been betrayed, kidnapped, bound, and left to burn, her Sylvy an inch from being orphaned.

On the G-Met side, Erik figured he fared best despite his tasing because he had hours of restorative sleep. Deb's right forearm had been grazed twice by bullets ricocheting off the crane—she swore the crane had it in for her. Paul had a sleep deficit, and Ms. Mahdi who'd monitored the events had to meditate through a panic attack.

Erik entered Ibeling's office, saw the cardboard covering the vinyl window and the chief's pinched brow, and prepared himself. Reviewing depositions and blurry video had given Almost Allwise Ibeling a migraine, and no matter what his words declared, his growl conveyed a grudge against the universe.

"Good, you've got suspects behind bars. However, you weren't authorized to take the shot at Promise Creek, Jansson. You checked yourself out of the

ER against medical advice, attached yourself to the SWAT team, and what—pretty please asked to borrow a rifle?"

"The armed officer was about to sneeze, sir," Erik answered.

"Oh, hi there. I mean, hi there, sir." Deb arrived, arm in a sling. "What'd I miss?"

"Jansson's *reasoning*." Ibeling rubbed his brow.

"The sneezing officer and I were the only ones in position for a shot," Erik continued, "and there was only the one shot to take from that position. The subject's hands, weapon, and profile were all that was visible. It was clear, however, that she had dead aim on Metzger."

It was a crack shot, which Ibeling acknowledged with a grunt. He fixed a dilated eye on Deb. "After Novak landed himself in emergency, you took off like Wile E. Coyote."

"I'd say more roadrunner, sir. I didn't fall off any cliffs or carry TNT. I should've had Wonder Woman cuffs to deflect the bullets."

Ibeling pressed fingers to his temples. "Renee Novak is going to sue for excessive force."

"It's on the video that she wanted me completely dead. *Blam* through the head."

Ibeling pressed harder. "So now she's Elmer Fudd? Be advised, Renee Novak has been duly charged with attempted murder of an officer. Detectives do you have a *shred* of evidence linking her to the shooting of Jean Nerstrand? She's not the confessing type. Also, Jack Cardenas remains at large."

"We have DNA evidence that ties him to the kidnapping and attempted murder of Karma Byrnes and Erik, I mean, Detective Jansson here." Deb nudged him with her good elbow. "We have a plan which, according to my partner—"

"Lacks details so is useless to share at this point." Erik's boy-scout expression merited a squint from Ibeling.

He shifted the squint to Deb. "I suppose I can't veto a plan I haven't heard. I expect an immediate and thorough investigation of Renee Novak."

If Erik could stand up to Ibeling's gruff, so would Deb. "Aren't we supposed to be on administrative leave because of stuff, sir?"

Ibeling shut one migraine-dilated eye and pinned Deb with the other. "*Stuff?*"

"You know, the debriefings, discharging a weapon, injured in the line of duty." She flapped her sling arm. Erik studied his feet.

"Then take a hike," Ibeling commanded. "You've earned a break, soon. Creative types say the best ideas come when they're off the clock. Bear that in mind." He came from behind his desk which had the effect of driving the detectives to the door.

There, hand shading his eyes, Ibeling stopped. "Good luck with the winter biathlon, Jansson. Metzger, thanks for reminding Greta about brownie pudding. I'd take that any day over French mud. There may be commendations. Out. Don't come back until you have evidence that's hard, you two."

In the parking lot, Erik put his hand on Deb's good shoulder. "Commendations, not condemnations, you can't get higher praise than that. And God bless brownie pudding."

IF ONLY RENEE NOVAK CATALOGUED HER CRIMES as thoroughly as she organized her residence. After the Ibeling meeting, Deb, arm en-slinged, went with Erik to the Novak house where the CSI van was parked in the driveway. The house had been a dream home. That is, as long as Dominic's indiscretions were leaf litter to blow away and Renee's dominion held them tight within mutual need. Surviving mutual sentencing was another matter. The two were denied contact, though neither Dominic nor Renee accused each other of anything. Renee declared, "I protect my family," and was silent. Dominic, the gladhander, jabbered on without implicating Renee. As part of a deal his lawyer was working on, Dominic admitted to a conspiracy to commit insurance fraud. Dominic had paid Jack Cardenas to set the Penn Avenue fire, dropped his support when the fire killed a man and couldn't pass as accidental, yet helped Cardenas hide for a time. Cardenas had been tempted back when Dominic offered money to be on standby to "clear up misunderstandings" after Jean Nerstrand's murder. The misunderstandings were Erik and Karma.

Bob Ott was guilty of fast work regarding building permits. But when Dominic approached him to secretly dispose of "misunderstandings," he pleaded a dislocated shoulder. After that, he saw that a repair order for fixing boarded windows at the Wasp house was cancelled. Skeptical, he went there to hear alarms going off and banging against the basement boarded window. He dislocated his shoulder for real freeing Erik and Karma.

Deb and Erik entered the Novaks' garage, empty of vehicles since they'd already been seized. Inside Foster of forensics grumbled, "cleanest garage I've ever seen." In his shapeless getup with floppy covers over his cowboy boots, Foster resembled a Dr. Seuss character. Deb was about to needle him if he'd had sauerkraut with his green eggs and ham when Foster took off on a rant.

"Look, Metzger. My time is twenty-four carat gold. Yours isn't the only crime in the dock. There's nothing out of place in this showroom, no obvious place to start. We're processing your perk's Mercedes, and Luminol found traces of blood that probably adhered to Nerstrand's tote bag. Your perk likely took the bag from the scene, tossed it in her trunk, and disposed of it in the body of water of her choice."

Deb hissed through her teeth. "Not enough evidence yet to tie her directly to the Nerstrand shooting."

"She can be tied to shooting you, Metzger. I understand her feelings there. Jansson, help me out."

Erik blinked.

"Because you would say, Partner," Deb coaxed.

"Ahem, Detective Metzger is lead for a reason, and as lead detective you require?"

Foster humphed, "Jansson, you traitor. Metzger, what am I supposed to do, start with your perk's favorite things, moonlight and mittens?"

Erik jumped in before she spouted fire. "It's come to my attention that a few of Renee's favorite things are scrubbers and cleansers."

Foster blustered, "So her fingerprints are on a bleach bottle, meaningless."

"*Arrgh*," Deb exhaled. "What's meaningless is silly arguing. My mom taught me that, and my mom did not raise an emotional illiterate. You're overworked, Foster."

He pouted. "My son's supposed to have the lead in his school's production of *Bye Bye Birdie*, and he's come down with strep. Try living with that."

"Oh, wow, hope he recovers." Deb was earnest. "We have a neatnik murderer. You said that a liner in Dominic's Yukon had traces of Jean's blood along with fibers from the trunk of his wife's Mercedes. Hear me out. Renee shoots her frenemy because her frenemy's a cheating bitch and Renee's a murderous bitch. We on the same page? Okay. Back at the scene, Renee picks up the shell casing, takes Jean's tote which in all likelihood has blood splatter and hair on it and—what was my next likelihood? Oh, Renee dumps casing and tote in her preferred body of water. She goes home, removes the liner from the Mercedes trunk and leans it against the trash barrel to toss. DON'T LOOK BORED WHILE I'M DETECTIVE-SPLAINING. Dominic comes back from his Albert Lea work-do, doesn't notice a little stain, so he uses it in his vehicle, where it leaves traces of Jean's blood. But Renee thinks he tossed the liner. Meanwhile." She looked to Erik.

"Renee details the Mercedes herself," Erik said.

"Yup," Deb said. "I spy a handheld vac plugged in on the counter. Those have re-usable filters, and I own one of those suckers and it's hard to make that filter like new. Bingo, your starting point, Foster, and best to your kid."

That's how Deb predicted bloodied hairs would be discovered in a device with Renee's fingerprints all over it.

THE SUN WAS ABOUT TO SET ON FRIDAY WHEN ERIK JANSSON and Anders jogged away. Behind them, Ulysses sat on a park bench to enjoy coffee, a bagel, and Lake Harriet rimmed with foliage.

"I think he'll be there when we come back," Anders said. "He's being treated for arthritis and bipolar disorder, but he'll never be able to hold a nine-to-five job."

"Lots of us don't want to hold those jobs, but I see your point. I doubt he'll pass muster as a reliable witness who saw a man with 'fire on his face.' When we catch Cardenas, it'll happen, we can charge him with plenty. I can't promise that we'll have sufficient evidence to charge him for the murder of Ulysses' friend Tom, but we're working on it." Erik couldn't share that it had taken his partner Deb trumpeting of justice for mistreated girlfriends, along with his smile, to convince the former girlfriend with the red van to hand over a piece of clothing owned by Cardenas. A stained smoky jacket that she stored as her insurance against Cardenas. It would take the lab time to work out the jacket's story, if it held the dirty truth that Cardenas had worn it when he killed a man with a wrench and started the Penn Avenue Fire.

Anders slowed his pace. "The thing about Ulysses is that he has wanderlust. He says he's more comfortable outside. The universe keeps him company, and shelter can be anywhere when the universe gets rough. In a normal room, he says there's nothing to do but be in his own head, and that's the loneliest place."

For the rest of the run, Anders panted about floundering on how to propose to his girlfriend, when she dropped by with cheesecake and a 'special outfit.' Marry me you fool, she said. Erik figured she was in a rush to take Anders off the open market.

On their return, Ulysses was gone from the bench. They found him in a clump of trees where he held a wet cat. "Somebody tried to drown him," he said. "He thinks he's mine so I better keep him. I'm naming him Anders."

Erik laughed that there's always a cat. If only a cat could find the rat Cardenas.

CHAPTER 42

ON SATURDAY MORNING, KARMA DROVE INTO THE PARKING LOT of Boom Island Park aware of the security car behind her. Surrogate father Mark had hired a private firm to tail Karma while Cardenas was at large. She'd been too numb after the rescue from the Wasp House to sense further threat and felt nothing except paralyzing fatigue and then relief. Whatever feelings had been tamped down would soon emerge. For the moment, Karma figured it was safe to meet a detective and directed the security detail to remain in the lot. She'd never been to Boom Island before, the rustic backside of Minneapolis with a miniature lighthouse Sylvy would adore. A knoll ended in steps down to the Mississippi River which was flat and bucolic above St. Anthony's falls. Not so bucolic that a boy hadn't drowned here—a teddy bear memorial marked the backwater where it happened. Another memorial, large and permanent, capped the knoll. Upright mosaic slabs depicted women of many shapes and colors in a natural setting. The pieces of tile represented brokenness brought together in tribute to the survivors of sexual violence. Karma wrapped her cocoon coat tighter, unsure of belonging, and touched her bandaged cheek. The healing wound itched. Then the backdrop of autumn trees, the intonations of a prayer group, and a hint of burning weed put her in a trance. She was gazing at the river when Detective Deb Metzger, arm in a sling, came up to her. The two women made small talk but that wasn't what brought them here. They walked to the monument.

Near the slabs, Karma saw imprinted on one side, "YOU ARE NOT ALONE." Another side noted that the memorial stood "on the land of the Dakota Ovate." Below that, "Survivors surround all of us, though we often don't know who they are."

"What happened?" Detective Metzger asked. "Not with Dominic. Way back."

"It doesn't have anything to do with this case."

"It does if the case opened an old wound, if something in the past alerted you to Dominic. Besides, what matters is that it matters to you."

"It wasn't rape." Karma followed a gull tilting in the air currents. "At least that's what I told myself. I don't know." She started walking in a tight circle, but Metzger's long strides beside hers stretched the circle into a slow loop. "I wanted to break up with this guy. It was the summer before my senior year in college and we were working in a resort town. It'd been thrilling at first because I'd never been so *wanted* by anyone. He'd gush about how beautiful I was and wanted sex all the time which, well, that's the age. Maybe he was um—"

"Controlling?"

Karma gave a rueful laugh, "Which I didn't realize soon enough. When it was time to return to school, he came to the room I'd rented, and I knew I had to be direct and said it's over, we aren't a fit. He wouldn't leave he said he loved me he said if we were together in bed I'd realiz . . ."

"Take your time."

"I said no, we're done. He was crying and pushing me against the wall to kiss me, to say no one could love me more. He held my arms so tight that the bruises lasted a month. I didn't think to scream. He thought we were having makeup sex."

"And you felt trapped."

"He wouldn't let me leave his arms—that's the nicest way to put it. I was terrified. He loved me, couldn't I feel that? I thought if he loved me, he'd go away."

"But that's not how it worked out."

Karma blew her nose.

"Karma, these women in the mosaics are here because they're so much more than victims and survivors. They live in full color. Try this angle. Take yourself out of your story. Put in a twenty-something woman, a babysitter of Sylvy's, if that happened to her, what would you say?"

Karma wanted to shout, *she was raped.* She couldn't. "He forced her. He should be in jail. Not that he will be. I feel like I've regressed."

Detective Metzger commiserated with a chuckle. "I feel like I regress every day."

Karma shot her an astonished look. "But you solved the case, you're powerful."

"It's a constant project. Karma, you've had and will have a wonderful life. You've been strong. I'm sure there's a saying about tragedies being part of that life. You need multiple chances to recover because you've been through multiple traumas. For one, being stuck alone with my partner, Mr. Moods. Gotta say, he's got guts and smarts."

"Does he like me?" Karma didn't expect that to jump out.

"I suppose Detective Jansson likes a lot of people more than he cares to show. Detectives can't wear their hearts on their sleeve. Well, some do." Detective Metzger's red face matched nearby leaves.

"I never told my husband about the, um, *incident*. We had a great marriage, love, sex, nothing lacking. But he died, a man dumped me, Jean was killed, and Dominic got so needy."

"Maybe you realized Dominic was a man who wouldn't accept no."

"He hadn't pushed me into sex."

"'No' about his business dealings, wouldn't accept things not going his way. Turns out that was even truer of Renee."

"After the rescue, this is weird, I was mad at Rafe who wasn't even there, wanted to shake him, like he should've fixed the whole thing with a crazy scheme."

"It was safe to be mad at him because you figured he'd never hurt you, and he did track down Dominic. Have you visited him at the hospital?"

Karma teared up. "Soon, he's been out of it."

Deb glanced at her. "I bet he'll look like someone who came through the fight of his life. Heroes are a wreck."

"That's a, um, positive way to put it. I'd talked to Rafe's 'Da' over the phone. I see where Rafe gets his charm. I'd never thought of Rafe as weirdly charming before. The weird could be reduced."

Metzger laughed, and a woman from a disbanding prayer group shouted, "Hey, Deb Metzger, I'd recognize that boom anywhere." Karma left the detective to head back to her car. The day began to bluster, with the sky shining in the east and in the west purpling into dark masses. Between Karma and the lighthouse, Detective Jansson stood on a picnic table.

FROM HIS VANTAGE POINT ON THE TABLE, ERIK PHOTOGRAPHED the chiaroscuro of the bright and bruised sky. The last of the season's white egrets flew by the blackest cloud.

"Detective Jansson?"

Karma below him with the light falling on her. "Are you like your grandfather who climbed on the roof for the view, that story you told? Addicted to adventure, damn the risk?"

He jumped down. "I want stability with a life on the edge, which may be too much to ask. It may have cost me my marriage." He wouldn't have confessed that if it weren't for the emotive sky. "And you?" He touched her arm, then dropped his hand.

She peered at the darkening sky. "I lost my husband to a maple tree. Risk . . . I can't . . . I panicked when we were trapped."

"Trauma survival isn't graded. Your knowledge of the place made the difference."

She glanced away. "I should go." Her first step brought her closer to him, and she smelled of fresh air and spice. He took her gloved hands.

"You know where to find me, Karma. Or rather, how to call me. No one knows where the new G-Met building will be. It will be in the reports how Rafe foiled Dominic's plans. What won't be in there is why. I don't think he would have taken such enormous risks if it weren't for you. I understand that his reward is a new nose."

Tears ran down the bandage on Karma's cheek. "His Da said it'd be cute as a button. I'm not so sure."

"Maybe Rafe's flaws become him, would that were true for all of us. This is turning into a Minnesota long goodbye." He dropped her hands.

She took his back, stood on tiptoes, and kissed his lips.

CHAPTER 43

Rafe's hand was cushioned with warmth, which helped him bear the pressure of nose splints and breathing apparatus. He concentrated on moving his head to see his beloved Da holding his hand and smiling.

"You're back, son. How wonderful! I'm staying until you shoo me away." Da's English accent trembled. "Your mother's coming in a few days. You'll appreciate this—she so thoroughly convinced herself that she was five years younger than she is that she entered the wrong birthdate on her driver's license renewal. Not uncommon in California, but she can't get on a plane until it's sorted."

"Da, agh." Rafe's raw throat coughed up a slug. No, that was his drugged tongue.

"Don't try to speak. The surgery went very well. They handle anesthesia much better now. The doctor removed old scar tissue from your septum and a bone spur." Da leaned close to Rafe's ear. "I blame your brother for that."

A nurse entered to replace the IV drip, and Da slipped into singsong Anglo-Indian. "Thank you very much, Nurse. I'm so glad you're taking care of my son." She beamed at Da as she left.

"The staff loves the Indian Doctor accent." Da mixed uppercrust British with American TV lingo. "All these important agencies want to hear from you when you're better, the FBI, the ATF, and the transit police, G-Met. Not transit? Anyway, my son, the expert witness! That bloody hypocrite who tried to whack you, that awful man, is jailed. As is his wife, who tried to nail a 'Detective Deb'—is that a children's detective?"

Rafe garbled, "Good." He wanted to move. He lifted his head and let it drop.

The nurse reappeared at the door to summon Da. Rafe reluctantly watched him go, but it was only to confer.

"You must have pleased the gods." Da patted Rafe on returning. "To gain what you want, simply receive. Beautiful Karma is waiting for you."

KARMA CONVINCED HERSELF THAT SHE'D DONE THE RIGHT THING in kissing Detective Jansson goodbye, and she settled into her car feeling secure, self-sufficient, and certain.

But as she drove to Rafe's hospital, her security detail provided no sense of security while her self-sufficiency and certainty went out the exhaust pipe. The activity of walking into the hospital, taking an elevator, and finding the room in the ICU unit steadied her until she remembered that she'd left the get-well card Sylvy made in the car. How thoughtless! The nurse who took her to Rafe's room said that Mr. Lutyens' father was with him and checked inside. The senior Lutyens, gracious and portly, came to the door.

"Karma." He clasped her hands. "How delightful to meet you in person. Call me Da. Rafe has told me so much about you and Sylvy. They're continuing to monitor his heart."

"His heart?" Karma felt a chest pang.

"Because of issues related to the anesthesia. He'll be fine. I'm leaving for a few minutes to have tea." His smile encouraged her to enter the room.

She did, and everything inside her turned upside down. This is how a man looks after being nearly beaten to death. Eyelids purple and swollen shut, splints alongside his nose and oxygen tubes snaking up the nostrils, an IV in one hand, the other bandaged—irrepressible Rafe repressed by tubes and drugs.

She sunk into the chair still warm from Da's presence and choked.

"Karma?" Rafe gurgled. "You . . . fine?"

There were a thousand things she should say, *thank you, I owe you, thank you for calling 911, take care of yourself, Syvy thanks you, thank you.* She should say that over and over. She opened her mouth.

"Rafe! You're too smart for your own damn good." She blubbered and held his hand like a baby's. "Too smart for your own good, you bloody wonderful idiot." She sobbed full bore.

"Shhh." He patted her hand, his splint hitting her knuckles.

"I forgot Sylvy's card. She says you're a hero and she loves you."

She could barely hear his answer, "Love too."

"Mr. Lutyens?" A nurse at the door. "Just checking. Your heart rate jumped up. I'd say normal for the circumstances." She left.

"Your heart?" Karma worried.

"Is fine," Rafe slurred. "Check." He tried to move his head in the direction of the monitor.

Instead, she put her head on his chest next to an EKG tab and felt the *ka-thump ka-thump ka-thump*. He lifted a bandaged hand to her hair, stroked it, and their heart rates slowed. Karma could rest like this for a long time.

CHAPTER 44

THE PLAN TO CAPTURE JACK CARDENAS had put Deb Metzger in a state. Nearly as unnerving was writing up the report in the Ibeling garage apartment. She looked away from her computer to the "commendation" she'd received from her G-Met peers, "the duct tape roll of honor." It was Saturday, over ten days since Dominic and Renee had been arrested, she couldn't finish the report, she had an appointment, and a storm was bearing down.

The plan had been hatched during Deb and Erik's "take a hike" spell the week after the arrests. Jimmy Bond Smalls hosted them in his man-cave-slash-wife's-music-room, while Deb provided the Wild Turkey. Their first bourbon saw a rehashing of failed attempts; the second rejected plans. Deeper into the bourbon, the detective trio drifted off topic. Jimmy confessed to worrying about his father's heart disease; Erik joked that if it weren't for insomnia, he'd never have time to read. Deb, in turn, confided that her Skype dinner with Jude had taken a bizarre twist. She might as well have been on the job listening to a beleaguered woman offload her issues. Nothing suave in Jude's narration of abandonment by her father, her mother's alcoholism, the trials of being an assistant to a demanding unwell woman, and the disappointments of Parisian life. Deb interpreted the last as meaning Jude had taken up with a French woman and it flopped. *Tant pis*, she toasted and slugged back bourbon. Jude was returning next week, her last job duty to deliver her ailing employer Nancy to her family. Erik recommended that Deb give Jude time to unpack her "baggage," and Jimmy that Deb should proceed with caution. "Because," he chuckled, "you're so good with caution." They clinked glasses to the challenge of love.

Which brought them back to Cardenas and his girlfriends and the original plan that had never been shared with Chief Ibeling. Cardenas was the jealous type who'd do in any man who confronted him over a woman, and he wouldn't do it by "using his words." A few days after the bourbon, a Black man in a Vikings sweatshirt loitered outside a woman's ground-floor apartment and was spotted by Cardenas. The Black man returned at dusk and pounded on the girlfriend's door—"*Cardenas, I've got police and a warrant. You, inside, you freaking bastard, get away from my woman.* Cardenas blew a gasket and threw the door open to sucker-punch the man in the gut. Only the man, Jimmy Bond Smalls with Kevlar beneath the sweatshirt, a warrant in his pocket, and patrol officers at his side, cold-cocked him first.

Deb stalled over writing "cold-cocked" for Ibeling to read when she remembered that as case lead she had another way out. Assign the report to Partner Erik who understood the term *euphemism*. She had somewhere to be.

SLEETY FLAKES BIT DEB'S FACE WHEN SHE ARRIVED at the sale property in a pleasant St. Paul neighborhood. The dour weather made the house look cozy with lights beaming from inside. The realtor, a middle-aged woman referred by Karma, burred, "Let's go in before we're caught in a blizzard. This property isn't huge at seventeen hundred square feet, but it's three bedroom with a den, two baths, partially finished basement."

The house had glossy wood floors and the kitchen had been updated. Deb, arm free from the sling, spun around the living area. White woodwork set off soothing blue walls, and there was a bona fide fireplace.

"It's just I hadn't been thinking about a house. I'm single with long workhours."

The realtor assessed her. "Karma said you might say that. She also said that you anchored a major case and that you're ready to anchor a home. You know how people dress for the job they want? You should buy a place for the life you want. That's what Karma told me, and I'm with her."

"It's a bigger commission, too."

"True," she laughed. "This place will go in a snap. Walk around, get the feel of it."

Deb toured each room. The bedrooms needed fresh paint and the bathrooms new fixtures. She didn't like that Mom had to loan her half the down payment, but Mom said that's what mothers with IRAs are for, and a raise for Deb was in the works "because of the optics." The house was small enough for one, big enough for two.

Deb returned to the front room where the realtor reminded her of the urgency because of the hot real estate market, and because they should be on the road within minutes to escape a snow dump. Deb was up in the air about returning Jude and her baggage. She was certain, however, that this was the home for her.

ERIK'S SUNDAY MORNING COFFEE STEAMED IN HIS FACE and steamed up his bedroom window. The October blizzard had created a white paradise, and it had become a post-case ritual that he and Ben, asleep with Stripe, would venture to the great outdoors. With eight inches of snow, cross-country skiers were descending on Theodore Wirth Park to groom the trails, and Erik intended that he and Ben would soon join them.

Sipping the coffee, he returned to the kitchen area to check the refrigerator—home, where the fridge is always full. Bare shelves indicated that he wasn't there yet, but next week a food delivery service would commence. Any philosophy of the good life should embrace small practicalities. The current syrup situation dictated that Ben could enjoy French toast dripping with the last tablespoons of sweetness while Erik could content himself with oatmeal. The sludgy meal reminded him that he had doubts about his future, that it would not end in biathlon glory.

Shooting he had down. His cross-country skiing, however, was sub-par. He had lung capacity and stayed vertical, but he did not fly over powder, and it bothered that he couldn't speed through everything. While he despised the idea of quitting—*because it was quitting*—the biathlon training required time that he couldn't find without sacrificing days with Ben. His poet-sister, who had the *sound* of wisdom if not its achievement, spouted a line about a constant war between obsession and responsibility. Obsession aside, his Iowa childhood had not afforded ski options. His college-era experience couldn't compare to that of the remote cousins on his mother's side, the Norwegians north of Bergen. They stepped out the door and onto skis the way Americans walk to the mailbox, they skied glaciers in June, they had the cultural memory of skiing to escape Nazis. Erik had the cultural memory of biking to the Pronto Pup stand. He should forgo the biathlon and settle for the middle-of-the-pack.

The caffeine reached his brain. Hell no he wasn't settling. The world is as vast as you choose to make it. He roused Ben.

THE SKY REACHED INTO THE BLUE BEYOND AS BEN AND ERIK skied side by side. The beauty was unseasonable. Maple leaves, red and orange, wore a down blanket. White-throated sparrows with yellow racing stripes on their heads huddled in the branches and whistled their confusion in a minor key. The clear cold on the face made the heart warm and full. Ben, skiing since he was two, sped along, hit a frozen lump, and plopped backwards. Erik helped him up, Ben raced a few yards and, acting the little kid, fell again.

"You do understand, Ben, this is about skiing, not making snow angel butts."

Ben raised himself and a smaller boy skied right into him. Both tumbled into the soft bank to the side of the trail.

"Detective Noir? Or should I saw Detective Blanc, given the surround-ings?" A woman skied up and stepped away from the trail toward the boys. Her ivory pompom hat enhanced the dark rose of her cheeks.

Erik had to catch his breath. "Good to see you, Maria. That's Ben."

"That's Micah." The boys swooped snow onto each other. "Being as obedi-ent as ever. I heard you—" she seemed to consider that the children were in earshot, but they were loudly plastering each other. "I heard you had adven-tures with a burning building. Glad to see you came out of it. There are com-puter simulations on escaping different structural scenarios, but they can't come close to the real thing."

"Were you ever caught?" Erik dropped his question. It seemed inappro-priate to ask this serene woman if she'd come close to burning to death.

"When I was eight, a cousin set a marshmallow on fire. He flung it from his stick and it landed in my hair. Flames right by my eye! Almost as traumatic was my mom slapping me to put them out. I had to sleep with the stench of burned hair. The next day I got a Pixie cut." She laughed lightly. "Well, we should ski on." She brushed the snow from her Yeti of a son. Ben brushed himself off, started down the trail, and calling after his dad to catch him if he could. Maria was about to ski off in another direction when she twisted back. "Speaking of cousins, you have a cousin at the University, in my building?"

"Yes," he grinned.

"Did you ask him about me?" There was a dare in that.

"Maybe." Erik took off after Ben. He knew when to make an exit. And when to reappear.

PRISCILLA GREW UP ON A DAIRY FARM IN MAINE, a state of woods, lakes, and rivers. She now lives in Minnesota, another state of woods, lakes, and rivers, not far from urban Minneapolis and St. Paul. She received a B.A. from Bowdoin College, a Ph.D. in English Literature from Boston College, and was a college professor. She has previously published a children's book, *Howard and the Sitter Surprise*, and a book on Robert Frost and Andrew Wyeth, *Abandoned New England*. She participates in programs that support literacy, affordable housing, and the prevention of domestic violence and abuse. For fun, she enjoys her husband's cooking and photographs birds.

The first in the Twin Cities Mystery series, *Where Privacy Dies*, was a finalist for a 2018 Foreword Indies Book Award, and the second, *Should Grace Fail*, was a finalist for a 2020 Foreword Indies Book Award. You can follow Priscilla on her website "Priscilla Paton" (priscillapaton.com), Goodreads (priscillapaton), Facebook (priscillapatonmystery), and Twitter (@priscilla_paton).

CPSIA information can be obtained
at www.ICGtesting.com
Printed in the USA
JSHW082004030223
36992JS00013B/29

9 781684 920815